What Others Are Saying...

"A charming story about life in a small town. You will actually believe the author is writing about a character from your own personal life. A sense of humor displayed throughout the book will bring a few chuckles. A nice read."

—Pat Reither, writer for Brighton (CO) *Local Color* Magazine

"What a refreshing, feel-good story Mary Ann Seymour has written about small-town life. I'm ready to pack my bags and move to Hayward. Who can't remember someone in their life like these characters? Wouldn't it feel nice if people everywhere helped and had the sense of community that these people do?"

—Dian Huss

Opal,

I hope you enjoy your little "visit" to Hayward. Happy reading!

Mary Ann Seymour

Around the Square

Around
the Square

By Mary Ann Seymour

TATE PUBLISHING & *Enterprises*

 TATE PUBLISHING
& Enterprises

Book design copyright © 2006 by Tate Publishing, LLC. All rights reserved.
Cover design by Melanie Harr-Hughes
Interior design by Sarah Leis

Published in the United States of America
by Tate Publishing, LLC
127 East Trade Center Terrace
Mustang, OK 73064
(888) 361-9473

ISBN: 1-5988649-3-9
061005

Dedication

For Dian and Diana whose concern for and willingness to
help others typifies the caring attitude of the people of Hayward.

Acknowledgements

My heartfelt thanks goes to my husband, Bob, who was not only my technical advisor but also my first critic, proofreader and editor. He also kept me going by often asking, "Are you writing tonight?"

A big thank you goes to the staff at Tate Publishing who have helped so much in this endeavor – Rachel Sliger who edited the initial lengthy manuscript, Melanie Hughes who listened to my ideas for the cover and worked to get the perfect picture, Mark Schantz who contacted me frequently to make sure everything was in order, and the many other people who have made this dream a reality.

One

"A walk, that's what I need right now. A long, quiet walk." Claire looked at the piles of boxes surrounding her. The movers had left a few hours before and at that moment she was envious of their ability to escape the mess and chaos they had left behind. For a couple of hours she had looked for necessities like towels, toiletries and, what seemed at that moment to be the most important of all, sheets and a blanket. The thought of throwing them on the bed, which the movers had set up, and burying herself in them was tempting. However, Claire knew she would later regret taking the ostrich approach to this entire task. She had made the bed, which gave her a minor feeling of accomplishment, and decided it was time to eat something for dinner. At that point, "something" was the remaining fixings for a sandwich, a handful of potato chip crumbs and an apple that looked as if it had been knocked on the floor a few times. She had not realized how hungry she was and devoured these as if they were a chef's masterpiece. There were three chocolate chip cookies left. She eyed them but decided they would be her bedtime snack along with the pint container of milk sitting in the otherwise empty refrigerator. Milk before bedtime often helped her get to sleep, but Claire doubted that this would be a problem tonight.

"Okay, now where are those shoes? I had them on when the movers left, so where did I put them?" She had the habit of talking to herself and hoped that she could have enough self-control to not do this in front of her new neighbors lest they think she was a little loony. While searching for the shoes she happened to glance in the bathroom mirror. "Ugh, what happened to you today?" A quick job with the hairbrush and a dab of lipstick was all she felt like dallying over. "This is not the best way to make a first impression on my new neighbors but this is going to have to do."

She finally found the shoes under the pile of towels that had not yet found their way to a shelf. Putting the shoes back on her feet that had decided to enjoy their freedom and swell over the past couple of hours presented somewhat of a challenge, but with shoes securely laced she grabbed the keys which she had placed on the table by the front door. As she closed the door, Claire faced a dilemma. Do people in this town lock their doors when they leave for even a short time? When she was growing up, her family always locked the doors. Her hometown was somewhat larger than Hayward and certainly did not have a high crime rate. Many of her neighbors never locked their doors, but for Claire's family that was a definite rule. She could never figure out why her parents, both of whom were raised in rural Nebraska, were so worried about some stranger entering their house. Maybe that was just it. It was their house, a house they had built together with their own hands and very little outside help. They were very proud of what they had built together. Maybe it was just so special to them that they never took for granted that it would always be safe.

Now the lock-or-not-to-lock decision was all hers. If she didn't lock it would she worry every minute she was away? If she did lock it would the neighbors and other townspeople be insulted, thinking that she did not trust them? Maybe flipping a coin to decide the issue would be a good idea. Or she could pick one of the daisies by the front porch, pull the petals off saying, "Lock it. Lock it not. Lock it. Lock it not." No, she would have to make this decision rationally. Claire swallowed hard, dropped the key in her pocket and descended the steps. She told herself not to look back. She also told herself that tonight her walk would be kept short, just a brief jaunt around the block in front of her house on the town square. She should be able to take frequent glances in the direction of the house. Surely nothing could happen under those conditions.

When she got to the sidewalk Claire had to make another decision. She decided to go left which, since her house was on the corner, meant she would cross Ash Street. Since she had vowed to stay on the outside of the square, she turned right again, crossing Oak Street and ended up on the corner of the lot occupied by the Methodist Church. Coming toward her from the opposite corner was a man. "Well," Claire thought, "Here's my chance to meet my first new neighbor." She didn't think he saw her since he veered off and headed toward the door of the church. As he reached for the door he noticed Claire and headed in her direction with outstretched hand.

"Good evening. I'm William Carlson, but my friends call me Bill. I don't believe I've had the pleasure of meeting you," he said with a most infectious smile. He had a good handshake, definitely not the limp kind that always made Claire want to quickly withdraw her hand. It was firm but not painful, and was definitely sincere.

"I'm Claire Menefee," she replied.

She started to say more when Mr. Carlson jumped right in with, "You must be the lady who just moved into the old Blowers place. Movers must have kept you pretty busy. Left about four o'clock, as I recall."

"You certainly have that all correct. I'm quite impressed."

"Oh, don't be. You'll find that news travels fast in this town. And believe me, it is pretty big news when someone new moves in. That sure doesn't happen often in Hayward," he added.

"Please don't let me keep you from church. Are there services tonight?" Claire asked, somewhat out of curiosity but mainly just fishing for any information she could get.

"No, I was just going in. I'm the minister of this fine church. Would you like to come in? I'd love to show you around. It's the oldest church in town." She probably would have accepted Reverend Carlson's invitation anyway but by now he had a firm grip on her elbow and was leading her toward the door. "It was funded by the Hayward family shortly after the town started to grow. They are pretty proud of it. I guess everyone in the congregation is, too."

At the top of the steps were oversized double front doors made from a dark wood with a beautiful grain. The brass door pulls were highly polished. On each side of the doors was a tall rectangular stained glass window each depicting a cross with a gold crown resting atop. A small white lamb lay at the bottom of each cross.

"Oh lamb of God we come, we come," the reverend sang. "One of my favorite hymns, Claire. Are you familiar with it?"

"Oh yes. I know it well," she answered, hoping she would not be expected to sing a duet with him. Claire did love to sing but preferably not on the front steps of a church at the end of a town square with a minister she had just met minutes before. She was hoping he would unlock the door so that they could enter but he didn't. In fact no key was needed at all as he reached out and pulled open one of the doors.

"You don't lock the church?" she asked, quite surprised.

"Oh no, and as far as I know it never has been locked. I certainly hope it will never come to that. You see, we feel that if a person has to break into a church then they are really in need of something, whether it be spiritual help or monetary gain. If it is spiritual refuge that one seeks here, then is that not our purpose? And if it is for some more earthly gain, then God should pass judgment on that and not I. In fact all of the churches in Hayward, the Catholics, Baptists, and Lutherans, stay unlocked, all except the Presbyterians. They must think they are in some high crime area in that west part of town," he said, laughing at what seemed to be some kind of inside joke. For all Claire knew, maybe the six blocks that stretched to the west did have some instances of crime. Right then she was glad she had not picked a house in that area, and that she could still see her house from the church.

Upon entering, Claire could instantly see why the members would be proud. The church gave an instant feeling of peace and stability. The foyer, though small, seemed welcoming. It was lighted by a large brass chandelier that was tasteful and not gaudy. There were small pews, complete with burgundy pew pads, against the side walls. She assumed these were there to provide temporary seating, maybe for those incapable of standing for very long. The carpet was a deep burgundy color. It covered the foyer and continued up the center aisle, up the steps to the chancel where it covered the entire area in front of the altar and under the pulpits.

She couldn't resist bending over and feeling the texture of the aisle runner. "This carpeting is lovely. And such a rich color. Is it new?"

"It was purchased earlier this year. Everyone was quite pleased with the decision. The communion stewards were the ones who suggested this color. It won't show if any communion grape juice gets spilled on it."

Reverend Carlson stood quietly and patiently, giving Claire time to look around. The center aisle divided two sections of pews. They too were made of a dark wood, and had been polished to a deep, lustrous finish. On the left outside wall were more stained glass windows portraying various symbols from the Bible. On the far end of the right hand pews was a good sized anteroom with folding chairs. A balcony ran around the back of the church and over the anteroom. The altar contained two pulpits, one larger than the other. Behind the smaller of the two was an organ. Although not an expert on organs, it looked to Claire like this had been another recent purchase. Between the pulpits was the altar, above which was a light that shone directly on the open Bible. Behind the altar was a wooden panel that she assumed was hiding the seats for the choir. Although the structure itself was obviously old, it was quite apparent that it had been carefully maintained and nurtured over the years.

"You are so right. This is something to be proud of," Claire said, still looking around.

"We don't fill the church every Sunday but on Easter and at Christmas time we need the balconies and have to set up all our folding chairs in there," he said nodding toward the anteroom. "And depending on who it is, we can really pack 'em in for some funerals, too. You do have time to see our fellowship hall and classrooms in the basement, don't you?"

Part of her wanted to say, "I'm sorry but I have to go watch my house," but the rest of her felt she had invested so much time in the tour already that she might as well go all the way. The stairs were accessible by walking through the end of the anteroom. As they walked down the rather narrow stairway Claire could imagine the sound it must make when all of the children were turned loose to go to their

Sunday School classes. The classrooms were down the hall to the right and seemed quite small, but then she really had no idea how many children there might be in the entire community. Fellowship hall was a big open room at the bottom of the stairway.

"This is our multi-purpose room. It serves as reception hall, dining hall, classroom, youth group central or just a general party room. You should see how it gets decorated for Halloween or Christmas parties. The kids and adults really get into that. Over here at this end is the kitchen. The women's group has worked very hard to make this as functional and up to date as possible." On opposite sides of a large serving window were full-length swinging doors, one marked "in" and the other "out."

"Let's go in this one just for fun," said Reverend Carlson, pushing open the "out" door. "Now you wouldn't want to try that during one of our big shindigs. You would really throw things into a tizzy. But it is kind of fun to go against the rules once in awhile."

The kitchen was remarkably spacious with a long work counter, two refrigerators and two ovens, and a big double sink. "The ladies would really like to get a garbage disposal one day, but I don't know how feasible that would be," he remarked. The area looked very efficient and provided space for quite a few active workers. Claire could picture the ladies, their dresses carefully covered with a variety of colorful aprons, busily buzzing and swarming around like a bunch of worker bees while trying to shoo inquisitive children away from the action. She figured that there also would be at least one queen giving orders or directions to the rest of the swarm.

"There is a rather unique feature of this church that I want to show you next," Reverend Carlson said, leading her out of the kitchen to an open archway on the wall opposite the stairs. She followed him into what turned out to be a tunnel. Although the tunnel itself had no light, the light from fellowship hall provided enough visibility to proceed safely. At the other end of the tunnel were two steps leading to a door. Without hesitation, he opened the door, stuck his head in and yelled, "Gracie, are you decent?"

A voice answered. "I guess it all depends on what you mean by decent."

"I think that means it's safe," he said, holding the door open so Claire could enter. Inside was a room walled with bookshelves holding an impressive number of books.

"Don't tell me this is the town's secret library?" Claire commented as she scanned the bookshelves, not even venturing a guess as to how many books this subterranean room held.

"Close. It's my library and it often doubles as a church library for some of the adult classes. People frequently ask me if I have read them all." He looked around the room as if he also was somewhat awed by the number of volumes. "I haven't read all of them cover-to-cover, but I have read at least parts of every one. I kind of have a thing for reading material. This is my hideaway as well as a ministerial study."

Claire jumped when she heard a noise behind her. She turned to see a petite lady about the same age as the minister. "Oh, I'm sorry, dear. I didn't mean to startle you. Bill, you should have told me that we had company." At this point Claire didn't want to jump to any conclusions about who this might be. Was her connection to the church or to Bill?

The new arrival extended her hand and then gently held Claire's hand with both of hers. "I'm Grace, Bill's wife. He didn't tell me he was expecting a guest or I would have had lemonade ready. I do have some iced tea if you would care for any, and there are some cookies left from today's music committee meeting."

Bill quickly responded that he had not expected to be so lucky as to have a guest and introduced Claire to his wife.

"Oh, I'll bet you're tired after dealing with the movers today," said Grace. "Getting a new home organized is never an easy task. Please let me get you some refreshments. And here, sit down and relax where you're not surrounded by boxes."

"Thank you very much, but I really can't stay," Claire responded. "I met your husband outside and he was kind enough to give me a tour of your lovely church. Am I correct in thinking that this is the parsonage?"

"You're right," said Reverend Carlson. "Quite handy to the church, isn't it? You probably didn't notice that there is a house that sits to the west of the church. The trees kind of hide it. The tunnel was added after the parsonage was built. I think a former minister asked that it be done after the three winters when the frigid temperatures and the snowfalls were record-setting. It's so much easier than trying to shovel your way out just to go a few dozen steps. We really have enjoyed having this easy access," he explained.

Grace gave a slight shrug and added, "Unfortunately, we are not the only ones who enjoy the tunnel. The children take great delight in running back and forth through the tunnel laughing and yelling. But then it's not just our house, it is really God's house, so we don't feel that we can say too much about their enjoying the time they spend here. We feel that the church has a better chance of keeping them as members if their early memories are good ones."

"This has been very enjoyable and I'm glad I had the opportunity to meet both of you, but I really must be going," said Claire. "I promised myself a brief walk around the square while I still had some energy left."

"It was nice meeting you too, Claire. Please know that you are always welcome to visit. Since we live so close, I hope you'll be a frequent visitor. And I hope you enjoy the rest of your walk," added Grace.

Reverend Carlson insisted he would walk Claire out although she assured him that she could find the way herself. They retraced their steps to the front doors where she turned to him and said, "Outside when I realized you were the minister, I figured that you were probably coming from home."

"Oh no, I was coming from having coffee with some friends at Maude's. I'll bet you haven't had a chance to visit Maude's, have you?"

Claire thought the name sounded familiar but at that moment could not for the life of her remember why.

"Maude's is the restaurant on the square. It's kind of across from your place on Main Street. It's really more of a café, but Maude likes to think of it as a full fledged restaurant. The variety isn't always the greatest but you can hardly beat her cooking when it comes to quantity, quality and flavor. Besides, what is lacking in variety is made up for in company. It tends to be where a lot of us go to visit and, I hate to admit, catch up on some gossip. That's how I knew what time your movers left today. A couple of folks were keeping an eye on them from one of the prime tables right by Maude's windows. I also like to go there to get some ideas for things to add to my sermons. When you have a few spare minutes you should drop by and get acquainted. Well, I'd better let you go so you can finish your walk. Oh, and Claire, I hope you will join us for worship any time, even if you're not a Methodist. You know you are always more than welcome."

Claire smiled. "It just so happens that I have been a Methodist all my life, and I imagine I will be taking you up on that offer."

"Wonderful. Maybe we'll see you on Sunday. You get a-goin' now before it gets too dark and you can't see the sights," he said and then added, "Good night, Claire."

Claire had totally lost track of time and had no idea what time the sun set in Hayward. The light was dimming but there was still enough light to take a quick look at her new surroundings. Main Street was the street on the east side of the church. She crossed there and discovered the post office on the corner. "That will certainly be handy," she said to herself. Next to that was *The Banner*. "I wonder how often that gets published. I can hardly wait to read it. If it's like other small town newspapers I've seen, it should be very informative and entertaining." There was one more shop on that block of Elm, Francine's Flowers and Fun which, judging from the items in the windows, seemed to be a gift shop as well as a florist.

Claire walked back up Elm and crossed at the corner. "I certainly don't want to get a ticket for jaywalking my first night here." She smiled at that thought. She doubted that jaywalking was high on the list of Hayward's illegal activities. At the very corner was a hitching post. Claire wondered if it was ever used. "I guess only time will tell," she thought. The corner store was Hayward's, a grocery store. Tomorrow she would definitely make a stop here. "I wonder how the produce is?" she said aloud, remembering her empty refrigerator and limited supply of canned goods. She quickly looked around to make sure no one was aware of the conversation she was carrying on with herself. Luckily no one was sitting at those front tables at Maude's, which was next to the grocery. She noticed as she walked by that there were a few customers enjoying large pieces of pie. Pie sounded much better than did those three chocolate chips cookies that were waiting for her at home. However, she did not think that this was the time to make her debut at this gathering spot. Believing that first impressions are often lasting, she felt it best to appear less like a stray. Claire quickened her step as she passed the big windows before anyone had a chance to notice her presence.

Main Street was filled with a variety of shops, some larger than others. The two smallest were a bakery and a barber shop. From the looks of the structure of these two it appeared that at one time there had been only one business here and was later divided into two. Having seen the barber shop which was obviously geared to men, she wondered if there was a beauty shop in town. At that moment Claire was glad that she had gotten a haircut right before leaving Colorado. That would be one thing she would not have to worry about for awhile. Finding someone she really liked to deal with her excessive amount of hair had always been a problem. There was even a time she had tried someone new and after struggling to cut and then dry Claire's hair, the hairdresser had politely asked her not to come back again.

A hardware store was next. The items in the window told her that it was more than a hardware store but was also very much like an old-fashioned general store. There were pots and pans, a set of Melmac dishes and a crock pot next to a ball peen hammer and a circular saw. There were even a couple of stuffed animals. Not being a very good cook, Claire felt that the saw would have come in rather handy trying to cut some of the roasts she had cooked in the past.

The next shop on Main Street was City Drug. An old-fashioned drug store brought back wonderful memories—the soda fountain with the colorful stools, sundaes, malted milks and banana splits in the pretty glass dishes, fountain cokes that always tasted better than those from the bottles, and the big glass containers in the drug section that held the mysterious red and green liquids. Claire looked forward to checking out this place to see if it measured up to her old memories.

The final two businesses in that block were Felton's, a clothing store, and the Farmers' Union Bank. Felton's window definitely did not display the latest in fashion—no bell bottom pants, no tie-dyed shirts, no mini skirts or polyester suits. Instead there were conservative but attractive cotton dresses, some cute summer children's clothes and a variety of sturdy denim wear. Claire wondered if Felton's really met the needs of the local female and teenage residents or if many headed to larger towns for more up-to-date fashions.

The bank building, like the other buildings in this row, was a large red brick structure. Large white stones went up the outside corners and on the wall next to Felton's. They also formed arches over the tall, vertical windows. It was definitely not like those wooden structures rapidly thrown up on a lot with a sign saying "Temporary location of such-and-such a bank" that always made people wonder if their life savings would really be there when they needed them. This bank building, however, gave Claire the feeling of strength and security, and that her money would be secure there, too. She had been curious to see the windows of this last building. Every other store window had displayed an American flag and the bank was no exception. This was definitely a patriotic display in a time when patriotism was not strong across the country. The conflict in Vietnam had eroded national harmony in many places but here in Hayward those unified displays of the Stars and Stripes seemed to signify that as a whole the members of the community still felt pride in their country.

At the opposite corner of Main and Maple was the town hall. Although not as grand as the court house, it was still a notable building with its sturdy stone foundation and brick walls. Next to the town hall on Maple was the Ford dealer. The sign also identified it as the farm implement dealer. A fine combination of cars and trucks and a couple of tractors sat on the lot. Since she had purchased a new car shortly before the move, Claire figured that this was one place of business she would not visit, unless, of course, she came to do just that—visit. She also wondered how many tractors drove through town on their way to the dealership.

West across Main was the very impressive looking Hayward Public Library. Having a library of this size in a town like this seemed quite unusual. While keeping with the red brick that was used in the court house in the square and businesses on Main Street, the similarity ended there. A wide flight of stairs led to an entryway bordered by six very large white pillars. Atop the pillars engraved in white stone were the words "Hayward Public Library." Claire was very curious about the history of this structure and decided a visit would be a priority, once a state of organization had been reached at home. Plus, once settled, or maybe even before, she would need some good reading material. But now she needed to stop ogling this magnificent building and continue on her walk as the daylight continued to fade into a warm, quiet, summer evening.

As Claire headed west across Oak, she saw an oversized elevated lot with a beautiful home, by far the largest that she had seen in this town. She had been to Hayward once before, years ago, but it had been a fast trip. Still she wondered how she could not have remembered a house like this. It made quite a statement of authority, not only in its architecture but in its prime location, sitting on that corner looking down over the square and the rest of the town. It was two stories with clapboard siding. That was not unusual but the white pillars that appeared to frame the front door made it stand out from the surrounding homes. White railings surrounded the front porch and continued along the porches on both sides. A balcony with matching railings sat above the front porch over the center pillars. A gable, similar to that on the library, sat on top of the pillars above the balcony. An oversized window was on each side of front door. It was difficult to tell how many rooms this house had. Looking at it from the front, Claire had the sense that she was looking at a hotel and not a private residence. From what she could see in the dim light the landscaping seemed to put an accent on this impressive structure. She would definitely be back to get a better look in daylight.

Claire crossed Maple once more and headed down her block toward home. There would be many other days to saunter down this street and check out the houses and yards. Right now the disappearance of daylight was telling her tired body that it was time to go home. When she reached her steps, she hesitated for a moment, somewhat nervously, and then silently walked up to the door. Taking a deep breath, Claire reached apprehensively for the doorknob and turned it slowly. "Well now, this could be interesting," she said realizing that there were no lights on in the house. The concern about who might be in the house waiting for her became second priority to finding a source of light, but she quickly located the light switch just where she hoped it would be. She did a quick job of looking around, checking behind the highest piles of boxes and decided that she was probably safe from intruders. But thinking that she had been trusting enough for one day, she locked the front door.

"Oh, the back door!" She had not even thought about that. Peeking into the kitchen, she didn't see anything out of place there either but, honestly, in that mess of cartons, a few partially unpacked, who could tell? She took a quick peek to make sure her chocolate chip cookies were safe and made her way to the back door to discover that it was already locked. She opened the refrigerator to get the milk to go with the cookies but decided to save the milk for morning. A glass of water would be her nightcap. Claire sat down, cookies in hand, and thought about her walk. As with the big house on the little hill, she did not remember much about the rest of Hayward from when she had driven through a few years before. But she felt comfortable with what she had seen tonight. "I think you did good," Claire told herself as she brushed off cookie crumbs and headed up to collapse in bed.

Two

"Oh, I wonder what time it is," Claire said as she yawned, squinting and looking at her watch. "Well, it's either eight o'clock or twenty 'til twelve. I hope it's not really almost noon. I couldn't have been that tired." After opening the bedroom curtains, she could tell both by the amount of sun coming in the window and a clearer look at her watch that it was only eight. "Come on and get in gear, old girl, you've got lots to do today."

She staggered into the bathroom and shuddered at what was looking back at her in the mirror. "Let's try to fix that face up before getting sidetracked with unpacking." A little makeup, blusher on the cheeks and some lipstick helped quite a bit, as did a quickie job with a hairbrush. She decided to brush her teeth, something she usually did after breakfast. But since she figured that milk was not much of a breakfast and that she soon would be making a trip across the square to the store, she decided to take care of that little chore right then.

Claire grabbed the first pair of shorts that she came to in her unpacked suitcase. She assumed it would probably be another hot June day. The blouses all were quite wrinkled but she picked the one that looked the most presentable. Ironing was definitely not on today's "to do" list. She had seen the ironing board come in but had no idea where the iron might be.

As she went down the stairs she discovered that she had never turned off the stair light or the porch light. As Claire reached for the light switch, she was startled by the ringing of the doorbell. "Eight thirty. People visit early around here," she said aloud and then hoped that the visitor, whoever it was, had not heard her. When she opened the door she was greeted by a smiling lady, about her age, holding a tray covered with a striped tea towel.

"Good morning. I'm glad to see you're up. I'm Betty Nutting, your next door neighbor. I thought you might need a little something to eat since I doubt that you made it to the store yet."

"What a nice thought. Please come in." Betty followed her into the kitchen, although Claire had a feeling she knew the way. She removed two boxes and some odds and ends from the table so Betty could set down the tray.

"Oh, I forgot to introduce myself. I'm Claire Menefee. And I do hate to eat alone."

"I was hoping you'd say that," said Betty as she removed the tea towel to reveal two mugs, a pot of what Claire hoped was coffee, a tiny pitcher of milk, a couple of sugar cubes, two forks and two good-sized cinnamon rolls. "I don't bake a lot. Leonard and I certainly don't need any baked goods but I figured this was a special occasion." She lifted the pot and poured the coffee into the mugs. "Do you use sugar or cream?"

"No, black is just perfect." Claire didn't want to appear too anxious as she lifted the steaming mug from the table. She wasn't sure which smelled better, the coffee or the warm rolls. "Boy, does this hit the spot. Things are pretty sparse in the food department right now. You mentioned Leonard, your husband I guess."

"Yes, my husband of twenty-six years. He's the town's doctor."

"Have you lived in Hayward long?"

"We've been here most of our married life. Leonard was my second husband. I married Lee in late December, 1941. Like many others, Lee had enlisted shortly after Pearl Harbor and we wanted to marry before he left. It was a very short marriage. He was killed in North Africa in '42. I met and married Leonard while he was doing his internship and I was a nurse at the same hospital. The war had disrupted medical school for him. It slowed him down in more than one way. Not only was he drafted and had to quit school for awhile but his right leg was amputated when he was hit with a grenade. Everyone tried to talk him out of going back to school but he was determined. Being a doctor had been his dream since he was little. Believe you me, he had to do lots of persuading the medical school to be admitted back. They didn't see any way he could really perform his duties effectively, especially in surgery. But one thing I have learned about Leonard over these twenty-six years is not to tell him that he is incapable of doing something. He'll go out of his way just to prove you wrong. I know you will recognize him when you see him. He's the only one-legged man around.

"Back to my story. After finishing his residency, Leonard looked for a town where he was really needed. And here we are. Enough about me. What about you? I'm not really trying to snoop. I just wonder what would bring you here."

"For years I have wanted to retire to a small town where people know and appreciate each other," said Claire. "So on many of our trips through Kansas, Arkansas, southern Illinois, Nebraska and Iowa, my husband and I would get off the main highways and look for interesting towns. I'd take notes on the ones we thought were possibilities and on some trips I even took pictures of the places that really appealed. It is kind of ironic that on one of the Iowa trips, the time when we came through and looked at Livonia, Kissock, Abbot Creek and Hayward, I didn't have the camera loaded right and none of the pictures turned out. But I was left with very positive feelings about this entire area. Unfortunately my husband died in a car accident three years ago and he never got to make the move we had dreamed about.

"I decided to retire from teaching, feeling that thirty-one years was probably enough. Then I had to get serious about a move. A good friend, Jane, and her husband, Bill, had retired a year ago and returned to Iowa where they had both been raised. They settled in Des Moines and I sent them on a few trips to look at different places. They liked this little pocket of small communities, too. To make it even better, Bill's sister is a realtor and was keeping her eye open for property for me. She had heard that Hayward and Livonia were both known for their friendliness and when she heard about this house she checked it out. She took pictures of the inside as well as the outside. In fact, I think one of the pictures has your house in it. The rest is pretty much history and here I am."

"Well," Betty paused, "it's not quite as bad a buying a pig in a poke. But I don't think you'll regret it. It really is a friendly little place, although sometimes it can be too little and too friendly. You'll soon find that everyone will know everything about you so if there is a part of your past that you don't want known, be very careful what you tell people or the entire town will know your deep dark secrets."

"Oh, yeah, like I have a lot of those," said Claire. "I would probably be a much more interesting neighbor if I did. I think you'll find that I am pretty boring. Do you and Leonard have any children?"

"Yes, we have three daughters all grown up and gone. Two of them married farmers and are not too far away. The other is in Indiana. What about you, Claire?"

"I have three children also, two sons and one daughter. One son lives outside of Denver, not too far from where I lived. Another son is in Michigan. Our daughter is in Arkansas. That is why central Iowa seemed logical. It's about the same distance to all three. Now, if you have time, I am really curious about Hayward itself and how it got started. I'm afraid that part is something I know nothing about."

"If you really want to get into it," Betty responded, "there is information about it in the library, which by the way was built by the Hayward family."

"I had wondered about that," Claire said, interrupting Betty's story.

"When Iowa was opened to settlers in the early 1830s, families from the states east of here came in hopes of having land of their own. Many came in family units. From what I remember hearing, the Haywards came as a clan. I think there were four older brothers that each had grown sons. All of them had families and could lay claim to land. There might also have been a father, or grandfather, of the family that came, too. Anyway, there were a whole bunch of them that claimed land next to each other. Put all fourteen or fifteen, or whatever the number was, parcels together and you're talking a lot of land. After they had all been here farming for a few years, it became logical to centrally locate some of the goods and services that all the families needed. That was the beginning of the town. A store and a blacksmith shop were set up in the middle of their combined acreages. A post office soon followed with the name, of course, of the landowners.

"The Haywards were raised to be unselfish, as the area would soon find, and they were determined eventually to make this a substantial town. And they certainly did not exclude others. Some of the outlying land was sold to settlers coming west, and some of the land around the growing town was divided into lots for homes. Promises were made for schools and churches. In fact, I think the first temporary school was an addition to the back of the store. The Haywards, being staunch Methodists, picked a prime location for their church. They had big plans for what they wanted and as growth took place it was closely monitored to make sure that the vision they had for an attractive, respected community was not lost. They felt that homes and businesses were equally important, and that is why one side of the square is for residences and the other for commercial use. One end of the square was to be for the civic activities. Originally a school had been built on that spot but when it needed to be replaced it was built a few blocks west of its original location. Then someone had the idea for a library. That's why the library is on the south end. And, as you know, their church sat on the north end. The church was rebuilt several times until the family got it to what you see today. As the town grew it attracted many Catholics. Since that was the second church to be built it was placed south of the school when it was on the library site, and that is where it remains today. It is not the original church, either. The Haywards wanted the center of government right in the center of town. I think that a town hall had been planned for the square but when Hayward was named as the county seat the court house was put there instead. The town hall then was moved to the civic end."

"Just out of curiosity, is there a reason that the town square is a rectangle and not a square? Did they once start out to really have it be square?"

"No, I don't think so. I think they wanted enough room on the east and west sides for businesses and homes but they wanted to showcase the church at the north by having it the only thing in that big lot. The same thing for the civic end. And speaking about the library, that's an interesting story, too. In the late 1800s, Andrew Carnegie was using much of his wealth to build public libraries throughout the country. The town council applied for Carnegie money but they were turned down. I have no idea why. Anyway, the Haywards were miffed that their nice civic-minded town was rejected so they set out to build a library better than the Carnegie money would have provided. Although you do find many Carnegie funded libraries through mid America, you will not find many as architecturally grand as this one."

"How could they afford to do all of these things? Was selling off farming land really that profitable?"

"Well, that is yet another Hayward story. It seems that not all of the sons were as excited about farming as their fathers were. When gold was discovered in the Colorado mountains in the 1870s, three of the family, in agreement with the others who would continue to farm the land in their absence, headed west. Somehow, the things the Haywards touched always seem to turn to gold and that is just what happened. They didn't even go to the same locations in Colorado, but every one of them struck it rich, two with gold and one with silver. I can't remember the names of the towns but one had a silly name, kind of like Copper Cup or Gold Cup or..."

I interrupted with, "Tin Cup."

"Right, Tin Cup. Doesn't have a very prosperous sound to it, does it. Anyway, the agreement was that while the miners themselves got bigger shares, the family and the town, would use the rest. Much of that money was used for the library and for the construction of the churches."

"Wow, that's quite a history. You sure know a lot about it," said Claire.

"By the time you've lived here almost twenty years, you will have heard the story quite a few times. It's probably not talked about as much as it used to be, though. There are not as many of the family that still live here in town. There's the mayor and his brother, both of their sons, and the mayor's sister. She lives right across the street from you. She's nice. I think you'll like her. She is proud of her family but she doesn't rub it in. There are Haywards in the surrounding towns, some of whom wanted to get a bit further away from here but still are in close contact. Some of them still farm and own some big farms. In fact the mayor and his brother still own lots of land but it is actually farmed by others. I hope I didn't bore you with all that."

"Not at all. I found it very interesting." Claire straightened in her chair. She had not realized how much she leaned over the table toward Betty as she listened to the story.

"Oh, my goodness. Look at the time," said Betty. "I'm sorry to blabber on so long when I know you have so much to do. I'd volunteer to help you with the unpacking but if you are anything like I am, you're probably still at the point of it being a one-person job. But please do let me know if there is anything I can do for you. That is another thing I think you'll find about Hayward—people sincerely like to help others any way they can. All you have to do is ask."

Betty started gathering up the mugs and plates.

"I can't thank you enough for the delicious cinnamon rolls and the coffee, Betty. That was certainly more than I had planned on for breakfast. It was wonderful to meet you. Please know you are always welcome."

By this time they were at the front door. Betty turned around and said in parting, "I know you are anxious to get settled but those boxes aren't in any hurry. Remember, you're retired now and there are probably very few things you should have to hurry about in this laid-back place. It was great talking to you. See you later."

Over half the morning was behind her and Claire was determined to at least get one room organized. Since she was there anyway, she decided to start with the kitchen. She found the paper bag with the shelf paper. That was a start. Finding the scissors would have been a good next step but since she had no idea where they might be, she decided just to rely on the old method of sharply creasing the paper and tearing it over a straight edge. The side of the table worked great and before Claire knew it she had all drawers and shelves lined and ready to receive their goods.

The first box she opened contained her everyday dishes. Those plastic dishes were beginning to show some stains. Claire thought they should be replaced but there was no hurry. "Oh jeez!" she exclaimed as she unwrapped something in damp tan paper. "That explains why I didn't remember finishing that cup of coffee." The packers had been in such a hurry they had packed the cup, coffee and all. That cup was definitely stained now but she would just have to live with it, she thought, putting it in the dishwasher. The glasses were going to be next, but the doorbell rang. She opened the door to find a short, pleasantly plump, blonde smiling from ear to ear. In her hands was a basket covered with a linen napkin.

"Hi, I'm Vernina Graves. I live on the other side of the Nuttings. I know you have not had time to get to the grocery store so I thought maybe you could use some lunch."

"Please come in. I'm Claire Menefee."

"I brought some chicken salad and fruit. You can put it in the refrigerator until you want to eat, don't you know," Vernina said handing her the basket.

Claire gladly took it from Vernina and said, "Won't you come in and have a seat?"

"Well, maybe, just for a few minutes."

Vernina sat down at the kitchen table while Claire removed the contents of the basket, putting the salad, two pats of butter and green grapes in the refrigerator. Since that little carton of milk was the lone occupant of the refrigerator, she could have put in two or three entire baskets full. The basket also contained two golden brown rolls, undoubtedly homemade, and two chocolate cookies.

Sitting down to join Vernina, Claire asked, "I know that word travels fast in this town but how did you know I had not yet been to the grocery store?"

"Oh," she answered looking a bit embarrassed, "my husband, Bryan, manages the grocery store for the Haywards. He called me about thirty minutes ago and suggested I go ahead with my plans to bring you something for lunch. I didn't want to appear pushy but I felt that you might want a little something until you could go shopping, don't you know."

"I don't see that as pushy. I see that as kindness and I truly appreciate it. I'll eat a little later but right now, tell me about yourself."

"Well, you know my husband works at the grocery store. I stay home and take care of the family. It's a job I love! We have three children. Maggie is ten, Ryan is eight and Libby is my baby. She just turned five. They keep me pretty busy, don't you know. Now I'd like to hear about you and I'm curious about why you came to Hayward."

Claire repeated the story that she had told Betty. She wished she had a tape recorder on which to save her story since it was beginning to seem that she might be telling it a few more times.

When Claire had finished Vernina sat silently for a moment. Then she said, "You sure have more courage than I have. I would never be brave enough to leave friends and a place I know to go to a town I don't know much about and where I don't know anybody. I admire you but I think you will really like it here with its nice folks, don't you know." Vernina stood, "It was sure nice to meet you, and if you ever need anything, please let me know. People here really like to help each other, so if you need something, just let someone know."

It seemed to Claire that she had heard that same thing somewhere just recently. She also figured she would be hearing it again. She handed Vernina her empty basket and walked her to the door, thanking her for her generosity. Vernina turned and waved a happy good-bye as she walked away. Claire smiled as she walked back to the kitchen wondering if she would ever have to cook again. The chicken salad made a delicious lunch. After eating it and the homemade rolls she decided that if she was going to have to do some cooking she would definitely have to improve her cooking skills. The cookies were devoured so fast one would think she had not eaten in days.

Fun time was over and work time was back. Claire opened more boxes and unloaded more kitchen stuff. The time passed quickly and when she had finished it was nearly four o'clock. She wasn't sure what to do with the empty boxes, so she flattened them and decided to put them in the garage. She unlocked the back door and carried them out to the carriage house/garage. Few houses had been built with carriage houses or garages. Many had been added later but Claire's was an original. It provided lots of extra space for storage or projects. The man who had built her house had done carpentry work on many of the houses along this street. When he was not working on houses, he was a furniture maker and had used the carriage house not only to store his wagon, but also as a workshop for his furniture business.

"I wonder what time the store closes. I'd better jot down a list and get going." Claire closed the back door behind her and grabbed her purse from the kitchen counter. She hunted through the purse to find a piece of paper and came up with only a deposit slip from her Colorado checking account. This would have to do for now. She wrote down the bare necessities and decided to get other things as they appealed to her at the store.

Claire felt a bit more comfortable about leaving the front door unlocked, since she could peek at it once in awhile during her shopping trip. She hurried down the walk, looked both ways, and not seeing even one car in sight, crossed to the square. The court house was in the middle of the block. Several types of trees flourished around the outside edge. One sidewalk ran down the center from north to sound and another from east to west. A variety of trees also bordered the walks. The park benches scattered at various locations gave the square an inviting, relaxed look. If she had more time she would have sat and enjoyed the beauty for a few minutes, but she was a woman on a mission and if she didn't stay on task the cupboards and refrigerator would remain empty for another night. Claire wondered what the chances were that her third meal of the day would be delivered to her. She figured she'd better not take that chance and hurried across the square.

A bell jingled as she entered the store. Claire reached for a shopping cart and was surprised to find there were only about a half dozen. When she looked around it became obvious why there were so few carts. The aisles were so narrow that one cart took up almost half of the aisle. To prevent traffic jams in the middle of an aisle, arrows were painted on the floors to show which way to go. This seemed to be a good solution to the problem but she wondered what happened if one got behind a slow shopper, as she felt she was going to be on this first trip.

"Howdy, you must be Claire," said the man coming toward her down the aisle.

He was shorter than Claire and was a little past chubby. She wondered if he often sampled some of his wares when business was slow.

"Let me guess. I'll bet you're Bryan," she said, quite proud of herself.

"You're right on. Bryan Graves. It's a pleasure to meet you." Bryan wiped his hand on his less-than-white apron and extended it to her. "I figured you would be stopping here before too long. I thought I might have to stay open a little later than usual if you didn't make it by normal closing."

"When is normal closing?" Claire asked.

"Let's see, today is Saturday so closing time is five o'clock. Every other day it is six, but we don't open at all on Sundays. But, Claire, if you find that you have a really, really big dietary emergency on a Sunday afternoon, call me at home or come over and I'll open up long enough for you to get what you need."

Grocers who open at your request. Meals delivered to your door. What was this place Claire had landed in, Nirvana?

Bryan added, "But to get me on Sunday morning you'd have to come get me out of church. That's pretty much where you find most people on Sundays. So, can I help you find anything or do you just want to look around a bit?"

"I think I'll just go up and down the aisles but I'll try to hurry." She opted for a hand-held basket instead of a cart and started on her hunt. She had not gotten far when the clock over the check stand struck five.

"Don't worry about that, Claire. Bud Hornsby just drove up. I expect Ellen sent him down for last minute fixin's for Sunday dinner. She seems to do that to Bud almost every weekend."

The shelves were sufficiently stocked with the basics—flour, sugar, spices, coffee, shortening, eggs, cheese, milk, bread, butter and so forth. There was only a very small jar of mustard. "Well, I'll go through that in no time," Claire grumbled, so she bought two jars. When the first basket was filled she set it down at the check stand and picked up a second. The produce was quite fresh, as she assumed it would be in this part of the country. The meat counter was rather picked over but what could she expect from a store that should have been closed by now? She heard the bell over the door jingle again. The other customer must have left. In a moment Bryan stood smiling behind the counter.

"What can I get for you, Claire? I suggest the pork chops. You're in pork country, don't you know. Sometime you'll have to get one of the hams. They are yummmmy!" He licked his lips to help make his point.

"I think I'll try one now, one of your smaller ones. Let's have a couple of pork chops, a chicken, and, let's see… How lean is the ground beef?"

"It's very lean and cooks up with hardly any grease. I can wrap up small packages for you if you like," he offered.

She finished giving Bryan her order and as he wrapped everything in white butcher paper, Claire checked out the candy counter. Always the little girl at heart, she could seldom pass up those tempting items that stores put by the check out counters for suckers just like her. It was a tough decision but she finally settled on a Milky Way, an Almond Joy, and a Hershey bar. A package of Juicy Fruit gum would be her final purchase.

Bryan totaled up the order. "Can I write an out of state check or would you rather have travelers' checks?" Claire asked.

"Your own check will be just fine."

"Would you like to see some kind of identification?"

"You must be kidding, right?" he laughed. "Why would I need that? I sure as heck know where to find you if this is no good." She had wondered if merchants here and in the surrounding areas would accept her out of state checks until she could open her local account. If this response was any indication, Claire didn't think she would have a problem. The only problem she had at the moment was how to get four sacks of groceries home.

"If you can hold on a moment, I'll lock up and walk you home," Bryan offered. Somehow this didn't surprise her. It just fit with what she had heard about these Haywardites. Bryan reappeared after a brief trip to the back of the store. "Everything secure there. If you can carry these two, I'll get the rest. You go on out and I'll get the lights and the lock." The lights went off, the door was closed, and across the square they went.

When they reached her porch, Claire told Bryan that he could leave his two sacks on the porch swing and she could get them from there but he insisted, "I've come this far, I might as well finish the job, don't you know." She managed to open the door while still holding the bags and led the way to the kitchen.

"Just set them anywhere, Bryan. Thank you so much. That was certainly above and beyond what I ever expected from my grocer."

"It's just the neighborly thing to do. Plus I like to keep my customers happy," he replied as they walked to the front door. As he stepped onto the porch he turned. "Welcome to the neighborhood, Claire. We're glad to have you here. You have yourself a nice relaxing evening." He waved and was off up the walk to his own house two doors away.

Claire returned to the kitchen, put the groceries away, and put the Milky Way and the Hershey bar in the freezer. "Those will be a nice treat for a hot day," she said. It felt good to have provisions again but now she had to decide what to fix for dinner. But, if her luck continued, this meal might be delivered just as breakfast and lunch had been. "What can I do while stalling before I actually might have to fix something? I guess the bedroom would be a logical place to go for awhile. Oh, gee, I haven't even unpacked my suitcases." She grabbed the rest of the shelf paper and went upstairs.

She actually managed to get the suitcases unpacked without getting side-tracked with another task. Jumping from one task to another was a bad habit she'd always had. It was going to be interesting to see how persistent she could be with unpacking and organizing. Claire took the shelf paper in hand and lined all of the shelves in the main bedroom, the bathrooms and the hall linen closet. She located the boxes of bed and bathroom linens and methodically unloaded them and placed the items in their new locations. Finally looking at her watch, she discovered it was almost seven-thirty. Making up the other bedrooms would just have to wait. She was facing the reality that dinner was her responsibility this night.

As she turned the corner at the bottom of the stairs Claire heard a bang from the kitchen. She ran to follow the noise. She found no person but did find a pie sitting on the kitchen table. "The back door," she said and opened it. Claire caught sight of a red dress passing through the bushes at the back of the yard. "Wait!" She yelled and the red dress stopped and turned around.

"Oh, hi! I didn't think you were home. I knocked and when you didn't answer I figured you weren't there. I didn't mean to be pushy. I kind of got in the habit of walking in when Shirley lived there. I'm Jane Dunn. I live right across the alley."

"Hi. I'm Claire, but you probably already know that."

Jane blushed slightly, "Yeah, I did. You'll discover that news does get around here."

"Would you like to come in for awhile? I have a freshly baked pie I would like to share."

"I'll come for a few minutes but I'll pass on the pie. I baked two and told the kids they had to wait for me to come back before they could have any."

The two of them returned to the kitchen and each pulled up a chair to sit down and visit. By now Claire was wondering if she really needed a house with a living room. She might have been better off to have picked one with a much larger kitchen.

"Tell me about your family, Jane."

"Jim and I have two children, Jenny and Jeff. Jenny is ten and Jeff is almost eight. Jim is the Postmaster and part-time mailman. When Jim took over the job of Postmaster he missed his old mail routes. So now he shares that job with Steve Williams. Many people, especially those on the outer edges of town, have post

office boxes, but those of us on the innermost blocks still get mail d(
loves to get out and visit with his customers so on some days he deliv
and Steve mans the post office."

"Don't those people who have to go to the post office resent not having their
mail delivered?"

"As far as I know, no one complains. I think a lot of people come to the main
part of town almost every day, anyway. Lots of us view shopping and dropping in
at the post office as mainly a time to visit," she explained.

"How long have you lived here, Jane?"

"We've been here for about six years. We lived in Livonia after we were married. That's where Jim had grown up, but when Jim got the postal job here in addition to working at the Ford dealer, we wanted to get closer. Jim was on his route
when the "for sale" sign was going up in the yard. We drove back over that evening
and made an offer on it the next day. Houses don't go empty here for long. This is
a popular little place to settle. It's safe and clean and friendly."

"I haven't had a chance to look around the whole town yet, but I haven't seen
a school. Is there one?" Claire asked.

"There is one a few blocks southwest of here, more on the edge of town. Years
ago there was a school where the library is now. I don't know how true it is but
there's an old story that when one of the early family of Haywards built that big
beautiful house across from the little school, they realized that they did not enjoy
hearing the laughing and screaming of lots of happy children. They also, I heard,
felt it was not the most attractive thing to have across the street from their property so they convinced the other members of the Hayward clan and other town
leaders to move the school. It stayed at the new location but the school itself was
enlarged when Kissock, Livonia, Abbot Creek and Hayward consolidated their
individual schools into one school district. The elementary school is here and the
junior and senior high is in a combined building in Kissock.

"I do need to be going, Claire, since the children are waiting for their pie.
Please come over and visit sometime soon. Shirley always just came to the back-
door. That saves you from having to walk around to the front. I hope you'll feel
comfortable doing that, too."

They walked out the back door and into the yard. Claire said, "Just out of
curiosity, I have a question for you."

Jane paused and turned, "What's that?"

"Don't think that I want to talk about myself, but you asked nothing about
me," Claire said with a puzzled tone in her voice.

Jane smiled sheepishly. "This weekend you're the big news here. It's so rare that we have newcomers. I'll bet that everyone within one block of the square knows you are here. And I'll bet most of them know where you're from and what you did before you came here. After you've been here awhile, you won't be news anymore. But people will often still know what you're doing just as they know about everyone else. At least you won't have to explain your whole history again. I need to hurry. Come over soon. 'Bye."

"Goodbye, Jane. And thanks for the pie." The red dress again passed through the bushes.

Claire went back into the kitchen and pondered what to fix for dinner to go with the pie. At this point she seriously thought of eating just the pie—all of it—but common sense prevailed. She got out some eggs and cheese and started fixing an omelet. A couple of pieces of whole wheat toast rounded out that part of the meal. Then came the pie. It was cherry and it was delicious. "A whole pie for one person. Hmmm. I wonder how long that will stay fresh. I'd better have another little piece now," she thought to herself. It was equally as delicious except there was a little bit of guilt added. But she didn't really care.

"If I keep eating like this I will have to increase the miles I walk," she thought. She washed and put away the dishes. The kitchen had been updated within the past ten years and was equipped with a dishwasher but she figured it was almost as easy just to wash these few as to rinse them and put them in the dishwasher. She covered the pie and set it carefully on the counter. One would have thought it was a valuable possession. Claire started to turn out the light when she remembered the back door. She paused for a moment then walked over to lock it. "Maybe sometimes," she said, "but I think at night it will stay locked." She turned key, switched off the light, and up the stairs she went.

Claire wasn't quite ready to turn in yet so she made the bed in one of the other three bedrooms. She had no idea when she would have any guests but thought she would have one room ready just in case. She knew her children and their families would visit sometime but she didn't know if any would come this summer, since they had all come to Colorado to help her pack for the move. Maybe some of her Colorado friends might even drop by sometime. "It never hurts to be prepared," she thought. She spread a quilt on each of the other beds and tossed some pillows on as a finishing touch. It looked good and gave her a feeling of accomplishment. Now she was ready to end this very busy but interesting day.

Three

She ran as fast as she could. They were coming faster. No matter how fast she ran she couldn't get away. What was she going to do? They were yelling at her. There had to be a place to go, a place to hide. There was the church. Maybe she could make it there before they caught her. Hopefully she could seek safe haven there. How many were there? She couldn't really tell. The footsteps got closer. The voices got louder. "Mine," they all seemed to scream. "Eat mine!" They chased her with rolls and biscuits, with pies and cakes, with fried chicken and baked hams. "Mine's the best! Eat mine!" Claire could hear the church bells ringing. "I think I'll make it. I must be getting closer. The bells are getting louder." Suddenly she sat up with a start. The church bells were ringing and thankfully they had awakened her from her dream, a bad fattening dream.

"What time is it?" she asked herself, shaking her head and trying to find her way back into reality. The clock showed nine o'clock. "I thought Reverend Carlson said church was at ten." Listening more closely Claire detected more than one set of bells ringing, some from farther away. She got out of bed and looked out the window toward the Methodist Church. Seeing no activity she decided that probably she was right and church was at ten. Since she was wide awake by then and there was plenty of time, she decided to go to the service. She opened the closet door and viewed the selection with a puzzled look. "How dressed up do these people get? Do the women wear hats? I hope that's not expected since I don't have any." She picked a pale pink sundress with a matching jacket, and even found the pink heels to wear with them.

After getting dressed and putting makeup on, she went down to eat breakfast. It was a nice feeling to know that things in the kitchen were organized. While having cereal with sliced peaches, she made a mental list of what to work on later that day. "I need to put the books in the bookcases and get out the other things that go in the living room. Then I'll load the good china into the hutch in the dining room. I should easily be able to do those things this afternoon. That will leave me time this evening to take a long walk." After breakfast dishes were taken care of and teeth brushed it was almost ten o'clock, so she grabbed her purse and headed out the door.

Many families were in front of the church and heading up the steps. There didn't seem to be many more coming after Claire. "I hope I won't be late. Nothing like making a spectacle of yourself by walking in late the first time you go." Luckily the service had not yet started and she slipped into one of the back pews. Her timing was good as the acolytes started up the aisle just as she got seated.

Seeing those children carrying the candles brought back many memories of Claire's childhood. She had sung in the children's choir for years and the acolytes came from that group. Everyone took turns lighting the altar candles and when it was her turn, there was no getting out of it. It didn't bother her to process with the group or stand up in front of the entire congregation and sing with the choir, but to have to go out alone, or even with a partner, to light those candles was a dreaded event for Claire. If she had been able to figure out which Sundays it was going to be her turn, she would have feigned illness and stayed home. However, the turns were random so the children never knew who it was going to be. She remembered how her palms would get sweaty just waiting for the dreaded announcement of who would be selected each week. As Claire watched these two cherubs walk past she could almost feel that same feeling of relief that this was not her turn.

After the candles were lighted and the acolytes had cleared the aisle, the organ music that had been soft and gentle suddenly changed to a booming rendition of *God of Our Fathers*. The size of the organist herself befitted the magnitude of this hymn. Just looking at her made one think that she could really belt out a song. With the first words of the hymn the choir began its procession down the middle aisle. Following them was Reverend Carlson. The choir partially filled the choir loft. The absence of choir robes added a multi-colored look. There were polka-dots and stripes, suspenders and bow ties, reds, oranges, blues, greens, whites and even bright purple. Claire wondered if they had robes and were just not wearing them during the summer.

The order of the service was comfortably familiar. During the children's service she was surprised at the number of young children who hurried up the aisle to sit and squirm through the part of the service planned specifically for them. Claire had no idea how many children were in Hayward, but she figured there were probably comparable numbers for the other town churches. This was a good sign that many young families were indeed in the area. One small girl, who appeared to be four or five, leaned over the communion rail making faces at the congregation. Claire wondered who would be bold enough to do this, and wondered if perhaps her parents were in the choir and she felt secure in knowing that they could not clearly see what she was doing to entertain herself and others.

During the children's message Claire looked around the church, which was filled with a variety of ages. Her attention was drawn to the balcony where she was not surprised to find the teenagers of the congregation. They were behaving themselves, at least at that moment. She wondered if any of them were doing what she used to do during many services while sitting innocently with the youth choir. She would take the short title of a hymn or use the name "The Methodist Hymnal" and see how many words she could make using only the letters in those words.

The choir's anthem was *You Led the Way*. Claire thought it would take a choir twice this size truly to do it justice. Coming from a much larger congregation she was used to a much larger choir blessed with numerous trained voices. That was far from what she was listening to at the moment. But what the choir lacked in number and quality was balanced by what they had in passion. The director, tiny Grace Carlson, really knew how to get the most out of that small group. After the final notes, Grace nodded to her performers and gave them the thumbs up signal. Claire wondered if she would ever do anything but this positive response. Probably not. Being a choir director seemed a lot like being a teacher. You never know what your class will be like from year to year but it really doesn't matter. You take whatever you get, work the best magic with them that you can and recognize the accomplishments that they make. Claire thought that Grace would be a wonderful teacher.

As the service progressed she also formed an opinion of the robust organist. Not only could she get a lot of music out of the organ, she also kept the congregation guessing as to what notes she might actually play during the hymns. In addition to this she seemed to take great pleasure in changing the keys of the hymns between the verses. She must have thought that everyone was a natural soprano. In addition to this somewhat sadistic habit of raising the pitch she often appeared to forget the speed with which she started a song. One verse would sound reasonably familiar, while subsequent verses could be played either faster or slower. Claire made a mental note of leaving a surprise gift of a metronome on the organ. Maybe the organist would think it was a miraculous message from God and use it to improve her consistency.

During the sermon Claire's mind did wander momentarily as she looked around to check out the congregation. The men were wearing suits or sport coats. Some of the suits seemed to fit better than others. She wondered if that was because some were worn on a regular basis and others only on Sundays or on other very special occasions. Another interesting thing with some men was the very pale sections across their foreheads. Definite lines ended the pale sections and below these were nicely tanned faces. After studying these interesting head markings, she decided that these were the farmers whose weekday hats kept the sun from darkening the tops of their heads.

Women wore lightweight but still nice appropriate church type dresses. Claire spotted only one hat, and it was easy to spot, too. It was bright yellow and was covered with feathers that fluffed out all around both the crown and the brim. It reminded her of an exploded canary. The lady wearing it appeared to have a bright yellow dress to match. Claire couldn't see anything more of that person but figured that this was someone whose wardrobe might be interesting to watch for in the future.

At the end of the service, the candles were extinguished and Reverend Carlson followed the acolytes down the aisle to the foyer where he would greet the members of the congregation as they left. Since she was in one of the last pews, Claire was one of the first to reach him. Instead of simply shaking her hand and thanking her for attending, he pulled her out of line. "I'm so glad that you came, Claire. Here, stand by me so I can introduce you."

Claire had never imagined that she might be put on the spot like that but under the circumstances she didn't seem to have much choice. So she smiled and stood on his right side. The reverend did a good job of introducing her and as far as she could tell he never hesitated even a moment to come up with everyone's name. It did prove to be interesting to Claire, too. There was no way she could remember these names but she might be able to recognize some faces when she saw them again. There were, however, a couple of names that she surely would remember. Mrs. Yellow Feathers turned out to be Lila Hayward and her yellow dress was actually a yellow silk suit. She shook Claire's hand with one of those limp hand shakes that make you wonder if there are any bones in the hand at all. Lila then introduced Claire to the man following her, "This is my husband, His Honor, Mayor Hayward."

Mr. Mayor's handshake was definitely that of a seasoned politician. "Chester Hayward. We are glad to have you in our fair little city, dear. Please drop by city hall and visit sometime."

"Right. I'll put that on my list of things to do tomorrow," Claire thought to herself. "Thank you, Mayor Hayward. I just might do that sometime," she said in return, trying to look sincere.

The last person to exit the church and thus greet the minister and Claire was a smiling woman named Meredith Andrews. When introduced, she took Claire's hand in both of hers and squeezed it gently. "I was hoping that I would have the chance to meet you soon," she said. "It is so nice to have some new neighbors in town. How is your unpacking coming? Is everything organized? Have you had a chance to enjoy your yard? Have you met many neighbors yet?" She paused for a very brief moment then added, "My, that was a lot of questions, wasn't it? I'd love to have the chance to visit with you. In fact, why don't you come to tea this afternoon? Sunday afternoon tea is a tradition for us, and Mother would love meeting you."

Claire might have been able to come up with some excuse had she not become somewhat catatonic just thinking of the questions about being organized. Instead she smiled weakly and said that afternoon tea sounded like a lovely idea.

"Oh, good. We are just down one block south of you, 209 Oak. Would about three o'clock work for you? We'll look forward to seeing you."

When Meredith was out of earshot, Reverend Carlson turned to Claire. "I didn't mean to corner you. I just thought this would be a good time to introduce you to many of our members."

"I appreciate that, and it was nice to see so many friendly faces. I hope they all don't think I will be able to remember them the first time I see them again."

By this time, Grace had joined them. "Did you make sure that everyone met our new neighbor, Bill? He doesn't have many chances to introduce new people so I'm sure he had fun showing you off."

"She got to meet everyone who couldn't sneak by without speaking to me," replied her husband. "She got to meet Meredith and was invited to tea this afternoon."

"I'm sure you will enjoy getting to know Meredith. And you should have an interesting afternoon, too, right Bill?"

Bill smiled and agreed, "Yes, it should be interesting."

Claire told Reverend Carlson that she had enjoyed the service and told them both good-bye. As she walked down the steps and strolled home, she wondered what they had meant about her afternoon with Meredith being interesting. She would find out soon enough. What she needed to think about now was how to best utilize the next three hours. She decided that unloading the good china and organizing the dining room would be a good two and a half hour job. She changed clothes, laying the dress she had worn to church carefully on the bed. "I assume that is an appropriate thing to wear to an afternoon tea," Claire said to herself as she searched her memory, wondering if she had, in fact, ever been to an afternoon tea. The dress was replaced with a pair of shorts and loose fitting top. Looking at herself in the mirror, she hoped that loose fitting clothes would not become a necessity because of all this good Iowa cooking. "Maybe I can get in a walk this evening or at least tomorrow morning for sure."

She grabbed an apple and ate it while unwrapping the china pieces and placing them in the hutch that filled up most of the space on one of the dining room walls. She had one and a half sets of china. The complete set had been Dennis' and hers. The half set had been Dennis' grandmother's. When she was in her early twenties, she and her sister had gone together to buy a set of Haviland china. Then they divided it. They also divided a very delicate, fragile set of crystal. Claire and Dennis had inherited these upon her death. These very old dishes were the ones that graced the top glassed-in section of the hutch. They had only been used on very special occasions.

Claire lovingly placed in the silver drawer the pieces of pearl-handled silverware that had been her grandmother's. She had been told that Grandmother Howard could only afford to buy one piece at a time and died before she obtained the entire set. It had always been a special treasure for Claire. She debated whether to put the sterling silver flatware in the hutch but decided to keep it in the silver chest where it had always been housed. She also decided that it would stay behind some shoe boxes in her closet. This had been its previous location so she was confident she would be able to remember where it was. Claire smiled when she thought of the possibility of forgetting where she had put it, remembering something that a friend, Laura, had done. Laura was so worried about someone stealing the family silver that she kept changing the hiding place. One day she decided to place it in one of the furnace vents in the basement and soon forgot where it was. For years Laura looked and looked for that silver with no luck. As her family grew, she and her husband decided to finish two bedrooms in the basement. While working on moving the vents to go to the new rooms, the furnace worker discovered the long-lost silver.

Claire's timing was good. She finished loading the hutch at about two-thirty. She took the empty boxes and added them to the growing pile in the garage, then carried the silver chest upstairs and stashed it safely behind the shoes. After a brief freshening up, she sprayed some cologne on neck and wrists and again put on her church dress. She made the sensible decision to switch to flats. She loved to walk, but not in two-inch heels.

It was a beautiful Sunday afternoon in June. Claire would have loved to amble slowly up the street and more closely observe the houses of her new neighbors but she didn't want to be late for her first tea party. She crossed Maple and once again marveled at the big white house on the corner. As she walked past the side of the property she noticed that there was a tall fence around the back yard. She soon found out why, as she jumped at the sound of a dog furiously barking. As it tried to jump the fence Claire quickened her pace and hurried on down the street. There were only five houses on that block. The yards didn't seem any wider but the big difference was the amount of land occupied by that big white place.

Meredith's house was the fourth from the corner of the block and was across the street from Saint Mary's Catholic Church. The house was the first red brick one Claire had seen. It had two stories and the only distinguishing feature was the wide front porch. Meredith greeted Claire before she even had time to knock or ring the bell.

"Hello, Claire, I'm so glad you could come. Please come on in." Meredith ushered her into the parlor where an elderly lady was already sitting.

"Who invited her?" the sweet-looking older lady demanded.

"Mother, I told you we were going to have company for tea. This is Claire. She just moved into the Blowers house," Meredith explained.

"She's a crook," her mother responded.

"Oh, Mother, you know she's not a crook. You just say that to anyone you meet for the first time."

The wrinkled little thing hunched forward and examined Claire through squinting eyes. "Well, she sure looks like a crook to me!"

A pinkish color began to show on Meredith's face as she introduced Claire to this little charmer. "Claire, this is my mother-in-law, Clara. Here, Claire, you can sit in this chair," she said pointing to the spot next to Clara. Claire was not sure which of the three of them was most uncomfortable about this seating arrangement.

"I have both hot tea and iced tea, Claire. Which would you like?"

Since the temperature was hovering close to ninety degrees Claire felt that hot tea would only make her sweat more than she already was from that rather uncomfortable greeting, so she opted for the iced tea. Meredith served it in a tall glass complete with a slice of lemon and a sprig of mint. "And which would you like, Mother?"

"I want coffee. I don't want any of that sissy tea," Clara stated emphatically.

"This is a tea and we are not having coffee," Meredith responded with a little less patience in her voice. "I'll pour you a nice cup of hot tea." Clara accepted the little china cup begrudgingly.

"Mother helped me bake these lemon bars. They're her favorite." Meredith held the silver tray covered with the pale yellow bars sprinkled with powdered sugar. As Claire reached for one a boney little hand gave her wrist a sharp slap.

"Mother! What are you doing?"

"That's our food. She should have brought her own. Someone should have told her to bring her own food!" Clara announced loudly.

"That would be silly. Claire is our guest. Here is one for you," Meredith said handing a small plate to her mother-in-law. As she did so a few flakes of powdered sugar fell on the table covering.

"I want two!" Clara demanded. So Meredith placed another bar on her plate, leaving another trail of powdered sugar.

Meredith and Claire visited while they ate but it was hard for Claire to keep her mind on the conversation. As they talked Clara was somewhat of a distraction. First she licked a finger, touched a bit of the spilled white powder and licked it off her finger with a rather loud slurping sound. She repeated this activity until all the sugar was gone from the table. Then she bent over and started to lick the powder off the top of her lemon bars. The pinkish hue in Meredith's cheeks had now turned to a rose color and filled more than merely her cheeks. Claire didn't know if it was due more from embarrassment or anger.

"Mother, since you don't seem very hungry, why don't you take your afternoon nap or go out in back and watch the birds like you enjoy doing?"

Clara bent over and picked up a purse that was on the floor beside her chair. "That's what happens when you get old. They always want you to take a nap," Clara grumbled.

"It was nice to meet you, Clara. You and Meredith will have to come have tea at my house sometime," Claire said, trying to be polite, as Clara started to walk away.

She turned her head and glared at Claire. "If you come here again, remember to bring your own food." Clara headed off through the dining room, purse clutched to her chest. Claire figured she was on her way out back to intimidate the innocent birds the way she had her guest.

After Clara had left the room, Meredith apologized, almost tearfully, for her mother-in-law's behavior.

"I'm sorry if I upset her. Is she always uncomfortable around strangers?" Claire asked.

"Sometimes she is pretty normal but more and more she acts like what you saw just now. We never know how she will be day to day or even minute to minute."

"I can't imagine the patience that must take on you and your husband's parts," Claire said sympathetically, not really knowing what else to say.

Meredith continued with a woeful look on her face. "There is a retirement home combined with a nursing home in Livonia but most families who have lived around here for generations, as Aaron's has, feel that it is their responsibility to take care of their aged relatives. That's the way they've always done it. So Aaron thinks she belongs here. But I'll tell you, it just gets harder and harder. He is gone during the days and doesn't have to put up with her all day long. He comes home at night and doesn't find it hard to be around her until she goes to bed between eight and nine. And besides, she is his mother so he has a stronger devotion to her than I think I do. Oh, I shouldn't be burdening you with all this. I just met you after all."

"Sometimes I think it's easier to tell someone you don't know so well. I must say, I admire you. I don't think I could do it. Does Clara carry her purse with her through the house?"

"You seldom see her without her purse. Since she believes all strangers are crooks she thinks she needs to carry it with her all the time. And do you think she carries anything valuable in it? No. She has some peppermint lozenges, a coin purse with maybe a dollar's worth of change, keys to her old farm house, and a squirt gun. You know what she is probably doing now? She throws bird seed on the patio, sits in a lawn chair beneath the maple tree and squirts the birds when they come in to eat. The birds don't seem to mind it since they keep coming back for more."

"That does sound little unusual, but as you said, it's not really harmful. Does your husband help you with her on weekends?" Claire asked, hoping for Meredith's sake that the answer would be yes.

"He's usually here one day a weekend. During the week he goes out to work on the farms. Both of our sons farm the family property. And he likes to try to get away on either a Saturday or a Sunday when he can play golf. He's playing at the country club today."

"The country club?" Claire replied in amazement. "There's a country club around here?"

"Yup, it's between here and Kissock, toward the river. During the Kennedy administration, the government decided that the farmers worked too hard and needed some form of recreation. So golf courses and country clubs were built in different areas of farm country. At the time we thought it was kind of silly, but now Aaron thinks it's great. Full-time farmers still don't have much time to spend golfing but many retired farmers and other businessmen use it. A few women do, too, so if you're a golfer, now you have a place to play."

Meredith and Claire talked about families and grandchildren. Meredith told Claire about growing up on a farm, how she met Aaron, how long she had lived in town and other bits of information about her life.

Claire told her about her previous job and town, how different it was growing up in a city and how she was enjoying Hayward so far. She couldn't believe it when she looked at her watch and saw it was about four-thirty. She thanked Meredith for her hospitality and invited her to drop by any time. "Maybe we could take up golf together. Clara could come and ride around on a golf cart and shoot at the birds."

Since she was in no big hurry, Claire decided to walk more slowly and admire the fine, old homes that lined Oak Street. She was guessing, based on the age of her 1890 house, that most had been built in the late eighteen hundreds or early nineteen hundreds. They were mostly Queen Anne, or Victorian, with two stories, stone foundations, and long vertical windows. Without exception, all of these houses had good-sized front porches. All the homes she had noticed in passing seemed to be clapboard. The one next to the Andrews' house was a little different in that the second floor had two separate sections jutting out from the roof, one on each side of the peaked porch. The next one was an asymmetric house with a wing built on the left of the front door. Claire felt that if she could have seen it from above it would have looked an L or a T. And then came the big white house in the Greek revisionist style.

She crossed the street to her block. The first house was a blue charmer. While most houses had steps coming off the front of the porch, this one had the steps coming off the corner of the porch and going diagonally toward the corner of the lot. Very healthy white alyssum lined both sides of the walk. The next house was a light forest green with peaked windows on the second floor. The white trim around the fascia and the windows and doors made it look very neat. The porch had no railing but its roof was held up by three small pillars, giving it an asymmetric appearance. A man was sweeping his walk as Claire walked by. He waved and walked toward her. She recognized him as William Swan, the realtor who had listed her house.

"Hello, Mrs. Menefee. I'm sorry that I haven't been down to see you yet. I hope you found everything in good condition. The Hoffmans had done so much renovating and updating that I knew it would be a good buy for someone. Now if you discover that things aren't quite right in the house you let me know and I'll take care of it."

"It's nice to see you again. The house was in great condition. Even the walls look as if they had been recently painted. But if I have any concerns, now I know where to go."

"Beautiful day, isn't it? It's a great day for a walk, although it could be cooler to suit my taste. I've lived here twenty years and I still haven't gotten used to the heat and humidity."

Claire continued on her house-watching walk. The next home was a lovely robin's egg blue. This house was perfectly symmetric, with a dormer protruding to the front over the porch. This porch was the first she had seen that was bounded by clapboard instead of railings. She thought of what a good hiding place that would be for a twilight game of hide-and-seek. The overgrown evergreen bushes in front of the porch would also be good for hiding, if you didn't mind being poked. As she walked she turned and looked back, and was glad that she had. The side of the second story had decorative trim boards. Some of these white boards were laid diagonally, some crossed to form Xs and those at the top arched to where the siding met the soffit. It was very unique, and Claire thought it quite attractive. Another thing a bit different about this house was that a brand new red Ford was parked in front. That was the first car she had seen parked on the street except during church. Claire assumed that everyone used the alley and put the cars in the back.

At 107 Oak was a house with average structure but interesting painting. On the porch roof and second story, instead of the siding going horizontally, it went vertically. And between the wide green boards were very narrow ones painted bright white. It reminded Claire of a pinstripe suit. There were hedges and grass but there was no other color than green and the white trim. There was not a flower in sight.

When she reached the next yard she was greeted with a cheery, "Hi, Claire. How are you?" Vernina Graves was swinging on the front porch with two girls sitting by her sides. "Come up and swing with us."

Claire turned up the sidewalk and headed toward the house. This house was white clapboard that was almost the reverse of the L house she had seen on the other block. The difference was the bay window on the right side. The porch, which had no railing, was on the left side. Neatly trimmed shrubs were evenly spaced in front of the porch. There was attractive gingerbread at the top of the front gable. Vernina scooped up the younger of the two girls and put her on her lap. "Mrs. Menefee, these are our daughters, Maggie and Libby."

"Hi, Libby and Maggie. It's nice to meet you. Are you just relaxing and enjoying the day?"

"We were talking about what to do tomorrow," replied Maggie, the older girl. "I want to go to the library so I can get some more books for the summer reading program."

"But I want to go swimming," whined Libby.

Claire was thinking that maybe they could do both when Vernina explained, "Mondays are cleaning and laundry days. Each girl has certain things to do to help me and it takes quite awhile to get everything done."

"Yeah," pouted Libby, "I have to take the sheets off all the beds and get out clean sheets. Then I have to dust under all the beds. I hate that job. How come Maggie can't do that?"

"Think about it, Lib. Who fits under the bed better, you or me? Besides, I would trade you if I could. Would you rather pick up after Socks?" Maggie responded.

"Oh stinky, stinky! You can keep that job!"

"Are you out for a Sunday stroll, Claire?" asked Vernina.

"Yes and I'm enjoying looking at all of these lovely homes. They all look so nice side by side. They're similar and yet they are all somewhat different. They certainly have more character than the houses where I used to live. Here you could give someone the directions to your house just by telling the street and giving a description."

"We felt pretty lucky to get this house," said Vernina. "We used to live closer to the edge of town but when this one came up for sale we grabbed it. We like being on the square. Bryan can sleep a few minutes later too, and he likes to be able to keep his eye on the store. It gave us so much more room for the children."

"And it gives Socks more room, too, Mommy."

Claire visited with Vernina and the girls for a few minutes, told them it was nice to meet them and backed up waving good-bye. She was so busy talking that she forgot that the porch had no railing. By the time her toe barely felt the floor, it was too late. She tumbled backwards. Luckily those neat bushes were there. Vernina and the girls rushed toward her. Claire was stunned and embarrassed for a moment, but as soon as she realized she was all right, she started to laugh. Then the girls and Vernina did, too. As gracefully as possible, feeling somewhat like a whale out of water, Claire rolled sideways off the bushes. She didn't mind that those three had witnessed her clumsiness, but she was thankful that no one else was around to see it. Claire brushed herself off, assured them that she was fine, and headed toward the front walk.

The next house was the most elegant on the block. Rather than going horizontal to the sidewalk as the other houses had done, the length of the house went from front to back. On the right side was a one story turret capped by something that resembled a Hershey's kiss. On the turret the vertical windows were topped with semi-circle windows. The front of the porch continued the rounded look with an arched fascia. The color was a pinkish tan and every bit of white trim was ornate gingerbread. A rounded bush was on each side of the front steps.

"Are you okay?" Claire heard a voice ask. At first she didn't see where it was coming from and then she saw Betty Nutting standing in the shadows on the porch. Now she really was embarrassed. Claire walked toward Betty, assuring her that nothing more than her pride was hurt.

"I thought I might have to go get Leonard up from his nap," Betty said with a little laugh. "I saw you coming up the street and I was hoping you could stop and visit for awhile. Would you like a glass of lemonade or iced tea?"

"Oh, no thanks. I just had a visit with Meredith Andrews and her mother-in-law."

"I'll bet that was an interesting experience, wasn't it? Leonard has encouraged Aaron to put his mother in the nursing home in Livonia but he'll have none of it. She really is in good physical health but he worries about the strain on Meredith. Some of us take turns staying with Clara for short periods so Meredith can get away to run errands or just get a break. Clara really can be pleasant at times if you catch her in the right mood. She loves to reminisce about life on the farm. But when she gets in one of those moods her behavior can be weird. She doesn't seem to be a danger to herself or others, but you never know. So you just need to keep a close eye on her."

"I can truly say I've never met anyone quite like her."

"I think you might find a couple of other characters in this town too, but I'll let you'll discover them for yourself in time."

"Do you ever walk for exercise? I love to walk, but it's always more fun with others."

"Exercise is not a big priority around here. Cooking and eating are the main recreational activities. But I'd love to walk with you sometime. I do work in Leonard's clinic when Sally Jensen can't. And I have some other community things that come up but other than that I'm usually free. You just tell me when and I'll see if I can go."

Claire replied without hesitation, "Tomorrow morning, eight o'clock. I really do need to get out and get some exercise. I feel as if it has been way too long."

"Great," Betty said enthusiastically, "I'll be ready. But you might have to slow down for me."

"I don't think that will be a problem," Claire said with a broad smile. "See you in the morning."

She bounced down the Nuttings' steps and headed for the front walk. She slowed her step a bit as she appraised her own house. Claire had liked the appearance of all the homes she had seen this afternoon, but she truly did like hers the best. It was very similar to what she remembered of her aunt and uncle's house in Nebraska where she had spent some fun summer days. The white house appeared to have three stories, the third being the attic that had a finished bedroom with a window that looked out onto Oak Street. It had a wrap-around porch with steps on both the front and the side. Carved posts supported the porch roof and complemented the porch railings. There was quite a bit of gingerbread detail but it paled in comparison to that of the Nuttings. The porch had a swing in the corner. As with every house she had seen, Claire's had large trees that provided both beauty and shade. Plantings of daisies lined the base of the porch. She had never been crazy about daisies but right then they looked very nice with red petunias in front of them. To complete the picture, dark blue lobelia was in the front row giving a nice patriotic look.

When she got inside Claire decided she had played too much today and needed to do some more organizing. She changed clothes and started loading book shelves. She couldn't stand not having everything unpacked and put away so she was determined to work hard tonight to see how much she could accomplish. The many boxes in the basement could certainly wait. Since they were out of sight, they were not of major concern. But the places that she could see were the places that needed to be taken care of—soon. Claire worked until seven, fixed a quick but poor excuse for a well-rounded dinner, and returned to the task until about ten. The last boxes were carted out back. "What am I going to do with all those?" Claire said, looking at the many boxes she had thrown into half of the garage. "I'll worry about those later." She returned to the house and, out of habit, turned and locked the back door.

Four

Betty was waiting promptly at eight the next morning when Claire stepped out on her porch and closed the front door. "Where do you want to go?" Betty asked.

"I don't really care," Claire replied but after a brief moment added, "but since I haven't been north let's head that way."

That turned out to be a good choice, for right away Claire got a good long look at the house directly across Elm from her house. Betty explained that it was owned by Clarence and Elizabeth Lambert. "Elizabeth is the sister of Mayor Hayward and Clarence is the president of the bank that the Haywards own. Elizabeth is really nice. She doesn't have that stuffy air about her. Clarence, however, is pretty sold on himself and his importance. But they are good neighbors." She went on to explain how in the very early nineteen hundreds the original house on the lot had burned and the Hayward clan had wanted it rebuilt in the same Greek revival style of the other two big Hayward family homes. But whichever Hayward owned it at that time wanted their house to be different, and it certainly was. Its severely sloping roof and a front door that resembled a little guard house made it stand out from the surrounding homes.

As they headed further east on this block there were more Queen Anne type houses to carry on the look of the main town block. But when they came to the end of this block the houses, although still having a Victorian look, were smaller. The sidewalk also ended. Betty said this was true on each side of town. The center three square blocks had bigger houses and each block had sidewalks. Then the houses generally got smaller and the sidewalks ended. Walking at the edge of the road was certainly no problem since rush hour traffic in Hayward was nonexistent. Claire commented to Betty about the lack of traffic and Betty explained that the town was designed to keep the business traffic limited to Main Street. In order to keep traffic out of the residential areas, stop signs had been placed at every intersection. The only uninterrupted through street was Main Street, which connected to a county road on the south end and a small state highway on the north. "Maybe you noticed that the speed limit on most streets is twenty. On Main Street it is twenty-five. Sheriff Johnson likes to sit right off Main Street and catch speeders as they come off the highway. That's about the only thing he has to do around here. I don't think that Butch Johnson would know a criminal if one was standing in front of him."

"I take it this is not a high crime area," Claire said, jokingly. "Do you even have a jail?"

"There is one in the basement of the court house, but I honestly can't think when there might have been someone locked up there." Betty thought as we walked. "It might have been old Zeke Myers. He got pretty drunk quite a few years ago on the fourth of July. He grabbed his rifle out of his truck and started shooting at the puffs of smoke from the fireworks. Said they were ducks. The sheriff took him to jail so he could sober up but I don't think they even locked his cell."

Betty passed on lots of interesting bits of information as they walked. She told Claire how, many years ago, the Haywards had pulled some strings to keep the highway from coming through the middle of town. They wanted the customers the road might bring but they didn't want their peace and tranquility disturbed. She commented about how there were a few newer houses on the outskirts of town, houses built in the forties and a couple in the fifties, many of which were owned by some of the younger families. She explained that as the area grew, different services were divided among the four communities. Kissock had the combined junior and senior high school and a bowling alley. Livonia had a small hospital, retirement and nursing home, and funeral home. Abbot Springs had the grain elevator and scale owned by Charles and Chester Hayward. The story was that it was built there because the Haywards didn't want all that dust in their own little Garden of Eden. It helped Abbot Springs to grow, too.

At the north end Claire could see a continuous row of trees in the distance. Betty informed her that was where the Hidden River was. "I have no idea why they call it that," she said, "since whenever you see a stretch of trees growing like that you almost always find a creek or river." They walked around the north section of town and Betty showed Claire where the carefully tended cemetery was. The garden club was in charge of the maintenance of the grounds.

They headed around the eastern edge. Every house had trees in the yard and most had colorful flowers blooming. From what Claire could see, most backyards of these outer houses had abundant vegetable gardens, too. She had not noticed that in the central area of town but that didn't mean they weren't there. As they walked Claire pondered doing some vegetable planting next spring. Her thumb was far from green but she thought it might be worth a try.

Beyond the cemetery to the north and beyond the eastern edges of Hayward were cornfields. On the rolling hills for as far as one could see were rows and rows of green plants that appeared to be about two feet high. Claire was reminded of something her husband's grandfather, who had grown up in Indiana, used to say about corn, "Knee high by the fourth of July." That holiday was not that far away so the corn seemed to be right on schedule.

When they came to the south edge of town there was an expansive stand of trees that marked the banks of Abbot Creek. Shortly after they headed west they came to the city park. It was a good sized park for a town of this size. It had a nice playground with swings, two slides, a sandbox and a row of good old-fashioned teeter-totters. Although it was not yet open for the day, there was a swimming pool. There were four horseshoe pits and a baseball diamond. A group of children was playing baseball as they walked by so Betty visited with them for a few minutes and introduced Claire to the group, none of whom really seemed to care one bit about her existence. Betty explained to Claire that she had helped to deliver about half of the players. Picnic tables were scattered in various areas and there was also a covered pavilion. There was even a bandstand.

"It looks pretty quiet here now, but you'd be hard pressed to find a table or even an empty spot on the grass a week from today," Betty said.

Claire stopped to think what today was. She had lost track of the dates since she had started her move and must have had a puzzled look on her face.

"One of our big celebrations is on July Fourth. There'll be a parade starting at the square and ending here. There will be a big pot luck and barbecue. You might want to eat light on Saturday and Sunday so you have room for all the food that will turn up here. And, of course, at night there will be fireworks."

They continued their walk and when they came to the south end of Oak they headed back north toward the center of town. Claire and Betty had covered about half the perimeter of Hayward and decided that was enough for one walk. Betty mentioned that if they had kept going around to the west they would come to the gas station and the Dairy King at the edge of town where the county road separated from the state highway. They decided to make that trek sometime in the evening and treat themselves to ice cream for dessert.

When they got to the block with the big white house, Claire asked Betty whose it was. Betty said that it was lived in by Mayor Hayward and his wife, Lila. Directly to the west of it, she explained, was the home of his brother, Charles, and his wife, Dorothy. The Hayward family had once owned many homes in town but as family members moved, they were sold. As they crossed Maple, Claire looked back to see how much of Charles' house she could see. From the side it appeared to be quite similar to the Mayor's residence, except on a slightly smaller scale. The white pillars were there and there was also a second floor balcony in the front. There was a wide front porch but it did not wrap around to this side. It also appeared to be a very fine structure.

"I met Mrs. Hayward, the Mayor's wife, at church yesterday. She was dressed, uh," Claire paused, trying to think of an appropriate adjective, but the most polite word she could come up with was "attractively."

"Lila does love her clothes. I'm not sure if she would like to see the other ladies in town spruce up their wardrobes to be more like hers or if she just likes standing out like a parrot in a flock of pigeons. She is an interesting woman. The story is that she met Chester at the state fair. She was the winner of her county's hog calling contest and qualified to compete in the state competition.

"The contest was about to start when an acquaintance recognized Chester and pointed him out to Lila. The Hayward family was pretty well respected throughout the state and was known to be pretty wealthy. Apparently Lila ripped off her contestant number, combed her hair, put on fresh lipstick and pressed her way through the crowd to get next to him. When her number was called and no one answered, she commented to Chester that she thought it was very rude for someone to enter the contest and then not show up. I guess she also told him during the performance of some of the female contestants that hog calling was a very unladylike activity and thought that any self-respecting woman with proper breeding would never even think to do such a thing.

"Chester must have been attracted by her comments about proper breeding because the Hayward family always wanted to be a little better than everyone else around them. And Lila was and still is an attractive woman. So that is how the romance started with poor innocent Chester not suspecting that Lila was not the upper crust she pretended to be. Lila still has that uppity air but she is also very civic minded."

As they strolled past 107 Oak, Claire commented to Betty about the condition of the yard. "All the other front yards in this block are so well taken care of. I know I really shouldn't talk because I have some weeding and trimming that I need to do, but this yard just doesn't look quite as nice."

"This is Ben Miller's house. His wife always wanted to get off the farm and live in town. When she became quite ill, he let his son move into the farm house and he bought this house for Susan. Since she died he has continued to live here, but his heart is really back on his farm. He goes out there almost every day, although at his age I don't think he does much of the work. But his interest just is not here and lawn maintenance is not a priority."

By now they were on the walk by their own houses. "That was fun," said Betty. "We should do this more often. I know I need to exercise more. All that ham and bacon and chicken fried steak are delicious, but they do take a toll on one's waistline."

"I'm going to try to walk at least five times a week so just let me know when you want to come," said Claire.

"I'm game for tomorrow. It's so much easier to keep it up if someone goes with me," Betty said, smiling and looking as if she were ready to go again right then.

"That is so true. Plus then I have someone else to talk to. I get really tired of talking to myself. Oh, by the way, when is the library open? I need to pick up some good reading material to put me to sleep each night."

"It's open Monday, Wednesday and Friday during the day and Wednesday evening until seven. I would go today if you can," Betty added. "Wednesday is the day they have the activities for the children's summer reading program."

"It's nice that the librarian would keep the kids interested in reading during the summer."

"Oh, it's not the librarian who runs the program. It's organized by a couple of the teachers who live in town. They saw the need and asked Miss Banter, the librarian, if she would be willing to organize a program. She told them that she was just too busy, so the teachers took it on themselves. This is the second year and I've heard there is better participation this year. I'd better go. Thanks again for the walk. See you tomorrow morning. We'll hit the west end of town." Betty headed for her door and Claire headed home.

After changing clothes it was not quite ten o'clock and Claire wasn't sure how early the library opened, so she decided to take care of some other errands. She went to the post office to get stamps. There she met Jim Dunn, the postmaster and Jane's husband. They visited for awhile and Jim mentioned how Jane was excited that another friendly person had moved in behind them. "Please do drop over and see Jane often. She loves company and she usually has some home-baked goodies around. She loves to cook and bake and I certainly don't need all of those delicious things she makes, but it would be rude for me to turn them down, wouldn't it?" Jim said, laughing while patting his overly sufficient midsection.

Next Claire needed to go to the hardware store. Seated outside the store was a man not too much older than she. This would not have been the least bit unusual had not it been for the fact that he was holding a rifle across his lap. "Hello," Claire said rather timidly, not wanting to offend this person. "It's a nice morning, isn't it?"

"Howdy," he said suspiciously as he checked her over from the tip of her head to the toes of her sandals.

Claire entered the hardware store and looked around until she found what she was looking for - nails to hang her pictures. "Can I help you find anything, ma'am?" a friendly voice asked from the end of the aisle.

"Oh, thanks, but I found what I came for and I thought I would just look around for a few minutes."

"I'm Bob. If you need anything just holler," he said and then he disappeared behind the aisle shelves.

Claire didn't find anything else she really needed so she took her big purchase to the counter. "Are you expecting trouble out front?" she inquired, nodding her head toward the front door.

Bob chuckled. "You must be talking about my dad. He comes with me to the store a couple of days a week. He feels that he's helping to keep the town safe by sitting there. We took the firing pin out of the rifle so he really can't hurt anyone." He figured the cost of Claire's handful of nails. "I'll bet you're getting ready to hang some things in your new home. I'm afraid I can't remember your name but I know you moved into the old Blowers house. That is one very well built house. Edgar built many of the houses on Oak, too. Don't you need a hammer to go with these nails?"

"No, I actually have a hammer, and I even know where it is and how to use it. And my name is Claire," she answered.

Bob told her the total and after she paid him, he handed her a little sack of nails. "My dad's name is Farley. You might call him by name when you leave. He tends to not trust strangers and it would help if you used his name. Thanks for your business, Claire."

She gingerly walked past the hardware store sentry. "Hi, Farley. My name is Claire. Thanks for helping to keep my new neighborhood safe."

Farley studied her again and said in a rather surly tone, "Well, you just can't let your guard down. You never know when they might sneak up on you. You be careful and keep your eyes open."

"I will," Claire assured him, although she had no idea who he meant by "they."

The next stop on her excursion was the bank where she needed to open an account. She stated her request to a very friendly, smiling teller. As smiley as the people in this town were, Claire assumed that they must have a good dentist around to keep all these smiles so bright. The teller referred her to another grinning face who offered her a seat and handed her the necessary forms.

As she was filling those out, a plump man who appeared to be quite satisfied with his importance approached her. Claire guessed, and was correct, that this was the bank president and her neighbor. He extended his soft, chubby hand. "How do you do? I'm Clarence Lambert, president of this fine financial establishment. I am guessing that you are our newest citizen and my new neighbor." Claire shook his hand thinking that must be what it would be like to shake hands with the Pillsbury Dough Boy. She introduced herself and complimented him on his friendly employees. This caused his head to straighten and his chest to puff out as if she had complimented a proud father on the handsome appearance of his intelligent children. "We do try to provide the best service to our fine customers. And if ever I can do anything to help you with your monetary requests or questions, just don't hesitate to let me know. It was wonderful to meet you, Claire, and thank you for choosing Farmer's Union Bank. Good day to you." He gave a small bow, turned and swaggered away. Claire thanked Ruby, the nice clerk helping her, who still had the same grin pasted on her face. Claire did not doubt Ruby's sincerity, but she had never encountered as many smiling people as she had met in Hayward.

Stamps, nails, bank account. Next, something to read. Claire had gotten into the habit of reading herself to sleep every night and she knew the day would soon come when she would not fall asleep from the exhaustion of the move and getting organized. She stood and admired the marvelous exterior of the Hayward Public Library. So much elegance for a town this size. She climbed the steps and entered through the large double doors. Straight ahead was a large oak desk and seated behind it was a thin, stern looking woman. Could it be possible? Was this somber looking person actually from around here or had she kidnapped the real librarian and hidden her away? The sign in big bold letters on the desk said, "Miss Bertha Banter, Head Librarian." Claire had the desire to ask for an assistant librarian but she had a feeling that there wasn't one. Miss Banter looked at Claire imperiously over the top of her glasses. "Yes?" she offered in an impatient tone, as if Claire were keeping her from something very important.

"Could you please direct me to the fiction section?" Claire asked as pleasantly as she could.

"Have you even looked for it yourself? Sometimes one can learn more from self-investigation than from simply asking others to answer one's question. But since there is no one else waiting, I shall show you."

"No one else waiting?" Claire thought. "There doesn't seem to be anyone else here at all."

Bertha tilted her condescending nose in the air as she came out from behind her little throne and led the way to the fiction section. When Miss Banter was sitting Claire had the distinct impression that she was rather tall. Now that she was ahead of Claire she was much shorter than Claire originally had thought. Claire wondered if she had an extra-high chair behind that desk to give the impression of being taller and thus more dominant than she really was.

"Thank you," Claire said, mustering as much civility as she could.

"Yes, well, do be careful with the books. Do not replace anything you remove from the shelves. This only creates chaos for the other patrons." Miss Bertha huffed to herself and marched back to her desk.

"So this is the lady who didn't want to run the children's summer reading program," Claire said under her breath. "It's probably a good thing, too. Who would want to come and visit with her every week?" Claire was quite pleased with the selection of fiction books. Bertha might not be the most hospitable librarian but she, or someone, had done a good job of stocking the shelves. Claire found a book by a favorite author and picked up two others that sounded interesting. "I wonder what I will need to do to check these out," she thought.

She felt rather like a child ready to be reprimanded as she approached Miss Banter and her seat of authority. "I would like to check these out, please."

"I would ask you for your card, but since I have never seen you before I know that you do not have one. I will need to see some form of identification and some proof of residence. I assume that you do live somewhere around here."

"Yes, I just moved to Hayward. I have a Colorado driver's license but I don't have any proof of residence yet."

Miss Banter looked suspiciously at her again. "Well, we just can't check out books willy-nilly. You just never can tell who might want to come in and steal my books."

Claire thought for a second and then suggested, "I just came from the bank where I opened an account. If I show you one of my temporary checks would you be satisfied?"

Bertha twisted up her skinny little mouth in thought. "Well, if Clarence Lambert can trust you I guess I can, too." She pulled out a form to request a library card and slid it toward Claire. Then she slapped a pen on the desk. Claire filled out the form and although she did not look up she could feel Miss Banter's glare. She handed the form to Miss Banter, who checked all the information, running over the words with her long, bony fingers. She turned to her typewriter and rhythmically hit the keys and typed a Hayward Public Library card for Claire. Then with a flourish she got out a stamp and stamp pad. With great passion and perfect cadence she stamped the pad, then the date slip on the inside of the first book. She did this again for the other two. She slapped each one closed and slid them across the desk toward Claire. "Two weeks," she added.

Claire turned to go, but being a glutton for punishment, she turned back to

Miss Banter. "One more thing. I heard that you have a section on the history of the town. I would like to look at some of those resources, please." The same cold stare greeted her.

Miss Banter looked at Claire for a moment, sighed deeply, then slowly rose from her chair and led Claire to two large tables at the far end of the library. "These are very valuable documents. They can never be replaced if destroyed. You must treat them with extreme care. Now what do you want?" Claire gave her a general idea of what she was looking for and Miss Banter slowly moved from row to row, removing numerous volumes that she then slammed down on one of the tables. "Leave them here when you are finished. I am the only one who reshelves them."

"Yes, I bet you are," Claire thought, "and you'd probably be really happy if no one ever came in and looked at anything to begin with." Thankfully Miss Banter had turned and left Claire alone. She picked up the first volume, called The Early History of Hayward, 1839 to 1870. Before she opened it she blew the dust off the top, causing her to cough. She glanced toward the desk, and sure enough, Bertha was giving her the eye. Claire didn't read it thoroughly but the information she scanned said pretty much the same thing Betty had told her on Saturday. The same was true of two other volumes that went from 1871 to 1890 and 1891 to 1910. The interesting thing in the latter was that there were pictures of many of the houses and businesses around the square. The trees, of course, were now larger and more plentiful and the yards groomed but in general they looked pretty much the same. Some of the names and types of the businesses had changed, but one thing remained. The Hayward name was very prominent. There were other books that looked interesting, like town directories and Hayward family histories. But Claire needed to head home. And besides, any additional reading would require further impositions on Miss Banter's precious time.

Claire stood and pushed in her chair, which made a slight scraping noise. She knew the look she was getting without even turning her head. She picked up the three books she had checked out and headed for the front door, forcing herself to say, "Thank you," as she headed out.

"Two weeks, don't forget!" Bertha admonished as Claire walked through the heavy doors.

She breathed a sigh of relief as she hurried down the stairs. "Well, that was quite the experience," she told herself. "I'll bet the people around here do no more reading than they do exercising. What a pity with a facility like that. But she won't keep me away."

When Claire got home it was lunch time. After a quick sandwich, she went out to the garage where the movers had deposited the tool box. She found the hammer and started hanging pictures. Getting things on the wall definitely gave a finishing touch to resettling.

Hanging pictures usually is not a dangerous task but accidents can happen. Claire had measured the spot for the nail hole and drove the nail with clean, well placed strokes. But when she picked up a large picture and did not get a good grip, it started to slip from her hand. She grabbed at the wire on the back, and as the picture started to drop the wire sliced through the skin on her finger, delivering a cut similar to, but much deeper than that caused by the edge of a piece of paper. It was a clean slice, Claire thought, although she could not tell much for all of the blood. She applied pressure with a paper towel and went to get a bandaid. The medicine cabinet was the logical place to look but unfortunately it had not been the logical place to put the bandaids when she unpacked. She sat on the side of the tub, unwrapped the towel and tried to evaluate the damage without fainting. The cut did not seem to need stitches and the bleeding was subsiding. When her light-headed feeling was gone, Claire decided that this would be a good time to get to know the people who worked in the drug store. She pressed the red-splotched towel back to her finger and went down to the kitchen. She traded that towel in for a napkin, not certain if she really needed pressure on it anymore. She snatched her purse and hurried across the square.

Claire had barely walked through the door of the drug store when she was greeted by, "Hey, kiddo, what are you up to?" A dark-haired man in a white lab coat looked at the napkin held tightly on her left hand and, answering his own question, said, "I'd say that you were up to no good. What did you do?" Claire explained what had happened. He came from behind the counter and asked to look at her hand. "I'm no doctor, that's for sure, but I don't think you'll lose your hand," he said to her seriously and then broke into a smile. "I think just a good bandage will do it."

"I thought that a bandaid might just be all I need."

He looked at it again. "Well that might be okay, but I need to practice my first aid anyway. So if you don't mind and if you're not in a hurry, I'll fix you up. Just have a seat." He disappeared momentarily and returned with a tube of some-thing, a box of gauze bandage, a roll of tape and a pair of scissors. After applying what turned out to be first aid cream to the cut, he cut a small piece of gauze and wrapped it around her finger. The he opened the tape roll. "Don't you just hate it, kiddo, when you can't find the end of the roll? You know it's there somewhere but you just can't see it. Ah, there it is." He cut a piece just long enough to go around the injured finger and fastened it securely. "Please don't tell Doc Nutting about this. He hates it when I steal his patients."

Claire thanked him and told him that he had a great bedside manner, adding that she would also like to buy a box of bandaids. "How much do I owe you?"

"For the bandaids, a dollar sixty-five. There's no charge for the office visit. My name is Rudy. I also double as the pharmacist. I think you must be the lady who moved into the old Blowers house."

"You're right about that. I'm Claire. It's a pleasure to meet you, Rudy." She retrieved two dollars from her purse and handed it to him.

"I'll give you back your change on one condition. You need to have our traditional welcome-to-Hayward soda fountain treat. Go have a seat and I'll be with you after I put these things away and wash my hands."

"More calories," was Claire's first thought, but then she figured that Rudy had been nice enough to help her. She didn't want to hurt his feelings by turning him down. Besides, she had not seen a real old-fashioned soda fountain counter in a long time. She sat down and looked around. It looked pretty much as she remembered the drug store from her childhood. The two big glass balls filled with red and green liquid were back by the pharmacy. There were rows of various products from aspirin to heating pads to boxes of chocolates. There was a magazine rack where a couple of boys were looking through the comic books.

Just as Rudy came to the back of the counter, the bell over the door jingled and a nice looking young man came through the front door. "Just in time," yelled Rudy. "You've got a customer." The young man joined Rudy. He put on a short white lab coat like Rudy's and over that he put a large white apron. As he dressed Rudy introduced him. "This is my nephew, Ron. He's studying to be a pharmacist, too. But to be a really good one, he has to learn how to tend a soda fountain. Now, Ron, Claire has had a very stressful afternoon and we're going to help her relax by treating her to one of our famous ice cream treats. You just tell him what you want, Claire, and he'll fix you up. And make sure you don't give her too much ice cream, Ronnie, because you know that cuts into the profits. And you take care of that finger, Claire."

Rudy headed for the back toward the pharmacy and Ron asked Claire what she would like. She asked him if he had a specialty and he said that everything he made was delicious. She decided on a chocolate soda. If that was an example, Ron was right when he said that he made all things well. It was delicious. She thought that one reason that it was so good was that it seemed to have an extra amount of ice cream. She savored every bite and even accidentally made that rude slurping noise as she sucked up the last drops. Claire congratulated Ron on his ice cream prowess, picked up the box of band aids that Rudy had dropped into a small white paper bag, slid down off the stool and headed for the door. As she opened it and the bell jingled, she realized that in her haste she had not even heard the bell when she had entered.

That evening Claire decided it was time to do some work in the front yard. She put on a pair of gardening gloves, something she seldom wore, but felt it best to use them to keep her newly bandaged finger clean. The weeds were spreading in the flower beds. She was on her hands and knees fighting a battle that seemed unending when she first heard it. It sounded like a wounded moose but Claire doubted there was a moose within hundreds of miles. She raised her head and listened again. She couldn't begin to describe the cacophony of sound she heard. Where was it coming from, and what in the world was it? She stood up and looked around. The sound had stopped for a few minutes.

Claire got back to work, thinking it was just some aberration, but no sooner had she returned to that uncomfortable kneeling position than the noise started up again. Now her curiosity had been thoroughly aroused. She again pushed herself to a standing position, joints creaking as she rose, and listened carefully to try to at least figure out the direction of the sound. It seemed to be coming from the courthouse. She crossed the street and followed the sound. Sure enough, that was the location of dissonance, but just what the source was she had no idea. Her only thought was that it was music lessons for some beginning musicians. Maybe there was a summer music program for the elementary students. Looking around the corner toward the street in front of the courthouse she could see many cars. "How brave those parents must be," Claire thought, "to sit and listen to that." She headed back to her house, skin crawling as she walked. She couldn't even walk in step to the rhythm because there wasn't any. Claire decided that the weeds could wait and went inside, hoping that the sound would not permeate the inside of her house.

Five

The recipe books were spread haphazardly on the kitchen table. The recipe cards had been searched more than once. Claire dropped her head into her hands. The day after tomorrow was the day. What in the world would she take? Surrounded by these women who seemed to pride themselves on their cooking ability, Claire's insecurity with her culinary skills was getting her down. Since the July Fourth celebration was a barbecue and pot luck, she assumed that meat dishes would not be needed so she eliminated her favorite meatballs simmered for hours in a mix of chili sauce and grape jelly. About the only other thing she knew she could make well was a chocolate layer cake. But in this heat, what were the chances of the top layer not sliding off the bottom one? Jello salads also didn't seem to stand much of a chance if the temperatures hit the nineties. "Ah," Claire said when she came to her grandmother's recipe for chocolate oatmeal cake. "That will just have to do." Since it was a sheet cake with no frosting to melt, it seemed like an acceptable choice.

She checked her supplies, made a list and headed for the store. She was amazed at how crowded it was. Lots of people must have waited until the last minute to get what they would need for the next two days. Claire wondered if the day before the Fourth would be one of those emergency days when Bryan would open the store for someone who realized her need for an item for the potluck. Would he open the store for her even if it was a Sunday? It was a good time to visit with many of the people she had met during the week. Claire paid Bryan and once again he thanked her for shopping at his store. The town's residents really didn't have much of an alternative but it was still a nice friendly thing to say, and it was good public relations.

As Claire left the store she noticed that Cub Scouts and Boy Scouts, proudly decked out in their uniforms, were placing little American flags around the square. These reflected the display of flags in every store window, giving the entire center section of town not just a colorful touch but also a definite feeling of American pride. This was something Claire had not seen in some time in the larger city where she had lived. She carried the groceries home and stored them in their proper places. Then she went out and sat on the porch swing, watching the Scouts going about their task. They finished at about the same time that the crowd at the grocery store diminished.

Claire decided that it was time for her to take a slow walk around and through the square. Except for cutting across to do shopping and on her hunt to track down those weird noises, she had never really studied what was there. The trees with their lovely canopies of green gave shade to most of the square. There were benches on each side of the courthouse, plus a few more scattered at random locations. In the front of the north corner of the courthouse was a large plaque memorializing those citizens of the county who had given their lives in service to their country. The first names were of those who fought for the Union in the Civil War and the last was the name of a Johnny Wagner who had died in Vietnam. Claire hoped that would be the last name to be carved on the memorial.

The courthouse building itself had the same Greek revivalist look that the library did. The pillars gave it a true look of importance. In front of the south corner was an old cannon that she judged to be from the Civil War. It bore no plaque so she didn't know if it had specific historic significance. Claire suspected that its current importance was as a good spot for climbing by the younger members of the community. Continuing on around the building she came to another bench. She sat and just took in the scene in front of her. A gentle breeze made the flags flutter in unison. Claire wondered what the upcoming July 4th celebration in mid-America would be like. She would soon find out.

The sound was so thunderous that it rattled the windows and awakened her from a deep sleep. Claire sat up, thinking that a rare morning thunderstorm was overhead. She looked at the clock and discovered it was only six o'clock. She dragged herself out of bed to make sure that the windows were all closed. But when she pulled back the curtains she saw only a bright summer sun. "How strange to have such loud thunder without clouds," she thought. "At least a storm won't be spoiling the festivities." She climbed back into bed but by then she was too much awake to go back to sleep. She slipped on a robe and went downstairs to eat breakfast.

At the bottom of the stairs she stopped. The early morning sun cast beams of light into the living room. Claire stood for a few moments, looking around at the warm, homey sight. By now all the nooks and crannies had been filled with her favorite things and she truly felt at home. The living room, the first room in the front of the house, was next to a small entryway. It had a window on the front and a window on the side, both windows looking out over the wrap-around porch. She walked through the living room into the spacious dining room. The dining room set, her favorite pieces among all her furniture, nicely filled the room. The large table would easily accommodate eight but with the extra leaves it could go to ten or even twelve. The thought of entertaining eleven others for dinner was absolutely the furthest thing from Claire's mind at that moment, but she thought the time might come when she would be brave enough to try it.

She continued through the dining room into the kitchen that ran the width of the back of the house. The kitchen had been modernized with new appliances, counters, floors, and, thankfully, plumbing. The realtor had told her that the original builder had made a small room off the kitchen below the stairs for his mother-in-law. That had since been turned into a nice-sized bathroom which was extremely convenient and saved her knees many a trip up the stairs. The stairs to the basement were off the kitchen and the basement, like the garage, provided wonderful storage for the many things with which she could not yet part. There was also a small closed-in porch on the back of the house. Like most of the house, it was pretty well shaded by the large trees, and was a wonderful place to escape to when she wanted to have a cup of breakfast coffee without getting any more dressed than a robe.

Today was one of those days. Claire carried out her breakfast of toast and homemade raspberry jam, another culinary gift from Jane Dunn, and a mug of steaming coffee. She sat and watched the birds fly in and out of the birdfeeder and birdbath, both of which were left by the Hoffman's. She spotted the Nuttings' cat, Bumbles, crouched secretively beneath the butterfly bushes, hoping for an appropriate time to pounce on an unsuspecting victim. The butterflies were flitting from flower to bush as if they had not a care in the world. The bees also were getting an early start today. It almost seemed as if all those creatures were out to get their daily errands and chores completed before the parade and picnic.

By 9:30 people had started gathering around the square. Betty and Leonard had carried lawn chairs out to their front walk. Claire took a cue from them, unearthed a chair from the garage and joined them in front. "What was that loud noise early this morning?" she asked.

They both laughed. Leonard answered, "That has become a tradition about the last eight to ten years. Ron Milstein, who helps his uncle at the drug store, buys the loudest firecracker he can find in the Chicago area and brings it here to start the day off with a big bang. The first couple of years we were quite startled by it. Now we just know it's coming and brace ourselves."

"At first I thought it was thunder. Then I thought maybe someone had fired off the cannon in the square," said Claire

"Now that's another story. For years Farley Simpson tried to get that old cannon to actually fire for the Fourth. The city council finally had to put cement in the barrel so he would stop fooling around with it." Leonard must have seen a look of confusion on Claire's face. "Have you met Farley? His son, Bob Simpson, owns the hardware store."

"Oh," Claire responded, nodding her head. "I encountered him keeping guard in front of the store. He seemed to be quite an interesting fellow."

"That he is," continued the doctor. "He's a World War II veteran. He did decoding for his unit's messages. One time he decoded a message incorrectly and his error resulted in serious injuries to his buddies. He never got over it and as time has passed he has gotten stranger and stranger. He even carries a small notebook with him most of the time and he thinks it's a code book. Every so often someone will say something to him or he overhears a conversation and he'll pick up a word that he thinks is in his codebook. He'll pull out that book, and then he'll get all worked up if the word is about something he thinks is dangerous. Sometimes he'll start his day writing the words for that day. It really is sad and he interprets some words into some weird substitutions. He's quite harmless, but if he approached some stranger with his useless rifle, I'm sure he could give him a good fright."

They sat and talked until ten o'clock when Claire heard it again. It was fainter than it had been when she had heard it before, but it was definitely the same sound. She looked around to see if she could locate it. As it got louder, she saw the source. It was a marching band, using the terms marching and band loosely. It had turned the corner by city hall and was near the beginning of the parade. It sounded better than it had the other time she had heard it, but still the notes were not quite true to the way they had been composed. The overall sound reminded her very much of a record her brother had given her in the fifties. The performing group for that record was called The Sauerkraut Band. With that group one knew they really had to be skilled musicians in order to make their songs sound so bad. But with this bunch she didn't have the same feeling about how they produced their sound.

Trying to sound as polite as possible, Claire commented, "I didn't realize that Hayward had a band."

Betty smiled, "We have a band about twice a year, now and often in December for the hanging of the greens. They are mainly former high school band members who get together a couple of weeks before they are to perform. They practice in the basement of the courthouse. They try to practice with the windows open but almost every time one of the neighbors can't take it and goes over and knocks on the windows and asks them to close them. That helps muffle to sound, but it still is audible. They really do try but, well, you know."

The parade turned off Main onto Elm and passed in front of the Methodist Church. Then it turned in front of Claire's house onto Oak. The parade was headed by the local Cub Scouts and Boys Scout carrying American flags followed by the Boy Scout flag, a couple of Iowa state flags, and what Claire guessed to be the town flag. Everyone stood respectfully as the color guard passed. Next came the band playing what sounded vaguely like *Stars and Stripes Forever*. The spectators clapped and a few shuddered visibly after the band passed. The cheerleaders from the high school followed the band trying to march in time to the music, which was no easy task. Their red, white and blue uniforms and pompoms accented the patriotic theme. Six baton twirlers followed the cheerleaders. Three of them were probably in their teens and the other three were much younger. One of the older girls misjudged her own strength and sent her aerial way too high for her to control. "Watch out!" someone yelled as it came down right behind the unsuspecting cheerleaders. The littler girls didn't do much twirling but mainly waved their batons back and forth. Still, their performance was a crowd pleaser and, Claire was certain, made their parents beam.

Next came a dozen or so veterans, some of whom could still squeeze into their uniforms. Claire recognized Farley in this group, mainly because he was carrying his rifle with great pride. While the rest of the group waved to the crowd, Farley's eyes were aimed straight ahead as if he were still in a military drill. Applause greeted these men and one woman as they continued on the route.

Mayor and Mrs. Hayward came next sitting regally in a Ford convertible. The mayor wore a short sleeved white shirt with a red and white striped tie. Claire suspected that Lila had selected his tie, for she wore a bright red suit that looked as if it would have been much too hot for this summer day. On her head was a large red straw hat. Around the crown was a very long blue and white striped tie. She brought down the sides of the tie bending the sides of the brim almost to her cheeks. The tie was fastened under her chin with the tails trailing over her shoulders and down her back. She looked as if she were ready for a turn-of-the-century road race rather than for a gentle drive for a few blocks at five miles an hour. The Haywards waved at their constituents, Chester looking sincere and interested. Lila, on the other hand, looked as if she were out for a photo shoot.

After Mr. Mayor was an Uncle Sam dressed in the traditional patriotic outfit. But this Sam was walking on stilts. He threw pieces of red and white peppermint candy as he strode very efficiently from one side of the street to the other. He got a good round of applause. Claire figured it was for both the talent and the candy.

Next was a float from the local 4-H group. Children and adults sat together on bales of hay, waving to the spectators. Children on bicycles decorated with crepe paper streamers followed the float. Playing cards had been inserted in many of the wheels. The sound brought back fond memories of when Claire's children also had done that. Next came the pet parade. Some unfortunate dogs and one pig had been dressed in various get-ups, but seemed to be taking it all in stride.

Behind the dogs and children came the sheriff, Butch Johnson, in his shiny black car with a big gold star painted on the side. Riding with Butch and waving to the crowd was his young deputy, Burton Taylor, known to most folks as Burt. The sheriff's car served as buffer between the dogs and a variety of tractors. Some were very old and Claire wondered how they still ran. Others were new and looked as if they had just been driven off the lot for the occasion.

The crowd clapped its approval as the tractors passed, since they marked the end of the parade. "That was nice," Claire commented to Leonard and Betty. "What time should I be at the park?"

"You could go now, if you want to. Some families do head right over so they can get the best tables. But most don't show up until about three. That's when the games are scheduled to start," answered Leonard.

Betty followed up immediately with, "That is when they are supposed to begin but as long as we've been here I have never seen them start on time. We still go about then and stake out a place in the shade. We'll be taking our collapsible table so you are very welcome to sit with us. The eating starts about six. Most people take ice chests to keep their food cool until then. As close as we are to the park there is plenty of time to come back and get whatever you are taking."

"I guess I'll head down about three. If there is shade my cake should do okay until time to eat. I guess I'll see you there."

Leonard and Betty waved and headed up their walk when Betty turned and said, "Make sure you wear comfortable clothes and shoes. Everyone will be checking out how well the newcomer does in the games." She smiled and continued toward the door.

Claire was not sure if Betty was kidding or if she meant it. Now she was stressed not only about how the quality of her chocolate chip oatmeal cake would compare to the dishes of the other cooks but also about her athletic ability. She could be in trouble.

Shortly before three o'clock she headed down Oak toward the park and had just passed the mayor's big white house when she was startled by the sound of the Hayward's dog lunging at the fence. Claire could see his head appear and disappear as he jumped, trying his best to get over. She wondered if he had ever jumped the fence and hoped if he hadn't that this wouldn't be his lucky day. Many cars passed as she headed south. As she got closer to the park both sides of the street were lined with cars. This obviously was an event attended not just by the Hayward citizens but by those from other places.

She spotted Leonard Nutting's Thunderbird convertible, smiling as she thought of the first time she had seen Leonard get into his car. In what was one smooth, continuous movement he would throw his leg over the side of the car, swing in the rest of his body and bring his crutch onto the passenger seat. When getting out he did use the door but his method of entry was the fastest she had ever seen anyone get into a car. "I wonder what he does in the winter?" she thought.

Betty saw Claire looking around and waved at her. The spot the Nuttings had found seemed to be prime property. It was close to the space that she assumed would be for the games and races. It was also far enough from the pool that the sounds of the screaming children and their splashing were muffled. Claire stuck the sack containing her table service and cake under the table, hoping that any ants would not find it before it was time to put it out for public scrutiny. Leonard was making his way through the crowd visiting with young and old.

Betty pointed out several people Claire had not yet met. Claire tried hard to remember what Betty told her, but she knew most of it would be lost from her memory by the time she might encounter these people. Some of the information, however, was quite interesting and bordered on gossip. She thought she should have been ashamed for enjoying that part, but she wasn't.

Their talking was interrupted by a man's voice talking to the crowd with a bullhorn. "That's Bud Hornsby," Betty told her. "He owns the Ford dealership. I think you met his wife Ellen on one of our walks." Claire remembered Ellen. She had been getting her mail when they went by and Betty had introduced them. Ellen had asked Betty if she had any advice on how to survive living with a teenager. Her son, Steve, had just turned 16, had a new driver's license and was driving her nuts. Both Betty and Claire encouraged her just to hang in there and that things would get better in a few years. Ellen said she doubted it since she also had a thirteen-year-old daughter, Katie.

Bud was evidently the game emcee. First there were games and races just for the children. Some of them had obviously run over from the pool to participate, since the shirts they hurriedly had thrown on stuck to their wet bodies. There were races of all varieties—three legged races, sack races, potato in the spoon races, and 50 and 100 yard dashes. All who took part got a ribbon. Many of the children had them pinned proudly on their shirts. The swimmers tossed their ribbons to parents and headed back to the pool.

Then came the adult events, and Claire felt a slight knot tighten in her stomach. "Cool it, it's all in fun," she told herself. The adult games were very similar to the children's although there were no plain dashes. Every race involved things other than just speed, requiring more overall coordination or just plain luck. The first race was the potato in the spoon. Whoever was in charge of the race must have gone to every store in Des Moines to find that many mammoth potatoes. This was done as a relay with teams of both men and women. Betty had already formed her six-person team which happened to include Claire and her immediate neighbors, Vernina, Jane and Jim Dunn, and believe it or not, Betty's husband Leonard. Watching him run his part of the race was truly amazing. He did the best of any of them at balancing the potato even though every time his crutch hit the ground it must have jarred his entire body. Betty's team did okay, coming in at about the middle of the group. But it sure would have been easier to carry those huge potatoes if they had not had to transport them on teaspoons. Claire had to admit, though, that it had been fun.

The next event that Betty got Claire involved in was the three legged race. This time it was run by the men first and then the women. Quite a few of the men came over to Leonard and jokingly asked him if was going to enter this race. Betty turned to Claire and said, "Quite a few years ago Leonard did enter this race with Daniel Homes. Daniel was a very tall, strong man. When the whistle started the race, Daniel just picked Leonard up and ran with him, Leonard's crutch touching the ground every few steps. They won by a large margin but were disqualified. He and Daniel didn't care. They just thought it was a good joke. People have never forgotten it and ask him every year if he's going to run it again."

The women's race was next. Betty had talked Claire into running with her. Some of the other matchups were quite interesting. For instance, petite Grace Carlson was with a girl who appeared to me about fourteen. "That's Katie Hornsby," Betty said nodding to the pair. Phoebe Peoples, whom Claire recognized as the church organist, had a partner of similar girth. In fact, they looked like a matched set.

"Who's that with Miss Peoples?" Claire asked.

"That is Miss Pearl Hatcher, the elementary school principal. They run together every year. I don't know if they can't find anyone else to run with or if they just enjoy each other. It seems to be one of the few fun things that Pearl does all year. I'm sure you will find her quite, uh, interesting when you have the chance to meet her."

They lined up, ready for the whistle. "Start with your inside foot and just pretend we are on one of our walks," Betty whispered. On the signal to start Betty and Claire got off well. They were very lucky to not be bumped by the Peoples-Hatcher team who were to their immediate right. Out of the corner of her eye Claire saw them bounce first into each other and then bounce away. They obviously had not come up with a start strategy even after all the times they had done this together.

Their strongest competition turned out to be Grace and Katie. Being the same size and about the same weight, they moved together in great form. But the fact that Betty and Claire had been walking together in more or less the same stride for almost two weeks gave them a good advantage and they edged out the petite pair at the finish line. They turned around to see that many of the couples were struggling but having a great time. Peoples and Hatcher were still trying to get into a rhythm, still bouncing off each other, and were running, or rather walking, in dead last place, except for those who had fallen and had not managed to get up. Claire wondered what would happen if the Phoebe and Pearl twosome did fall down. Would they be able to get up or would they need help from the stronger members of the crowd? Despite all the trouble they seemed to be having, the two were still enjoying themselves. They laughed as they slowly approached the finish line. When it was finally crossed they both threw up their hands and said, almost in unison, "We made it!" The crowd laughed and applauded them. That incident was reassuring to Claire and indicated that these events were definitely more about fun than winning.

Next came the pancake flipping contest. This was not the official pancake race. That one, sponsored by a flour company, would be later in the year. But this was good practice for those who took the event more seriously. Having never flipped a pancake in her life, Claire decided to opt out. But some of her new friends had different plans. Vernina came over and handed her a skillet with a lovely tan pancake lying innocently in it. "Here, I brought an extra just for you," she said with a twinkle in her eye. "It'll be fun, don't you know."

Claire wondered just who it would be fun for. She doubted that it would be fun for her and she was sure that the pancake would not be having fun either. She guessed the only ones to enjoy it would be the crowd checking out how the newcomer could handle this skill. Jane was the one of the few faces Claire recognized besides Vernina's. But when she looked around at the starting line she spotted Clara Andrews, her skillet clutched in both hands and her purse draped over her arm. Claire turned to Vernina, "I can't believe that Clara Andrews does this race."

"She is really quite good. I've heard that she used to win it almost every year. She doesn't have the speed anymore, don't you know, but she still has the technique."

Claire turned to ask Vernina exactly what the technique was but the whistle blew and they were off. The first requirement seemed to be to flip before running. She accomplished that all right, but when she added running to flipping things did not go too well. Her second flip was too high and with too much forward motion. As she tried to chase it down Claire's skillet almost hit the lady next to her. Luckily she was on a chase of her own and never knew what almost hit her. Claire decided that she needed to temper her tosses a bit if she wanted any kind of control over that little brown disc. Subsequent flips were not bad but the speed was nearly nonexistent since she was concentrating so much on tossing and catching. When she finally crossed the finish line, Claire discovered that she had come in last. Even Clara had beaten her. People still clapped. Claire took that as a kind of sign of acceptance.

Vernina came over, laughing. "It could have been worse. At least you never dropped it, did you? I'll take the skillet but you hold onto the pancake."

Claire wondered just what she was supposed to do with it when the bullhorn announced, "Next is the pancake throw."

"Oh great," she thought, "I throw even worse than I flip." A large platter of pancakes appeared from out of nowhere and the interested contestants each took one. The men went first in this game. It turned out to resemble the discuss throw.

Most of the men had a pretty good technique with some the younger fellows even getting a couple of spins with their bodies before releasing the pancake. Claire tried to study what seemed to work the best but knew there was no way she would do that turning first. She thought that approach would only result in her throwing it in completely the wrong direction. Most of the women just stood sideways and gave it a good heave but some of the teenage girls tried the spinning technique. A couple did quite well and put the rest of the contestants to shame. Since Claire had spent hours in her back yard in Colorado tossing a Frisbee with her children, she thought she'd give that technique a try. Her throw wasn't too bad and fell in the area already quite covered with broken pancakes. It was a fun event and she definitely preferred it to tossing cow pies, a contest that was held in some places in Colorado.

There were horseshoe contests with mixed teams, a big game of Bingo was held on some of the picnic tables, and other games were held in different areas of the park. The contest Claire found most interesting was a croquet tournament on an enlarged course and played with six croquet sets and six teams. Betty explained how it worked. Each team started at a different place on the course and tried to be the first to get back to where they started. They all had to pass through the wickets in order as in regular croquet but the twist was that when a player hit his ball against an opponent's, he could place his own ball next to the other ball. Then, while bracing it with his foot, he would hit his own ball propelling the other ball off in a direction opposite of where it needed to go. Watching it for the first time, Claire had trouble keeping track of what was going on and it seemed more like controlled chaos than anything. However, the players didn't seem to have any trouble. There were lots of "Oh no's" and "Oh look what you did to me" and "I'll get you for that" but it was all in good fun.

Bud Hornsby grabbed the bullhorn and announced that in five minutes the final event before the softball game would be held, the shmoos. Claire was still engrossed in watching the croquet bedlam and found it interesting that all activities instantly were left as they were, to be resumed at a later time. Rudy Milstein walked by as she turned to move toward where the crowd was gathering. "Hi, kiddo, are you going to do shmoos?" Claire told him that she might, or might not, depending on what shmoos were. "It's what we call water balloons and we toss them back and forth between partners trying to keep them from breaking. A few years ago someone said they looked like those little characters from the L'il Abner cartoon strip and they've been called shmoos ever since. I need a partner. Want to try it with me?" It sounded relatively harmless so Claire joined him and they went to get their balloon.

To start the contest there were two long lines of partners facing each other. At first they were about two feet apart. On the signal the balloon was gently tossed to the partner. Then everyone took a step back. The signal to throw was given again and the balloon was tossed back to partner one. This continued with the difficulty increasing as the distance widened. Along the lines were sounds of water splashing and people remarking as their balloons broke, often soaking the partner with the unsuccessful catch. Rudy and Claire did quite well and were among the last six or seven pairs but then she became one of the unlucky victims as she grabbed Rudy's off-target toss a bit too hard. "Sorry kiddo, that was my fault." He came over to her to check out the damage. "Good. You're not too wet. You should dry okay in this heat."

"Oh, yeah," she thought, wondering how well one dried out in ninety percent humidity. Rudy and she stood and talked while the shmoo throwing finished.

"How's that cut healing?" he asked. Claire told him that she thought it was doing well since she hardly even thought of it anymore. He walked her back to the table where Leonard was giving prenatal advice to a very pregnant young woman while a toddler pulled impatiently on the hem of her dress. Rudy added his opinion to the conversation, which seemed to involve vitamins. Claire sat down and was soon joined by Betty, who told her whom she had run into and passed on some interesting information she had gleaned.

Rudy turned and said, "I'm going over to watch Ron in the softball game. Oh, by the way, did you enjoy Ron's Fourth of July wake-up call? He seems to find louder ones every year. You ladies drop by for a limeade some afternoon. Bye, ladies. Bye, Leonard. And Leonard, you keep writing those prescriptions." He nodded and turned toward the baseball field.

"That is one nice man," Betty said. "Everyone loves Rudy. He treats everyone in such a friendly, sincere way. I can't imagine that drug store without him."

Right then out of the corner of her eye Claire caught sight of a large tray of fruit being carried through the middle of a group of people. As Claire looked closer she discovered that it was not a tray of fruit but instead was a hat of fruit. Apples, oranges, grapes and plums decorated the brim on a large white hat. She had a pretty good idea who was wearing it. She could tell her presumption was correct when the fruit headed in her direction and the people around it went their own ways. Lila Hayward came right over to Claire and grabbed her hand. "Is this not the most wonderful Fourth of July celebration you have ever seen? Aren't the games just wonderful? Have you been participating like a good little Hayward citizen? Just wait for the food. It's just to die for! And how are you two doing on this delightful day?" she asked, turning toward the Nuttings. They responded politely and then Lila was off to work the rest of the crowd.

Claire turned to Betty and quietly said, "I had the urge to ask her if there was going to be a hog calling contest as one of the events but I was afraid I would not have been able to keep a straight face. By the way, where does she get those hats? I assume she doesn't just walk over to Felton's Clothing and pick them out."

Betty laughed. "I really have no idea where she gets them. I imagine she does some catalogue shopping or goes to Des Moines. I can't imagine any reputable department store carrying some of the creations she wears. Maybe she makes them herself."

Many people had settled back into their pre-shmoo activities but Claire's stomach was starting to ask when it would be time to eat. She could smell the meat cooking and that added to the rumblings that were going on deep inside her. Betty nodded toward where the bingo game had just broken up. "How would you like to help set up the tables for the pot luck?" she asked Claire.

"If that will help us eat sooner, I would love to," she responded, jumping up from her seat.

Rolls of paper appeared and were placed over numerous tables. No sooner had the paper gone on the tables than women came forth with their arms full of dishes and pans of all shapes and sizes. There were vegetable dishes, more kinds of potato salads than Claire could ever have imagined, pasta salads, fruit salads, Jello salads, homemade breads and rolls, and real butter. Then came the desserts—pies, cakes, cookies, brownies and containers of homemade ice cream. Just as the food had appeared as soon as the paper was laid down, people with plates in hand appeared as the last bit of food was set on the table.

The main course was barbecued pork. Claire wondered how many hogs had died for this feast. It was hard to choose what to take. The salads were especially tempting. She decided to pass up the yummy looking ones with cucumbers. She had reached the age when putting slices of cucumbers on her puffy eyes agreed with her body more than putting them in her stomach. Everything smelled wonderful. Everything tasted as wonderful as it smelled. Like most others, Claire went back for seconds, or to get firsts of things that she hadn't tried before. She noticed that the cake she had brought was almost all gone, one small piece remaining. "Success!" she said to herself. But what appealed to her most was the homemade ice cream. Her dad had had a hand-turned freezer but it was used only on rare occasions. And those rare occasions often turned out to be on unseasonably cool days. Sometimes the family would not even be able to turn the freezer outside but took turns with that chore while sitting in the basement. Even on those chilly days there was nothing like that taste. She always thought that the effort involved added to the flavor but she had done nothing to assist in the making of these ice creams and they were scrumptious. There were different flavors but she stuck with vanilla.

There was one more contest after dinner. That was the watermelon seed spitting contest. There were separate contests, one for the children under ten, one for the teens, one for women and one for men. Although encouraged to participate, Claire managed to talk her way out of it. She had always had the fear that if she did try this she would inhale the seed and choke. Plus she never felt it was a very ladylike thing to do. Everyone, contestants and observers, had fun with this post-dinner event.

As the sunlight waned, the mosquitoes increased. Some people are seldom bothered by the vicious bloodthirsty little beasts. Claire, however, was not one of those. They loved her and she was spending a lot of energy trying to shoo them away. Leonard reached under the table and pulled out a bottle of insect repellent. "I try to keep my patients happy and healthy," he said, handing her the bottle. The stuff smelled bad. It must have smelled bad to the mosquitoes, too, since they didn't bother her any more that night.

The fireworks display was very nice. It didn't equal what she was used to in a bigger city, but there were lots of "oohs" and "aahs" and they kept the crowd happily engaged. After the last bang, people began to gather up their belongings. Claire offered to help Betty and Leonard, but Betty said they would take care of everything after Leonard tended to a burn suffered by a youngster who got too close to a sparkler. Since Claire was by herself, she was one of the first to leave the park.

As she walked home she reflected on the day and felt it fulfilled her desire for a celebration built around love of country and care for each other. Claire was thinking of how much fun the games had been when she jumped almost off the sidewalk. It was the Haywards' dog once again taking on the role of protector of his property and any surrounding areas. She hurried her pace and was glad when she had crossed over Maple and was in her own block. Most of the houses were dark, although some had the forethought to turn on porch lights before going to the park. Behind her Claire could hear cars leaving and heading up Oak, and voices of the people as they too walked home after a very busy, fun-filled day.

Despite being busy putting simple finishing touches on her new home, Claire managed to finish reading the library books before they actually were due, so she decided to make another trip to the town library. She walked across the square instead of using the sidewalk on Oak. It was nice to walk under the trees providing a canopy over her head while the birds serenaded her. She thought that if it didn't warm up too quickly she would sit on one of the benches and read one of the newly checked out books. As she climbed the stairs she saw a sign she had not noticed before hanging to the right of the front door. It read, "Library is open. Do not use book drop!"

"Well, that could have been said in a friendlier way," Claire thought, but somehow she was not surprised. She opened the door and was greeted by the icy glare of Miss Bertha Banter. She suddenly felt like a child who might have been sent to the principal's office for some misdeed. "Where should I return my books?" Claire asked. She said the words in a quiet voice, not so much because it was the proper volume for a library but because of being intimidated by this scowling, surly person.

Bertha looked down her nose at Claire from her extra tall chair, which allowed her to look down on everyone. She tapped on the desk. "Here. Just put them here," she answered in a demanding way. Claire carefully placed them in a pile in front of Miss Banter and started to walk away to find her next selections. "Wait! You may not go yet!" Claire turned around to see what the librarian was talking about. "You need to stay here until you are cleared."

"Cleared? What do you mean 'cleared'?" Claire asked in disbelief and exasperation.

"I have to inspect the books to make sure they are being returned in the same condition in which they left the library." Bertha checked the fronts and backs. She fanned through the pages doing a brief examination of the body of the books. She closed each book and examined the tops and sides of the pages. "You may go now," she said in her usual brusque way.

"Do you check every returned book that thoroughly? Doesn't that take a lot of time? It seems that as busy as you seem to be around here you might not have time to do such methodical examinations of every volume." Claire's sarcasm about Bertha's demanding work load seemed to go right over her head as she glared at Claire in return.

Bertha straightened in her chair, trying to make herself look as large and prevailing as possible. "There is absolutely no need to check the books returned by the regulars who have proven to me that they have the appropriate respect for the city's property. Until that level of trust is achieved I check all the returned items. Keeping my books in the best possible condition is a responsibility I take very seriously. Now, unless there are more questions or requests, please proceed with whatever you came for. I have many things to do and I have no time for idle chit-chat." Bertha began to shuffle through stacks of cards that were in a set of drawers sitting on her desk.

Claire walked away, rolling her eyes in disbelief. It was no wonder there was no one else in the library. Someone would have to be very desperate for something to read to frequent this cold, prickly place. She shook her head, trying to shake off negative feelings. She refused to let this little library Nazi disrupt her reading habits. Claire strolled the aisles in the fiction section and found five books she thought looked interesting. She wondered how many she was allowed to check out at one time but she did not want to keep Miss Banter from her important business by asking another question. Since Claire previously had checked out three books, she decided to settle for that same number again. She debated with herself about which ones to keep. When her decision was made, she started to lay the temporary rejects on one of the tables at the ends of the rows below the sign boldly stating, "Do not reshelve books!" She quickly looked around to make sure the coast was clear and then hastily replaced the two books. She knew it was no big deal but took pleasure in doing something that Miss Banter had specifically forbidden. "So there," she said in her quietest library voice.

Claire took her selections to the check out table and found that the book warden was not there. She waited patiently rocking back and forth from heels to toes. She looked around and didn't see Bertha at all. After a few minutes Claire began to wonder if some horrible fate had befallen her deep in the depths of the library stacks. Maybe her heart just gave out somewhere amid the periodicals. But then she didn't seem to have much of a heart so that was probably not a concern. Maybe she got hung up trying to reshelve a book on a top shelf. Maybe a heavy book fell off the shelf, hitting her in the head and knocking her out. Maybe she fell down the stairs while taking something into the basement. Or maybe she just slid off her big chair and was lying helplessly right behind the check out desk where no one could see her.

After a couple of minutes Claire was beginning to get worried when she was startled back to reality when right behind her came that unpleasant voice, "Are you ready to check out?" She turned to see Miss Banter giving her that same hostile glower but behind that solemn face she envisioned Bertha's being pleased that she had made Claire jump.

Claire took a deep breath to try to regain her composure. "Yes, I am. I have found a few that look quite interesting," she said, not wanting to appear anxious.

"I doubt that you would be checking out things that you were not interested in, would you?" Bertha said coldly, probably enjoying this put-down. She moved toward the back of the over-sized desk when Claire noticed her shoes. They had thick rubber soles and they made absolutely no noise on the wood floors. No wonder she was able to sneak up behind Claire like that. She was probably hiding somewhere in the stacks just waiting for an opportune time to make her move to scare this unsuspecting customer. Claire wondered how many times she had done this before.

Claire handed Miss Banter her three books. "Do you have a library card?" Bertha calmly asked.

Claire wanted to scream, "Of course I do, you silly woman! How else do you think I was able to check out those other books!" Instead, Claire handed her the card that she had carefully tucked into her pocket before leaving the house. Bertha looked at the card, looked up at Claire, and looked at the card again. Claire felt like she was going through some kind of security clearance. She must have passed because Bertha once again pulled out her stamp and stamp pad and systematically and rhythmically stamped the due date in each book. Then she handed Claire her card atop the books.

"Two weeks," she said.

"Thank you," Claire mumbled as she turned to leave. It was a good thing that the front door was attached securely. She pushed it so hard out of frustration that it opened to its full extent and bounced back toward her. She stomped down the steps with what must have been a look that reflected her feelings. For at the bottom step she ran into, literally, Bud Hornsby who was headed to his Ford dealership.

"I am so sorry," Claire said, "I guess I wasn't looking at where I was going."

Bud laughed. "I'll bet you just spent some time with Miss Banter. You're not the first person to come storming out of those library doors. It really is too bad that she upsets the patrons so much. I know grown men who are afraid of her. Ellen used to be scared of her but she isn't bothered too much by her anymore, so now she checks out books for me."

"How does she keep her job with an attitude like that?" Claire asked.

"I don't know. I guess you would have to ask the mayor or the town council. I hope you can enjoy your books despite what you must have gone through to get them. I'll see you later." Bud headed off to work and Claire headed home.

Claire was no longer interested in calmly sitting in the park and reading. She just wanted to get home and calm her nerves. She stomped across the grass, avoiding the sidewalk like all good Haywardites probably did, and headed home. When she got to the house she headed straight for the kitchen to find comfort food. "Chocolate! That's what I need." Claire rifled the cabinets looking for that delightful brown substance. Any kind would do—chocolate cookies, chocolate covered raisins, bridge mix. Even just chocolate chips. But no luck. Now she felt even worse than she had before. Then Claire remembered them. They were in the freezer where she had stashed them after her first grocery shopping trip. She opened the top freezer door and waiting for her amid the frozen vegetables lay a Hershey bar and Milky Way. Now the decision was which one to choose. She decided on the Milky Way and carried it to the back porch as reverently as if it were a family treasure. Claire sat down and, as she started to salivate, unwrapped the candy. That first taste was heavenly. Of course her first urge was to devour it quickly. Since it was frozen it was impossible to eat it too fast, so she nibbled at it very slowly, enjoying each small, cold delicious bite.

Six

The small U-Haul trailer pulled up to 203 Oak early Monday evening. A man and a woman in their late thirties unloaded the trailer, taking turns carrying items into the house. The trailer was unloaded in less than two hours and was towed away. The blue four-door sedan was back later that night and pulled into the garage in the back of the house.

Weeks ago Claire had been invited to attend the Tuesday morning quilting group that met at the Methodist church. She decided that might be a fun hobby to pick up again, so she joined them in the church basement at ten o'clock. It was an inter-denominational as well as a cross-generational group. She guessed that the women ranged in age from their eighties to thirties. There were many familiar faces and she could even put names with many of them. Grace Carlson, Phoebe Peoples, Ellen Hornsby, Jane Dunn and Elizabeth Lambert, her neighbor across the street to the north, were among those she knew. Betty Nutting often joined the group but that day she was substituting for Sally Jensen, who was taking a few days off from the clinic. Meredith Andrews and Clara were even there.

At this stage in the quilt's progress, sections were being put together before they would all be combined to be quilted. There were small gatherings around the room to work on the sections. Claire sat in a group with Meredith, Clara, Ellen, and a lady she had had not met, Francine Simpson, wife of Bob who owned the hardware store and daughter-in-law of Farley. Clara looked at Claire suspiciously and Claire heard her whisper to Francine, who sat next to her, "She's a crook, you know."

"Now, Clara," Francine said patiently, "I am sure that Claire is not a crook."

"Well, she sure looks like a crook to me," Clara said, squinting at Claire

Except for Clara's suspicions of her, from what Claire could hear, the topic of conversation in each group was quite similar.

Ellen looked at Meredith and Francine. "I see you have a new neighbor. What in the world happened to Lois?" Meredith leaned over and told Claire that Lois Teller was an elderly widow who had been pretty much homebound.

"I guess that her daughter and son-in-law felt they just couldn't let her stay by herself anymore. An opening came up in the nursing home and they took it. They moved her out last week. I didn't find out until Saturday," Francine explained. "They came over and thanked us for helping to watch out for her for so long."

Meredith continued, "They came and talked to us, too. Clara had always liked Lois. I think it was a good move but it happened so fast. They decided to rent the house for now, furniture and all. I guess they took only a rocking chair and a dresser to Lois's new place. They said that they had a response right away about renting the house."

Ellen continued to question, "Do you know anything about the new people?"

Meredith turned to Francine and said, "I don't know anything. Do you?"

"They just told me that it was a couple and they'd be coming soon, but I didn't think it would be that soon!" answered Francine.

Francine continued, "They sure didn't seem to have much to unload from that trailer. It looked like mainly clothes and a nice big television. The two of them seemed to struggle to get it moved in. I would have had Bob go help them but he wasn't home. I'll probably go over this evening and take some cookies or a pie."

"Well you had better be darn careful," Clara chimed in, "because you know they're crooks." Meredith just rolled her eyes and sighed. "Here, better take this," Clara continued, reaching in her purse and pulling out her squirt gun.

"Mother, that squirt gun won't frighten anyone. Now put that away."

"Well, it couldn't hurt anything," Clara said, angrily stuffing her weapon back into her purse.

A flurry of color by the door caught most eyes. A bright orange dress with a matching straw hat, bedecked with silk brown-eyed Susans, rushed into the room. "Have you seen them? Did you know that I have new people behind me? I went over this morning and knocked on the door and no one answered. I am sure they were there. I think I heard movement inside. Can you imagine not answering the door when I come to visit?" There were a few muffled comments as Lila flung her hand to her forehead and threw herself into a chair.

Ellen tried to calm the distraught first lady of Hayward. "Lila, maybe no one was there. Or maybe someone was on the phone and couldn't come to the door. Maybe someone had just gotten out of the tub and wasn't dressed. There could be all sorts of reasons why no one opened the door. Maybe you should go back later today and try again."

"Oh, I suppose that is possible," sighed Lila. "I just so wanted to be the first to welcome them to town. Maybe I'll just sit here with you ladies for awhile. It is much cooler down here than outside. You just get back to what you were doing. I'll be fine."

Claire could see eyes meeting eyes around the room and heads shaking. She was getting the definite feeling that Lila was not the most popular lady in town. She assumed that Chester must be better liked than his fashion plate wife. Maybe he sent her out of town on shopping trips during election times to improve his chances for a victory.

People were back to their sewing, and conversations were much more varied. "What happens to this quilt when it is complete?" Claire asked.

Ellen answered. "We've done different things with it in the past. Sometimes we have given it to needy families. We've sent some smaller ones to the seniors' home in Livonia. One went to a family whose home burned. And one year we raffled it off to help raise money for college costs for a young man whose father was killed in a farming accident. We always seem to come up with good places for them. As far as I know the group has not decided where this one is going."

The morning went very fast and Claire enjoyed her time. It was good to be socializing with a group of women again. It was also, as she had expected, a good way to get to know the who's and what's of the town. Lila had left early, after composing herself from the initial shock of being rejected at the door of her new neighbors. Claire knew that as soon as anyone found out anything about the newcomers, the word would spread. She had witnessed how fast gossip or actual information traveled around here. And she was glad that she was no longer the new arrival and the big topic of conversation. "Maybe I should meet these people soon and welcome them as a person who knows what all that scrutiny is like," she thought, "but I don't want to overwhelm. If Lila gets to them first, they might not be too anxious to meet many more people for awhile."

"Why didn't you answer the door?" he asked her sharply. "Don't you think that looked suspicious?"

"I don't care. I don't want to meet anyone. Why'd you have to pick this place, Tony?" she whined.

"Don't call me Tony. You can't be calling me Tony. My name is Mike. How many times do I have to tell you? I have to be Mike, and you have to call me Mike."

"Mike, shmike, why'd you have to pick that dorky name?" she whined again.

"I don't recall that I had much say in the matter. Just get used to it," Tony said in a harsh tone. "And if I say Missy you better answer right away."

"Missy! Mother of God, whoever thought I would be a Missy? Prissy Missy. I hate it. Why couldn't I just keep Rita? I'm going to blow it, I know."

"You know perfectly well why you couldn't keep Rita. And you better not blow it, I'm warning you right now. Let's get this stuff put away and make it look like we're all settled."

"And Tony, I mean Mike, do we have to keep this ugly furniture? It must be a hundred years old. I hate it! Can't we buy some stuff that doesn't look like it was from the dark ages?"

"Listen, Rita, uh, Missy, you'll learn to love it or at least you will pretend to love it. Maybe later we can replace some of it. But not now. Besides, keeping this stuff helps make it look like we actually belong here. I have a feeling these people might get a little upset with too much change."

"More coffee, gents?" Maude asked the group that sat around one of the front tables. She filled up the cups and then lingered to hear what was being said about the new couple in town.

"Lila went over and gave them an official welcome. But I must say she wasn't too impressed. She didn't think they were too friendly. She didn't like the way the gal, I think her name was Misty or something like that, dressed. Said it was too provocative," the mayor shared with the group.

"Well, I've seen how she dressed and I kind of liked it," Steve Williams said. "I was on my route and walked by while she was out in the yard. I thought she looked pretty good. But don't tell my wife I said that."

"I saw them coming out of the bank. Did Clarence say anything about them?" asked Frank Felton, whose clothing store was next to the bank.

"Now Frank, you know it would not be ethical for Clarence to talk about his customers," Chester responded. But after a brief pause he added, "But yeah, they did open a joint account. He said it wasn't for a huge amount but he had the feeling that there would be more added later. But that's just between us. Do you hear me, Scoop? If anything we talk about here gets into *The Banner*, I'll have Clarence call your loan, and I'm not kidding this time."

"You have my word," said Bruce Gibson, who had heard this threat many times before. But this time he felt that the mayor probably meant it. "But what else do you know?"

No one had the chance to answer before the group was joined by Bud Hornsby. "Room for one more?" Bud pulled up a chair from the next table as the other four repositioned their chairs to make room. "What's new, as if I didn't know?"

Rudy Milstein, who had left Ron in charge during his lunch break, aimed a question at Bud. "Do you know anything about the new couple?"

The smug look on Bud's face gave it away before he even had to say anything. "Yup, I know a few things. Just what would you like to know?" Bud was enjoying being in the spotlight and prolonged their curiosity while he gave Maude his lunch order.

"Spill it," said Scoop impatiently.

Drawing his first word as long as he could he said, "Well, they are from Chicago. Mike, that's the guy's name, said he recently received a very large inheritance. He and his wife decided they wanted to get away from the rat race of a big city and come to a small town to slow down and enjoy life. Said they picked here because he had a cousin or aunt or knew somebody who worked at the nursing home in Livonia and told him that Lois' house had just become available, furniture and all. They packed up a few things and here they are. Can you imagine just packing up and leaving like that? Anyway, Mike said that even though he really didn't need to work because of all the money he was going to be getting, he didn't want to sit around the house all day. He said that leaving a fast-paced life was one thing, but coming to a dead stop was something else. He said years ago he had worked in a Ford dealership that was no longer in business, first repairing cars and then selling them. Then he had a variety of jobs. He wondered if I could use some help, even if it was just part time. I asked him a few questions and he seemed to know what he was talking about. So we worked out a deal. He'll start half time and then maybe we'll increase his hours. This should give me a lot more time to get out and play golf."

"I'm sure Ellen will be thrilled with that idea," joked Rudy.

"I think I'll drop by and interview Mike and—what's his wife's name?" asked Bruce, edging forward in his chair, looking as if he was ready to charge down the street at any minute.

"Oh, I don't know. I don't even remember his talking about her at all. But you can find that out. That is why we call you 'Scoop', isn't it?" Bud answered with a laugh.

"I was surprised that you never ran an interview with Claire Menefee," commented Rudy.

"Well, if you recall, she came right before Scott was born. He and Gloria kept me pretty busy morning and night for awhile."

"I did notice that there were a few skinny editions there for a couple of weeks. It was kind of like reading a half page of news and the rest advertising. By the way, you ran my ad bigger than we agreed. You're not going to try to charge extra for that, are you? I won't pay for it," said Frank, secretly pleased that the bigger ad had been quite eye-catching and showed off some of his summer clothing specials.

"No, of course not. I did that with quite a few just to take up space. Now that Scott is sleeping better, and we're all sleeping better, I can get things back on track. How'd you like the birth announcements you got? I designed and printed those myself." Bruce didn't really want an answer but said it as a little reminder that his printing business extended beyond just the newspaper. He got up from the little male gossip group, left the money for Maude at the cash register and was out the door at a pretty fast pace.

The article that Scoop ran about Mike and Missy Brock contained mainly the same information that Bud had repeated. He did get a bit more information about Missy who, to Scoop, seemed to be much less enamored with this sudden move than was her husband. She said that she wasn't crazy about gardening but she figured she could learn. She was a little concerned about the selection of goods at the clothing and drug stores but figured she could get used to it. She wasn't sure that the theater on Maple Street behind the bank would provide the quality of entertainment she was used to but she figured it would just have to do. And she definitely was not fond of the "maniacal vicious dog" that lived in that big white house next door and she was sure she would never get used to him. Scoop had to tweak her words a bit to make Hayward sound not so provincial. He decided that he would write nothing about her comment on the mayor's dog, although he knew that those were the same sentiments of most of the townsfolk.

Not wanting to show favoritism for Missy and Mike over Claire, he also interviewed her. He knew that by now almost anything he could write about her would be old news but it just seemed like the right thing to do. Still he managed to write a column that gave some information that many people might not have known. He told about her family which right away made her article different from that of Missy and Mike since they steered away from any mention of family. He told about her hobbies and what she had been involved with and enjoyed since her move to town. Mike and Missy, of course, had not had time to get involved in anything but when it came to hobbies, their list was pretty nonexistent. Mike did mention that he did enjoy an occasional game of poker. Missy could not think of much of anything that she enjoyed except watching television. Scoop wondered how well she was going to enjoy being here. He suspected that there were not many other ladies with whom she could discuss the characters and plots of the afternoon soap operas.

Claire had read a couple of issues of the *The Banner* but she was much more interested in this latest edition. She was curious about what Bruce had written about her. She was somewhat pleased to find she was not on the front page. Instead there was a feature length article about the Bennetts, the county farm family of the year. There was a large picture of the family on the front page. On the middle pages were more pictures, some showing each of the children doing one of the many chores that have to be done around the farm.

The articles about the Brocks and Claire were on page three. Claire read the article about her twice and felt it pretty much followed just what she had told Bruce. She had come from a place where people were often misquoted in the paper so this was a relief to see his writing was actually what she had said. Then Claire read the section about the Brocks. She got the feeling that Mike was a much more outgoing person than his wife. But then, she thought, maybe Mrs. Brock was just shy and uncomfortable around strangers. Besides, maybe Missy just didn't want people here to know very much about her. Even though Haywardites were pretty open, Claire had to remind herself that not everyone is.

This issue had a variety of articles. One encouraged the children to keep up their reading since the summer reading program would be ending in two weeks. The names of the participants were listed as were some of the prizes they could win. Among these were US savings bonds, donated by Clarence and Elizabeth Lambert, stuffed animals from the Simpson's hardware store, an Iowa State baseball hat from Felton's clothing, and certificates for ice cream and sodas donated by Rudy Milstein. There was also a thank you to Hayward Groceries for the donation of paper bags that had been used to make vests for one of the activities.

The results of the county fair were listed. Many of these names were beginning to sound quite familiar to Claire. In the sports section, she learned that the Hayward Sharks had a good showing in the regional swim meet, taking two seconds and six thirds. The winners of the golf tournament were listed. One was Aaron Andrews. Claire was sure that Meredith was happy for him but that she would have rather had him around the house more often to help with Clara rather than out sharpening his golf skills.

There was an article reminding the children that next week would be Vacation Bible School in all of the churches in town. Claire thought this was an interesting approach to VBS. By having it toward the end of summer vacation maybe the turnout was better since the kids might be more bored and ready for something else to do by then. She wondered why all of the churches had theirs the same weeks. Perhaps some programs were more fun than others and some of the congregations were afraid of having their little ones indoctrinated into a different church. Anyway, whatever the reason, Claire wondered if she would be asked to help. She might be willing to assist with snacks or crafts but certainly was not ready to take on planning and delivering lessons. She had done enough of that to last her for a long time.

Claire glanced through the classified sections just to see what was there. There seemed to be the typical things. There were sections listing pets and livestock for sale. There was a variety of tack and horse trailers. There were cars, none of them very new, and lots of trucks. Although there was no real estate for sale or rent in Hayward, there were a few rentals listed in Livonia. There was one farm sale coming up but she didn't recognize either the name or the location. If anyone was in need of a piece or two of furniture, they might be helped by the listings of used items. And, of course, there was a lost and found section. The Perkins were asking help finding their goat, Frannie, who had reportedly been last seen along county road 52 chewing a red and gray plaid shirt. This listing ran right above that submitted by someone looking for help to find the culprit who had removed a red Pendleton wool shirt from the clothesline where it was airing. Claire had a feeling that the Perkins might soon be getting an angry phone call. There was an ad for a "nearly new" Briggs & Stratton lawn tractor engine, with the proviso that "buyer must take the mower to which it is attached."

The Tuesday quilting group rehashed the articles about the Brocks that had appeared in *The Banner*. Those who had actually had the chance to meet them added their perspective. Vernina said that Bryan said Missy was not very friendly when she came in to buy groceries. "He didn't say that she was downright rude, just more cold and unfriendly."

Ellen Hornsby had not yet met Missy but had talked to Mike for a short time. "He seemed nice. We didn't talk about really much of anything, about the weather and stuff, you know. But I didn't know that people from Chicago sounded like that. I thought he seemed to have more of an east coast accent."

Gladys Felton added, "Frank hasn't met her yet but said that he'd be hanged before he would carry clothes in his store like the ones she wears." The ladies chuckled about that as some smoothed their skirts making sure they were not showing too much of their legs.

Elizabeth Lambert quoted her husband as saying, "'It's good to have some new money, I mean people, in this town.' I asked him what he meant by that but he just mentioned that the Brocks had opened an account and new accounts were always good for business."

Francine Simpson said she had taken them a peach pie. "Mike raved about the thought of a homemade pie. He said his mother had been the queen of the pie makers but he hadn't had a good one in years. Well, his wife turned to him and gave him the meanest look. I have the feeling that she doesn't like to cook."

"I don't think she likes to eat," chimed in Phoebe Peoples. "I saw her for just a moment when they both were going into the post office. She is way too skinny for my taste. Do you think men like it when women look like that?"

"You got me," added Francine, "I have often felt that what they say and what they think are two different things. I think they say what they think we want them to say just to keep peace."

Jane smiled proudly. "Well, Jim says he likes me this way, on the plump side. He says there is more of me to love." Claire looked at Jane as she made that remark and thought she looked as if she was putting on a little weight. Claire thought she and Betty should invite Jane to join them on their walks.

Meredith said that she too had received a much friendlier reception from Mike. She had invited Missy over for tea but had been rejected. "She wasn't rude, just quiet, said she still had a lot more organizing to get done."

"I'm glad she didn't come. She's a crook," chimed in Clara in her ever-accusa-tory tone.

They all had a small sense of guilt when a gentle voice behind them said, "Maybe we should just give her time. Not everyone likes to be hovered over. They have just been here a little over a week, after all." Claire recognized the voice as that of Grace Carlson. Of course, Grace was right. They were all being too quick to judge someone who just seemed a bit different from the Hayward mold. Her truthful comments had just been delivered when, with her usual dramatic flair, Lila rushed into the room. Claire was getting the feeling that Lila liked to come to these gatherings late so that she could draw more attention to herself.

"I have met them, have any of you?" Lila left no time for an answer. "I went over with some of my prize winning gladiolas. I picked almost the best ones from the backyard. And all that she could say was, 'Thank you.' They were beauti-ful—pinks and reds and yellows—and all she could say was, 'Thank you.' Then she looked around and I kid you not, the look on her face was like saying, 'Where am I going to put these?' I wanted to just rip them right out of her scrawny little arms and say, 'Listen, Missy, if you don't want them I'll take them back.' Come to find out that her name actually is Missy. Who would ever name their daughter Missy, anyway?" Lila looked as if she would swoon at any moment, so Claire stood and offered her chair, into which Lila immediately collapsed.

Feeling that her words would fall on deaf ears Claire rephrased what Grace had said. "Maybe we are judging too hard, too fast. I loved meeting you all at once because it was my choice to be here and make this my new home. Maybe it was her husband who talked her into this move. Or maybe he made the decision by himself and she really didn't want to come. I say give her some space and some time."

Heads nodded all around. Even Lila seemed to agree a bit but added, "But you don't have to live by them. Besides, she said she was afraid of our dog. Can you imagine anyone being afraid of Mellow?"

"Yes!" almost everyone said in unison.

"What, you mean you all are afraid of little Mellow. We called him Marsh-mallow when he was a new puppy because he was so sweet and pudgy. Now we just call him Mellow. You wouldn't feel that way about him if you just got to know him." Lila added emphatically, "Some people are just too quick to judge."

Seven

As Claire guessed, she was asked to help with vacation Bible school. She quickly said that she would help with the snacks. Claire figured that mixing Kool-Aid and counting out cookies wouldn't involve too much brain power. There were only four classes to take care of: pre-school, kindergarten and first, second and third, and fourth through sixth together. Claire had wondered if she might need to bring some of the cookies but that had been organized by the women's group before she was recruited. On Monday there was a variety of drop cookies. On Tuesday there were bar cookies. Wednesday the cookies were all in the shape of stars and crescent moons, the stars iced in yellow and moons in white. Thursday was brownie day.

Every day Phoebe Peoples, who was in charge of music for the week, would make a trip through the kitchen to make sure, as she explained, that everything was okay in the snack department. She carefully would eye the cookies and, after making her selection, always said, "I think there are a few extra. I'll just sample one." One turned into two or even three, but she was right. There were always extras. Claire did a good job of resisting those extras, even the thick chocolate chip ones. But on Thursday the brownies were too much of a temptation. After snacks had been delivered to all of the classes she sat down to enjoy a brownie and a glass of milk, a welcome change from the sweet Kool-Aid of the other days.

Friday saw the arrival of six-inch gingerbread men. They would be individually decorated by each child. As closely as Claire could figure this was done to be symbolic of how God had created man in his own image, or something to that effect. Evidently this was a tradition and something looked forward to by children and Sylvia White, who was in charge of the crafts. The frosting of the cookies took the place of a craft for that day so she did not need to plan for anything. The decorating done by the smaller children was very basic with more frosting on fingers and hands than on the cookies. On the other extreme, those done by the older children were very elaborate. Licorice whips outlined the ends of sleeves and pant legs, silver balls sprinkles and red-hots were used as buttons, earrings or polka dots, M&Ms were eyes. Some even planned ahead, bringing garlic presses from home to make frosting hair. Whereas the little guys ate theirs as soon as they slapped on some frosting, many of the creations of the older children were laid carefully aside to be proudly displayed and then taken home.

Everyone was glad to see Friday come, even though the week had gone fast and had been fun. About mid-morning, Grace, who was in charge of the entire VBS week, went to each classroom telling all the adults that there was going to be a quick meeting as soon as the children had gone. Claire figured this would be kind of a wrap up and critique of the week. It turned out to be a bit more and was a typical example of the caring attitude that she heard so much about.

As teachers finished with their children they all sat together in a small circle. When everyone was there Grace came through the tunnel followed by Reverend Carlson. Claire figured he was coming to thank them for a job well done. But when she looked at his face, it had not simply a look of gratitude but one of concern.

"First, ladies, I want to thank you for your help in making this yet another successful vacation Bible school. I hope you know how much you all are appreciated by every member of this congregation for devoting your time for the betterment of our children. Now I need to ask for your help in something else. This morning while you were helping with the gingerbread men…we did have gingerbread men again, didn't we?" he asked looking at Grace. She nodded and he continued, "…Ben Miller decided to start painting his house. He had just started when he fell off the ladder. Doc Nutting was there right away and said he had a broken arm, but he called an ambulance and took him to Livonia for x-rays just to be sure. If all that is broken is his arm he is very lucky at his age. Anyway, I called the other churches and they are spreading the word, too. We're going to get as many folks as possible to work this weekend and finish the painting job for him. We'd like to have some food there for the workers so if any of you ladies could help out in that department it would be greatly appreciated."

Claire turned to Grace and asked, "Is that the dark green house with all the white vertical lines?"

"Yes, that's the one. It will be a bear to paint."

Claire turned to Bill and asked, "Do only the men get to paint?"

He looked a bit startled and said, "Well, I suppose anyone could paint. Any adult that is. I just said men because I don't know many gals who enjoy painting. In fact I don't know many men who enjoy it, either."

"I would much prefer standing on a ladder with a brush in my hand to standing in front of a stove with a spoon in my hand. So if it doesn't bother anyone, I would rather paint."

"So would I," piped up Francine Simpson, "and I know that Bob will furnish the extra paint brushes if volunteers don't bring their own."

It was settled. The women present would be happy to help, and they would contact others in the church to contribute food for the workers. Francine and Claire headed down Oak and stopped in front of 107. "What was that old guy thinking?" said Francine. "That is one difficult house to paint. How did he ever think he would be able to get all of those white stripes painted? That will take a very steady hand."

"Maybe he was going to make a change when he painted it and not do all of those narrow vertical stripes."

"Unless it is approved by the city council, no one on the center three square blocks is allowed to change the color or appearance of a house. That's one reason Hayward has retained such a strong Victorian appearance," explained Francine.

They stood for a few minutes pondering the task to which they had just committed themselves. To break the silence Claire finally said, "We can do it. We'll just view it as a good challenge. And maybe there will be some man who has really steady hands who will want to tackle those stripes."

"Don't count on that," Francine laughed. "No, don't count on that."

Claire woke up at five-thirty. She had no idea what time this painting project would get started but she didn't want to appear as a slacker and be late. Before going to bed she had dug old painting clothes out of a box in the basement. Claire had examined the shirt and old pants sentimentally, looking at the variety of colors of drips and splotches, each color that of a project done while painting children's and grandchildren's rooms and other decorating projects. "Well, I don't have a dark green yet. That will be a nice addition," she had told herself.

After getting dressed, Claire took her usual coffee and juice to the back porch where she sat watching a rabbit hopping around looking for something to eat, but finding not much to its liking. It finally gave up and wedged its way through a hole in the fence and into the Nuttings' yard. Claire was a bit nervous about the day's work. Would she offend some of the male population by straying from the food preparation department to the labor force? And if she did, would she care? Besides, she was taking Francine with her.

It was a little after seven when Claire walked around to the front and looked down the street to see if there was any activity at Ben's house. Two trucks were already there and the occupants were talking on the sidewalk. "Here I go," she thought, squaring her shoulders and heading to 107.

She greeted the two men whom she didn't know and introduced herself. They introduced themselves and said they owned farms next to Ben's old place. The three of them stood and surveyed the project. "Sure is fancy," said one. "A bit harder than painting a barn," said the other. Another truck with three men arrived, one older, who had also farmed near Ben, and his two sons. They dragged a couple of ladders out of their truck.

"What's the plan?" the older gentleman asked.

The rest of them shrugged and said they were just here to help like everyone else. Then the group heard a loud, "Good morning," coming from down the street. It was Mayor Hayward, dressed in overalls that looked as if they had never been worn. Past Chester, the volunteers could see others heading toward them as well as some other trucks and cars. The mayor walked around, shaking hands with everyone and thanking them for coming. When he felt that everyone had been greeted properly, he cleared his throat and said, "We need to come up with a plan." Then there was dead silence.

After a minute or two of silence Claire suggested that they should check and see if any areas needed to be scraped or primed. There were four ladders so one was set up on each side of the house and the group was divided into four teams to check for repairs and pre-painting steps that needed to be taken. The cadre of volunteers continued to grow and swarm. The smell of coffee and cinnamon rolls also arrived. The food was set up on the front lawn of the Graves' house. Volunteers gathered around eating the delicious warm rolls. Claire was glad that she had volunteered for this project. It was worth it just to get one of those rolls.

By this time there were lots of helpers, probably more than were actually needed. Not only were there old neighbors of Ben's, but everyone from his current neighborhood was there too—Bill Swan, Dr. Tim Payne, Doc Nutting, Bud Hornsby and his son Steve, and neighbors from across the alley. Clarence Lambert showed up for a short time with his brother-in-law, Charles Hayward. Both Jim Dunn and his assistant at the post office, Steve Williams, were there which made Claire wonder if there would be any mail delivery that day. Aaron Andrews was there but said he had to leave about noon since he had a one o'clock tee time. Bryan Graves came by on his way to the store to apologize for his absence but said he couldn't find anyone to mind the store because so many people were involved in the painting project. Steve Hornsby, who had worked part time in the grocery store the previous summer, quickly volunteered to substitute for Bryan. He said that he would really love to stay and paint but felt that it was his civic duty to work at the store for free so Bryan could help his elderly neighbor. He was off to the store with Bryan before his father could even object.

Ron Milstein came, but he didn't look like his heart was in this project. He said that he and Rudy had flipped a coin to see who manned the drug store and who came to paint. Ron had lost but Rudy said that was probably best since he could find the bandages and splints faster than Ron and he had a feeling they might be needed. Ministers from each church were there, which was good because it was looking as if this project was going to need lots of guidance from above.

The crew checking for repairs reported that luckily there was not much that needed to be done before the painting could start. Bob Simpson had brought a couple of cans of water-based primer that could dry fast so a small crew got started on those few spots right away. Chester, apparently feeling that he was the logical one to take charge, suggested dividing the workers into six crews, one for each side of the house and two for the garage in back. He went on to delegate those who would be the green painters on the top story and who would be on the bottom. Then he appointed the white paint crew. In the role of the head cheerleader, he said, "Let's hit it folks, and do it up right for good old Ben!"

Claire saw a few flaws in Chester's plan but was not about to say anything. She was hoping that someone else would voice concern but everyone took brushes in hand and divided up the paint into the smaller buckets that Bob Simpson had brought. Francine stepped over to her and said, "This could be interesting, couldn't it?" The two women had not yet been included in any of the crews but they figured that their turn would come.

Ladders, painters, and paint cans were going all directions. Francine and Claire walked around to observe the mission and the chaos. Everyone was so anxious to help that the adrenaline was flowing. Francine mentioned that she had never seen some of these men move so fast. They debated about whether or not to suggest that the main floor painters might want to wait until the painters above them were through, but figured that anyone should be sharp enough to figure that out. It wasn't long until someone below realized that this was not a good idea. Luckily the recipient of the spilled paint was wearing a hat so most of the green paint was deflected from his head. But his formerly blue work shirt was now a lovely splotchy green. The word was spread and the ground floor crew was more aware of when work was going on directly above them.

"Hey Jim, watch out there! You just got green on that trim I just painted."

That and similar complaints were heard on all sides. With ladders everywhere and people scurrying about in every direction it looked like an ant hill that had just been disturbed. It would be a miracle if no one was knocked off a ladder. It would also be a miracle if the foundation as well as the grass didn't end up being covered with green and white paint.

"Coffee break!" someone yelled. Ladders and paint brushes were abandoned as workers bedecked with specks of green or white or both walked to the front to get a cup of hot refreshment. As the workers gathered on the lawn, Francine looked at Claire, "Say something."

"No, you say something. You know these people much better than I do."

"Okay," Francine said. Clearing her throat, she inserted thumb and ring finger between her teeth and emitted the loudest, shrillest whistle Claire had ever heard. While it was painful for her ears since she was standing so close to Francine, it certainly got the attention of everyone assembled on the grass. Smiling at her Francine said, "Claire would like to make a suggestion."

Those were not the words Claire expected to hear, but now the ball was in her court. She took a deep breath and quickly composed her thoughts. "Francine and I have been very impressed with the effort that all of you are showing to get Ben's painting done. While walking around, however, we have seen some near-accidents."

"And some real accidents, too, right Herman?" someone said, pointing to the man who had the green paint poured on his head. Laughter went up from the crowd. "I think that is an improvement in his looks," someone else yelled. "Yeah," added a third, "I always said he was green behind the ears." When the laughter and comments had subsided Claire continued.

"Francine and I think it would be a better use of time and resources to be a bit more patient about painting the trim. We suggest that those doing the trim wait until the green siding above and around them is done. That way there won't have to be so many touch-ups to cover up green splashes. That might mean holding off for a little while or putting more people on the green crews."

Doc Nutting stepped up beside Claire and joined her in giving advice. "We don't want any injuries. Those on the ground have got to be more aware of where the ladders are. And although I am not superstitious, it's really a bad idea to walk under a ladder."

As the painters finished their coffee, they returned to their jobs but at a much less frantic pace. Those who were on the white paint crews took greater notice of what areas could safely be painted. Some even sat on the lawn, waiting until it was their turn.

"Get a big bucket!" someone yelled.

"No, get a washtub" yelled another frantically.

Francine and Claire looked at each other as if to say, "Now what?" They followed the sound of the excited voices to the back where they found Bryan Graves holding a four-legged green, black and white thing. Claire was pretty sure it was his dog, Socks, but at that point it was hard to tell. Bryan held on as well as he could to this strange looking creature while someone else tried using a hose to remove as much of the paint as possible. Some of the paint was being washed off but, as Socks struggled to be free, he shook as hard as he could to remove paint, water and Bryan's grip. Most of the painting had stopped as people gathered to see what was happening. Although Claire was sure that Bryan thought otherwise, it was a pretty funny sight.

Vernina and Ryan soon showed up with a rope which Bryan, with much effort, managed to fasten to Socks' collar. Bryan pulled Socks to the back of the yard, away from the garage, stood back and just let the poor animal shake off paint and water the best he could. "Maggie and Libby are filling their pool with soapy water," Vernina said, trying to offer encouragement to Bryan who was quite wet and colorful by this time. Once Socks stopped shaking, Bryan pulled him into the Graves backyard. "I'll take over now," Vernina offered.

"No, I'll do it. There's no sense in anyone else ending up looking like this." Poor Socks was led to the pool where Bryan picked him up and set him in the waiting wash water. By now the dog seemed resigned to the fate that awaited him. His head dropped and he stood patiently while the washing began.

The men laughed as they headed back to their posts. "What part was Bryan doing?" Claire asked.

"He was up on that ladder," someone volunteered nodding his head toward a tall extension ladder that reached the peak of the back of the house. "The trouble started when Bryan's dog saw him up there and started to climb the ladder to get to him. Bryan turned around to see who was bumping the ladder, started to lose his balance, and dropped his whole bucket of paint when he reached back for the ladder. It was something to see."

"I'll go get some more paint and take over for him," Claire said.

"Oh, I don't think you should. Let some man go up there," the man said looking at her as if she was not fit enough to climb a ladder that size.

"I would really like to do it. I've painted more than one house in my time. And heights don't bother me at all," Claire assured him.

"Okay, miss, if you're really sure."

Claire went to the station by the garage that had been set up as the headquarters. "With all these accidents, do you think we'll have enough paint?" she asked.

Doc Nutting was manning paint central. "Luckily Ben got his paint at Bob's store, so he could mix up some more if we need it." Claire poured the green paint into the bucket, found a brush and headed for the ladder. She could feel activity around her stop as she started to ascend. Her legs were shaking somewhat.

They always did that whenever she was getting used to the feel of a ladder. But Claire hoped that the shaking was not visible to the staring eyes below. When Claire reached the top, she sighed, looked upward and said a little "thank you" then turned and waved to her audience. She turned and continued where Bryan had left off.

A great deal had been accomplished when the next food crew arrived with lunch. There was sliced ham and turkey, homemade rolls and thick slices of bread, fried chicken and potato salad, and a big vat of sloppy joes. There was also a variety of Jello salads. Claire continually wondered how these Iowans managed to keep all of these Jello salads from melting in the summer heat. Potato chips, fruit, cookies, iced tea and lemonade were all plentiful. All the work came to a halt and the workers, who ate as if they had been deprived of food for days, devoured the provisions with gusto. Lunch break was winding down when there was a "Yoo hoo" from down the street. Everyone turned to see Lila waving and smiling at the group. She headed straight for Francine and Claire. "I bet you wondered where I was," she said with great excitement.

"I'll bet I didn't," Claire said to herself. Lila, of course, was wearing a hat but this was by far the most conservative one Claire had seen on Lila yet. It was just a normal, unadorned, wide-brimmed straw hat. She was wearing slacks that had smudges of dirt on them. Claire assumed these to be ones Lila had used while gardening. The top part of her body was covered with a painter's smock. It had not one spot of paint on it and Claire wondered if Lila had run into Des Moines last night to pick up a little something to wear to today's painting social.

"I'm here to paint. Where should I start?"

"Are you sure you want to do this, Lila?" Francine asked. "It can get pretty messy and we do have quite a few volunteers."

"Of course I want to help. It will be good for the morale of the men to see me joining in," she said, smiling from ear to ear. She must have equated herself to General Eisenhower visiting with the troops before D-Day.

Claire led her to the back of the house where the side beams were being painted. That way she could kind of enjoy Lila and her "help" while she was finishing the uppermost part of the siding. One of the men showed Lila the best way to use the brush without getting excess paint and how to apply it without leaving brush strokes. She had been at her post for no more than three or four minutes when the workers heard a distressed "Oh dear, oh dear! Look what I've done!" Lila stood with outstretched hand. "Oh, now I will have to do my nails all over again. How could I have been so clumsy!"

From where Claire was she could see nothing on Lila's hand but whatever it was upset her enough that she dropped the brush and hurried off around the corner of the house. Although Claire was sure he didn't mean for it to be heard by others, one of the men below shook his head and said, "What a weirdo!"

The body of the back of the house was completed. The men working on the trim continued to work. Claire turned and looked at the garage. It looked as if it was almost finished, too. She checked out both sides of the house and was pleased to see that those too were close to completion.

Francine showed up beside her. "Looks pretty good, doesn't it? But now you and I have a job to do." Claire had a feeling she knew what that was. Turning the corner at the front of the house, quite a few people were standing with hands on hips staring at the top striped sections.

"Why do you suppose anyone painted it that way to start with?" one older man asked.

"Someone was probably just trying to show up his neighbors," another suggested.

"I think it's lovely," said a lady who had gathered up the remainder of her food contributions and was headed for home, "but I'm sure glad that I don't have to paint it."

"Well, I sure as heck can't. My hand's not that steady anymore," ventured Dr. Payne who had already been on the trim detail. Claire was hoping he meant that his hand was not that steady after doing so much tedious painting and not that his hand was unsteady in general. The idea of trusting her teeth to a dentist with shaky hands was not a comforting thought.

Francine stepped up and said that Claire and she would give it a try if they all agreed to not stare at them while they worked. That seemed to be fine with the group, many saying that it was time for them to head home anyway. Everyone in front seemed to thank everyone else for helping and then Claire guessed they went around to the other sides to check out the work, thank those people too, and say their goodbyes.

Luckily that first big exodus had not taken place before the big black car with the gold star on the side pulled up and double parked in front. Butch Johnson got out, walked around to the passenger's side and helped out Ben Miller. Ben stood in the street surveying the hive of activity. Butch held on to his good arm and helped him up the walk toward the porch.

"I am so lucky. I am just so very lucky to have friends and neighbors like all of you," he said. Someone carried a chair off the porch so he could sit on the sidewalk and watch. As people left he told every worker thank you and called each and every one by name. As the afternoon continued and various sections were completed more of the workers left and Ben continued to express his heartfelt thanks. Doc Nutting came from his paint distribution center and suggested to Ben that he really should go inside and lie down for a rest but Ben sat fast, saying he couldn't leave these people finishing the work he really should be doing himself.

Francine and Claire started from opposite ends of the upper front section. "This is tricky," Francine said.

"What we need are some angled brushes. I assume that Bob has those at his store."

Francine let loose another one of her loud whistles and within moments Bob yelled up at her, "You called?"

"Could you run to the store and get a couple of angled brushes? That will make it faster and neater to paint these ridges."

"You got it," he answered and they watched as he dashed off across the square. The two sat on the sloped porch roof and visited while they waited. Claire really could have used more of a rest but Bob was too fast. He was back in no time and climbed up and handed them the new brushes. Those made a huge difference. Although keeping the paint on the thin horizontal boards and off the base color was still difficult and required concentration and a steady hand, the angle on the brush helped immensely. The eaves and fascia boards had already been painted as had the decorative semi-circle on the front. All that was left to do were uprights. Claire could hear people leaving below. The two women were definitely the tail end of the crew but they wanted to finish this so that they did not have to come back. Finally the two painters met in the middle of the upper roof. The only part remaining was the section over the porch.

At first glance it looked as if it would not take very long. After all, this section was less than a third the width of the top section. But when they looked more closely they also discovered that the white uprights were closer together and skinnier. For this it was decided that one of them would start in the middle and work out and the other from the end and work in. That way the ladders would not be vying for space in the middle. Claire's arms were getting tired and keeping the white paint off the green was getting harder, but she was determined to finish and do a good job. Maybe it was because she wanted to prove to the male population that women were perfectly capable of painting houses. Maybe because she wanted to keep up with Francine who was about twenty years younger and Claire needed to prove to herself that just because she was in her fifties she was not going to be deterred from doing the things she liked. Maybe it was because she wanted to prove herself to this town. Or maybe it was because she just wanted to do a nice job for this older gentleman and help give him an attractive looking house that he could be proud of. It was probably a combination of all of those.

By the time she had finished philosophizing Claire was almost to the middle and the job was almost done. She finished the last strip and wanted to throw her arms up in triumph but was afraid she would throw herself off the ladder, so she silently congratulated herself. When she reached the bottom of the ladder Claire was greeted by Francine, who had finished a few minutes before her, and a tearful Ben Miller who shook her hand with his left one and then threw his arm around her.

"Thank you, thank you, thank you. I had worried for weeks about how I was going to paint those strips by myself. I was afraid that I was going to have to hire a professional painter to finish the job. You and Francine did it better than a professional."

"I was trained by a pro," Claire responded. "My husband's grandfather was a house painter. When we bought our first house he helped us paint and he taught me how. We'll give the credit to him. And you are very welcome."

"I feel that I should invite you all in for dinner," said Ben, noticing that the crowd had decreased. In addition to Claire only Doc and Betty, Bob and Francine, Vernina and Bryan were still there. Bryan by far looked better than the rest of the remaining painters since he had done an extremely thorough job of removing the paint from himself after giving Socks his unscheduled bath.

"I have a better idea," said Vernina. "I brought some of the sloppy joes and there is still a lot left, don't you know. Let's all come to our house and have supper." Betty said she had a salad and dessert to contribute.

"Give me some time to clean up," said Bob who was hoping to salvage some of the painting equipment and sell it at a big mark-down. While Ben sat on the front walk, still admiring the new paint job, the rest of them walked around and picked up the site. Bob and Francine went home to clean themselves and the paint brushes. Vernina and Bryan went home to heat up sloppy joes and check on a slightly pale green dog that was tied up in the back yard. Doc and Betty went to gather up what they could for the meal. Claire went home to clean up and try not to sit down. She was afraid she would never get up if she did. She felt that she should contribute something to the meal but had nothing prepared. Then she remembered the few bottles of wine she had brought when she moved. "I wonder if these people drink wine," she said to herself as she pulled two bottles off the shelf. "If no one wants it, I might come home and drink it all myself."

Claire turned on a light so she would not come home to a dark house, pulled the door closed behind her and headed off to spend the rest of the evening with her delightful, caring neighbors.

Claire had never known either of her grandfathers, since both of them had died before she was born. When she met Carl, her husband's grandfather, she decided that he must be one of the best grandfathers ever. He was funny and caring, patient and positive. And he was in constant motion. He was a cute little bald man after her own heart, since she had never been one to spend a lot of idle time, either. Now, for some reason, Ben Miller reminded her a lot of her husband's grandfather. It certainly was not that he was in constant motion because he wasn't. But the fact that at his age he was going to attempt to paint his own house all by himself was something that Carl would have done without a second thought. Of course, Carl was a professional painter but still, attempting a job like this while in one's mid-seventies was a job that very few professionals would have attempted on their own.

Claire decided that getting to know Ben Miller would be a good project. She visited him the day after the painting project was completed. She knocked on the door, uncertain what kind of response she would get, but she was greeted with such a huge smile that she knew she had made a good decision. He ushered Claire in and pointed her toward what he said was the most comfortable chair. He apologized for not having any refreshments but Claire assured him that they were not necessary.

Ben again thanked her for finishing painting his house and returning it to looking like the house that his late wife had loved so much. As she looked around the interior of the house Claire wondered if his wife would be too pleased about how it looked on the inside. But she stopped herself, remembering some of the times that the tidiness of her home had been put on the back burner while she recovered from injuries or illnesses. He started to talk about his wife but stopped himself. "Oh, I'm sorry. I'm sure you did not stop by to hear about Helen."

Claire quickly interrupted him. "No, please, I would love to hear about her." Saying those few words was like opening a flood gate. Ben told her about how Helen and he had met and about their courtship and marriage. He told stories, some happy and some sad, of their years of living on the farm. He told about her illness and her desire to move into town for those last years of her life. Ben removed a large red handkerchief from his pocket to blow his nose a couple of times as tears brimmed in his eyes while he reminisced about the woman who had obviously been the most important person in his life. He said, with guilt in his voice, that he dragged his feet on moving because he had loved living on the farm, and now he wished that he had not waited so long so that she could have enjoyed more time, as Helen called it, "living the city life." Claire could commiserate. She felt sad that she had been able to fulfill her dream to live in a small town but her husband had not.

"My, my, my, listen to me carry on. Please tell me about yourself. I've heard some things about you. You know how word spreads through this town. But I would like to hear it from you." Claire repeated to Ben pretty much the same story that she had told to Vernina and Betty that first Saturday and then again to Scoop Gibson. But with Ben she was able to share the story of grieving for a lost spouse. None of the other friends that she had made in Hayward could share those same feelings with her. And Ben was a gentleman, although almost old enough to be her father, who could nod and sniff and know what she was talking about when she told of that painful period of adjustment after her loss.

They talked about many things, both local and more worldly. The time got away from them and Claire couldn't believe it when she looked at her watch and discovered that she had been there for two hours. She stood up and Ben rose to his feet. They walked toward each other and instead of merely shaking hands, they hugged each other.

"Thank you so much for coming. You'll never know how much this has meant to me. Please come again—any time."

"I will, Ben. I will." Claire headed down Ben's walk and turned and waved. He was wiping another tear from his eye.

Claire invited Ben to dinner two days later. She had a hard time choosing the menu. One would have thought that this was a dinner for a celebrity. Claire finally decided upon pork chops cooked in a mixture of applesauce and barbecue sauce and a corn-macaroni casserole. She had not yet become addicted to the Jello salads that seemed to be a mainstay in this part of Iowa, so she added a tossed green salad instead. For dessert she made a peach pie. Pies were one thing Claire felt pretty confident about. Chocolate cake was another solid choice, but what would she do with the remainder of a chocolate cake? Who was she kidding? What would she do with the rest of a peach pie, either? What was left of a peach pie after two pieces were removed just sounded like less than what would have been left from a chocolate cake.

Then her dilemma became which table to use. Having the two of them sit at the dining room table seemed so formal, but would eating at the kitchen table be insulting to a guest? Judging from the less than formal appearance of the interior of Ben's house Claire opted for the kitchen table. That would, after all, have a homier feel. And if it was going to be the kitchen table, the china and silver would definitely not be in order. She decided to put a tablecloth on the table, although it did take some searching to find it. Then she had to drag out the ironing board to press out the many creases. The finishing touch was a bouquet of daisies from the front yard, and she added a few red petunias to trail from the top of the vase. They were a nice complement to the red and white checkered table cloth.

Claire happened to glance out the window at five until six and saw Ben standing on the sidewalk in front of her house, but it was exactly six o'clock when the doorbell rang. She figured that he had been checking his watch for at least those five minutes to make sure that he arrived on time. When Claire opened the door, she was greeted by a beaming smile and two twinkling eyes. Ben held his good arm behind him as he came through the door. Then while saying, "Here, this is for you," he pulled it out and presented her with a box of chocolates. "I told Rudy that I wanted the best he had," Ben said proudly.

"Oh, Ben, how very sweet of you. Please come in and sit down. Dinner will be ready in a few minutes."

Ben looked around as he sat down. Claire wondered if he thought the room looked too sterile compared to the well-lived-in look he was used to.

"You have a lovely room here. It is so neat and tidy. Helen always kept things neat and tidy. I try, I really do, but somehow things just seem to pile up. Then it just gets to the point that I am not sure where to start to make things look better. And now with this cast, I have even more trouble keeping things organized."

"Does it bother you not to have things as neat as Helen did?" Claire asked.

Ben thought for a moment. "No, not really. In fact sometimes she made me a little nervous because she always wanted to have everything just right. When we were still on the farm she wasn't so bad. She was kept busy with all the farm chores and cooking for the help, especially at harvest, that she just kept things looking orderly and clean. But when we moved to town everything always had to look really neat. I could hardly lay down a magazine but what she came swooping by and put it back where it was supposed to be. I often felt that she just lurked around waiting for me to put something in the wrong place or leave something out so she could hustle in and let me know that wasn't where it was supposed to be. I could understand to a point that for her this was her dream house and she wanted it to be just right, but she honestly overdid it. I would often look for excuses to get out of the house, not because I wanted to be away from her, you understand. I just wanted to be away from her persnickitiness."

"I'll bet that Helen isn't worrying too much about perfection in your house now. She probably just wants you to be happy and safe and healthy. Speaking of healthy, I think it's almost time to eat. Let's go on into the kitchen. Oh, I hope you don't mind eating in the kitchen. Just two people at the dining room table didn't seem to feel quite right."

"Nothing wrong with eating in the kitchen. It's much friendlier that way."

Ben followed her in and looked around. "Nice kitchen, too. Pretty modern. Helen always wanted a dishwasher but we never got one in time. She didn't like doing dishes so I did them a lot for her. But she insisted on putting them away herself. I'm sure she was afraid I would put something in the wrong spot and she wouldn't be able to find it. I'd offer to help you get dinner on but I am not sure how much help I'd be with only one arm, and not my good arm at that."

"You just sit down. Putting this on will be easy." Claire put the food on the table and sat down. Her seat had barely hit the chair when Ben asked, "Would you mind if I said the blessing?"

"That would be very nice," Claire smiled and nodded.

With a bowed head and a quiet voice Ben prayed, "Dear God, thank you for this food you have provided for us. Thank you for this nice lady who has become my friend. Thank you for the kind townspeople who came to my aid when I needed help. Please show me a way to pass this kindness on to someone else. Amen."

"Thank you, Ben. Now to prevent having to pass things I think you can reach things from where you are or I can certainly help you." As she said that, Claire realized that unless his manners were not as good as she thought, he might pick up the pork chop in one hand and chew on it. "Would you like me to cut that for you?"

Ben laughed. "I haven't heard that since our boys were little. Yes, that would be very nice."

They talked as they ate, not discussing anything of real substance. Claire asked Ben what he did during the day to keep busy. "I just kind of putter around. I can't do as much as usual until the cast comes off. I hope to be able to play golf once I'm healed. I didn't take that up until after Helen died. She always thought it was a silly game, swatting some poor little ball while trying to make it disappear into some dark hole."

"Do you like to read? That is something that you can do without having two good hands."

"I do read some. I pick up a magazine once in a while at Rudy's and one of my sons gave me a subscription to *Reader's Digest*. But I don't have many books."

"I have some you could borrow. But how about checking some out from the library? The selection is pretty good."

A slight blush rose over Ben's face and his eyes diverted downward. "I am kind of embarrassed to admit this, but that librarian lady scares me half to death."

Claire laughed and hurriedly said, "Oh, Bertha Banter tries to scare everyone. I'm not crazy about her myself, but I am determined not to let her intimidate me and keep me from coming back. I wonder why she acts that way? Do you know much about her?"

Ben shook his head. "I don't know anything about her except that she is mean."

"I wonder," Claire interjected, "if she is lonely? I've never seen her in town with any friends. It seems that she does her job at the library and then disappears. I don't even know if she lives in Hayward. Sometimes I think people hide their fear or sadness or loneliness by trying to act firm and cold or maybe even mean. Wouldn't it be sad to live your life that way? Would you like another pork chop?"

Ben took her up on that offer. In fact he accepted Claire's offer of seconds on everything. "Boy, can that little man eat!" she thought. Standing at about five foot six he could put away food as if he were an offensive lineman for the Denver Broncos. She had cooked five pork chops, thinking that the leftovers would be good for another dinner or two. That idea disappeared almost as fast as the pork chops and corn casserole did. She wondered how long it had been since Ben had had a real meal. Two glasses of iced tea and two pieces of peach pie later, Claire cleaned off the table and they went to the front porch to enjoy the rest of the nice evening.

Joey Simpson and his friend Ryan Graves pedaled furiously up Oak Street, jumped off their bikes and hurried into Joey's house where Farley Simpson sat reading. "Grandpa, Grandpa!" Joey yelled, "You should see them. There are either five or six, we couldn't tell for sure. You should see them, Grandpa."

Farley dropped the book he was reading. Turning to Joey and Ryan he asked, "What are you talking about, boy? Slow down and tell me what you saw."

"Rabbits, grandpa, white rabbits."

"White rabbits you say? Hold on a minute." Farley rapidly took a worn book from his pocket and flipped through the pages until he came to the one he was looking for. His eyes widened and he asked with great excitement and concern, "Where did you see these … rabbits?"

"They're at the park, by the big split trees down by the creek. You should see them. Come with us and we'll show you where they are," Joey answered, sensing the excitement in his grandfather's voice and raising his level of excitement in return.

"No way. You are not to go back there. They could be dangerous. You stay here. I'm going to get the sheriff. Do you understand me? Do not go back there," Farley firmly admonished the boys. He stuffed the book back into his pocket, grabbed his rifle and ran out the door. He jumped on the first bike he came to and headed for the square in search of the sheriff. At his first stop he got lucky as he found Butch Johnson taking one of his many coffee breaks at Maude's. He was sitting with Mayor Hayward and Clarence Lambert, leisurely enjoying their steaming cups.

Farley burst through the door, rifle in hand, and ran to the table where the three looked up in surprise. It had been a long time since they had seen any adult move that fast. "Sheriff, you gotta come quick. They've come and they're down at the park."

"Slow down, Farley. What in the heck are you talking about?" Butch asked.

Farley pulled the book out of his pocket and waved it at the three as he answered, "I can't explain now. Come on, we can't waste any time. And you might want to call for reinforcements. There's more than one of them." With that Farley was out the door, on the bike and pedaling as fast as he could down Main Street, headed toward the park.

"I wonder what that old coot is up to this time. I guess I'd better check it out," the sheriff said, slowly rising from the table. "You'd better come with me, Chester."

Chester cleared his throat, "I would but I really need to meet with Bill Swan. City business, you know." Butch doubted his story but was not about to question him. Butch would have asked Clarence for his assistance. But Clarence, sensing that something dangerous might be happening, felt that he needed to be at the bank, ready to stand guard and lock the front door, if necessary. He had already made it to Maude's door. He walked as briskly as he could toward the security of his bank building.

"Wimps!" Butch said under his breath and hurried to his car which was parked right in front of Maude's. He started the engine, radioed his deputy Burt for back up, flipped on the lights and siren and headed toward the park. He caught up with Farley just as he got to the parking lot. "So what's going on, Farley?"

"Quiet, you fool. You probably already told them we were here with that blasted siren of yours. Get down and follow me." Farley and Butch, bent low, started to creep toward the creek when Burt pulled up in the parking lot.

"Hey, what are you guys doing?" Burt yelled.

Farley turned around and made a slashing motion across his neck as if to say, "Cut the noise." Then he motioned him to get down and join them in their stealthy movement toward trees.

Burt caught up and whispered, "What are we after?" Butch looked at him and shrugged. The three kept moving silently along toward two large trees that had split early in their lives and each tree had grown into two big trees.

"Joey saw them around here," Farley whispered to the other two. "Split up," Farley ordered quietly, completely taking over the maneuver.

"But what are we looking for?" Butch asked again in as quiet a voice as he could manage considering that his patience was beginning to wear thin.

"You'll know when you see them. Get going and be careful. Signal if you find them."

The three split up and circled the area of the split trees. It was just seconds before Butch yelled to the others. "I think I found them. Over here."

Farley and Burt hurried where Butch stood looking at the ground with a big grin on his face. Farley arrived and looked down. "Well, they're nothing but a bunch of baby bunnies."

"Okay Farley, what in the world were we supposed to find? What did Joey tell you, anyway?"

"He told me there were five or six white rabbits."

"Right. So here they are. What were you expecting to find?" Butch pushed for a better explanation.

Farley pulled out the dog-eared book from his pocket. "Well it says right in here in the code book that 'rabbits' is code for 'paratroopers' and 'white' is code for 'Germans.' I thought it sounded a little strange but these days you just can't take any chances. Those Germans are pretty clever and they can sneak up on you from anywhere."

"Oh, Farley," Butch said disgustedly. "You need to throw that stupid code book away. The war has been over for years. There aren't going to be any Germans parachuting into Iowa. Go home and put that book and that rifle away."

"I'm not throwing this book away. Mark my word, it will come in handy some day. Then you will have to eat those words. You just wait and see!" Farley turned, shouldered his weapon and started marching back up Oak Street.

"Old fool! What a waste of time!" Butch grumbled.

"Yea," agreed Burt, "but it is kind of pathetic. Imagine living thinking that the defense of the entire area rests on your shoulders. It's a wonder he can sleep at night."

The two men walked back to their cars. Before they got in, Butch put the bike Farley had been riding in his trunk and turned to Burt. "How about a cup of coffee after I take this bike back to Farley? I think we deserve it after such a harrowing experience."

"Good idea. I'll meet you at Maude's."

Their doors closed and they headed back to the gossip center of town to share with others the tale of their adventure in the woods.

The quilting group was up to its all-too-frequent habit of doing more gossiping than quilting. The biggest recent event was the alleged landing of the German paratroopers by the creek. Claire could sense that the ladies wanted to talk about it but they were sensitive about how Francine might feel about their discussing it. Luckily she brought it up herself, probably sensing that this was a topic of curiosity. It gave her a chance to vent about how she felt about it, too. Claire had a feeling that Meredith could commiserate with Francine since both were living under the same roof with somewhat unique older parents. Claire missed her parents very much but at the same time was thankful that she had never gone through a similar situation.

"I imagine you have heard what Dad did last week," Francine started. "He really had Butch and Burton going there for awhile. Dragging them all the way down to the creek, having them crawling on their hands and knees through the bushes. It was really too bad that the word had not spread to Scoop Gibson. That would have made a great picture for the front page of the *The Banner*."

"I think Farley had Clarence a bit shaken up when he came rushing into Maude's like that. Clarence went right to the bank and called me from there. He told me to lock the doors but he wouldn't tell me why. He gave me a pretty good scare." Elizabeth continued to relate what she knew. "He called me back a while later and told me it was nothing and that I could relax. All he said was that Farley had gone off half-cocked about some soldiers. But that is about all he wanted to say about it. If you don't mind telling, what did happen?"

Everyone edged closer in her chair as Francine related the sequence of events of the entire incident. Claire wondered whom Francine had heard the story from. She imagined that the way Farley told it might have been quite different than how the sheriff would have explained it. When Francine finished, all the eager listeners sat back in their chairs and many shook their heads.

Claire didn't really want to be snoopy, but her curiosity got the best of her. "Does he use that code book often, like on a daily basis, or does it just get pulled out when something like that the rabbit sighting comes up?"

"He can really go off on a tangent if someone says something out of the ordinary to him or if he sees something he's not familiar with. Even if he hears something on television that he thinks is unusual, he might look in his little book to check to see if the term or item is already in there. Or he might add the word and next to it write what he thinks it means in code. And he takes it everywhere with him. Do any of you remember when he had his appendix out a few years ago? We rushed him to the hospital so fast that he didn't even have time to grab it. When he came out of the anesthesia, the first thing he did was feel for the book in his pocket. Of course, in those hospital gowns there is no pocket and his trusty little book was nowhere to be found. He about had a heart attack over that. He was sure it was a plot by the hospital staff to keep him from figuring out all of the subterfuge that was going on in the hospital. It wasn't long before the nursing staff begged us to please go home and get it so they could get him quieted down. Once it was in his hands, he flipped through the pages and I guess he didn't see any words related to the hospital. Then he settled right down and started complaining about the pain. Before that he was not even aware that he was hurting."

"That is pretty sad," commented Ellen. "I can't imagine having to live with all that suspicion all the time. And it must be hard for you, too. And how about Carly and Joey? Does he scare them?"

"There are some difficult moments. But the kids don't seem to be bothered by him as much as Bob and I are. They just kind of seem to think, 'Oh, there goes Grandpa again, off on one of his pretend adventures.' That's what Joey started to call these episodes last year and that seems to make his behavior acceptable for the kids."

There were some other sympathetic remarks made and then they actually got back to the reason they were there. Then it happened again. Lila made her dramatic entrance and emphatically sat down in an empty chair in the middle of the group. It took her a moment to spew out her current grievance. So while she gathered her words and waited for everyone's attention, Claire took note of the outfit of the day. The short-sleeved beige dress appeared to be linen, which didn't seem to be a very practical fabric, especially if one didn't like lots of wrinkles on hot humid days. The hat—again the hat—was a finely woven straw with a gauze-like ribbon around the crown. The ribbon ended in a wide, flat bow. That in itself wasn't too bad but to the natural colored hat and ribbon had been added a big orange silk flower. Claire was beginning to wonder if Lila didn't have any hair on the top of her head and this was a way to cover it.

When the buzz of conversation had died and she had everyone's undivided attention, Lila commenced with her diatribe about what had her so upset this time. "Well, did you tell them, Francine?" Everyone assumed that she was talking about the incident with Farley and the sheriff. They all agreed that Francine had indeed informed them of the embarrassing event. "Well, I think it is scandalous and something should be done!"

They all sat kind of dumbfounded after that comment. No one knew quite how to respond. Finally one lady spoke up and asked, "And just what would you want done, Lila?"

In a typical Lila huff, she responded, "I'm not sure but things like that cannot be allowed to go on in Hayward."

Francine tried to remain calm and answered, "I think everyone is pretty much aware of what happened and if anyone sees anything like it happening again, I think they will call Bob or me."

"Call Bob? Why on earth would you want anyone to call Bob and tell him about it. What would he do? Run over and check it out?"

"That is probably exactly what he would do, Lila. It is really nothing to get that excited about."

"But don't you think the men in town might get a little excited about it if they all knew?"

"Oh, I don't think so Lila. The men have seen things like that before. I don't think they'll be shocked if it happens again."

"And you don't care if your husband checks it out. That is what you said, right?" Lila asked again.

By now they all were beginning to get the feeling that Lila had flipped her lid, which would be hard to do with that big hat on, or she was talking about something completely different than the rest of them were. Claire was the brave one who felt that someone had better get clarification on what topic they were all discussing. "Lila, maybe you should tell us exactly what you are talking about."

"Well, I'm talking about that Brock woman, of course."

In unison they all said, "Ohhh." They should have known that Lila once again had a grievance against Hayward's newest citizen. Francine's "Ohhh" was a little more pronounced than everyone else's and she nodded her head.

"Didn't you tell them, Francine? I can't believe that you didn't tell them already!" One would have thought that Chester had just suffered a coronary the way she was carrying on.

Calmly Francine said, "Why don't you tell them, Lila. I'm sure you can do a better job of it than I can."

"Well, yes, that is probably true," Lila seemed almost relieved that she was going to break this big news, whatever it was, by herself without any assistance from Francine. "I was at Francine's yesterday right after lunch looking at the new wallpaper she had hung in their bedroom. I just happened to look out the window and there she was, the Brock woman. She was sunbathing in her back yard and she was hardly wearing anything. At first I didn't see that she had anything on at all but I looked more closely and discovered that she was wearing bikini bottoms. But there was no top! I was shocked! Right there where anyone could see. It is disgraceful, just disgraceful!"

They all pondered the news, each placing her own value judgment on what she had just heard. No one seemed to want to comment for fear of infringing on other people's opinions. Finally Francine spoke up. "You have to admit, Lila, that she was not exactly where everyone could see. In fact I think the only way she could have been seen from where she was lying was if someone looked right out that very window where you did. She was, after all, in her own yard which is surrounded by a fence."

"I don't care. It is still indecent! I think something should be done."

Thankfully Jane Dunn entered the room and everyone's attention turned to her. With a somewhat dazed look on her face she walked over to a chair and plopped herself down. "Jane, are you all right?" Claire asked.

"I just came from Doc Nutting's," she said quietly. Claire immediately thought the worst and, judging by the looks on all of the faces, everyone else did, too. Luckily, Jane quickly went on to explain, "I'm pregnant."

Everyone rushed over to hug and congratulate her. After the flurry was over, Jane continued. "I really had no idea. I just hadn't paid much attention to…you know. But at least I know one thing for sure. Now I know why I thought I looked like I was getting fat. At least I have a good reason."

Eight

There was that feeling in the air. Claire knew that feeling. She had lived with that feeling for over thirty years. It was a sensation that was met with mixed emotions. It was a good feeling that parents got this time of year. It was a feeling that not all children enjoyed. It was the feeling that the beginning of school was just around the corner.

This would be the first year in thirty-one years that Claire would not be starting school. She was not quite sure how she felt about it. She knew she was not missing the time spent before school actually started getting the room set up—arranging furniture, setting out books, putting up bulletin boards, making name tags, labeling things in the room. The list could go on and on. She knew she was not missing those dreams, usually more like nightmares, the weeks before school began. There were the dreams where she was in the wrong school or where the children brought their parents to school and left the adults sitting in the desks as the kids waved good bye and left. There were the dreams when she overslept and rushed to the school and couldn't get in through any of the doors. And then there were those horrible nightmares when she forgot to wear underwear or even worse forgot to wear any clothes at all and stood buck naked in front of the class. No, that part Claire would not miss at all.

She would not miss that first day of school when she was as nervous as the children. Claire always worried about whether she would have to pry the crying little children off their parents or worse yet, pry the crying parents off their little children. She would not miss having to hold those criers with separation anxiety who would try to bolt for the door even if it had been an hour since their parents left.

But she had a feeling that she might miss the camaraderie of being with the other teachers. Claire probably would miss seeing the well-washed, beaming faces and clean neat clothes on the first day of school. For some children that, unfortunately, would be one of the last times they would be clean from head to toe. She figured she would miss the looks on the young faces, the looks of respect as they assumed the teacher knew everything and was going to teach them everything they wanted to know on the first day. She would miss their smiles as they turned around and waved good-bye at the end of that wonderful first day of school.

Right now, however, it was truly a feeling of relief that her time was her own and her schedule did not revolve around tardy bells and recess duties and lunch schedules. It was a relaxed feeling of freedom. Claire decided it might be good just to stroll over to the drug store and take Rudy up on his suggestion to come by for a limeade. She had asked Betty if she wanted to join her. Betty said she would after she made a trip to visit an old friend in the nursing home in Livonia. Claire decided to wander around the store to kill the time while waiting.

"Hey, kiddo, what are you up to?" said Rudy as she passed by the pharmacy counter. "I'll bet you came in to get your new box of crayons for school."

"Not this year," she replied. "But I was curious about the latest thing in school supplies."

"I don't think I have anything too trendy. It's just pretty much the basics—paper, pencils, glue, crayons—you know, kiddo. At least they don't still use those slates like I used." Claire was pretty sure he was kidding, so she just chuckled.

"Betty and I want to sample your limeade but she won't be here for a little while. I thought I'd just look around while waiting."

"Well you just make yourself at home, kiddo. And if you get tired of wandering before she gets here, feel free to sit and wait in that chair. It's not limited to those waiting for a prescription to be filled."

"Thanks, Rudy, I might take you up on that if I have to wait for very long." Claire headed down an aisle that was stocked with school supplies. There were spiral notebooks and binders, loose leaf paper and Big Chief tablets, pencils and ballpoint pens, glue, scissors and tape, small staplers and paper clips, rulers and compasses. And, of course, there were her personal favorites—crayons. There were boxes of eight, sixteen, thirty-two and the big wonderful fat boxes of sixty-four crayons, sixty-four beautiful colors all with nice sharp new points. Claire remembered how disappointed she always was when the newness wore off her crayons and they were not sharp anymore.

A couple of young children came in with their mothers. The children both wanted the big fat box of crayons but the mothers stuck with the smaller boxes instead. "Good for you," Claire thought, remembering how hard it was to get simple pictures colored the way she, the teacher, wanted them to look. Too many crayons were too confusing for little people and rainbows might end up with magenta, apricot, chiffon, lime, navy blue and blue violet stripes instead of the true red, orange, yellow, green, blue and purple. Too many choices aren't always good when you're five or six.

She left the families to argue about what other school supplies were necessary and what was non-essential. In a way Claire missed doing that with her three children but in other ways she was relieved that she no longer had to have the discussions about wants versus needs. She wandered a few other aisles and decided to look at magazines as she waited. Claire had never been a big magazine reader although she did enjoy *The Readers' Digest* and *Colonial America*. She had not been there long when Betty showed up with Clara tagging along behind.

"Hi, Betty. Hello Clara. It's nice to see you again." Clara scowled at her.

"I hope you weren't waiting long," said Betty. "Let's have a seat. I really need something cold to drink." The three of them sat in a row on the stools at the fountain, Clara in the middle with her purse sitting on the counter.

"What will you ladies have?" asked a smiling Ron who was in front of them almost before they were completely seated.

"Your limeade comes highly recommended," Claire told him.

"That is really Rudy's specialty, but mine's not bad either. How about you, Betty?" She also ordered limeade. "And what can I get for you, Clara?" Ron asked, bending over the counter and looking her square in the face.

"Are you hard of hearing, kid? I'm not either, so back off. I want a milk shake, extra chocolate and extra thick. And I don't want any of those wimpy straws. I just want one big spoon. Have you got that?"

"Yes, ma'am," said Ron nodding his head and backing away.

"Clara went with me to Livonia. She wanted to visit with Lois Teller," Betty explained.

"How is Lois?" Claire asked trying to get on Clara's good side.

"Well, in the first place she's darn old. In the second place that place makes everyone feel even older. She's even too old to know that she is miserable over there. But I knew she was, no matter what she told me. It's a pity; it's just a pity." Clara shook her head with a look of sympathetic sadness on her face.

Betty looked at Clara in disbelief. "I talked to Lois for awhile and she said she liked it there. She said she felt safe and that she didn't have to worry about what she was going to eat or how she was going to clean her house and do her laundry. I'd say she is doing quite well."

"No, she is just too old and crazy to know how miserable she is. It's just a pity."

"It was nice of you to go see her. I'm sure she enjoyed your visit," Claire said trying to put a positive spin on this conversation.

"I'm sure she did. Anyone would be glad to see me," Clara said, suddenly smiling and sitting a little straighter. It was as if her dour personality had disappeared and Miss Congeniality's had taken its place.

Ron brought the milk shake first. "Here you go, Clara. I hope it is the way you like it." Clara took the long-handled spoon and lifted a small bite. "Why is it brown? I wanted strawberry."

"I believe you ordered chocolate," Ron said politely. I had the feeling he had been through this with her before. "In fact, you ordered extra chocolate."

"Well, I'll eat it but don't expect me to pay for it if you can't get the order right."

Ron left and returned with two tall frosted glasses of limeade. It was very good, not too tart and not too sweet, and it was very refreshing on this hot, muggy August day. Betty told Claire about her visit with her friend while they sipped and Clara spooned. The bell over the door rang. Betty and Claire turned to see who had entered. It was Missy Brock. She looked around briefly then strutted over to the soda fountain. She sat at one end, avoiding eye contact with the three other customers. Clara saw the movement out of the corner of her eye. She studied Missy for a moment and then reached in her purse and started to remove her squirt gun.

"Clara, put that away right now," demanded Betty in a hushed voice.

Clara removed her had from her purse but continued to stare at Missy. "I don't like her looks. I'm sure she's a crook," she said.

Luckily Missy didn't seem to hear Clara but sat on the stool, legs crossed with her short skirt halfway up her thighs. Her left foot swung back and forth drawing attention to her bright red spike heeled shoes. Ron went over to take her order. "What can I do for you this afternoon?" he said with his perpetual smile.

"I don't suppose you have a beer, do you?"

"No, but we do have root beer."

"Ick! I hate that stuff! How about a cherry phosphate?"

"Now, that I can get for you." Ron turned to fill her order.

Claire turned to her and decided that this was as good a time as any to introduce herself. She also introduced Betty and Clara. "Yeah, I've met that Clara," Missy muttered. Claire went on to explain that she had moved to town just a few weeks before Missy had. She might have told her more but she got the distinct feeling that Missy couldn't have cared less, despite her faint smile. The phosphate arrived so Claire was quite sure that their conversation was over. She told Missy it was nice to meet her, as did Betty. "Yeah, likewise," Missy responded and quickly looked away.

Claire told Ron that she was paying for the drinks, over Betty's protest. He told her the store kept a running tab of Clara's milk shakes and sodas and that the Andrews paid for all of them at the end of the month. "This one is on me, anyway," Claire told him. She and Betty got off their stools. Clara was still fishing in the bottom of her glass for the very last drop. "How was your milkshake?" Claire asked Clara.

"It wasn't too bad, but I would have rather had the vanilla that I ordered. These youngsters just don't seem to be able to get anything right."

Betty's car was out in front but Clara said she would rather walk. Claire told Betty she would walk Clara home. She made small talk just to break the awkwardness of the silence. They passed Mayor Hayward's house, and Mellow made his usual charge at the fence. "That darn dog!" said Clara. "Someone ought to just shoot that loudmouth mutt." She pulled out her squirt gun and aimed it at the backyard fence. "Darn, I'm out of ammunition," she grumbled when she realized there was no water in her gun.

"Maybe you can get him next time," Claire offered.

"Well, someone should. He's a nuisance."

The rest of the way to Clara's neither of them said anything. Claire had run out of things to say when she got no response back from Clara. They walked up to the front door where instead of just walking in, Clara rang the doorbell. "I like to make her think that she has company," Clara said with a sparkle in her eye. "Hurry up, Meredith. I'm an old lady. I could go at any minute!" Clara yelled impatiently after waiting a few seconds. When Meredith came to the door, Clara marched right in saying, "The babysitter brought me home," and headed right on through the house.

"Thank you for bringing her home. How was her visit with Lois?"

"I think it depressed her to see her friend living in a nursing home. Betty tried to convince her that Lois was really in good hands and was much safer and healthier in that setting, but Clara wasn't convinced. I think she was a little afraid that the same fate might befall her some day."

"If Aaron has his way, she will be with us to her dying day. Or until mine, whichever comes first. I didn't know you were going with them this afternoon."

Claire filled her in on the rest of the afternoon activities. "Your mother-in-law sure does enjoy her ice cream. I hope she enjoyed that part of her day."

"Oh, I'm being rude. Won't you please come in for a bit?"

"Thanks for the invitation, but I think I'll just go for a walk and enjoy the day. Tell Clara good bye for me. I'll see you later."

"Thanks again for bringing her home, Claire. I'm sure she enjoyed her time with you more than she would ever let on."

Claire headed down Oak and when she got to the park she walked a couple of laps around the baseball field. She wondered how she would spend her waning years. Would she end up living with one of her children, being a burden that they would never have the heart to acknowledge? Would she end up like Lois, being moved out of her home because she was unable to take care of herself? Neither was a pleasant prospect. Claire shook off those thoughts and headed west.

Subconsciously Claire thought she knew where she was going since she had walked this path many times, and it was not long before she was passing the elementary school. Although school had not yet started, there were many cars parked in the small parking lot. Just as she had suspected, even teachers in a small town spend a good deal of time before school just getting their rooms ready. This was the fourth day that week that she had strolled by here and found the same cars. "Now that I do not miss," Claire said out loud. Most people have no idea of the amount of time teachers put in ahead of the opening day, but she knew, and she appreciated the teachers who were dedicated to taking this time to make their classrooms run so well. She stood in front of the building for a few seconds, imagining how different it would look in a few more days. Claire figured this was about the time that school would be out and the silence of today would be replaced with the bustle of children bounding out the door headed for home. "Nope, I don't miss this at all!" she said firmly and headed toward home.

Labor Day weekend was extremely quiet and extremely wet. A front with lots of humidity stalled over Iowa and dropped relentless rain. It was not a very cheerful way to end the summer season. Claire didn't walk, although the rain didn't always keep her from doing a mile or two, but she just wasn't in the mood. She decided to spend some time getting the basement in order since she more or less had just dumped things there earlier in the summer. She also did some more thorough cleaning that she had been putting off. She went to church on Sunday and heard about the need of another Sunday school teacher. She listened with some degree of guilt. Claire had done that one year and fretted more about that hour of teaching on Sunday morning than she did an entire week of being with the children.

She went through her cookbooks trying to get inspired to try lots of different recipes. She tried a new recipe for lemon chicken and made enough to take some to Ben Miller along with a couple of slices of raspberry pie. She gave herself a manicure and used nail polish she had bought after Rudy said it was a brand new shade he had just received. She spent a good deal of time reading and on Monday evening she finished her last library book. "Now that will give me something to do tomorrow," she said.

Claire woke up earlier than usual on Tuesday morning and had trouble getting back to sleep. So she got up, put on her walking clothes and went down to eat breakfast but, not being very hungry, opted for only a glass of orange juice and a big glass of milk. She sat on the back porch and enjoyed the beauty of the flowers still sparkling with the remnants of the weekend rains. The grass seemed extra green, probably due to the three days of abundant moisture. She checked her watch a few times and decided to head out for her morning walk.

Claire headed west on Oak and saw Jane handing out lunch boxes to Jenny and Jeff. She hugged and kissed them and then waved as they headed off for another year of school. As she turned toward the door she saw Claire and waved good morning. Claire waved back. "Jane should be walking with me," she thought. "She seems to be gaining more weight each time I see her."

Claire continued west for a few blocks and encountered numerous children, faces scrubbed and hair slicked down, heading toward the school. She turned south and took the next two blocks at a leisurely pace and just happened to walk by the school a couple of minutes before the bell rang. Even though the school was a lot smaller than the one where Claire had taught, it was still a familiar sight—children visiting with their friends, parents visiting on the sidewalk and moms of kindergarten children tightly holding the hands of their small children. She was never sure who needed that hand holding more, the children or the parents. The bell rang and the children headed to their respective doors. They were always much more anxious this first day of school to get to their classrooms and meet their teachers. Claire had a feeling that most children knew the teachers in the school already, not only because they might have older brothers and sisters but also because it was a smaller facility where familiarity with others was much more common. The mothers of the kindergarten children reluctantly let go of the small hands and waved goodbye but lingered by the closed door for a few extra minutes, visiting with the other parents who were also having mixed feelings about this step their children were now taking in growing up.

Claire managed to keep busy for the next couple of weeks. Betty and she walked every morning and sometimes she also walked in the evening, shortly before dark, often taking a route that took her by the school. She read a lot and checked out new books almost every week. Even though Claire felt that she might be considered a regular by then, Miss Banter still carefully examined every book she returned before giving her permission to check out new ones. Claire took pleasure in trying to be nice to Bertha because it was always interesting the lengths she would go to reject Claire's overtures.

She visited the drug store often, not really because she needed anything but because she enjoyed visiting with Rudy. Claire enjoyed his humor and his down-to-earth philosophy of life. She missed talking with Ronnie, who was back in school to finish his pharmacy degree. But she had to be careful about spending too much time at the soda fountain.

Claire met Meredith and Clara for lunch at Maude's. She felt that she should do more with Clara to give Meredith some relief but wasn't sure if she was quite ready to spend much time alone with her. Maybe the three of them could go into Des Moines sometime for lunch. At least that would give Clara and Meredith a change of scenery.

Claire spent time cooking and baking with Jane Dunn, who was such a good cook and taught her so much. But doing all this cooking was one of the reasons she had increased her walks to two times a day. Jane continued to grow but she was not concerned about gaining too much weight. "If Doc Nutting is not worried, why should I be?" she said one day when Claire asked her about just how much she had gained so far. "And you know that old saying, 'I'm eating for two now.'"

Elizabeth and Claire had become better acquainted and spent many afternoons just visiting over a glass of iced tea or lemonade. Elizabeth had a wonderful sense of humor and was not at all uppity like the rest of her Hayward family. She even told some very funny stories about some of her relatives, both living and dead.

With Ben Miller's supervision, Claire spent a good deal of time doing some beautification projects in his yard. One day they went to Des Moines to buy some foundation plantings and other bushes and some spring bulbs. She had wanted to suggest such a project but was not sure how Ben would take her suggestions. She didn't want to insinuate that his property was in need of help, which it definitely was. So she was relieved when he brought up the subject. He insisted that they take his pickup which was probably good since Claire knew they couldn't get many things into her car, and she did not relish the thought of soil lining the trunk. The only problem was that she would have to drive since Ben's broken arm hadn't healed yet. Claire never had driven a truck before but the two managed to make it there and back without any major problems.

Claire attended the weekly quilting group and enjoyed seeing the progress as the quilt sections were sewn together and the large top was put on a quilting frame so the actual time-consuming quilting could begin. She also volunteered to help polish the pews at church. Polishing furniture had never been a favorite household chore of hers but it was amazing the things she would do these days to take up some of the time.

Despite all of the activities that she had thrown herself into, there was still a sense of something missing. It took her about two weeks to figure out what it was. Then Claire woke up one morning, got dressed, ate breakfast, and checked her watch a few times to give the people involved a chance to get their daily schedule underway. She walked out the front door and headed once again down the street and toward the school.

When she got there Claire went into the office and introduced herself to the lady sitting at the desk. A name plate on the desk identified her as Theresa Stevens. "Good morning, Mrs. Stevens," Claire said, having a fifty-fifty chance of getting the Miss vs. Mrs. correct.

"Good morning," Mrs. Stevens replied cheerfully. "May I help you?"

"Yes, I'm Claire Menefee and I would like to visit with Miss Hatcher for a few minutes, if she is available."

"Please have a seat and I'll see." Mrs. Stevens rose from her chair and quickly walked the ten steps to the office of the principal and disappeared through the door. It was just seconds before she popped her smiling face around the door and said, "Miss Hatcher will see you now."

Claire thanked her as Mrs. Stevens quickly hurried back to her desk. Claire entered Miss Hatcher's office with slightly sweaty palms. Although this had been totally her idea, she still had an uneasy feeling, as if she were being summoned into the principal's office. Maybe it was because she had not heard the most complimentary comments about the personality of this lady.

"How may I help you?" Miss Hatcher said with a somewhat stern look on her face. Claire wondered if Miss Hatcher thought she might be a complaining parent.

"Would you mind if I sat for a few minutes?" Claire asked. Miss Hatcher motioned to the chair that was positioned squarely in front of her desk, the chair that Claire assumed was in that position to be more intimidating for a student—or for a parent—who might have been called in for a visit with the principal. "My name is Claire Menefee. I moved to Hayward in June. I recently retired from thirty-one years of teaching in Colorado."

She heard Miss Hatcher mumble, "Lucky you!" under her breath but Claire continued.

"I wondered if you could use me as a volunteer."

Miss Hatcher looked at her in disbelief. After a few moments, she asked, "After thirty-one years, why in the world would you like to come back to this? Aren't you just sick and tired of being around kids?"

"I realized since school started that I really do miss being around the children. I always enjoyed them and felt that they kept me young. I have time on my hands and thought maybe your school could use some extra help."

Miss Hatcher pondered her offer for a moment. Finally she shook her head as if she were in disbelief, sighed and said mockingly, "And what is it you would like to do to help my little school?"

"I thought maybe you could better tell me what you need. I could tutor individual children, work with small groups, work in the library—I'm open to suggestions."

She thought for a few moments and then said, "The library, yes I suppose that is an area where we could use some help. Would you like to take a look?"

Claire willingly agreed, so they left the office and headed down the hall until they turned off into a dark, dreary looking area. Miss Hatcher felt around for the light switch but having the light come on did not do much to improve the lacklus-ter look of the room. Claire took a quick look around and wondered just how much flexibility the school would give her to make a few cheerful changes.

"This is it," Miss Hatcher said. "The library was repainted over the summer and the painters didn't do much to get things back where they were supposed to be. Also, we share a librarian..." she began and for a brief moment Claire was fearful that she was going to say they shared time with the city library. Luckily she finished her sentence, "... with the junior and senior high school building." Claire mentally gave a sigh of relief. The principal continued, "We are supposed to get her two days a week, usually Wednesdays and Fridays. As you can see, however, she has not been able to spend much time here. The superintendent seems to think that getting the older children started with their library business is more important than it is for the younger students. So we have hardly seen her at all. Can't even think of her name. I imagine whoever it is could use your help. Look around. I

have some matters that need my attention. Let Theresa know what you decide."
She turned and marched authoritatively down the hall.

Claire wandered around checking things out. "This wouldn't be a room where I'd want to spend much time," she thought. The room itself was not very light but she figured the quality of the lighting was out of her control. There were bare walls and very little color. The checkout desk, or what she assumed to be the checkout desk, was piled high with books, magazines and other papers. "If I were six years old I think I would be scared to get too close to that pile. I'd be afraid it might topple over on me," Claire muttered.

There were numerous book shelves that were far from filled. The selection appeared to be quite outdated and limited. The non-fiction section had not kept up with the times in terms of history and science. The picture book collection, although not terrible, was old-fashioned in comparison to the colorful books now available. At first glance, the fiction section for older readers seemed to be the most adequate although these crowded books would have appeared more appealing if they had been spread out to fill up some of the bare and dusty open shelves. Tables and chairs were spread out all over the room. Maybe that was how the teachers liked them, but to Claire that was not the most effective use of the space.

She sat down in one of the chairs, her knees creaking a bit as they bent more than usual to reach the student-size chair. "This could be quite a project," she said looking around the room, thinking of some changes that she would like to make. "But don't get ahead of yourself. This is not your library." Claire decided that it would be worth contacting the librarian directly to offer her services. She arose, looked around again, and turned off the lights. Although she had the strong urge to walk around and peek into all of the classrooms, she was a good little visitor and walked directly back to the office.

Theresa looked up as Claire walked through the door. "Did you like our little library?" she asked cheerfully.

Realizing Theresa had put her on the spot, Claire quickly thought of the most tactful response she could. "I wish my school had a library when I was young. Now I think it would be a fun place to help." This seemed to be an acceptable response, for Theresa again smiled broadly. "I think I would like to talk to the librarian and see if she even is interested in having someone help her."

In her cheerful tone Theresa excitedly said, "Her name is Susan Davis and I'm sure she would welcome any help you could give her. You see, this is her first year here and I think she is feeling somewhat overwhelmed." She started, first calmly and then after a few moments more frantically, looking through the papers on her desk. Laughingly she said, "I know I have her home number here somewhere. I had all their phone numbers here just a moment ago." Still, as papers were flying, she managed to keep that smile. After what seemed like an uncomfortable eternity, Claire offered the suggestion that it might make more sense for her to contact Mrs. Davis at the other school rather than bothering her at home. "Oh, I'm sure it would be no bother, but that might be easier." After seconds of rummaging, she found a note pad, wrote out a number and handed it to her. Claire thanked Theresa and left her to deal the mess she had made on her desk and surrounding floor.

She wanted to call Susan as soon as she got back home, but thought it would be better to wait until the end of the day. The hours passed incredibly slowly. Claire was as nervous and excited as if she were waiting to hear about a job interview. Finally the old grandfather clock in the living room struck three and she made the call. After waiting a few minutes for her to be paged, a tired voice answered, "This is Mrs. Davis."

Claire introduced herself, wondering how many times she had done this in the past three months, and told her that she would be willing to volunteer in the Hayward school library if that would be useful. This explanation was followed by a few moments of silence. Claire was beginning to think that either they had been disconnected or Mrs. Davis had fainted.

Finally she responded, "You mean you actually want to come in and help in that library?" Claire assured her that was indeed what she wanted to do. Next she demurely asked "Do you want to help with the books?" At first Claire thought that was a very brainless question when offering to help in a library but then she thought she figured out what was being asked.

"I could help with sorting and shelving. I could check out and check in books. I could read to groups of children. I would be willing to help in whatever way you need me."

"Oh my, I would love to have some help. I feel that I am stretched really thin by being in two schools. The high school is quite demanding and feels their students are the most important, and I have to work the junior high students into the library schedule, too. I feel like I've neglected the Hayward building. And have you actually been in the library? Depressing, isn't it?"

"I agree that it could use a bit of sprucing up. Maybe I could meet you and we could talk about how I could help. I live here in Hayward, so I could meet you at school, if that would work for you."

"I'm due to be in Hayward tomorrow, but I have a dentist appointment with Dr. Payne as soon as school is over. If you don't mind, maybe we could meet somewhere after that. It shouldn't be too late."

"That would be great. Since I live right by the square, how about meeting at the drug store? You give me a call from Dr. Payne's office when you are finished and I'll walk over and meet you."

Claire gave Susan her number. Susan thanked Claire for her interest and added that she looked forward to meeting her. Claire had the feeling that part of it was curiosity about why a non-parent would want to volunteer time in an elementary school library. Claire was equally anxious to meet Susan. On the phone she sounded so shy and timid. She could not imagine how Susan would do with junior and senior high students. Personally, Claire had always found them rather scary.

Claire arrived at the drug store before Susan did. "Hey, kiddo, what are you up to?" Rudy said with his usual greeting.

"I'm meeting someone here any minute now. How have you been, Rudy?"

"Fit as a fiddle. Couldn't feel much better and loving every minute of life. Can I get anything for you? We're running a special on liniment and corn plasters." She was thankful that at the moment she was not in need of either one of those. "We just got in some new shades of lipstick, if you care to take a look." Claire might have but then she heard the bell over the door.

"Maybe later, Rudy. I think this is for me," she said cocking her head toward the door. She turned and walked toward a slender, young woman who looked as uncertain of herself as she had sounded on the phone. "You must be Susan."

"Well, yes, I guess I must be," she answered with a friendly smile on her face.

"I'd like to get a Coke. Do you want something?" Claire asked, heading toward one of the stools at the fountain.

"Oh, I really shouldn't since I just had my teeth cleaned, but that does sound good."

Susan ordered a plain coke and Claire ordered a chocolate one, another one of Rudy's favorite concoctions. Susan said that she was grateful for Claire's offer of help. She was new to both of her schools and felt quite overwhelmed. She explained this was her first job in a school. "I have a degree in library science and I hoped to work in a city library." Immediately Claire's imagination placed this sweet innocent thing sitting behind the desk of the Hayward Public Library welcoming the patrons with a smile and actually making them feel comfortable.

Susan continued, "The school opportunity only came up in late August. You see, I just got married in July. My husband got a degree in agriculture and came back to manage the family farm outside of Kissock. When his mother found out the schools needed a new librarian, she told me to apply. I wasn't really sure I wanted to. I kind of wanted to just be a wife for a while. But she kind of pushed the issue. She is a long-standing member of the school board and I guess she thought it would be impressive if her new daughter-in-law worked in the schools. So here I am, overwhelmed and spread too thin for someone who is not sure what to do in one school, let alone in two."

"Of course, I don't know anything about the secondary school, but what do you want to do here in Hayward? Or what would you like me to do to help?" asked Claire.

"I'm really not sure. I have seen so little of it. So far there seems to have been very little checking out of books. I know I have not had time to do that yet and it is already the third week of school. I think the teachers have done some, but I would like to be able to do that, too. And did you see that pile of books on the desk? I don't know if the painters knocked them off the shelves or if that was how they were returned last June. Anyway, all of those need to be reshelved. And the place is just downright depressing. Two days a week or less is all I have to spend there and I bet the children feel the same way about it."

"You mentioned some of the same things I thought about. I could certainly reshelve books. And if you showed me your check-out system, I could do that while I was there, too. I thought that Mondays might be a good day for me to come in. Since you will be there on Wednesday and Fridays that would let children check out on Mondays and I could reshelve the books that had come back so you would not have to worry about that on Wednesdays."

"I think that would be great. Wednesday is the day I know I am in Hayward all day. Fridays it might not be all day. Friday afternoons are quite busy in high school and I have been warned that I might have to be there for some extra time."

Claire had the desire to ask just who had told her that she might have to spend some extra time in Kissock and if Miss Hatcher knew about this arrangement, but she bit her tongue knowing full well that it was none of her business. "Let's plan on that then. I'll talk to Miss Hatcher and see if there are any forms for me to fill out or anything."

"Claire, do you have any ideas about how I could make the library seem more cheerful?"

"I wondered about bringing in some artificial plants. Real ones would be nice but with no light in that room that would never work. I also thought that the table and chairs could be organized in a more inviting way. How are they used now?"

"I am embarrassed to say that I really don't know. I haven't had much contact with the teachers. I don't even know the names of many of them. They seem to keep to themselves the times I've been there. I have mainly just tried to familiarize myself with procedures and the materials. And there are shortages in terms of the quality and quantity of books."

"Yes, I noticed that right away. When will you know if you are going to be in Hayward all day this Friday?"

"I'll know by Thursday afternoon. In fact, I will just put my foot down and say that I have to be there all day, by golly."

"I don't want to be bossy, but I think you should make a point of asking each teacher, or as many as you can talk to, how they would like to use the library. That will help you decide how to arrange the tables. I would sure be willing to come over Friday afternoon and help you unless you will be in a hurry to get away."

"You know, I've learned pretty quickly that when you work in a school, the time you would like to be able to leave is not when you actually can leave. I'd be more than happy to stay as long as it takes."

They agreed to meet on Friday afternoon and as they were leaving, Rudy caught them. "I didn't mean to eavesdrop but I wondered if you might be interested in a couple of armchairs for the library. The reason I ask is that sometimes Lavelle's Furniture has second hand furniture that they try to resell. When I was taking out trash this morning I saw a couple of chairs they were unloading off their delivery truck. I looked them over and they didn't look too bad. I'll bet if you asked Floyd he would let you have them. Lloyd is always trying to resell the stuff they pick up when they deliver new pieces. Floyd doesn't want to bother with it, says it makes the store look junky. Lloyd usually doesn't work on Wednesday afternoons so this would be a good time to go ask, if you are interested."

Susan got excited at the thought of something fun and more non-traditional in the library. She thanked Rudy for the tip, told Claire that she looked forward to meeting on Friday, and headed off to Lavelle's furniture.

When Claire got home she went into the basement and right away found exactly what she wanted. There was no room for it in this house, but she had a narrow end table that would be nice by those chairs, if Susan could get them. She looked around for anything else that had possibilities and found two plastic potted plants. Up close it was easy to tell they were not real but from a distance they looked pretty good. She thought that if they were on top of a couple of the book shelves they would be fine.

Claire actually drove her car to school on Friday afternoon, since she couldn't figure out how to carry both the end table and the plants if she walked. She got there just as the children exploded out the doors. The feeling of relief and the freedom of being away from school for two days was something students and teachers all felt. Usually the teachers had enough will power not to show their enthusiasm, and resisted the temptation to race the children to the doors, running and yelling as they exited the building.

Claire stopped at the office to let Theresa know she was there. She had called on Thursday to see if there were any forms to fill out as a volunteer. As Claire suspected, there were none, but Theresa was impressed that she had thought to ask. Miss Hatcher was also in the office when Claire arrived. She looked at her and shook her head. "I still can't believe that you actually want to spend more time with children. They just get on my nerves." She shivered as she spoke and as she walked back toward her office added, "When I retire I don't want to ever set foot in a school again." Claire thought Theresa was embarrassed by the bluntness of that comment. She just shrugged and smiled her sweet smile.

Claire went down the hall where she saw the top of Susan's red hair partially hidden behind a pile of books that appeared to be ready to reshelve. "Yoo hoo," she said, and the head rose and eyes peeked over the tops of the books. "How are you?"

"I'm doing pretty good. I'm glad that the official part of today is behind me and that now we can concentrate on doing something fun with this room. Floyd Lavelle was more than happy to let us have the chairs. He said it would be a great tax write off. They are kind of a funny shade of purplish red but we can live with it. He said he would deliver them about…" Susan looked at her watch, "…about now."

"I found an old end table in my basement if you would like it. And I have a couple of plastic plants, too."

Susan was excited about the additional contributions so Claire headed toward the front door to retrieve them from her car. Outside the office there was a gathering of Miss Hatcher, Theresa Stevens, and two men, one considerably older than the other, and two purplish red armchairs.

"This is not a home, Mr. Lavelle. It is a school. I can't imagine why you are delivering furniture here."

"Your librarian asked me to deliver it. She convinced me that they would make a warmer, more comfortable feeling for the library."

"Well, this is a school and it is not supposed to be comfortable. The children are here to learn, not have fun. I do not understand that woman's thinking." Claire was wondering if Miss Hatcher was related to Bertha Banter. They seemed to have similar ideas about the atmosphere in their respective buildings.

By now they were joined by Susan and many others who Claire assumed had heard the raised voices. Susan stepped up and defended her decision. "We want the students to feel that the library is a welcoming place. We don't want them to avoid coming because it is so cold and unfriendly. I'll bet these teachers will agree with me that the library should be an essential and hospitable part of a school setting." She turned toward those gathered around her with a pleading look in her eye. Claire doubted that that look was needed. The teachers nodded and mumbled that they agreed that the library needed some changes.

"Well, I disagree but it seems that I am in the minority. We will give this cockamamie idea a try but if it gets too lax in the library, the furniture will have to go." Miss Hatcher turned abruptly and stomped into her office where she closed the door with more force than was necessary. The group in the hall gave a quiet little cheer and many of them patted Susan on the shoulder as they headed back to their respective classrooms.

"Thank you, Mr. Lavelle, for bringing the chairs. I'm sorry if she made that uncomfortable for you."

"Don't think a thing about it. My children went to school here and they didn't always make life easy for Miss Hatcher. I'll bet if Lloyd had made the delivery she would not have made such a fuss. Where would you like these to go?"

Susan led the way down the hall as Floyd and the younger man carried the chairs. Claire continued on her way to get the contributions from her car. When she returned to the building Floyd held the door for her. "Those will be a nice addition," he said, looking at the items Claire carried. "And I think that librarian lady will be a nice addition, too."

"Thank you, Mr. Lavelle, and I think you are right."

"Please, call me Floyd. Everyone does. If you need any furniture you know where to come. I'll give you a good deal. Now you have a nice afternoon."

When Claire got to the library, Susan was sitting in one of the chairs looking like the cat who swallowed the canary. "That was pretty bold of me to do that, wasn't it?"

"Yes, it was, and you have now let everyone know that you are ready to stand up for what you believe. Good for you. So what do we do now?"

"I talked to most of the teachers and they all had pretty much the same thoughts. They don't mind doing the checking out some times but they would all like a time when either you or I could be here to help with that. And they would like to have me teach some classes on library skills. And the teachers of the older children would like to have some research time in the library. I think that is a great idea, but we all agreed that the non-fiction selection is really small and outdated."

Susan looked around the room, studying the layout. "I guess I would like to have most of the tables and chairs together in the center of the room in front of the check out desk. I'd like to put the two smaller tables more toward the outside so students could work there if they needed to be separated or needed a quieter place to study. Then maybe these two chairs and your table could go by the back wall."

It sounded like a good plan to Claire but that entailed a lot of moving of furniture and bookshelves. "So what can I do to help?" asked a familiar voice from behind her. She turned and there was cute Theresa, smile and all.

Susan explained her plan. "I'll be back in a few minutes," Theresa said. Not only was she back in a few minutes, but she brought reinforcements. Five teachers and one custodian, Clifford Wilkens, appeared to help. Susan exhibited drill sergeant qualities Claire never would have known she had but she organized that group with great efficiency. First she had them unloading and moving some of the emptier book shelves. She and Claire unloaded and relocated the check-out desk so it was closer to the door. Then they moved most of the tables and chairs to a cluster area in the middle of the room. The newly contributed furniture was placed toward the back. All the moving was finished within about thirty minutes. They all stood and admired the new look. "It's a start," Susan said. The helpers were individually thanked as they departed, and they in turn thanked Susan for trying to improve the room's atmosphere.

The last person to leave was the seemingly well-fed jovial fellow, Clifford Wilkens. Even though the lighting in the library was not very bright it still reflected off the top of his balding head. "I am sorry that I didn't get your library cleaned up better for you but the painters didn't finish until right before school started and then I didn't know how you wanted things set up. The old librarian didn't even want me touching anything in that room." Claire wondered if the former librarian was related to Miss Banter or if this was a common characteristic of Iowa librarians. Clifford continued, "All she wanted was for me to keep the floor clean. So please let me know if you need anything."

After Clifford left Claire said, "That was certainly easier than I thought it would be. I think you have good advocates in Theresa and Mr. Wilkens. Be sure you stay on their good sides."

Claire stayed and helped Susan reshelve the displaced books. They also got a lot of dusting done in the process. One of the last things Claire did before they called it a day was place one of the plastic plants on the check out desk and the other on the table that sat between the two chairs. Susan had decided that would be a good spot for her to have reading time with the younger children. Claire asked her to give her a quick lesson on check out procedures and said she would be there Monday morning to reshelve and check out as necessary.

As she walked to her car, Claire felt not only quite dirty but felt they had accomplished a lot. Susan had stood her ground and had stated strongly for all to hear that the library would be a friendly place. Claire believed that that same feeling had also been strengthened in the classrooms of those teachers who had witnessed her strong stand and had come to help in the trenches.

Since she was now a volunteer but not on the clock Claire didn't feel the need to arrive at school at exactly 8:30. She got there at about 8:35 instead. She checked in at the office where Theresa offered a cup of coffee to start the day. Claire was not a big coffee drinker but that did sound good right then. While she was waiting for Theresa to return, Miss Hatcher entered on the way to her office.

"Well, you really did come back. I still can't imagine why you would want to do this. You won't find me hanging around a school once I finish putting in my time. Anyway, thanks." The last comment was not said with the same sincerity as what she had expressed at the beginning of her conversation.

Claire certainly could not understand her attitude. How could anyone with such apparent dislike for children want to spend her entire working career in a school? She acted as if she were serving out a prison sentence rather than doing her chosen job. Thankfully Claire had never worked for a principal like that. Nor did she remember having a principal similar to this one as she was growing up.

Theresa returned with the coffee. "I forgot to ask you what you wanted in it," she said, holding the cup tentatively.

"I take it black," Claire said reaching for the cup. "Thank you very much."

"We're very glad to have you here. We all know that Mrs. Davis is overloaded. If there is anything I can do for you, just yell." Then giggling she added, "Well, it probably wouldn't be good to really yell down the hall, would it? And yelling in a library is not good either."

Claire thanked her for the offer and headed toward the library. She flicked the lights on and for a brief moment admired the room that looked much more inviting than it had when she had first seen it a week ago. Then her eyes wandered over the check out desk where the first job was waiting. There were new stacks of books anxious to be properly replaced in their spaces on the shelves. By spending the time putting away the books, she became more accustomed to the library and what subjects were where. She was somewhat familiar with the Dewey Decimal System but could tell that it would take awhile before she would be able to quickly send the students to the correct location in the library to find certain books.

After the books were put away she familiarized herself with the equipment. There were filmstrip projectors and movie projectors. There was an opaque projector which reminded her of the dozens of bulletin boards she had developed with the use of a similar, handy machine. There were also half a dozen guided reading machines that could be used to help increase reading speed. There was a rack with maps—world maps, United States maps, Iowa maps, and maps of the western and eastern hemisphere. There were also a few old globes, one that was somewhat flattened on both sides. She imagined that at one time it had been dropped but it slightly resembled how those who lived prior to Columbus and his peers might have imagined the earth's shape. All of this equipment needed some dusting, so she did need to ask for some help.

Claire strolled to the office and asked Theresa where she could find Mr. Wilkens. She explained in a jumble of words and a flurry of arms motions that his office was clear at the end of one of the halls. It didn't seem like a very logical location to Claire but Mr. Wilkens didn't seem too bothered by this. When she commented about how far away he seemed to be from the rest of the school, he laughed and said, "That's how I get my exercise." Then he added, after turning around and looking behind him, "Plus it gets me a long way from the front office. They did put in a phone so that the office can call me when they need me." Mr. Wilkens, who asked that Claire call him Cliff, gave her some cleaning supplies and even carried them back to the library. He helped for a short time until it was time for him to go set up for lunch. She couldn't believe that the time had gone so fast. She had planned to stay for only half the day on Mondays but there was still something she wanted to do before leaving. As the teachers entered the teachers' lounge for lunch, Claire introduced herself and chatted with them briefly. Most of them had either seen her during Susan's encounter with Miss Hatcher and Floyd Lavelle or had heard about her. They were very congenial and expressed their thanks for her volunteering

She had been furnished a list of the teachers and the numbers of their classrooms and peeked her head into the classrooms whose teachers she had not talked with in the lounge. Claire wanted to know from the teachers whether they wanted to have their classes have an established check out time on Mondays while she was there. Most of them were interested and signed up. Some extended into the early afternoon, but she said that would be all right. The only one she had not yet found was listed as a Marian Fossel. She had been to her room once with no response but returned to it after locating everyone else. The door was still shut so she again knocked, as she had the first time. Claire didn't want to be pushy but thought that as long as she was there anyway she would just open the door and see if Mrs. Fossel was there and had not heard the knock. But when she tried to turn the knob, she discovered it was locked.

Claire went back to the office and asked Theresa if she knew if Mrs. Fossel was in the building. "I'm sure that she is," Theresa replied.

"I've been to her room twice. I knocked but the door seems to be locked."

"Yes, I imagine that it is. And I am sure that she is there. Marian is not our most..." she paused as she seemed to be looking for the appropriate words. "She is not our most interactive teacher."

Wilma Knight, a fourth grade teacher, had entered the office and was listening to our conversation. "Come on, Theresa, tell it like it is." Then Wilma turned toward Claire. "Marian is a soap opera fan. She locks herself in her room every lunch hour. She denies it but we are pretty sure she lies on one of the tables in her rooms and watches her soaps. She insists that she is grading papers but a couple of years ago she forgot to lock the door and one of the kids walked into the room and found her. That was the school-wide gossip for weeks, until Mr. Walker forgot to put the lid on his fish tank one weekend and all the fish jumped out and landed on the floor. Talk about coming in to a smelly room. Whew! Anyway, I am sure Marian heard your knocking but just didn't want to answer the door." Wilma seemed to laugh to herself as she walked out of the office.

Theresa tried to be diplomatic. "I'm sorry that you were unable to contact Mrs. Fossel. I'd be happy to give her a message for you." Theresa started rummaging around through the papers on her desk, looking for a notepad so that she could leave a message.

"I just wondered if she would want to set up a check out time for her class during the time I am here on Mondays."

"Well, I imagine that if it were going to make her life easier, she would be glad to take you up on that." Color started to rise in Theresa's face. "Oh, I didn't mean that Marian is lazy," she hurriedly added.

Claire had a feeling that was exactly what she was hinting at but she tried to make her feel better. "I didn't take it that way at all. Who wouldn't want to do something if it would make their job easier? I know I would have. You could tell her that I will try to contact her next Monday or she could tell you if she is interested."

As Theresa continued to search for a paper to write the message, Claire headed back to the library and checked to see if there was anything else that needed to be done before she went home. She thought things looked very nice compared to how the room had looked when she had first seen it a week ago. Her stomach growled loudly, reminding her that it was past its normal lunch time. "Next week I might want to bring lunch," she said out loud, being glad that no one was there to hear her stomach or her one-sided conversation. She turned off the lights and walked back to the office.

"Bye Theresa, I'm leaving now. I'll see you next week."

Theresa waved a scrap of paper in her direction. "I have your message for Marian. I'll give it to her this afternoon. Thanks Claire, you have a nice week."

As Claire walked out the front door she thought, "This leaving school at midday feels good, and a six day weekend isn't bad, either. There were many times when I would have liked to have done that." She smiled and headed for home with a spring in her step that had been missing those many previous years when she left school at the end of a very long day.

Susan called Monday evening to check on how things had gone. Claire responded, "I got a lot done. I spruced up things a bit and signed several teachers up for check-out times. Everyone I talked to seemed pleased with the scheduling idea. That should give you a lot more flexibility on the days you are there."

"I can't tell you how much I appreciate this, Claire. I feel that a big burden has been lifted from my shoulders. This Friday is another day when I have to be back at the high school at the end of the day. I don't think I told you, but I was hit up to be the sponsor of the cheerleaders and we have to get ready for the football game that night. Hey, Claire, why don't you come? Friday night football is a big deal around here. I'll bet lots of your neighbors will be coming."

"I might just do that, Susan. I love the feeling and excitement of high school football. I wonder if Steve Hornsby plays? He is one of my neighbors."

"I'll bet he does. Most of the boys seem to play. I've heard that the coach has to do a lot of recruiting to fill the roster each year. I hope you can come. Wave at me if you do. Thanks again, Claire."

The Tuesday quilting group was smaller than usual. Judging by the comments of many of those in attendance, this was a busy time for canning and freezing.

Having never been into that herself, Claire would not have otherwise been aware. She just always knew that this was the time of year when she baked apple pies. Once the children had grown up and left home, the little baking Claire had done decreased even more. But in September and October she did make a few apple pies for her own indulgence.

The group that was there was as jovial as ever and Claire was the subject of the first round of conversation. "I hear that you are helping in the school library," said Grace Carlson. "That's very nice of you. I'm sure you will be very helpful."

"I hope so. That cute new librarian seems to be quite overwhelmed right now, but I'm sure that once she gets organized she will be very good."

"I assume that you've met Pearl Hatcher," Jane Dunn asked. "What did you think of her?"

Not wanting to be critical of someone she had recently met, Claire quickly thought of some neutral comment to make. "It was she that suggested that I help in the library. Other than that, I have not talked to her very much."

"That is probably good," continued Jane. "She is not the warmest person."

"She is mean and crotchety," chimed in Clara.

"Now, Mother, that's not nice," reprimanded Meredith.

"Yes, it's true! She probably scares all of the little kiddies, too," added Clara.

Grace, with her ever-positive outlook, jumped into the conversation. "Pearl used to be a wonderful, caring teacher. She taught for years and then assumed the job as principal. After a few years in that job, she seemed to enjoy it less and less. I think she is just burned out."

"I definitely think she needs to retire," said Jane emphatically. "Jenny is kind of used to her abruptness but Jeff is still scared of her. Of course, that is a good deterrent to keep him from getting into any trouble."

Claire was relieved that the conversation came to a halt when Lila made her characteristically late appearance. Lila's outfit indicated that she was beginning to switch from her summer wear to fall outfits. She wore a rust colored skirt with a flowered blouse in coordinated colors. Her hat was a rust colored skimmer with a simple tan hat band. She entered with her usual panache, but for once did not seem stressed about anything. Everyone greeted her as she sat down, looking like the cat that had swallowed the canary. It looked as if she could hardly wait for someone to ask her what was new.

After a few moments of silence that seemed like minutes, Grace broke the ice and asked Lila why she looked so happy. Lila smiled and paused for a moment to make sure that she had everyone's undivided attention. "Last night we had just returned from a trip to Des Moines and were headed into the house, when

I noticed old Zeke Myers come staggering down the street. I told Chester to go on in and I would head Zeke home in the right direction. Instead, I told him that there was a nice looking lady at 203 Oak who thought he was pretty cute and I was sure that she would like it if he serenaded her under her window. I mentioned that she was pretty hard of hearing so he would have to sing quite loudly for her to hear him. He was quite flattered and thanked me and then weaved and staggered down the street toward the Brock's house. Then I left the rest up to Zeke and went inside. Awhile later I did hear a lot of screaming and yelling. I guess maybe Missy was not very appreciative of her suitor." Lila laughed as she thought about what she had done. The rest of them just sat in amazement.

Meredith was the first to comment, "I wondered what all that noise was."

"I thought it was a sick cat," laughed Clara who seemed to be the only one beside Lila who enjoyed the story. "That's what that woman deserves." Then the look on Clara's face changed and she went from smiling to looking dead serious. "She and that husband of hers are crooks, you know."

Nine

On Saturday morning Claire was working in the back yard trying to clean dead stuff out of some of the flower beds. She was on her hands and knees and was looking at the ground but she had the feeling that someone was watching her. She raised her head and looked around. Seeing nothing, she turned back to her gardening. Then she a heard a funny noise. Claire looked around again but saw nothing. So it was back to business again when she heard the sound once more. It sounded like muffled giggling. Thinking that she probably should investigate, she pushed herself up from the ground and walked toward the alley. She was not all the way there when two little heads barely poked around the end of the fence.

"Peek-a-boo," Claire said at the two heads. They responded with more giggling. "Libby, is that you?"

Two small bodies emerged from their hiding place.

"You're right, Mrs. Menefee," Libby answered. Then she turned to the girl beside her. "See, I told you that the new library helper lady was my neighbor. I told Carly that you were but she didn't believe me."

"Looks like Libby was right." Claire extended her hand. "It's nice to meet you, Carly. I don't believe I know your last name."

"It's Simpson, Mrs. Menefee."

"Oh, you're Francine's daughter. I met your mom at the quilting group. What are you girls doing this afternoon?"

"Oh, we were just playing at my house, but then when Carly didn't believe me I just wanted to show her where you lived."

"Do you think it would be all right if you joined me for a glass of lemonade? Maybe you should call your mother and make sure."

"My mom is in the backyard. I'll just run home and ask real fast."

The girls went running down the alley as Claire brushed off some dirt and dried flowers from her knees. They were back almost before she was finished.

"She said it was fine but told us to not stay too long."

"You two can help me. I think it would be nice to have it on the porch, don't you?"

The three of them went into the house and each returned with a glass of lemonade. They sat down and visited about the start of school. The girls were both in Mrs. Goering's kindergarten class. They said she was very nice and school was fun.

"My brother has Mrs. Fossel. He and his friends don't like her very much. They think she is kind of mean," said Libby.

"Maybe that's because it is still the beginning of the year. I bet she'll be nicer once she gets to know all of the students better." From what Claire had heard about Marian Fossel, she didn't have much hope that things would change but she certainly could not say that to the girls.

"You know," Carly said leaning over toward Claire as if she were going to share a secret, "they say she sleeps on a table in her room at lunchtime."

"Now that doesn't sound very comfortable to me, does it to you?"

"Did you hear the story about her ants?" asked Libby.

"Do you mean ants like the insects or the aunts that are like uncles?" Claire responded with curiosity.

"I mean like creepy little bugs. Joey told me that on the first afternoon of school she sat down in this nice comfy chair that only she gets to sit in. She was reading a story to the class and after a few minutes she began to wiggle. She tried not to look worried but she kept wiggling. Then all of the sudden she jumped up and yelled, 'ouch.' She turned around and pulled apart the cushions of the chair. And guess what she found?"

Claire raised her eyebrows and leaned closer. "I don't know. What?"

"There was a whole bunch of ants that had moved into her chair. Joey said she screamed and sent one of the boys running to get Mr. Wilkens. When he came he just stared. Joey said all that Mr. Wilkens said was, 'Will you look at that!' She made him take the chair out and spray it with something. She took the class out for recess for the rest of the day. He said she kept itching her seat when she thought no one was looking. The boys all thought it was funny."

"I feel sorry for the poor little ants," said Carly.

It was quiet for a moment until Libby told Claire that she liked all of her flowers.

"What are those tall ones?" asked Libby.

"Those are hollyhocks." They walked over to get a closer look. "Have you ever made dolls from these?" The girls shook their heads. Claire pulled a few flowers from the stalks and handed them to the girls. Then she showed them how they could fasten three together to look like tiny ladies with a long colorful dress, one in pink and one in lavender.

"That is neat! Let's go show my mother. Thanks Mrs. Menefee. Thanks for the lemonade and the pretty flower doll."

"Yeah, thanks Mrs. Menefee," added Carly.

They took off running down the alley again, proudly holding their new dolls.

Monday morning was very busy. The check-out blocks went well for the younger children, and they were in and out quickly. The books for kindergarten through third grade were not actually outdated because fiction for those ages seems to endure. But there were so many more interesting choices available for young readers these days, and it was too bad that nothing recent had been added to the collection.

Things really slowed down when the fourth, fifth and sixth graders came in. Many of the students were looking for non-fiction books, many in the science area. However when the average publishing dates of the science books were around the early nineteen fifties, those books were not very useful. There was virtually nothing about space travel or the space race. There was no reference to the changes in medicine that had occurred in the last two decades. There were no biographies that held the interest of today's students. The two encyclopedia sets were from the late forties.

This was painful for Claire to see. Here were children anxious to learn, and the materials that would have helped them were all too often missing. She didn't want to interfere, being a newcomer to the community as well as just a volunteer, but Claire couldn't help herself. She asked the teachers if they had concerns about this. They all said they wished there were more reference books but said they tried to do the best with what they had. They also acknowledged that there was very limited funding for the library and said that more of the district's money went into the adopted text books that were updated as often as possible. Claire didn't even want to know how recently the science and history books had been updated so she didn't delve into that any further. She also asked if there were good up-to-date materials in the Hayward library. Most said they didn't think it was much better than what the school had. Also a few commented that no one was overly anxious to use that library because of the cold reception they got there. Claire certainly knew what they were talking about.

She finished her time, turned out the lights and checked out with Theresa at the office. While talking to her, Claire was startled by a loud noise that reverberated through the halls. Theresa smiled as Claire jumped and then, as if in response to her questioning look, said, "That's just Mrs. Knight. She does have quite the loud sneeze, doesn't she? She always tries to run out into the hall when she feels a sneeze coming on, but then everyone in the school can hear her, too. I guess I'm so used to it that I don't even notice it anymore. But I can certainly understand why you jumped."

As she walked home, thoughts ran through Claire's mind about what could be done to enhance the library's book collection. She came up with no viable solutions that she personally could do but thought maybe she could talk to some others and perhaps something could be done to help.

That night she called Susan and talked to her about her concerns. Susan agreed completely. Claire told her that she thought she might bring it up at the quilting group and ask for ideas. Susan thought that was a great idea and was very thankful that Claire had thought of it. "I know that the library needs a lot of help but I am too new to know how to go about it. Plus I really haven't had time yet. Please call and let me know what happens tomorrow. And thanks again, Claire, for everything you are doing for the school and for me."

At the Tuesday quilting group, the quilt was nearing completion. Claire figured that it would take one or two more sessions to finish it. She was working on getting up enough courage to bring up her concerns about the school's library when a new topic of conversation, or rather gossip, took over.

With a smug look on her face, Vernina said, "Guess who I saw together having dinner in Livonia?" She waited anxiously for a few moments, but there were no guesses. "Well you would never guess in a million years, don't you know. It was that sweet Ben Miller and Bertha Banter!"

The responses were very similar. "You have got to be kidding." "I can't believe it." "You must be mistaken." "Is the world coming to an end?"

Grace, who was just as surprised, tried to say something a bit kinder. "Well, that is very nice. I wonder if they had a good time."

"Well," Vernina started, drawing out that word as long as she could, "I didn't see smiles on either of their faces. They didn't seem to be talking to each other very much either, don't you know. I was just there with my cousin for a piece of pie and a cup of coffee so I didn't get to watch them for very long. But from what I saw it didn't look like the best date either one of them had ever had."

"Imagine, Ben Miller on a date," said Betty. "I'm happy for him. But, I'm not sure that Bertha is the one I would have picked for him to restart his social life. But then it is certainly none of my business, is it?"

Heads nodded in agreement and then fingers went back to work on the quilt. After a few minutes of near silence Claire decided it was time to bring up the book shortage. Luckily she was helped with this when Jane, who was looking quite pregnant by now, asked her how she was enjoying helping in the school library. "I enjoyed seeing the children excited about checking out books. And the teachers were very happy to have some help and were very friendly."

"Then you must not have dealt with that Mrs. Fossel. She's an old grouch!" chimed in Clara.

"That is not polite," reprimanded Meredith.

"It's the darn truth. I wouldn't want any of my children in her class, the old grump," replied Clara emphatically.

"No, I didn't have her class yesterday. Maybe she will come another day." Claire quickly got back to the main subject. She explained about her concerns and the shortcomings she had seen in several areas of the library's collection. She could see by the looks on the faces around her that she was making her point.

"What can we do about it?" asked Jane.

"I don't know. That's what I'm wondering. I thought maybe as a group we could come up with some ideas. As individuals I'm not sure what could be done, but as a community we might be able to put together some things that would help."

"Couldn't we just ask the school board for more money for newer books?" asked a worried looking Gloria Gibson as she gently bounced baby Scott in her arms.

"I doubt that it is that simple," responded Elizabeth Lambert. "Clarence was on the school board for years and he always complained about how tight their resources were. I'm sure the school board would love to help out if they could."

"We could have a bake sale, don't you know," offered Vernina.

"We could have a huge yard sale," suggested Meredith.

"Yeah, and I know some stuff I would like to contribute," said Clara looking at Meredith with a mischievous look in her eye.

"Those are all great ideas," said Betty, "but would one of those raise enough money to buy what is needed? And how much money are we talking about here?"

"I don't really know. We would have to ask Susan Davis to figure that out for us. But I guess that she would be thankful for any funds that could be provided," said Claire.

"Would it be a good idea to form a committee to work with Susan and see what ideas we could come up with to try to raise some funds?" asked Betty.

Everyone nodded in agreement. Gloria was getting more excited at the thought of being able to do something to help the school and volunteered to talk to Bruce about getting any information they needed into the newspaper. It was decided that there should be an organizational meeting next Monday evening to see what could be done. Gloria wrote down the necessary information, gathered up baby Scott and the assorted baby paraphernalia and headed for the door. "If I hurry I can get this on the front page of Thursday's paper so everyone will see it."

"I wonder if someone should talk to Pearl Hatcher about all of this," said Jane. "I would think she would be grateful for the support, but you never know about her."

"I would be willing to do that, but I'm not sure that I would be the best one," Claire said. "I'm not sure that she is crazy about me. In fact, I think she thinks I'm a little crazy."

"I would be more than happy to talk to her. And I'll take Bill with me. He can be very persuasive when he wants to be," volunteered Grace. "He can approach it in a totally non-accusatory way and emphasize how it is in the best interest of the children."

The women nodded in agreement and some even commented about experiences where Reverend Carlson had persuaded them to do things that they really didn't want to do.

"I'll call Susan Davis tonight and tell her what we have come up with so far. And I'm sure that she would be very happy to go with you, Grace. She could probably line up most of the teachers to give their support to this project, too, if you think you need more voices," Claire said.

"I think that Mrs. Davis, Bill and I will be a good start and not too intimidating," Grace answered. "I'd better go tell Bill about what I just volunteered him to do." Grace got up and disappeared into the tunnel that led to the parsonage.

Those who remained got back to the quilting. There was not much conversation for awhile and Claire had the feeling that the others were thinking of ways to help raise some funds. And then it was if by divine intervention or magic or women's intuition or something that at the same time about six of the old time quilters said, "How about the quilt?" Claire looked at them and one went on to say, "We could auction it off to the highest bidder and the money could go to the school." Another lady had a little different idea, "Or we could raffle it off. People around here love raffles. They like taking a chance. Raffles let lots of people participate."

"That's a great idea, but wouldn't you need to talk to the entire quilt group before any decision was made about the quilt?" Claire wondered out loud.

"Sure," said Jane, "but I can't imagine that anyone would object. We can discuss it next week."

Fingers got busy with their stitching and before they realized, it was noon. Sewing things were picked up and the quilt was carefully put away in its designated safe spot. As everyone left, many talked about possible ways to raise funds for the school.

Claire walked toward home with Betty. Claire was about to head to her door when they saw Ben Miller rummaging around in his front yard. The ladies looked at each other and almost in unison quietly said, "Ben Miller and Bertha Banter?" They started to giggle like adolescent girls. "We don't even know why they were there," Claire said.

"And I suppose you think he has a new job as a book salesman and they were having a business meeting. Or maybe Bertha has suddenly become interested in farming and is just using Ben as a resource."

"No, I don't think that at all. I just think it was interesting since I know that Ben has always felt intimidated by her. He told me that himself."

"We could go ask him if anything is new in his life," Betty said smiling.

"I know you're kidding, but I would like to know. I might ask him sometime, but I don't think this is the time. I'd better go eat lunch and give Susan Davis a call. If you find out anything more about Ben and Bertha, let me know. That way I won't have to pump him for information later."

Claire headed in and went straight to the phone. She told Susan what had been discussed. Claire also told her that the group thought she would be one to talk to Miss Hatcher about the possibility of a fund raiser. Susan sounded a bit apprehensive until Claire told her that the Reverend and Mrs. Carlson were willing to come with her as concerned community members. That seemed to make her feel much better. Claire asked her to come to the meeting planned for Monday night. As she said the words "planned," she realized that very little had been planned for that meeting. She asked Susan to call her that night so they could talk some more. Claire really didn't want to be the one to head the meeting but she figured between the two of them they could come up with some ideas about an agenda for this first meeting. She just hoped that there would be a good turnout.

On Wednesday morning Claire was out doing some cleanup work in the front yard when I heard a "Hi there." She looked up to see Ben walking carefully up the walk carrying two steaming mugs of coffee.

"Hey, you got your cast off. How is it feeling?"

"It's doing okay. It feels good to get it off. Now I can do a lot more things around the house. You look as if you are working much too hard," he said. "I think you need a break."

She took one of the mugs from him and then they sat down in the porch swing. "How are those new bushes doing, Ben? Are you remembering to water them at least once a week? You want to get them pretty comfortable in their new location before winter comes."

"Yep, I've done that. I've even pruned some of the trees." Claire didn't have the heart to tell him that this was probably not the best time of year to do that since she was so glad that he was getting out and working in the yard. The entire neighborhood had noticed and appreciated his efforts.

"What else have you been up to, Ben?" she asked, wanting to get right to the point of what she really wanted to know.

"Not much. Just kind of been hanging around. Oh, I did go out to dinner last week. Went over to Livonia. It was pretty good."

"Did you go by yourself?" Claire continued trying to sound innocent.

"No, I actually took a lady."

"Oh Ben, that's great! I know it is none of my business, but who did you go with? And did you have a good time?"

"Well, in a way I guess it is kind of your business. It was kind of your idea."

"My idea? What do you mean, Ben?"

"I took Bertha Banter, the librarian. You said that maybe she was mean because she was lonely. I thought about that for a long time and thought you might have something there. So I bolstered up my courage and marched myself up the steps of the library and through the door and right up to that check-out desk. I was just going to come right out and ask her when she spun around in her chair and looked at me with than stern look and I panicked. When she asked me what I wanted I said the first thing that came to my mind as she stared at me with those beady eyes and that big nose. So I blurted out, 'Do you have anything about vultures?' Can you believe I asked her about vultures? "Anyway she rambled off some number that was the area for bird books. I wandered over to the area she had directed me to and just grabbed a couple of books off the shelf without even looking at them. I took them over to check them out. While she was looking through her file for my library card information, I swallowed hard and came right out and asked her. At first I think she pretended that she hadn't heard me. Then she asked me what I had said and I told her again. She grabbed the books from my hand and stamped a due date in them. Then, without even looking up, she said, 'What time and where are we going?' I told her and then she said that she would go. Of course she kept that same huffy attitude the entire time.

"When I got outside, I discovered that my knees were shaking. I couldn't believe that I'd actually asked her. I couldn't believe what I had done. But I was committed and I felt it really was a nice thing to do."

Claire had turned sideways in the swing and was facing Ben, totally engrossed in the story. "So how was the evening?"

"I guess it was all right. She barely smiled all night and she didn't say much. I didn't say much either. I don't think either one of us quite knew what to say. She did say the food was acceptable. I thought it was quite good. She said it was a little noisy which I guess meant that she wasn't hard of hearing. She said she didn't want any coffee because it makes her too stimulated. I can't imagine her over-stimulated, can you?"

"No, that's something I can't visualize."

"She did thank me when I took her home, and she did kind of mumble something that sounded like, 'It was nice to get out for the evening.' I think she enjoyed it but it was really hard to tell."

"Do you think you will try taking her out again?"

"Oh, I don't know. I'll have to think about that for awhile. I might have to see how she acts when I take back my books. Anyway, I did it. I tried to make her less lonely."

"That was very nice, Ben. You are truly a gentleman."

Ben humbly hung his head for a minute and then he changed the subject and asked what was new in Claire's life. She explained to him about the book situation at the elementary school and told him of some of the suggestions that had been made at the quilters' group. When she told him there was going to be a meeting Monday night he said he would try to come.

"Where will it be?" he asked.

Claire paused and thought. She thought really hard. Either her memory was getting worse than she realized or there had never been talk about where the meeting would be held. She wondered if there was a standard meeting spot that everyone knew about and that is why it never came up. "I'm embarrassed to tell you, Ben, but I'm really not sure."

"My guess would be the basement of the court house. Lots of groups meet there."

Then Claire remembered the horrendous sounds coming from the basement of the court house in the summer and later found out that was where the community band practiced. "I'll let you know when I find out for sure. We would love to have your support."

Ben stood and she handed him her cup. "Thanks for coming over, Ben. It's always good to visit with you." Ben walked down the steps and headed home. "What a cute little man," she said to herself. "And what a fun neighbor to have."

On Thursday afternoon there was a knock on the door. When Claire opened it, she was surprised to find two little Cub Scouts smiling up at her. She thought they were about to give their sales pitch for whatever money raiser they had going at the time. Instead they handed her a piece of paper and one little guy said, "Please come to a meeting on Monday to help raise money to buy books for our library. We really need some new books."

This was a great surprise. She figured that Gloria must have put a bit of pressure on her husband to use his printing business to get out the word about the meeting. Playing a bit of the devil's advocate, she asked the boys why they needed more books for their school.

The other cub responded, "Because the ones we have are old and in bad shape and my teacher says that we need some new ones. And since my teacher says that we need new books, then my mom and dad say that we need new books, too."

"Thank you, boys, for handing these out. That is very nice of you."

"We had to," one responded.

"Why did you have to?" Claire asked.

"Because Mrs. Dunn said so."

"Mrs. Dunn, Jeff's mother? Why would she tell you that you had to?"

"She is our den mother and she said it was our civil responsibility to help our school and our town whenever we could."

"I'll bet you mean your civic responsibility. I agree with her, and you are helping all of the children in your school by doing this."

The boys looked pretty pleased with themselves when she said this. "Good bye, lady," they said as they turned and headed across the street to the Lamberts. Claire read the note. It was succinct and gave the necessary information. The meeting would be at 7:00 in the community room in the basement of the court house. Ben had been right.

Friday Claire went to the grocery store and was pleased to see a flyer in the store window. "Hi, Claire, how you doing?" asked a smiling Bryan.

"I see you have a flyer about the meeting on Monday. Thanks for doing some advertising for us."

"You'll find that they are in every store window, too. I think that is a great idea you had. Vernina came home all excited about it. I can't imagine anyone, well hardly anyone, in this area who wouldn't support it. Can I help you find anything today? We have some really nice pork chops and roasts and lots of different kinds of apples. Pork chops and fried apples. The thought of that makes my mouth water!"

He was right, that did sound good. She made the rounds and did her weekly shopping, picking up the normal things plus about a dozen apples. Claire thought that she would use seven or eight of those for a pie, which would leave her with some for baking or frying or just eating. The abundance of apples was always one of her favorite things about fall.

She carried her groceries through the square and was crossing the street in front of her house when she saw Jim Dunn on his mail route. He arrived at her walk just as she did. "Howdy, Claire. Good to see you. You certainly have the town all abuzz about your book idea. I'm certainly willing to help any way I can."

"I see that Jane is doing her part." Jim looked puzzled. "I hear that she forced her sweet little cub scouts to go out and do their civic duty. The two little guys that came here were sure cute."

"She thought that was a good activity for their Thursday afternoon den meeting. That wasn't what she had originally planned but Gloria called her Thursday morning and said that Scoop had run off lots of flyers and thought that the scouts could help pass them out. Jane jumped on that. As the pregnancy has progressed, her stamina has decreased. She thought that sounded like a great way for the guys to burn off some energy. Have an opening ceremony, give them a snack, send them off to pass out the flyers, have a closing and send them home. She said it was the easiest meeting she ever had. Better get a move on. See you, Claire."

As Claire went inside, mail and groceries in hand, she shook her head thinking of Jane doing Cub Scouts. Claire had done that once and it was not her favorite volunteer activity. Maybe it was because she was volunteered for the job. Dennis had been the Cubmaster when their boys were in Cub Scouts and there were no volunteers to be den mother for their younger son's den. So she found herself doing it. She thought what she didn't like about it was that she was with children all day and then had to rush home after school and have a house full of boys for an hour. They were nice little guys but she never felt that she had time to get organized before they arrived. Claire admired Jane for doing it. She imagined that she would be good. Jane was such a happy, positive person and Claire imagined that Jane and the scouts did enjoy each other. But she was thankful that it was Jane that was doing it and not her.

"No! I am not going! There is no way I want to mingle with those people."

"Yes, you will go. And you will be civil and you will be polite and you will be friendly. And you will at least look interested. You've always said that you want to be an actress. Well, here is your chance."

"Why do I have to go? Why do you give a hoot about their stupid little school and their stupid book problem? I couldn't care less."

"That's your big problem. You couldn't care less about too many things. But listen. I think there is a lot of money in this town and in the area. Lots of big money. If we get involved in this book project we might be able to tell if this place is richer than it looks. And we can probably locate where the big money is. But you've got to look good. For heavens sakes, wear something frumpy looking like that rest of these women do. Try to fit in and not stick out like a sore thumb."

"I don't have clothes like the rest of them, thank goodness. I guess I'll just have to stay home. Too bad."

"You will not stay home. You get yourself up to that poor excuse for a clothing store and buy something plain, if you need to. But you will be going with me. And you will have a smile on your face. And leave some of that makeup off, too. Do you understand that?"

"Yeah, yeah, I got it."

Claire was pleased to see so many people entering the community room in the basement of the court house. She knew many of the people by now, or at least they looked familiar. She wondered if those she didn't know were all from Hayward or if some were from the other communities that sent their children to school there. As people came in, most greeted each other like the good friends that they were. They chatted and laughed and approached the meeting with the air of an ice cream social. When the room was almost filled, Mayor and Lila Hayward made their appearance. Claire wondered if Lila had detained Chester outside until the crowd was already inside. She always enjoyed seeing Lila show up at different events because she loved to see what the mayor's wife was wearing. Tonight she chose a fawn brown matching skirt and jacket with a subdued white blouse. Around her neck was a necklace of large fall-colored beads. To top off the outfit, she wore a hat with a fall colored tapestry crown and a band of small fawn colored felt leaves. The brown brim was turned up which gave it a jaunty look. Claire actually liked this outfit. It was attractive, attention getting, and, in her opinion, very tasteful.

But Lila's entrance was upstaged and most conversation ceased when Missy and Mike Brock entered. As Mike led Missy to a seat next to Bud and Ellen Hornsby, whispered comments went around the room. Claire heard questions like, "What are they doing here?" "They certainly don't have children, do they?" "Do you think Mike had to drag her out of the house?" and even "Who in the world are they?" A forced smile was on Missy's face as she tried to look less uncomfortable when she spoke briefly to the Hornsbys. Most townsfolk had become familiar with gregarious Mike as he had made himself known around the business area of town. Many people had at least heard of Missy Brock and the overall perception was not positive. The flashy clothes she usually wore had been replaced with a simple blue and white cotton dress. It was very similar to the dresses that the other women wore. Her makeup no longer resembled what might have been seen in a low budget movie, but was limited to a pale pink shade of lipstick and a pink color rubbed on her cheeks. But the similarity ended there. Her hair was done in a dramatic upswept manner and was held in place with a large pearl studded comb. Large pearl drop earrings dangled from her pierced ear lobes. To finish off the incongruous outfit, Missy had stuck with her normal style of footwear – white sandals with spike three inch heels. Even if people had not heard about Missy before, they now wanted to know who she was.

The crowd was so large that those who were last to arrive had to stand at the back of the room. When everyone was settled, Reverend Carlson stood up and began the meeting. Those involved with starting this project had decided that Bill would be a great choice to chair the meeting. He welcomed everyone and summarized basically what the posters and newspaper article had said. Then he introduced Susan Davis, who took the floor.

"Thank you all so much for coming. I can't tell you how pleased I am to see so many of you here this evening. It is wonderful that you are so willing to hear our ideas about how to improve the education of the children in our area. I feel so lucky that I was hired as the school librarian in both Hayward and Kissock. I have enjoyed working with the children and the other faculty members." Susan went on to describe the shortcomings of the school's library collection and how she felt it needed to be updated.

Susan then introduced Miss Hatcher, who certainly did not need any introduction. "Oh, dear," Claire thought. "I hope she doesn't come across as her usually negative self." She was pleasantly surprised, for Pearl definitely came with her happy face. She talked about appreciating how hard the school board worked with the limited money it was allotted. She expressed her appreciation to the staff and students who worked very hard with what was available but added that she knew that so much more could be done with newer resources. She ended her talk by having all of the staff of the school that were in attendance stand up and be recognized. Most of them seemed to be there and they received a warm round of applause.

Bill Carlson resumed the floor and asked if anyone had any questions. There were none so he continued. "If anyone has any suggestions on how we could raise some funds for the school library, I'll write them on the board." There were a few moments of awkward silence. Then someone in the back yelled out, "We could have a bake sale."

Bill wrote "Bake Sale" on the board. "How about a tractor pull?" "I think the kids could have a walk-a-thon with people making pledges for how many laps they walk around a certain distance." These also were noted. "We should have a big rummage sale." "How about a school carnival?" "We should raffle off something."

Several more ideas were added to the list. When no more suggestions seemed forthcoming, Bill continued. "These are some really good ideas to get us started. What I think we should do now is select a committee to take these ideas and see what plan it can come up with. I am sure that everyone is anxious to help so just raise your hands and I'll add your name to our board."

The first hands up were those of Mike and Missy Brock. In fact, he had her hand in his as they were raised. "We may be newcomers but we would be pleased to help with this project. In fact, we would be honored if you would let us be the chairpersons of this fine undertaking. Isn't that right?" Mike said looking down at Missy.

After a second, and a stern look from Mike, Missy concurred, "Yes, we would be just thrilled to death to do what we can for this fine project."

"Well, that is just wonderful. For those of you who may not know, this is Mike Brock and his wife, Missy. They moved here just this summer and it is wonderful of them to be so willing to get involved in our community effort. Let's give them a round of applause." The crowd, still somewhat stunned by the fact that someone who had such short-term ties to Hayward would take on such a seemingly over-whelming task, applauded politely. Bill continued. "Now that we have our leaders, the rest of you don't have to worry about being chosen for that position. Raise your hand if you would be willing to join the committee."

Bill wrote down those names that included Betty Nutting, Vernina and Bryan Graves, Bud and Ellen Hornsby, Elizabeth Lambert, Grace and Bill Carlson, Jane and Jim Dunn, Burton Taylor, and Bob and Francine Simpson, and Claire. There were many others that Claire didn't know. She was wondering if Lila was going to want to get in on this planning group or just show up and look good at one of the activities when she raised her hand. "Well, I just really want to help. You all know I do but I just don't think I have the time." There was a barely audible, collective sigh of relief from those who had volunteered. "But I would be more than happy to help at some point. You just think of a task for me and I would do it to the very best of my ability."

Pastor Stover from the Baptist church and Reverend Thomas from the Lutheran church said they also would be more than happy to help in some capac-ity but did not want to be on the planning committee. Those were the sentiments of many others. Among those was Bruce "Scoop" Gibson who volunteered to give free publicity in the newspaper. Also the teachers who were present expressed their desire to help in some way. The overall sentiment seemed to be "Tell us what to do and we'll do it."

Bill thanked everyone for coming and adjourned the meeting. Those who had volunteered stayed to plan their next steps. Mike started off with, "Well, where do we go from here?"

Betty said, "This was a good meeting tonight, but I think we also should have meetings in Kissock and Livonia. I am sure that there are people there who would be interested in being involved in some way."

"Great idea!" said Mike. "How should we do that?"

Bud Hornsby said, "I don't think we all should go to both places. I think we should divide up and go to one or the other. Oh, and I don't think both meetings should be on the same night. That would give more people a chance to come to one or the other if they had conflicts."

Grace added, "I think that Susan should speak at one and Claire should speak at the other since she was the one who really got this all started." Claire certainly was not crazy about that idea but she supposed it did have merit.

"Let's just explain the problem, get ideas, and add to our committee. Then we can all meet together again," said Mike. Claire was beginning to think that maybe this guy was going to do all right as chairman. But when it was suggested that Mike go to one meeting and his wife go to the other, Missy had an instant panicked look on her face. Claire wondered how effective she really would be.

Betty said she would set up a meeting in Livonia and Susan said she would do the same in Kissock. Assignments for each location were made. Mike set the next meeting date for the committee for a week from Saturday. Claire was skeptical that the other meetings could take place by then but Betty assured her that it would be okay. "Some people just look for a chance to get together. We'll get the word out tomorrow. And I'll bring my aunt's snickerdoodle cookies and some punch."

"That will bring them in for sure, don't you know," said Vernina. "They are the best!"

The meeting broke up with people discussing ideas about the project as they headed up the stairs and out the door. It seemed more like the breaking up of a block party as the Oak Street residents and Jane and Jim Dunn all headed home. They all joked about the large percentage of the committee that lived by each other. "At least we don't have to go far for our meetings," laughed Elizabeth. "And Betty won't have to carry those cookies very far, either."

The other two meetings were well attended, considering that there was not as much publicity as there had been in Hayward. The size of the organizing committee had now grown to about thirty. The Saturday meeting was pretty large but the members were well fed since Jane brought coffee cake and muffins. And Betty brought her delicious cinnamon rolls like the ones she had delivered to Claire that Saturday morning about three months earlier.

After wisely giving the group time to visit, Mike began the meeting. Introductions were made but Claire felt that except for Mike, Missy, Susan and her, this step was not very necessary, since so many of the committee members already knew each other. The ideas that had been listed at each meeting were reviewed and discussed. There were pros and cons for most of them. Some were so popular that many of the members did not want to eliminate them. Mike had a bit of a hard time trying to keep tempers from flaring as some people proposed to get rid of ideas that others liked really well.

Claire sat back and listened to those who knew their neighbors and their habits. She took a deep breath and raised her hand. She got the feeling that Mike was glad to see a hand go up for permission to speak rather than have so much bantering going on back and forth.

"Yes, miss, what would you like to say?" Claire was hopeful that before this was over Mike, and maybe even Missy, would learn the names of their committee members.

"It has been very interesting to listen to the discussion of so many ideas, and it would be really hard to not do most of them. I was wondering if it would be possible to do most of the activities and combine them into one big event. We could have it all on a Saturday at the school. The day could start with the walk-a-thon. There could be a carnival with different activities, with the bake sale at the same time. And the quilt that the quilting ladies have generously donated to the cause could be raffled off at the end of the day. A yard sale could take place on the front yard of the school and, if the weather should be bad, it could be in the gym instead."

"I think that is a great idea!" said Jim Dunn. "Having everything at the school seems really fitting. Maybe we could invite folks into the library so they could see the problem themselves."

"I really like the idea of the carnival," said Burt Taylor, "and what I'd really like to see is a dunking tank. We could make lots of money if we could get Miss Hatcher in it. She gave me a lot of trouble in school. I know there are a lot of my friends who'd love to dunk her." A far-away look came over Burt's eyes. Claire didn't know if he was thinking about the encounters he had had with Miss Hatcher or if he was envisioning sinking her in the tank. There were probably others who felt the same way, including Claire, but politely no one made a comment about his suggestion.

Everyone seemed to agree that the idea was a good one and was relatively workable. Susan raised her hand. "I hope I am not committing the teachers too much, but some of them had mentioned the idea of the staff making box lunches to auction off somehow but they didn't know how to make that work. I think that could be a part of the day's activities."

People were really starting to get excited about things and even more ideas were being added. "What if we had a dance in the gym in the evening? It could be open for all the families. We did one of those years ago when old Bob Braddick retired after being the school custodian for 30 years. Do any of you remember that? It was a lot of fun." The older gentleman from Livonia was pleased with his suggestion and almost everyone else was, too. Claire noticed that Missy rolled her eyes at this idea, but that was nothing new. She did that so often Claire was beginning to wonder if she had a vision problem. Or maybe it was a nervous tic of some kind.

"A dance would be fine with me, but would we lose some of the Baptists?" asked someone else.

"I don't think there are many who are that conservative," responded Bill.

"And if they don't want to dance, they just don't have to come, don't you know," added Vernina.

"Now if folks are going to be there for the evening, maybe we should have a dinner beforehand. I wonder if Maude could come up with a menu that would be easy and we could make a lot of money from that."

"It sounds as if everyone likes that idea," said Mike. "So where do we go from here?"

"I think maybe we should think all of the ideas through very thoroughly," Claire suggested. "Let's break into smaller groups and list the pros and cons of each. Then we can get together and see what ideas we want to keep. And we can also see what problems we might run into."

Mike counted the people off to divide them into groups. For a moment Claire thought she was back in elementary school but it was probably as efficient as any other way. They were given twenty minutes to accomplish each task and then all the groups came back together. It came as no surprise that all of the ideas were adopted. One idea was added when Jim Dunn said that he was sure that the school would let the Boy Scout troop use their water to have a car wash.

There were some obstacles that the groups thought of, but all in all, they were small and, at least at first glance, seemed to be relatively easy to overcome. Mike listed all of the proposed activities on the chalkboard as well as the concerns. He said that Missy was also writing down all of those. Claire hoped that she was able to handle the task since her eyes were again doing funny things. In fact, the only one who didn't seem excited about this project was Missy. She didn't seem to be interested at all. She was much more interested in checking to see if there were chips in her bright red fingernail polish. Claire wondered if Mike had bribed or even threatened her to get her there.

It was decided that the big committee would be divided into subcommittees with each one responsible for planning one activity. This time everyone volunteered for the activities in which they were most interested. Claire was careful to wait to choose her group. She was afraid that she might get in the same group as Missy. Suddenly the thought of being on a committee with Lila seemed much more pleasant than working with that woman. Maybe Missy wouldn't sign up for a group at all and would just follow Mike around with her little note pad.

As the groups were starting to gather in different parts of the room, Claire had a thought. "Excuse me," she said loudly, "but have we decided on a date for this event?" Everyone looked at each other. That was something that had not been discussed at all. Everyone sat down again. It was nothing more than a question but it was as if the air had suddenly gone out of the balloon.

Bill, in his typical gentle way, stood up. "Now let's think about this for a bit. We are close to the end of September now. Could we pull this off in October? How complicated are all of the arrangements going to be?"

Claire was curious what the response would be. Where she had come from there would have been no way that an affair like this could have been put together in that period of time. But she had a feeling that these folks could pull together and get things done pretty quickly.

Betty spoke up. "I think we could do it by the last weekend in October. That would put it three days before Halloween." There were nods of agreement and so it was decided, at least at that moment, that October twenty-eighth would be the target date.

Grace spoke up. "When we meet in our groups, talk about whether that is realistic date. If any group thinks that won't work, then we can talk about changing it."

Ellen Hornsby, who had frantically started rummaging through her purse looked up and said, "Hold it for a moment." She returned to her search and then held up a small date book. "Let's see. October 28.... yeah, that's okay. That Friday game is a home game so that should work for us football fans."

The small groups met for a short time to think of any reasons that the October date was not a good one. Claire was amazed at how efficient these people were at reaching decisions. She had seen so much socializing at other gatherings that she thought that there would be more time spent off topic. But they stuck to the topic at hand and regrouped in about ten minutes. Even more surprising was the fact that every group agreed that any obstacles were small and could be worked with. So the October 28th date was a go.

Mike was getting more efficient as the chairman. "Before we go back into our groups, let's decide when to meet as the entire committee. I think next Saturday would be good since that will still give us three weeks. Does that work for everyone?" There were nods of agreement all around. "Each group should have in mind any publicity you want and the equipment you will need. Is there anything anyone can think of to discuss now? Good. Then we will see you all next week."

The small groups got back together to decide when to meet again. Claire was undecided as to which group she wanted to work with so she meandered around from group to group listening to their discussions. Some stayed to get more done immediately. Others set meetings early in the coming week. The groups seemed to be pretty equally divided except for the dinner group. Elizabeth was there with a couple of women from Livonia so Claire decided to join them. That group discussed possible menus and providers of the food. They decided that Elizabeth and Claire would check with Maude to get prices and the other two would go to Joe's Barbeque Diner in Kissock. They decided that their publicity would be tied to the entire day's activities, but it would stress that people did not have to come to anything other than the dinner if they so chose. The committee agreed that was enough for today and all headed home.

Elizabeth and Claire happened to leave the building shortly after the Brocks did. Although they were out of earshot, their body language showed that they were not having a loving discussion. At one point Missy stopped, turned to Mike, stomped her spike-heeled shoe on the ground and with one hand on her hip, shook her other hand in his face. It didn't appear that he appreciated her comment very much, for he grabbed her hand and stuck his finger right in front of her face. After delivering his message, she turned with a huff and they proceeded through the square headed in the direction of their home.

"Now they don't look like a happy little couple, do they?" Elizabeth said.

"Nope," Claire agreed, "but then I have never seen her look happy. What do you think their story is? I just think there is more to them than they have let on."

"Well you know what Clara says about them," Elizabeth said. And in unison the two said laughingly, "They're crooks!"

The car pulled up in front of the house. The driver turned off the engine and looked around for a few moments before he got out of the car. "Nice little burg," he said to himself. He walked up to the front door and rang the bell. He waited a couple of minutes and rang the bell again. Still no answer. He looked at his watch and then looked up and down the street. He then headed toward the square.

"Busy day in town today, I guess," he thought to himself as he approached the square that was surrounded by parked cars. He continued on his way, carefully looking around him as he walked. He thought it odd that there were so many cars and yet there appeared to be so few people in the stores. He decided to get a cup of coffee at a friendly looking place called Maude's. Many of the tables were filled with groups of people, mainly men, sitting around fingering coffee mugs while talking and laughing. He picked a spot toward the back where he could watch the comings and goings.

He had barely been seated when a plump middle aged woman with an infectious smile hustled over to his table, a pot of coffee in her hand. "Good morning," she said in a manner that seemed to fit the atmosphere of the entire restaurant. "What can I get for you this fine day?"

"Good morning to you, too. I'd just like a cup of your best coffee," he said, smiling back.

"Well, I just happen to have some right here." Maude bent over and filled a mug with a flourish that she had developed over the years. Her movements made it seem more as if she were creating a small waterfall than just a little cup of coffee. "I don't believe I've seen you in here before. I'm Maude and it's good to have you visiting us today."

"Well thanks, Maude," he answered, not offering any information to her about his presence in Hayward.

"Can I get anything else for you right now?" Maude added, trying hard not to show her disappointment that she had not learned anything more about this stranger.

"Well, I do have a question for you, Maude. On my way in I noticed lots of cars parked around the square. Is there a big sale or some other special event going on today?"

"Oh, those belong to the committee meeting in the courthouse. They're discussing ways to raise money for the school library. A lot of people from around here have gotten involved. They always meet on Saturday mornings. It's real good for business. Some of them come in for breakfast before the meeting and some of them drop over for lunch when it's done."

"Hey, Maude, more coffee over here," someone yelled from another table.

"Thanks for the information," the stranger said as she smiled and walked away.

After his second and third cups of coffee, poured by a shy, teenage waitress who wasn't too willing to offer much conversation, he paid for the coffee and walked back outside. Looking at his watch, he decided that the meeting could not go too much longer since Maude had mentioned that some of the committee members came to her place for lunch. He decided to stroll back to his car and wait. Instead of going straight back he circled the long way around the square admiring the look of the town. "I think this was a good choice for them," he said to himself. "I don't think I would mind this place myself."

He walked down the north side of the square and past the Methodist church on the other side of the street. He remembered happier times when going to church had been a regular part of his life, and then he continued south along Oak. Walking slowly, he took in the striking appearance of these old homes that had been maintained with great care. The paint colors blended well with the colorful hues of the flowers that graced every yard. The lawns, trees and bushes all looked as if they had been recently manicured. He shook his head thinking how different this neighborhood looked from the one where he was raised. And he wondered if living here was truly as idyllic as it looked.

He had crossed Maple and was concentrating on the large pillared house on the corner that he had just passed when he was startled back to reality by the loudest barking he had ever heard. Looking toward the sound, he saw the fence shake and the head of a very large dog appear and reappear as it jumped in its attempt to get over the fence. "Whoa, I wouldn't want to mess with that one," he muttered as he hurried his pace down the street.

He had just reached his car when he heard the barking start again. He turned around and saw a couple also hurrying past the corner property. "Finally," he thought. He stood by the car and waited. The pair seemed to be having a heated discussion and did not notice him until they were almost even with the car. They were startled when they realized he was standing looking at them. He said nothing as they looked at him, not sure how to handle the situation. Finally the newcomer spoke up.

"You do remember me, don't you?"

The couple nodded in agreement and the man said, "Yea, we remember you Mr. Chambers." They looked at him nervously for a moment.

"I just dropped by to check on you and see how things are going. How about we go inside and just have a little visit." The three walked to the porch where the woman pulled a key out of her pocket and unlocked and then opened the door. They walked inside and the door closed quietly and securely behind them.

The next meeting of the entire committee went very smoothly. The plans for every event were well underway. Claire wondered if everyone was as impressed as she was with what had been planned and, in some cases, accomplished by each committee. The group with the biggest job was the carnival committee. It was led by Carla Perkins from Kissock and Burt Taylor, who was still determined to get Miss Hatcher in the dunking tank. Carla had taken on this job willingly because prior to her marriage she had taught in a school that had a harvest carnival every year. She was familiar with simple games and activities that could be done in the different rooms in the school. She said that she had already talked to Miss Hatcher and had her approval.

"Did you ask her if she was willing to sit in the dunking thing?" someone yelled from the back of the group and everyone laughed.

Carla smiled and nodded toward Burt. "That is his responsibility." Then she continued to explain. "I've talked to the teachers and have their cooperation. The teachers will not be responsible for the games. We'll have parents to get those organized, and I have lists of everything every game needs. We will ask for volunteers to help throughout the time of the carnival."

The other groups reported, and every activity seemed to be well thought out and organized.

Mike had asked Scoop to attend this meeting so that the publicity could be discussed. He not only brought his notepad but he also brought his camera and snapped a few pictures. Scoop had asked to have a picture of the Brocks since they were chairing the event but Mike declined, saying that the committee members themselves were the ones who deserved all of the credit.

It was decided that not only would articles and ads be run in the paper but fliers would be distributed and posters displayed around the three towns. Scoop said he would print the fliers. The scouts, everyone was sure, would be willing to take them from door to door as they previously had. Susan, who was managing to stay one step ahead of everyone, had already gained the cooperation of the art teacher in junior and senior high for the students to make the posters.

Everyone left the meeting on a positive note. That is, everyone except Missy, who kept her nose buried in the notebook in which she was taking the minutes of the meeting. Many people would say hello or goodbye to her and she would offer only the faintest smile, nod and give a brief response. Again Claire wondered why Mike bothered to bring her to these meetings at all. Anyone could have written down the information like Missy did. Claire had a feeling that getting Missy to come each time could not have been a pleasant experience for either one of them. "Oh, well, it's none of my business," Claire said, not realizing that she had actually verbalized it.

"What did you say?" Elizabeth asked.

"Nothing. I was just thinking out loud."

After the meeting Claire had some errands to run. She had often extended simple little errands into longer ones to give her the chance to visit with more of the shop owners and their employees. Today she really just needed to pick up some groceries but decided to start at the other end of the block instead. Since it was Saturday the bank was closed, and she didn't need to go there anyway. Felton's was next. She loved to drop in every so often to see if any of the new clothing arrivals caught her eye. Today Felton's was teeming with teenage girls.

"This is the busiest I've seen it in here," she commented to Gladys, who stood happily watching the girls search through the fancy dresses.

"It's a big time of year. Next weekend is homecoming and the biggest dance of the fall. We always order lots of the newest fashions for this. They always come in on Friday evening so the girls rush over here to get a good pick. Then what we don't sell by next Friday afternoon, we send on over to the dress shop in Cummings. And what they don't sell they pass on to another store. It's great when the homecoming celebrations are spaced a couple of weeks apart like this."

Amid the giggly girls was a much older lady. "Is that someone's mother?" Claire asked.

"That's Irma Fisher. I don't think she has any children. But I do know that she is one of our regular customers. Notice that I said one of our 'regular' customers and not one of our best customers. Irma often visits us on Fridays or Saturdays and then again on Mondays. She'll buy a dress at the end of the week and then return it on Monday, saying that it didn't fit or the color was wrong or give us some other excuse. She has done this for such a long time it has just become routine."

"That seems like a pretty silly thing to do to just buy something and then bring it right back. Does she have that much trouble making up her mind?"

"We don't think she brings it right back. We are pretty sure that she wears the dress out for some event over the weekend and then returns it."

"And you let her get away with that?" Claire asked in disbelief.

"For one thing, we can't prove it. She lives outside of Kissock and it seems silly to run over there just to spy on her on weekends. And the customer is always right, you know. For another thing, Irma is a widow and lives on very limited income. From what we hear, the only fun she has is going out with some of her friends who pay her way. She also does a lot of volunteer work both here and in Kissock. If you get sick and need someone to come visit you, count on Irma. If you break your leg and can't clean your house, give her a call. She knows that she can't give financially so she tries to give to others through service to them. I heard that she volunteered to help Ben Miller when he broke his arm, but he turned her down because he was afraid he would never get rid of her."

"But I guess you shouldn't ask her for help on the weekend," Claire said jokingly. She decided that this probably was not the best day to peruse the dress racks so she headed on her way.

Farley Simpson was again manning his post by the door of the hardware store. "Good morning, Farley," she said.

Farley released the grip his had on his rifle, raised one hand and touched his hat. "Howdy," he said briefly.

"It is a beautiful morning, isn't it?"

"Yup, I imagine that it is."

Claire should have just moved on but couldn't resist making one more comment. "Are you expecting trouble today, Farley?"

"Nope, not really expecting it but you have to be alert just in case trouble comes. If you have any trouble or see or hear anything suspicious, you just call me, ma'am."

"I will definitely remember that, thanks. See you later, Farley."

Claire popped her head in the bakery intending merely to say good morning to the Taylors but she should have known better. The smells of the freshly baked goods were just too enticing. She found herself standing in front of the display cases trying to make a decision. Claire felt much like she had as a young child when she stood in front of the cases trying to decide what sweet treats to buy with her shiny nickel. It was a difficult decision but she finally selected a loaf a whole wheat bread that was fresh out of the oven. She had to fight the urge to tell Irene to not wrap it and that she would just sit and eat it at the small table by the wall. But will power and common sense prevailed and she happily left the shop with the bread tucked securely in her grasp.

The Saturday lunch bunch was filling up Maude's, supplanting the Saturday morning coffee and rolls group. Claire had not been to Maude's often but had thoroughly enjoyed the food when she did go with friends. Her committee had chosen Maude's to provide the food for the dinner at the school. Sloppy joes, buns, chips, baked beans, baked corn, and gelatin salad would be the menu. The committee was planning on adding store-bought cookies but the Taylors had stepped up and volunteered to donate sheet cakes and brownies for dessert. To help Maude with her planning, tickets would be sold ahead of time at Maude's, the schools and at locations in both Kissock and Livonia. Maude had already put out the word that the restaurant would be closed that night. She thought that would be a good way to encourage her Saturday evening crowd to go to the fund-raising dinner.

At the grocery store Claire carefully placed the freshly baked bread in a basket and quickly gathered the few items that she needed, making sure that she also included a pound of real butter. She had been a margarine user for years but loved real butter on fresh bread or rolls. She paid for the purchases and hurried across the square. Her mouth was watering just thinking about a lunch of simply bread and butter. She might add a carrot or a piece of fruit, just to soothe her conscience, but the bread was really all she wanted.

Homecoming weekend was an exciting time for the community. The game itself was close but the hometown boys managed to pull out a 21-20 victory in the final minute. Homecoming floats were driven around the field with occasional pieces of the stuffing falling off. The homecoming queen and king and their court were announced with cheers from the crowd and tears from the queen and her excited mother.

Evidently the tradition for Saturday following the Homecoming game was to have the royalty and the cheerleaders and the football team, and apparently anyone else who was interested, drive through the center of all three towns. Claire assumed that the time for their appearance was prearranged since many people surrounded the square to cheer as they drove past. Some were in cars, with a select few in convertibles. Many rode in the back of trucks. It was indeed a jubilant, though brief, event.

The homecoming romp was the reason that the final meeting of the entire fund-raising committee was set for one o'clock instead of in the morning as the previous ones had been. Each committee gave a final report and minor problems were resolved. The next-to-last committee was in the middle of its report when Mayor and Mrs. Hayward entered the room.

"Please, carry on," boomed Chester in his best mayoral voice.

"And I just came to offer myself and my expertise to any group that needs it," stated Lila who was dressed rather modestly in a blue gathered skirt with matching cardigan sweater, an orange and blue plaid blouse, and a simple straw hat adorned with a blue ribbon and a large orange flower. "You just let me know which group needs me the most and I will be glad to help you out."

Lila started socializing around the room so fast that Claire didn't think she noticed that no group jumped at her offer. When Lila and Chester had made it to the back of the room, the last group, the dinner committee, reported stating that ticket sales had been brisk and that everything seemed to be well under control.

Lila jumped up, "That's what I can do. I can sit at the door and take the tickets. And Chester can help me. That way we can also greet and thank everyone for coming. That will be perfect!"

Claire gritted her teeth and managed to keep from blurting out what she was thinking. "Yeah, why don't you just show up and look as if you've been involved. Just take the credit for something you had nothing to do with." She was sure that others were feeling the same way but didn't have the courage – or were too polite - to say anything. Claire realized that she should not have been so resentful since the Haywards had made a sizable donation of seed money to cover start-up costs.

Mike diplomatically jumped right on Lila's suggestion. "That sounds great. That will show that the Hayward family is supporting this great project." He went on to do a quick review of what had been discussed just to make sure they had every detail covered. "A week from now we will be in full swing. It should be a lot of fun. You all have worked very hard and Missy and I have been impressed by the thoroughness of each committee."

"Oh, yeah," Claire thought, "I'll bet she couldn't even list the committees. I'll bet she couldn't name five people that had been at every meeting. I'll bet she doesn't give a hoot about this whole thing."

The meeting was adjourned but most people stayed to talk. If they weren't talking about the fund raiser they were talking about last night's football game or the mini-homecoming parade. And some, if they felt they could not be overheard, were discussing the boldness of Lila and how she wanted to jump into the spotlight without raising a finger to help. Others had finally had it with Missy Brock and were commenting about her stand-offish attitude. Claire had heard no comments like this before. It was like the tension for pulling this all off was starting to get to people and cattiness was showing. She was really surprised that she had not seen it sooner even though she felt much the same way. Gradually folks left and Claire and Elizabeth strolled home.

"Can you believe that sister-in-law of mine? She has been that way ever since she married Chester. I can't understand how anyone who was brought up with the work ethic that I know her family had could turn out to be so selfish and self-centered."

"Oh, I wouldn't worry about it, Elizabeth. She is certainly not a reflection on you or Clarence. What is Dorothy like? I don't see or hear much of her."

"I like Dorothy a lot but she is super shy. When she married Charles, people said it wouldn't last, said she didn't fit in with the rest of the family. Charles has never pushed her into the public eye. She has been content to be a good mother and wife. She is very nice when you get to know her but she would never go out of her way to meet people. She is much more content to sit and read or knit. I know that Charles would like to have her get out more, but on the other hand she takes very good care of him, the house is always spotless and orderly, and she is an excellent gourmet cook. She tries lots of foreign recipes, which is not the type of cooking that most of the other wives around here do. I know they are coming next Saturday, but while Charles will be circulating among the crowd, Dorothy will be politely friendly to those around her. Otherwise she will sit quietly during the dinner. They might dance, though. They are really very good dancers. But Dorothy would be very uncomfortable if she felt that anyone was actually watching the two on them on the dance floor."

"Wow! What a contrast to Lila. How do the two of them get along?"

"Lila tolerates her and is nice to her to her face but I know she thinks that Dorothy is dull and boring. She can't stand the way Dorothy dresses. Many times she has offered to take both of us into Des Moines to go shopping. I have gone a couple of times, mainly out of curiosity, but Dorothy never has. She makes many of her own clothes, which Lila thinks is ridiculous. I often wonder how much money Dorothy has saved on clothing by making her own versus what Lila spends. I suspect that Charles is probably glad that he got that end of the clothing expenses instead of Lila's."

"And you seem to be a nice happy medium between the two of them," Claire said smiling at Elizabeth.

"I would like to think so, thank you."

By now they were in front of Claire's house and they each went their separate ways. Claire thought as she walked toward the door that even though this was a small town, it seemed to have more than its share of eccentric characters. "That is one thing that makes this place so much fun," she said out loud bouncing up the front steps and into her house.

"What's this official-looking envelope?" asked Missy as she handed the bulky, oversize package to Mike.

"It looks like the registration papers I requested have finally arrived. Actually, I guess I shouldn't said 'finally,' since I just wrote for them about two weeks ago. That's pretty fast for the government."

"OK, but what is this Securities and Exchange Commission?"

"I'm going to file the papers with them to become a Registered Investment Adviser. They're going to put their seal of approval on our plans."

"How are you going to get them to do that?" said Missy.

"They have a loophole big enough to drive a tractor through. I just fill out all these forms and send them in, and after 45 days, if they haven't told me otherwise, I'm officially a Registered Investment Adviser. I keep reading in the Wall Street Journal about how they're so understaffed that they're about two years behind on their registration checkups. By the time they get around to us, we'll have closed up shop. Besides, I don't think any of the people around here will actually check with the SEC, anyway, so I can use the forms we're going to send in as proof that I'm registered."

"I want you to drag out that typewriter we bought so you can get started on these forms. I'll tell you what to say, and you can fill in the blanks. Oh, and another thing. I need to have you go down to that library and look up the addresses and phone numbers of printers and office supply places in Des Moines and Chicago. Just tell the librarian that you need to look in the phone books for some old college friends in those cities, and I'm sure she'll be glad to find them for you. Just make sure she doesn't see what part of the phone book you're looking at."

Missy looked puzzled. "Why do I need to do that?"

"Because after you're done with that I need to have you call around and locate some office equipment and a place that will do some printing without asking a lot of questions. For what I have in mind, I don't want to be buying that kind of stuff here in Hayward or anywhere nearby. And don't make the calls from here. I wouldn't be surprised if this hick town has a telephone company with an operator who might be able to listen to everyone's calls. You need to go on a shopping trip to Des Moines and make the calls from a pay phone over there. I'll tell you what to ask for when you're ready to go."

Ten

The weather forecast had not looked good for Saturday with predictions that the rain of the past two days would continue through the first half of the weekend. Luckily Saturday morning broke sunny and warm; it was a better day than anyone could have asked for. Although Claire's assigned duties did not begin until shortly before the dinner, she knew she nervously would be hanging around the school hoping that every aspect of this massive undertaking would be going well.

She did manage to wait until eleven-thirty to head toward the school. As she approached, Claire could see children making their laps around the school yard in the walk-a-thon. She had heard via the grape vine that many relatives who did not live in the vicinity had been hit up for pledges for this event. The actual starting time had been ten-thirty so it was good to see that there were still many children walking.

The yard sale was going on in front of the school. From what she observed, it seemed to be mainly the exchanging of one person's cast offs for the undesired goods of another. But as long as money was collected for the good of the cause, no one seemed to care. And everyone seemed to be quite pleased with his or her purchase.

The best benefit of the rain of the past two days was the amount of mud that it had produced. This did a good job of creating customers for the car wash. Claire regretted not having brought her car but she truthfully had not even thought about it. The car had seen little action since she moved. So far most of her needs had been met around the square in Hayward.

The entire high school football team, with a little encouragement from the coach whose wife was on the committee, had volunteered to help the scouts with the carwash. Some of the cheerleaders had also volunteered. Claire suspected that their motives were not purely altruistic as they joyfully interacted with the players. There was a lot of giggling and spraying and general horseplay going on but the group still managed to turn out cars that were mostly clean and relatively streak-free.

As she approached the front door, Claire saw Susan busily organizing containers on a large table. When she got to the table she was pleased to see the variety of containers and the obvious amount of time that some of the teachers had put in on decorating their box lunches. There were baskets, wrapped shoe boxes, and a hat box. There was even one round box that had two small circles attached and was painted to look like Mickey Mouse.

"Susan, these look great! They should bring some good bids. Are you going to tell us who brought which one?"

"Oh, yes, of course. That is going to be part of the fun," she answered

"Is Miss Hatcher going to be the auctioneer?"

"No, she backed out this morning. Said her voice was too hoarse. I didn't believe her but I felt it best to not argue with my boss. Now if the bullhorn would get here we could start."

"Who is bringing the bullhorn? Sheriff Johnson?" Claire asked.

"Oh, here it comes now," Susan said looking out toward the gathering crowd.

Claire turned in the direction of where Susan was looking and saw a bright yellow bullhorn held high in a lavender-gloved hand above a bright purple wide-brimmed hat. The fluffy lavender feathers that circled the crown fluttered in the breeze as Lila rushed toward the front table.

"I am so sorry, dear, but we had a hard time finding it. I think Chester hid it when Bud returned it after the July fourth picnic. Chester doesn't think that a bullhorn is something that a lady should have but he just doesn't understand how often it does come in handy." Lila laid it on the table and smoothed out the purple flowered dress with her lavender gloves. Looking over the variety of lunches she nodded her approval. "Nice, very nice. These should bring some good bids. Now where would you like me to stand?"

It was a good thing she had not directed that question in Claire's direction or she probably would have told her exactly where to go. Luckily Susan was quick to answer and she did it very tactfully.

"I'd like you to stand here and help me look for the bidders. But since this activity was my responsibility, I will be the auctioneer." Lila did not seem too pleased with the response as she stiffened a bit. She turned toward the crowd and put on her big look-at-me-I-am-the-mayor's-wife smile.

Susan mounted a red, white and blue box that Claire thought she probably had borrowed from the band director at the high school, turned toward the crowd, most of whom were seated on the lawn by now, and raised the bullhorn to her mouth. But before she could even say one word to silence the crowd, they were all startled by a loud sneeze, followed quickly by two others. The sneezes did what the bullhorn never got a chance to do. They immediately got the attention of the crowd.

"Oh dear, excuse me," came an embarrassed apology from the front of the group. With a rather red face, Wilma Knight said, "I always thought my sneezing would come in handy some day." Those around her laughed and someone patted her on the shoulder to try to ease her embarrassment.

Susan proceeded as if that was what had been planned all along. "Now that we have your attention, let's get on with the fun." She explained how the bidding would work. Then Lila picked up the first box, held it up to show the crowd, turning and smiling as she did so. It reminded Claire of someone on television showing off a product during an advertisement. Ironically, the first box had been prepared by Wilma Knight. The bids came quickly and rose fast. When the bidding was done, Wilma joined the student who had purchased her lunch, looking quite proud that hers was the first to be sold.

Most of the rest of the boxes also sold well with little variation in prices. The one exception was the basket brought by Vickie Thornton, a third-grade teacher in her second year at the school. Not only was she one of the youngest members of the faculty, but she was also the cutest. She had beautiful red hair that came to her shoulders in soft curls. Her sparkling blue eyes were enough to melt the heart of any man and they apparently had. The bidding on her lunch took the longest time as four young men, each very handsome in his own right, vied to have the winning bid and the right to eat lunch with Miss Thornton. The crowd really got into the bidding war, too, as many had their own favorite young man. Cheers from different sections of the crowd arose as the suitors would once again raise the ante. When the final bid was accepted, a blushing but coy Vickie took the arm of the winner and they walked off to enjoy the lunch.

The final box to be offered was the very creative Mickey Mouse box. Lila held it high for the crowd, which responded with many compliments. The bidding started a bit higher on this box, probably as a compliment to the creativity of the designer. Some bidders came late and did not hear the name of the person who had prepared the box and some didn't really care. They were just caught up in the festive atmosphere. The final bid went to young Burt Taylor who had just joined the group after checking to make sure that all of the carnival activities were ready to go.

Burt made his way to the front of the group to pay and to see which teacher – maybe one of his old favorites or maybe a new cute young one – had provided this lunch. The look on his face told it all when Pearl Hatcher herself arose from a chair in the shadows of the front door and introduced herself as the Mickey Mouse person. The crowd roared with laughter for many of them knew how Burton felt about his old principal.

"So we meet again, Burton," Pearl said with the same stern look that Claire imagined she had given him many a times when he was back in her charge.

Burt, whose cheeks were quite pink by now, simply nodded politely and responded, "Yes, ma'am." He walked to retrieve the chair Miss Hatcher had been using and carried it to the table where she waited. "Would this spot be agreeable for you?"

Pearl sat down in the chair. Burt pulled up the box Susan had been standing on and sat by Miss Hatcher. Claire felt sorry for him. He had worked so hard on the carnival and somehow this didn't feel like a very nice reward for his efforts. But life is sometimes tough and filled with surprises and for Burton, this was just one of those times. And for all Claire knew, maybe Pearl was not too happy with the situation either. She hoped for both of their sakes that Pearl had packed a delicious lunch.

The carnival started at one o'clock and seemed to be a big hit. As she walked through the building, Claire was amazed at the variety of activities that Carla Perkins had put together in such a short time. There were ring toss and fishing games, bingo and milk bottle bowling, races and face painting, and many other popular games. The bake sale was also a big hit. By the time she got to that room, most of the items had sold signs on them. Cookies and brownies were sold by the dozen or individually. Many children were walking around munching on the treat of their choice.

In the front of the school where it got good audience participation was the dunk tank. Not only was Burt in charge but he was scheduled to be the target during the last block of time. Claire wondered if he was hoping that interest would wane by then. As she looked over the list of those brave enough to put themselves in the seat above the water, she was somewhat surprised to see that the pastors of all of the churches had volunteered for ten minute blocks. That was probably enough since all of these gentlemen were well past fifty. Another volunteer over fifty was Cliff Wilkens, the popular custodian.

Among the other names were Bud Hornsby, Bryan Graves, Jim Dunn, and Scoop Gibson. All of these were well known figures in Hayward. Claire figured that although the children might not have known them all that well, their parents would have. Owning a car dealership and a hardware store, running a grocery store and being the postmaster made these men very recognizable figures in town. Sheriff Butch Johnson was signed up for a half hour, probably talked into it by his deputy. There were a couple of teachers, too, as well as a few people from the other communities. One of the biggest draws, according to Burt, would probably be John Brook, the high school football-basketball-baseball coach. He put Coach Brook toward the end in hopes of keeping lots of people around.

One name that was not on the list was that of Miss Hatcher. Claire really hadn't thought that Burton could get Pearl to agree to it. Everyone thought that having the chance to try to dunk Miss Hatcher would bring in lots of money. Claire personally would have liked to have taken a few shots at her.

Right by the front door where everyone entered the carnival, Grace Carlson sat at a table selling tickets for the quilt raffle. The quilt, which in Claire's opinion turned out to be quite beautiful, was displayed across a portable chalkboard next to the table.

"Hi, Claire, how is everything going?" asked Grace.

"I think things are going very well. People seem to be having lots of fun. There is certainly plenty to do. How are the tickets going for the quilt?"

"Really well," she beamed. "I try to not let a family go by me without buying at least one ticket. Of course, many people buy more than one. I think we should do very well. Have you bought your ticket yet Claire?"

"I bought it when Meredith was pushing the tickets at the last committee meeting."

Grace got a rather worried look on her face. "By the way, did you see Farley by the dunk tank?"

Claire thought for a moment. "No, was he supposed to be there?"

"No, he really wasn't supposed to be anywhere. He wanted to sit here by me. He pulled up a chair right here by the front door. Now that in itself would not have been so bad, but he had that rifle with him. I thought that he would scare people away so I suggested that he go over behind the dunk tank to keep an eye on things and make sure that people didn't get out of control."

"What was he doing, anyway?" Claire wondered out loud.

"Oh you know Farley. He mumbled something about watching out for the enemy sneaking into the school. When I said 'dunk tank' he got a perplexed look on his face and opened that little book that he always carries. He flipped through the pages, found what he was looking for and put the book away. Then he simply said, 'Darn good idea,' and headed off in that direction."

"Well wherever he was, he didn't seem to be too obvious. Plus with Burton over there, I don't think he'll be a problem. It must be very hard to live your life like that. I wonder if he ever lets his guard down."

Grace just shrugged and then turned her attention to selling a raffle ticket to the family approaching the door. With the sale complete she looked at her watch. "I'm glad you're here. It's Bill's turn in the tank. Would you mind taking over for a few minutes? I think that I want to watch but I'm not really sure. I feel that I should be there for moral support and have some towels ready, if need be."

Claire sat down as Grace hurried away. Business was light and she sold only five tickets in Grace's absence, four to one family and one to a little freckle-faced girl who came running out from the building saying that her grandma wanted to buy one. When Grace came back Bill was walking beside her, hand in hand, and he was dry as a bone.

"It looks to me as if you got lucky," Claire said checking him over top to bottom.

"You could say that. I surely would not pick many of these people to be on my softball team. Not one of them came even close to the target. Russ Stover didn't fare as well, though. He got drenched about five times. Five times in ten minutes. What are the odds of that? I think it was old Barney Farnsworth that got him most of those times."

"I thought Barney had moved," said Grace.

"He did, but then he moved back to Livonia." Bill turned to Claire and explained, "Barney is quite the drinker and rumor has it that more than once he showed up at Sunday morning services either a bit tipsy or hung over. Russ was not pleased about that, especially since he is very anti-alcohol. So almost every Sunday some part of his sermon dealt with the evils of alcohol. One Sunday, I heard, he even pointed at Barney who had fallen asleep and was snoring during the sermon. When Barney heard what had happened he yelled at Russ and told him that he was not God and he was being too judgmental. He said that he was moving out of this unforgiving place and would never darken the doorway of that Baptist church again."

"I guess he felt he got his revenge today," said Grace.

"Too bad he probably slept through the sermons about forgiveness," said Bill.

Grace went back to her table and Bill decided to visit the other parts of the carnival. Claire went into the gym, which also served as the lunch room, to start getting ready for the dinner that would be starting at six o'clock. The lunch tables were set up and extra tables and chairs had been borrowed from the churches. Elizabeth arrived with a large roll of red and white checkered paper table cloths. She and Claire started covering each table while discussing their impressions of what they had seen during the day. They both felt that things were going well.

"You know," said Elizabeth, "even if we don't make as much money as Susan might like, I think this was a great community builder. It got the entire area working and having fun together. And that is a really good thing. The parents get together through their kids' school activities, but unless you still have kids in school, you too often lose that opportunity to interact with the folks from Livonia, Abbot Creek and Kissock."

"I just realized that I have not seen either of our illustrious leaders here all day today. Have you seen either Missy or Mike anywhere?" Claire asked Elizabeth.

"Now that you mention it, no I haven't. I wouldn't mind it if Missy just stayed home. That sour look on her face might put a damper on this nice, happy event."

"Yeah, she certainly doesn't have the most positive effect on people, does she? But I thought Mike would be here."

They were so busy talking and spreading out the table cloths that they didn't notice that Betty had arrived with the plastic ware for the dinner. She walked up behind them and calmly said, "Good afternoon." Even those quiet words startled them making Claire jump.

"You scared me."

"I'm sorry. You were deep in conversation and I didn't want to just stand and eavesdrop. You might have been talking about me for all I know."

"If we had," Claire smiled at her, "it would have been very complimentary, believe me. No, we were just speculating on when the Brocks were going to show up."

"You mean they haven't been here yet? Leonard and I were out past Kissock delivering a baby and we just got home about twenty minutes ago. How have things been going?"

"The turnout has been good and people seem to be having lots of fun," Claire answered.

"I did see Butch Johnson dripping on his way to the patrol car as I got here. But he said that despite his many dunkings he still had a good time. He said he figured that as many people as had taken turns throwing at him he must have made a lot of people angry over the years. I told him I didn't think that was true at all and thanked him for being such a good sport."

After they got the tables arranged and the serving tables set up, they left to change clothes for the dinner and dance. Even though she had driven to the school to deliver the dinnerware, Betty decided to walk home with the other two. They had fun joking and laughing on the short walk.

"Did you get Leonard's tux pressed for the evening?" Elizabeth asked jokingly.

"Leonard in a tuxedo? Now that would be something. I don't think he's worn one in his entire life. He's not even crazy about wearing a coat and tie to church on Sundays."

Claire was not sure just what the proper attire was for the evening. She didn't know if church wear was too dressy so she opted for a rust colored dress with a full skirt. She thought that would work for dancing, just in case the opportunity arose. She also chose to wear black flat shoes rather than heels, again thinking those would be better for dancing. Plus, at five feet nine inches she didn't want to appear to be taller than she was.

Elizabeth drove them back to school since they now were without comfortable walking shoes. They got there shortly before Maude and her helpers did. The three were quite surprised when Mike Brock carried in the first load bringing in the big warmers for the large trays of food. Missy was close behind him loaded with bags of buns. Everyone went out to help carry in the lighter things, leaving the heavy items to Mike and Maude, who was used to throwing around the big pans.

On one trip Elizabeth and Claire had a chance to question Maude. "I didn't know that the Brocks were going to help with the food."

"That was not the plan, but things don't always go according to plans. My niece, Linda, and her husband were going to help me as they often do. But Linda's baby decided to come way ahead of time so they were a little busy today."

Elizabeth and Claire looked at each other. "So that was where the Nuttings were," said Elizabeth.

"Right. And when Linda called first thing this morning to say she was sure she was in labor, I called the Brocks since they are in charge of this thing. Mike said they'd be there to help out right away. He was there in about twenty minutes. Missy didn't come for about two hours. But without them I would have been tracking down you two."

"I'm really glad that you called them first. Cooking for this many people does not sound like much fun," Claire said.

"Each to his, or her, own," laughed Maude. "I had a great time. And that Mike was a lot of fun to work with. And I am really glad that he was there to help carry some of the heavy stuff. You two weaklings don't look like you're up to that task." Maude turned and shoved huge bags of potato chips toward them. Claire was really glad that she was in charge of carrying those rather than a pan or two of hot baked beans.

Elizabeth and Claire had volunteered to be in charge of taking the tickets at the door. That way they could greet everyone and see who was coming. Even though Claire certainly did not know everyone, Elizabeth did a good job of filling her in on many of those who were unfamiliar. There were some people from other towns that Elizabeth did not know, but Claire was amazed at how many she did recognize and could name.

Among the early arrivals were the Andrews. Aaron, with a sun-burned face, looked as if he had just come from a day of golf. Clara was between Meredith and Aaron. "Good evening," Claire said. "We're glad that you are joining us. Are you hoping to get some dancing in tonight, Clara?"

Clara thought for a moment. "I was a darn fine dancer in my time but I don't think any of these men today even know the proper way to dance anymore. If you find me one who really knows what he is doing, you send him my way." Then she turned, pushing her way indignantly past Meredith, and headed for the gym.

"Mother and Dad really were good dancers," explained Aaron. "But I'm sure that Mother hasn't set foot on a dance floor since Dad died, and probably for years before that, too. It would be really something if there were someone she could dance with tonight. She would never admit it, but I'm sure she'd enjoy that."

Clarence came at about the same time but didn't look very excited to be there. "Is he all right?" Claire asked after Clarence had left the table and walked toward the gym.

"Oh, sure," answered Elizabeth. "He just doesn't like gatherings like this. And he hates to dance. I doubt that I will get him to stay past dessert."

There was a bit of commotion in the line waiting to present their tickets. Claire craned her neck to see what was happening but when she saw swirls of sheer burgundy and the bobbing of a burgundy pillbox hat, she knew that Lila had arrived. Lila pushed her way past those already in line and hurried to the table with the mayor tagging behind her. "Oh, I am so sorry that I am late. Here I had promised to take the tickets and greet the folks but I just couldn't make it on time. You two can just go on now and I'll take over."

Elizabeth looked Lila squarely in the eyes and said politely but firmly, "We really have a good system here, Lila. I think you should just go on and circulate through the crowd."

"What a good idea. I am sure people have been wondering where I am." She turned back to her husband, "Come on Chester. Let's go meet our people."

Lila made a totally unnecessary twirl, causing her full skirt to swirl around her. Claire thought the dress was quite pretty but too fancy for the occasion. "At least," Claire thought, "if she drops sloppy joes on herself it won't show very much on that color."

Among those next in line were Vernina and Bob Graves and their children.

"Great turnout, don't you know," said Vernina with her distinctive big smile. Within a few minutes, the Dunns –Jane, Jim, Jenny and Jeff – were at the table handing in their tickets. Jane looked very tired.

"Hi, neighbors," Claire said. "How are all of you doing this evening?"

Jenny and Jeff responded with a brief, "Fine."

Jim said, "I'm great, but Jane doesn't seem to feel too great these days."

"I guess I'm just getting old," said Jane. "The first two pregnancies were so easy. This one is just harder. But I'll be fine."

"I certainly hope so," Claire replied. "Please call me any time if you need me. Okay? I mean it."

"Okay," smiled Jane weakly, "I will."

When the Simpson family came, Carly was all smiles. She was wearing a blue and white gingham dress with lace trim. There was a big white bow in her hair that looked as if it had been curled for the occasion. Joey did not look quite so happy. When Claire complimented him on how handsome he looked, he blushed slightly and replied, "I didn't know I'd have to wear this tie just to come to school."

Elizabeth seconded Claire's sentiments. "Well, you look very grownup. I know you will have fun. The food looks great. Do you like sloppy joes? And the brownies are yummy! I know. I sneaked a little sample."

Joey didn't look convinced as he a Carly walked toward the gym.

"Is your father not coming, Bob?" Claire asked.

"He's here. He's just not coming inside. He doesn't feel that a big part of the population of three towns should be in the same place without someone keeping guard. He is hiding in the bushes out in front," Bob explained. "I told him that I would bring some food out to him."

Francine continued. "He said that when on guard duty one shouldn't eat, but we convinced him that once the crowd was pretty much inside it would be okay for him to take a little dinner break. I just hope he doesn't scare anyone out there."

The main rush had slowed down when a familiar smiling face came through the door. It was Ben Miller. And next to him, without anything even close to a smile, was Bertha Banter. "Good evening, Ben. It's nice to see you again, Miss Banter." Ben answered back while Bertha acknowledged with just a nod of the head.

After they had walked away from the table Elizabeth said, "I don't know what he sees in her. I've heard from more than one person that they have seen the two of them together in different places. He is so pleasant and she is just a grump!" Claire just smiled as she watched the pair walk toward the line for food.

Ticket collections had slowed to almost nothing so Claire told Elizabeth to go on and eat with Clarence. First, though, Elizabeth insisted that Claire go through the food line. Maude and her two recruits were still serving up a storm as satisfied customers returned for seconds or even thirds. Mike still had a smile on his face and visited with the folks. Missy, on the other hand, looked as if she had just about had it. Her hair, which was normally neatly arranged, hung limply around her face. The overdone makeup that had become her trademark had pretty much disappeared during the preparation and serving of the food. She kept shifting her weight from one leg to another, probably because the heels that she had foolishly worn to Maude's that morning were now rudely telling her that she had not made a wise choice.

Claire carried her dinner back to the ticket table, just in case there were late arrivals, and Elizabeth went to look for Clarence. Claire was about halfway through her sloppy joe sandwich when Mike and Missy rushed out the gym door and headed toward the front entrance.

"Leaving already?" Claire asked.

Missy just gave Claire that "if looks could kill" stare. But Mike turned and said, "Oh, we'll be back. We just need to do a bit of freshening up. Being a cook all day is harder than I thought."

"See you later," Claire yelled as they hurried out. They had barely exited through the door when she heard a scream. No one in the gym seemed to hear it so Claire decided she should investigate. Upon reaching the door, she saw Mike and Missy standing completely still, their hands raised above their heads. In front of them, with his rifle aimed straight at them, was Farley.

Not knowing quite what else to do, Claire used the most authoritative voice she had used since her teaching days and asked, "What seems to be the trouble here, Mr. Simpson?" She would have addressed Farley by the rank he had in the army but had no idea what that might have been so "Mr." was as commanding as she thought she could sound.

"I caught these two trying to sneak out. I thought I should detain them until I could figure out just what they were up to." His eyes jumped from one to the other as he spoke, as if he expected one of them to make a move toward him at any moment.

"It's all right, Mr. Simpson. They were just headed home to put on different clothes. They've been working in the mess hall all day and need to change. It's okay to let them pass, and when they return, be sure to let them back in."

Reluctantly Farley lowered his rifle. Mike and Missy slowly side stepped a few paces and then hurried off into the evening's darkness.

"You did well, Farley, but I don't think there will be any more trouble tonight.

Why don't you go on in with your family? The dancing will be starting before too long."

"Nope, I don't think I should do that. You can just never be too careful." Farley turned and walked back to his self-appointed lookout spot in the bushes.

"Someone could probably write a book about him," Claire said to herself as she went back in to finish her dinner. The food lived up to the promise Maude had made that if they chose her, no one would be disappointed. Beans never did agree with Claire but these were so good that she figured she would just have to face the consequences tomorrow. The brownies from the Taylors were scrumptious, but then Claire knew they would be since she had become one of their best brownie customers. She wondered how many other people in Hayward bought as many of them as she did. Every dinner or pot luck Claire had been to in Hayward seemed to have two or three pans of some kind of brownies. She began to think that she was the only one who did not know how to make these yummy chocolaty treats.

After Claire finished eating she decided that it was safe to leave the ticket table. She took her plate and utensils into the gym and, while depositing them, scanned the crowd for someone to sit with. Betty and Leonard seemed to be a logical pair so she walked over to an empty seat by them. Across the table from the Nuttings were Meredith, Aaron and Clara Andrews. While they all sat and talked, in through the door came a man Claire did not know. He carried a very large suitcase in one hand and a speaker in the other.

"The music has arrived," said Leonard. "I've never heard him myself, but I've heard that he does a good job playing lots of different types of music. That should keep all of these generations happy."

"He'd better be darn good or I'm out of here," piped in Clara in a voice that could be heard at the neighboring tables.

"Mother, please," said Aaron, "You need to keep your voice down."

"Well, I didn't think this was the library," she replied in a cynical tone.

Claire watched as the DJ got set up. When there was first talk of having a dance, she worried that the music would be provided by that same little group, loosely referred to as a band, that had marched at the beginning of the parade on the Fourth of July. She was relieved to learn that they were going to hire a DJ instead. It got even better when she learned that the one they had hired, who played at most of the high school dances in the area, was the brother of one of the teachers in the school. He was willing to work at half his going rate.

Claire wondered just what kind of music he would play and what memories it might bring back, not only for her but for many others. Music seemed to bond members of different generations, giving them memories of certain songs that those who came after could never possibly understand. And, of course, there was the music of the younger generations that the older generations often could not understand or appreciate or even approve of. It would be interesting to see just what he picked to play.

Claire was also interested to see who danced and with whom. Would couples stick just to spouses? Would there be mixers to get more people involved? Would women be as open to asking the men for a dance instead of the more traditional men asking the woman? Would some people just sit, wishing that someone would ask them to dance? Would she be one of those destined to sit all night? She was getting anxious to get started and wondered what was taking so long. Others seemed to be wondering that same thing as she sensed an air of impatience in the crowd. Then Missy and Mike Brock rushed in and headed for the DJ.

Clara glared at the couple as they hurried across the gym floor. "Well, if it ain't Mr. and Mrs. Crook."

Aaron spoke firmly but quietly to Clara. "Pipe down, Mother!"

"Well, I call 'em as I see 'em," Clara retorted, emphatically crossing her arms across her chest.

In the short time that they had been gone, there had been quite a transformation in the tired, apron-covered couple who had left. Missy's hair was done up in a twist that was held in place by a large red sequin-covered barrette. Her dress, also a bright red, had a scoop neckline, tightly fitted bodice and a very full skirt. Around her tiny waist was a sequin-covered belt. Her dress, though flashy, was very pretty and did not have the harsh, slutty look that most of her clothes did. On her feet were very high heeled red open-toed shoes, the kind of shoes they were used to seeing on her.

Mike looked refreshed. His damp hair looked as if it had just been washed. He had on a long sleeved black and white striped shirt and black polyester bell-bottom pants. His pants were tighter than those worn by the other men but looked very much in style with the times outside of this rural setting.

After talking to the DJ for a couple of minutes, Mike took the microphone and addressed the crowd. "Attention, everyone, attention! I want to thank you all for joining us tonight and closing out this very busy but fun day with still another few hours of entertainment. Although we have not begun to figure out just how much money we raised for the school library book fund, I feel that it was a very successful day indeed. I want to thank those who were instrumental in making all of this possible. Rather than naming all of those wonderful volunteers, I would ask that those who helped plan and carry out this event stand so we can thank you for the wonderful job that you all did." To a round of hearty applause, the volunteers reluctantly stood. Taking a quick glance around the room, it seemed that almost everyone who had been involved was there. Then Mike went on to introduce the DJ and said, "Let the dancing begin!"

The songs he started with were current popular hits, so the teenagers were the first on the floor. A few older couples joined them, much to the mortification of the teens who were embarrassed to have their parents dancing in public. As the songs continued, the number of dancers grew. The music from the late fifties seemed to have the widest appeal. That was the era of the beginning of rock and roll, which appealed to the younger members of the crowd, but had enough traditional tunes that the older dancers could also associate with that period.

Then the DJ dropped back in time to songs from World War II. That brought many of the older adults out of their seats and onto the dance floor. Ben Miller came over and asked Claire to dance. "Is Miss Banter not dancing?" she asked.

"She said that she didn't want to but she noticed that I couldn't keep from tapping my foot in time to the music so she told me that I should go find a dance partner. So here I am."

Ben reached out his hand to Claire's as she got up, and led her to the center of the floor. It had been a few years since she had danced, but Ben was a very good dancer. He gave good cues with his hand on her back and it wasn't long before she was moving easily with his guidance. When the music ended, they thanked each other as he walked her back to the table.

"That was fun, Ben. I think you could find a lot of ladies who would love to dance with you."

Ben smiled and winked. "You must have read my mind," he said and he looked around to see whom he would ask to be his next dance partner.

The WWII era music continued and those who had danced to those songs in an earlier time in their lives fox-trotted easily around the room. It took Ben a minute or two to decide but, after heaving a big sigh and squaring his shoulders, he headed toward Clara. Many people watched as he approached her wondering what her response would be. Claire was somewhat surprised that she popped out of her seat the minute he was in front of her. The two of them walked toward the dancing crowd. Clara put her hand on Ben's shoulder with such gusto that her purse flew over their heads and crashed against his back. Ben's knees buckled a bit when the weight of her purse hit him but he tried to continue as if nothing unusual had happened. It was fun to watch the two of them. Clara seemed to soften as they danced to *The White Cliffs of Dover* and *String of Pearls*. Claire thought at that moment that Clara looked like she felt she was about thirty years younger.

The music tempo changed as the younger dancers took the floor to do the twist. The next six or seven songs were again from the late fifties through the six-ties. The DJ announced that he was taking a short break. The entertainment for the break was going to be the drawing for the quilt. Since the quilt had been made in the basement of the Methodist church and since Grace had organized the raffle, Bill Carlson had been selected to do the drawing. To make it totally fair, a blind-fold had been placed over his eyes. Claire felt this was quite unnecessary. She, for one, certainly trusted Bill, but maybe the Baptists, Lutherans and Catholics were not as trusting as she was. Plus she thought it just added to the jovial atmosphere to tie a red bandana around his white hair. Grace stuck a very large fish bowl filled with the raffle ticket stubs in front of his hand. He reached in, poked through the stubs and came up with one. He handed it to Mike who was standing by to make the announcement.

"And the lucky winner is…" he paused for a few seconds to help build the anticipation, "Bertha Banter!"

Everyone turned toward Bertha, who sat with a stunned look on her face. She turned toward Ben, who smiled and shrugged his shoulders. As the crowd applauded, Bertha slowly got up and walked toward Mike. As he put his arm around her, she stiffened. Claire wondered how long it had been since a man had done that. She certainly did not look too comfortable with Mike's gesture.

"Congratulations, Bertha," he said, shoving the microphone in her direction.

Bertha looked terribly uncomfortable but did manage a faint smile. "This is truly a surprise. It is a beautiful quilt and I am sure that I will find the perfect place for it. I will enjoy it, I am sure." She headed back to her seat, staring at Ben as she did. Punch and cookies were passed out as people milled around waiting for the DJ to return. It seemed to Claire that many people were renewing old friend-ships and beginning others. Mike appeared to be having a great time. He was the center of a group of many of Hayward's business leaders and they were socializing like they had known each other for years. Another time she saw him introducing himself to another group of men. From the looks of their weathered faces, not to mention the very pale tops of their heads, she guessed that they were from the farming sector rather than business crowd.

Ben came to the punch bowl the same time Claire did. "Bertha sure looked surprised when her name was drawn," said Claire.

"I'm sure she was," smiled Ben with a mischievous look on his face, "since she did not even buy a ticket."

"You sneaky little dickens," Claire said. "I was kind of surprised to see her here at all. I wondered if she felt that this fund raiser was a conflict of interest for her since she has to appeal to the city council to get funding for 'her' library."

"I can assure that she didn't want to come at first. Then I leveled with her and told her that it would not look good if she were the only one in the entire town that wasn't supporting this fund raiser. I'm sure that was a bit of an exaggeration but I want her to soften up and be more caring about this community and her customers. She finally agreed that she would come with me but she assured me that she would not have any fun."

"That must not have made you look forward to this evening very much," Claire said sympathetically.

"Oh, her bark is worse than her bite. I was sure she would have a fine time once she got here."

"And is she?" Claire asked.

"I think so. The only time she really had that scowl on her face was when the DJ was playing the music that the kids like. I had better get back to her or she might think I'm flirting with you."

The music started again and the dancers once again flooded the floor. After a few more records, the DJ announced that he would be doing a long segment to honor the town's veterans and would be playing lots of the familiar songs from WWII. He started with *Don't Sit Under the Apple Tree* and a couple of other peppy tunes. Then he began to play some slower more sentimental numbers. *You'd Be So Nice to Come Home To* was almost finished when Claire noticed that Farley was standing in the doorway, his rifle held loosely at his side. He looked so sad and she wondered what memories were rushing through his confused head. When the strains of *I'll Be Seeing You* started, Claire took a big risk, walked over to him and without saying a word, gently took the rifle from him and set it on a table. Taking his hand she led him to the dance floor. It took him no time at all to get into the rhythm of the song. She didn't know whether to try to talk to him or to just let well enough alone so she let him quietly move to the music. She decided that silence was probably the best approach at the moment. When the song ended, she thanked him and complimented his dancing ability.

"Used to be quite a dancer," he replied, still looking somber.

"There are a lot of nice ladies here that would love to dance with someone as smooth on his feet as you are. You should go ask one of them to dance."

"Yes, ma'am, I think I might just do that." Farley nodded his head slightly to her and headed off to find a new dance partner. Claire was curious who he would choose. He paused briefly then headed for Clara.

"This should be interesting," Claire said to herself. Much to her surprise, Clara didn't hesitate at all but joined him right away. "Now that is a cute, but very unique couple," she said, hoping after the words left her mouth that no one had overheard her.

After that Farley danced with many of the ladies, most of them his age or older. He actually looked as if he was having fun. There were no real smiles, but that ever-worried look was gone from his face. When he danced with Clara he got quite a bit of audience attention, but as he continued people paid him no more attention than anyone else.

Clara got the crowd's attention again when Mike asked her to dance. Claire was standing close by when he asked her and initially the only response that he got was, "You must be kidding." But with pressure from Meredith and Aaron, she reluctantly agreed. Now that was an odd couple – Mike in his tight black bellbottom trousers and Clara in a pink flowered cotton dress and her white orthopedic low heeled shoes. When the song was over, he politely returned her to her seat, thanked her and went to find a different partner.

"Now that wasn't so bad, was it, Mother?" Aaron asked.

"His hand was sweaty. He doesn't know the Fox Trot. Couldn't follow him. He needs to spend some time with Arthur Murray," she answered in disgust.

Mike did a good job of dancing with lots of ladies. It seemed as if he had set out to get to know as many of them as he could. Missy, to the surprise of most of them, also did a good job of circulating. In fact, every time Claire saw her she was with some other man. She had turned on charm that many never knew she had. There were times when groups of men encircled her as she laughed and joked with them. Between the dancing Farley and the smiling, gregarious Missy, Claire felt like she should have gone outside to see if the moon was full. These were certainly some strange but nice changes and she wondered if they would last.

Closing the door behind them, he picked her up and whirled her around. "How did I do tonight?" she asked, feeling sure that she already knew what his answer would be.

"You did good. In fact you did better than good. You did great! You were terrific! You wowed them all."

"Well, it looked as if you did pretty good yourself," she responded. "Every time I saw you it seemed that you were rubbing elbows with some interesting local yokels."

"You're darn right. And don't sell those local yokels short, either," he grinned before he kissed her soundly on her bright red lips.

Eleven

Since it was the Sunday morning following the big event, Claire wasn't sure how many people would be in church. Even though the dance was over at ten o'clock, she was sure that was later than many folks were used to staying out on a Saturday night. The choir didn't sing. Grace had decided not to prepare an anthem for that day since she was not sure how many of her faithful choir members might want to sleep in after their big night out. Phoebe Peoples filled the void with her usual energetic, though somewhat erratic, organ playing. Bill's sermon was about individual giving for the good of a larger need. Then he talked about the success of the fund raiser, thanking the community as a whole for the support they had given. He even acknowledged the leadership of Mike and Missy Brock. Then as a total surprise to many, Bill had them stand up and receive a round of applause. Claire had never seen them in church before. In fact, she was quite positive that this was their first time in this church, anyway. Had they been there even one time before, it would have been a topic of conversation at the quilting group as well as many other places of gossip in the community.

At the end of the service, Missy and Mike stood beside Bill to greet people as they filed out. The progress of the congregation's leaving came to a stop and people stood still for an uncommonly long time. Claire wondered what was taking so long so she craned her neck to see if she could tell what was causing the bottle neck. She couldn't see a lot but the sight of a large black wide-brimmed hat, ornately decorated with extensive gold stitching, gave her a pretty good idea of what was going on. Either a lost flamenco dancer was asking for directions or Lila Hayward was monopolizing the conversation with the Brocks. How ironic this seemed after all of the insulting comments Lila had made about Missy. Claire would have liked to have been closer so she could hear what Lila said. She wondered how sincerely Lila could come across. Or maybe she really had changed her feelings about the Brocks.

When Claire finally got to the doorway, she shook hands with Mike and Missy and thanked them for their work on the fundraiser. Mike reminded her that the committee was going to meet one more time the following Saturday to get a final count on how much had been raised. Everyone seemed to feel that it had been a tremendous success and was anxious to hear the final numbers.

Betty Nutting had been behind Claire in the line so they walked home together. "Seeing the Brocks this morning was kind of a surprise, wasn't it?"

"Yes, but I think it was good. It never hurts anyone to attend church, except for some teenagers who think they are being terribly mistreated by being dragged to a church service."

Betty laughed. "I do remember those days. But I meant it just seemed odd that this is the time they chose to come."

"Maybe they were invited. I wonder if anyone had thought to do that before. It will be interesting to see if they continue to attend."

Betty talked as we walked. "And I noticed while you were speaking with them that they took all of the credit for the success. They didn't say anything to you about your contribution. They sounded as if they pulled this off all by themselves."

"I kind of thought that, too, but it's done and it went well. We should just be happy that everyone did their part and we had such a success. It really doesn't matter who gets the credit for it."

Betty added, as Claire turned up her walk, "You're right. I just hate it when you're right and I'm not. Are we on for walking tomorrow morning?'

"You bet. See you then," Claire responded and ran up her steps.

Since this was her first Halloween in Hayward, Claire really had no idea how much candy to buy. She figured that she would look around the grocery store to see what she could find when she was greeted by a, "Howdy, Claire."

"Hi, Bryan. How are you doing?"

"I'm doing well and the store is, too. It's candy season, don't you know. Between Halloween and what was purchased for the carnival we've had quite a run on the sweets. I'll bet Tim Payne loves this time of year. All that sugar has got to increase his dental business. Can I help you with anything?"

"I came to buy some stuff for Halloween but I have no idea how much to get. Do you have any idea how many trick-or-treaters I should plan for?"

"You would think that I would, wouldn't you, but I don't. I never pay much attention. Vernina always buys what she hands out and I'm the one responsible for taking the kids around town. I have always suspected that Vernina helps the supply disappear while we're gone. Now, don't you tell her I said that. So I'm afraid I can't be much help."

"Do you have any idea what are the most popular things with the children?"

"Oh those little masked varmints will eat just about anything, don't you know. I think Vernina picks what she likes and we have never had anyone egg our house because they didn't like what she passed out. It's a good thing you came this afternoon though. There will be a rush tomorrow."

"Thanks, Bryan. I guess I'll look around and see what I can find." Claire headed toward the candy counter while visions of Hershey and Milky Way bars danced in her head. She scanned the entire candy counter, overwhelmed by the decision. She thought about bubble gum but didn't know what she would do if she had lots left over. Chewing bubble gum at her age was not nearly as much fun as it used to be. Suckers would be easy and she thought Susan might use the leftovers as prizes for some of the contests she ran in the library. The bags of Hershey kisses were very tempting but how many of those little pieces would make a reasonable treat to drop in a bag? The candy bars would be a very nice treat but to buy the number she figured she would probably need would be very expensive. Finally Claire decided on a couple of bags of suckers and a couple of bags of chocolate kisses. She thought that any chocolate that was left over would be a nice treat for herself. "I might be visiting Tim Payne myself if I end up eating a lot of those. And I'll need to walk to Kissock and Livonia every day to walk them all off." She then looked around quickly to make sure that no one had overheard her. She thought, "Someday you are going to say something stupid and someone will hear you. That is a habit you really should break."

Claire finished the rest of the shopping, picking up lots of fruits and vegetables, trying to soothe her conscience from the guilt of the candy splurge. A loaf of whole wheat bread and the leanest pieces of meat in the case completed her purchase.

Bryan bagged the groceries and walked her to the door where he gently placed them in her arms. Smiling he said, "I guess I'll be seeing you tomorrow night, Claire. You might send one or two of those kisses my way, if you think you have enough."

"I might be able to spare a couple. Bye, Bryan."

"Are you nuts? Do you realize how much all of those must have cost?"

"Of course I know how much it cost. I bought them, didn't I?'

"All of that for those wretched little brats? What in the world are you thinking?"

"That's just it. I am thinking. They will make quite an impression, don't you think? Don't you imagine that will give the impression that we have lots of money to spend? In order to make money, you have to spend some money."

"Maybe, but I still think you're nuts. And what are we going to do if we have extras. I'm not touching those!"

"You won't have to do a thing with them. I'll handle them all. And I'll bet you that we won't have to worry about having any extras."

With the apparent success of the recent fundraiser still on everyone's mind, Mike confidently strolled into Maude's for a mid-morning coffee break. Briefly he stood in the doorway, surveying the crowd. He spotted Clarence, Mayor Hayward, and a third man Mike didn't know sitting at a prime table close to the window. "Good visibility," Mike thought to himself. He nonchalantly walked toward the empty table next to the group he had targeted and started to pull out a chair.

"Mike," a voice said, "how about joining us?"

Mike smiled before he turned around. "Oh, good morning, Mr. Mayor and Mr. Lambert. I was distracted and didn't even see you. I'm Mike Brock. I don't believe we've met," Mike said, extending his hand to the third man at the table.

Rising to shake Mike's hand, William Swan introduced himself. "You may not know me, but everyone in town pretty much knows who you and your wife are after all of the effort you put in on the fund raiser."

"Pull up a chair," invited the mayor. "Bill is our city attorney and can sue anybody you like," Chester said laughing.

"I could also sell you that house you're renting or find you a real nice piece of property in the area," William added.

"How's the car business these days, Mike? Did you leave Bud holding down the store?" asked Chester.

"It's kind of slow, but it is a great place to work. Bud's a pretty easy-going boss."

"I guess with all that money you got in your inheritance that you don't need to rely on many car sales." The minute the words had fallen from his mouth, Clarence knew he had let a confidence slip. "Oh, Mike, I'm sorry. I never should have said that."

Mike feigned a stern look at Clarence for a few seconds but then his annoyed look gave way to a friendly smile. "Oh, that's all right. It's not important. My inheritance is not all that big." Fully aware of the amount of money that Mike had deposited in his bank, Clarence looked at him warily. Mike leaned forward and lowered his voice. "Actually, it wasn't really an inheritance, anyway. The truth is that I used to be a commodities trader. I did pretty well. In fact, I did so well that Missy and I opted for an early retirement in a more relaxed setting like Hayward, away from the high pressure of the commodities business."

Chester pulled his chair a little closer to the table and leaned closer to Mike. "Where did you work? Who did you work for?"

"I started out working for my dad in the business, but after a few years he said I knew more than he could teach me, so he shoved me out of the nest. The last few years I worked for myself. When I decided to retire, I sold my seat on the Chicago Board of Trade. I still keep up with the markets, and dabble a little in it for my own account, though."

"Ahhh!" said Chester leaning back in his chair, thinking over what he had just heard. The group continued talking about things they often discussed to pass the time – the weather, the traffic around the square, the success of the year's harvest, and the winding down of the Vietnam war.

After finishing his coffee, Mike said, "Well, I guess I'd better get back to Hornsby's and see what's going on. Bud doesn't care when or where I take my coffee break, so maybe I'll see you here again tomorrow."

As Mike was passing the window in front of the store, he turned to wave at his new friends. They all waved back, to which William said, "He certainly seems to be a nice addition to our town…and to your bank, Clarence. Makes me wonder, though. All the farmers around here trade in corn and soybean futures to lock in their feed prices, but I've never met anyone who actually made any real money at it just by trading the paper."

"If he's as good as he seems to be, I wonder if he'd consider coming out of retirement and helping some of us make a little extra money…or maybe a lot of money," said Chester. "I'm sure there would be quite a few folks who'd be willing to follow his expert guidance if they thought there was some money to be made. Just think how much more generous everyone would be in improving the town if they had a little extra change in their pockets!"

Clarence put on his best banker's face – the one he donned to turn down a loan request, and said, "I don't know, fellas. As much as I like Mike, and as much as he seems to be a real go-getter, you've got to remember that we don't know much about him. Let's be real careful before we take any kind of leap with our money."

"You're probably right, Clarence," said William. "I understand the law and real estate, but you're the real money guy in town. Why don't you talk to him and see if he'll give you a little more proof to back up what he just told us."

"Good idea," said Clarence. "Let me think about how to approach him and get some more details."

"I think I've got some fish on the line," said Mike, as he and Missy ate dinner. "Now all we have to do is wait until they let me reel them in."

"What makes you so confident?" asked Missy.

After Mike described the meeting with the three men at Maude's, he said, "I could see the greed in their eyes when I told them that story about what I did in my former life. I think they bought the whole thing. And I'll bet you anything that they're going to have Clarence invite me in for a friendly chat so I can prove what I told them. Then they're going to ask me to help them make some money in the commodities market, too."

"What kind of proof do you think they're going to ask for?" said Missy.

"That's just it. I don't think any of those guys know enough about commodities trading to know what to ask for, so I'll act surprised about the request, and then ask Clarence if my Registered Investment Adviser forms and some of my trading account records would be acceptable. Of course, I'll try to talk them out of it by describing all the risks, but I think all they'll see are all those new dollars in their bank accounts!"

"Now I know why you had me using all that office equipment to dummy up your so-called history. And getting all that stationery and those blank brokerage statements printed on our last trip to Chicago…even when I complained about how much money you were spending. I always knew you were smart. Now I know with the success of that hokey fundraiser you have definitely established some trust."

"That's right," he said, handing Missy a martini glass. "Let's drink a toast to greed."

Their toast was interrupted by the ringing of the doorbell. Upon opening it Mike was greeted with that well known phrase, "Trick or treat!"

Halloween night was pretty much what Claire was used to in Colorado. The children were cute. Their costumes were creative and most of them were home-made as opposed to the plastic store-bought versions. Kids rang the doorbell, yelled "Trick or treat," held out their bags, and most remembered to say thank you. Claire did, however, notice a general sense of disappointment when she dropped her treats in their bags. No one said anything but she could tell that they had hoped for something else. She decided to ask the children at school what kind of treats they liked and remember what they told her for next year.

Jeff and Jenny Dunn with their dad, Jim, made her house their last stop for the evening. Although they gave her the expected polite thank you, Claire got the same less than thrilled response from Jeff when she dropped a sucker and a few kisses into his bag. She looked at Jim and said, "I think I will need to make my treats more interesting next year. I feel as if I am not meeting expectations."

"I hope you are not worried about that. They are just little beggars, after all. Plus the standard was set very high this year. The Brocks are giving out big, full sized candy bars to everyone. The kids thought they hit pay dirt when those were deposited in their loot bags. They're all talking about it as they pass each other on the street. The kids who hadn't been to the Brock's house yet hit the pavement running in that direction. Maybe that's how they did things wherever they came from but they have sure made the rest of the town look like pikers. Their pockets must sure be deeper than mine."

"Come on, Dad. Let's go so I can go eat some of this stuff."

"Okay. What do you two say to Mrs. Menefee?"

"Thanks."

"How about, 'Good night. Have a nice evening,'?" prompted Jim.

"Good night, have a nice evening," Jeff said, tugging his dad toward the steps while Jenny repeated the same prompted phrase.

"Good night, Claire."

"Good night, Jim. Tell Jane hello." Jim was on he steps when Claire yelled at him. "Wait!" She walked over to him and dropped a handful of chocolate kisses in his hand.

Because Claire had a bad headache first thing Monday morning, she had not made it to school. So instead she decided to go to school on Wednesday. She knew that was Susan's day to be there but figured she could probably still be of some use. Besides, she was anxious to talk to Susan about the success of the fund raiser.

Susan was busy with a class of students when she first arrived. So Claire started with some reshelving. She was not trying to eavesdrop as Susan gave her lesson on the non-fiction sections of the library and excitedly told the students that they were now going to be able to bolster the collection. She asked for suggestions from the students. Hands shot up and it seemed as if everyone had an ideas. Claire was not sure whose class Susan was addressing, but when she heard the loud sneezes coming closer and closer to the library, she was pretty sure that it was Wilma Knight coming to retrieve her class. Sure enough, through the doorway came Wilma tucking a lace handkerchief into the sleeve of her dress. The children stood, lined up and dutifully followed Wilma out the door and down the hall.

"Good morning, Claire. How are you feeling? Theresa said you had called Monday to say you were not going to be able to come. Maybe it was just the let down after that busy, busy weekend."

"It might have been. But it was short term and I'm fine now. I'm anxious to hear if there have been many comments from the children about the fund raiser." Claire looked at Susan waiting to hear all that she had heard.

"Since I wasn't here until this morning I don't know much about what might have been said on Monday and Tuesday, but today Halloween is the big topic of conversation. Lots of the children are talking about the big candy bars they got from one house. They seem to think that was really something. I cannot imagine spending that kind of money on Halloween candy, can you?' The minute the words left Susan's mouth she had a worried look on her face. "That wasn't you, was it, Claire?"

Claire smiled and laughed. "Absolutely not. I passed out suckers and tossed a few Hershey kisses in their bags." Reaching in a bag and pulling out the simple suckers, she continued, "I had a few left over and thought maybe you could use them as rewards for contests or something. And I agree with you about those candy bars. I have better uses for my money."

"Do you have any idea how much money we cleared? I want to get lists from each teacher and start ordering things as soon as we know."

"I haven't heard. It will be fun to find out on Saturday. Even if we didn't make as much as you'd like, it was still a great community event. I know I sure had fun."

"I did, too. And even my husband danced. I couldn't believe it. I couldn't even get him to dance at our wedding reception."

On Friday Mike decided it was time to test the waters. With a confident air and a smile on his face for everyone he met, he headed to Maude's. He had just reached for the door handle when he heard Clarence behind him saying, "Good morning, Mike." As he turned around, Clarence continued, "Chester is out of town this morning, and William told me he has some legal work to do for a farm sale, so I thought maybe we could just take a little stroll over to my office. The coffee's not as good as Maude's, but there's something I'd like to ask you."

"Sure," said Mike. "I'd be glad to. What's on your mind? Are you in the market for a new car? I'm pretty sure you're not looking for a new John Deere!"

"No, nothing like that," Clarence chuckled. "But let's wait until we can have some privacy, since this is a somewhat sensitive matter."

They walked in silence until entering the bank. After getting coffee for both of them, Clarence ushered Mike into his office and closed the door.

"O.K., Clarence. What's this sensitive thing we have to talk about? Missy didn't bounce a check, did she?"

Clarence laughed nervously. "No, no, nothing like that. Well, I don't know any diplomatic way to say this, so I'll just get right to it. We were all quite impressed with what you shared with us about your background and experience, and we were just wondering…"

Mike interrupted him. "I knew I shouldn't have said anything. This always happens. It used to happen at cocktail parties and even at Cubs games all the time. People asked me what I did, and when I told them they'd get this funny look in their eyes. It was all they could do to keep from asking for some hot tip about the commodities market, and most of the time they went ahead and asked anyway…" Noticing the somewhat confused look on Clarence's face, he stopped. "I'm sorry, Clarence. I guess I've put up some pretty strong defenses since I retired. Go ahead."

"Let me start over. I think I may have given you the wrong impression," said Clarence. "We're not looking for any hot tips. It's just that we thought that if you were still – as you say – dabbling in your own account, you might be willing to sort of come out of retirement and manage some money for some of your new friends."

"Clarence, I'm really flattered, but the commodities market is really risky, and there aren't any guarantees. In fact, I can almost guarantee that you'll lose money at some time. Now, if you're really interested, I could probably hook you up with a couple of my friends who are still in the business. I'm sure they'd do a great job for you."

Clarence leaned forward in his chair and rested his arms on his desk. "No, Mike, that's not what we're interested in at all. We've been really impressed with the effort you've put in for your new community, and, since I know that you're one of the largest depositors in the bank, you've shown that you have in fact done well. We wouldn't ask just anyone to do this for us, and we certainly wouldn't ask you to do it out of the goodness of your heart."

"Clarence, I really appreciate your saying that, but I really had planned to stay retired. If I were going to do something like this – and let me emphasize the 'if' - I don't think I could handle individual clients again. But what I might do – and I'll have to give it a lot of thought – is create some sort of pooled fund where the investors are sort of a 'club' and all the buy and sell decisions are made for the entire pool, not for individuals. Everyone would share in the profits – and losses – in direct proportion to his investment. I guess I'm just thinking out loud here, but do you think something like that might work?"

"That's what I had in mind, too. How many people could be in the pool? Right now it's just the three of us..."

"Sorry to interrupt," said Mike, "but there would be four of us. I wouldn't even think of doing this without committing my own money as well."

A smile was starting to appear on Clarence's face as he leaned back in his chair. "Well, Mike, it sounds like you're starting to give this some serious thought. As I said, there'd just be the four of us to start, but if we did O.K. it would be hard to keep this secret. Do you think we could let others into the pool?"

"I guess that would be a possibility," said Mike, "but I'd want to make sure they could afford the potential losses. Because of the securities laws we'd have to set a minimum asset level to allow them to participate, and we couldn't have any more than 35 in the pool at one time or we'd have to register ourselves as a security. To make it worthwhile for everyone, we'd need to set the initial investment at a minimum of, oh, let's say $10,000. Do you think that would be a problem?"

"It sounds to me as if you're ready to get started," said Clarence, the eagerness showing in his voice.

"Well, I'm not quite sure. I guess you just sort of got the juices flowing again, and like I said, I was more just thinking out loud about how this might work. You all have to fully understand that there are no guarantees. I would hate to alienate the new friends that Missy and I have made." Mike paused for a few seconds as rubbed his hand across his jaw and rested his chin in his hand. "Let me think about whether this is something I really want to do and how I'd set it up. Oh, there's one other thing. I know it's embarrassing to ask, so I'll bring it up. Somewhere in the back of your mind you're probably thinking, 'Is this guy for real?' Right?"

As Clarence tried to protest, Mike continued. "That's all right; don't give it a second thought. In my former life I believed in full disclosure, and I still do. If I decide to take this on, I'll provide copies of my SEC registration and my trading statements for the last three years. Would that be O.K.?"

"Of course, Mike. You're right, I wanted to ask about that but I was too embarrassed. Just between you and me, I didn't even know what to ask for."

"Well, Missy and I made the decision to retire together, so I need to involve her in any decision to 'un-retire.' I'll give you my answer in a week, and if I decide to go ahead with this, I'll also have the plan for how it will work."

"What are you doing with that clunky calculator and all those statements I just typed? And what have you done to that nice leather portfolio we just bought? It looks like you dragged it up and down the street!" asked Missy.

"For one thing a brand new portfolio wouldn't fit with someone who supposedly had carried papers in it for years. Also, I'm certain I can fool Mr. Country Bumpkin Banker with these statements, because he won't know what he's looking at. But you don't get to be president of even a little country bank if you're not good with numbers. I'm just double checking and making sure everything matches up, and that every month's ending balance is the next month's starting balance. A banker would notice something like that right away."

Three hours later, after punching numbers on the calculator and shuffling the pile of statements, Mike turned to Missy. "Perfect," he said, "not a single number out of place. Besides that, after handling these statements all night, they look like they've been around awhile, and not like they just came out of that new typewriter. I think I'll call Clarence in the morning and set up a meeting for next Thursday. By then I can have my "proposal" drawn up for him to look at, too. Do you think you'll be able to fit some more typing into your busy schedule?"

Most of the committee sat anxiously waiting for the meeting to start. Each group had turned in their money to Elizabeth, who had then handed it over to Clarence, who in turn passed it on to a designated bank employee who noted the proceeds from each activity and figured the total profit. The members of the sub-committees seemed to be sitting together waiting for the results. Claire felt as if they were divided into teams, excited to find out who would be the winning squad. Everyone knew that the overall total was what was important but there was still that competitive atmosphere with each group hoping that their earnings would be the most impressive.

Susan Davis was the most edgy of anyone. She would sit for awhile but then would get up and walk around the back of the room. Then she would sit for a time, drum her fingers on her chair, and then repeat her walking.

Elizabeth sat next to Claire and, if she knew any of the results, was keeping them secret. Clarence himself was in attendance for the first time. He huddled next to Mike as they examined the papers that he had pulled from his briefcase. When Mike had been shown all of the papers, he nodded to Clarence, and stood up to face the crowd.

"Thank you all for coming together one more time. I know that you are all excited to find out the results but there a few things I would like to say. First, Missy and I would like to thank you all for having the trust in two relative strangers to take on this big project." Missy actually gave a somewhat sincere smile to the group. Mike continued, "Next I want to thank all of you in this room for your hard work. You all pulled together to make this happen."

Betty, who was sitting on the other side of me, whispered, "It's about time he shared some of the credit."

"A leader is only as good as his team," Mike continued.

"You better believe that," whispered Betty again.

Mike lifted the papers that Clarence had given him. "Now for the fun! Let's see how we did." Group by group he listed the amount they had raised. Each group cheered and was cheered as he read. Many folks looked as if they were trying to keep a rough running total as he read the results of the first three or four groups but it became too hard for most, so they just enjoyed hearing the success of each part.

By now Susan was pacing back and forth. She knew the news was going to be good but, like the rest, she wanted to know just how good.

"Okay, now for our total. Too bad we don't have a drum roll. That would be fitting for all of the hard...."

Someone from the back yelled, "Just get on with it!"

Mike took a deep breath, puffed out his chest like a proud brand new father showing off his beautiful son, "Three thousand, two hundred sixty-four dollars and fifty cents!"

A loud "Yahoo!" came from Susan right before the loud clapping and sheering started. When the cheering had died down, Mike again thanked everyone for their hard work. Susan moved to the front of the room. "I, too, want to thank you so much on behalf of your children. They will benefit very much from what you have done for them. Monday I will start looking for the best buys I can find to improve our library collection." Everyone cheered again.

As the group disbanded, most people went to the Brocks to thank them for their leadership. Missy was actually very cordial with those who stopped to talk to her. She really could turn on the charm when she chose.

Betty and Claire walked home with Elizabeth and Clarence. Clarence commented about the total amount. "That was indeed a job well done. It seems that Mike did a good job of spearheading that."

The three women looked at each other but said nothing. Claire wondered if they had been too critical of the Brocks. Perhaps their style of leadership, a style where you seem not very involved, really did work. They truly did delegate the work and depended on all the others following through with their parts. But then what else would she have expected from this community that had, from her first weekend here, demonstrated care and concern for others? With that kind of attitude, could this project have failed no matter who the chairman was? She guessed they would never know.

The spike-heel shoes lay in the middle of the floor where they had been kicked when the two of them first entered the room. Her feet were draped over the arm of the overstuffed chair that she hated and an empty martini glass was in her hand. He walked across the room, the shaker in his hand. She held out her glass so he could refill it. Then he sat on the couch across from her.

"You are quite the little actress. You even had me convinced that you enjoyed that stupid job."

"Yeah, but it was kind of fun, all those people fawning all over us. I had a hard time getting into that dorky role but I could tell those yokels were really into it. And that was a pretty sizable profit they managed to get."

"It wasn't bad but there is a lot more where that came from. Clarence told me that some of that profit was from anonymous contributions. I thought there might be money in this town and that hokey fund raiser just proved it. I, or rather we, just have to figure out where all of the deep pockets are. And we have to figure out the best way to empty those pockets. I just have to continue to be a trusted friend to those three money hungry fools. And you should do more with the wives of the deep pockets.

"Oh, no. That's where I draw the line. You can't expect me to socialize with these hicks!" she whined. "My acting skills can only go so far. If I spend too much time with them they might see right through me."

"Or you might really get to like them. Did you ever think of that?"

"Not in my worst nightmares. Do you see me as the apron-wearing, quilting, sewing, baking wife? No way. You want quilts, you join that quilting group. You want freshly baked pies, you trot yourself down to that bakery. You can't expect me to become something I'm not."

He walked across the room to where she was sitting. He reached out and touched her face, stroking her cheek gently. He moved his hand under her chin and lightly rubbed her throat and neck. Looking directly in her eyes, he bent close to her. "If you think enough about what we might get out of this, I bet you could pretend to like anybody. You might even want to go out with some of those rich farmers' wives and help them shuck the corn and slop the hogs."

She would have protested his suggestions but his lips closed over hers before she could say anything.

When the quilt group gathered, the big topic of conversation was the success of the fund raiser. They all congratulated each other on the parts they had played and prided themselves on the fact that the quilt raffle by itself had brought in quite a bit of money. Many people were surprised that the Brocks had done such a good job of chairing the event.

"Chair shmair," said Clara. "From what I heard all they did was watch everyone else do all of the work. And then they stand there looking all sweet and humble and take all the glory. And if I were you I would recount that money and make sure that it's all there. They are just two slick crooks, I tell you. Just look at their beady eyes."

Meredith looked embarrassed by her mother-in-laws comments. "You know that's not true. They did their job as the chairmen. They delegated responsibilities to others on the committee. That is why it all worked out so well."

"Bunk!" Clara replied disgustedly.

The group then started talking about the next project that they would be working on. Claire had no ideas since quilting was still a relatively new art for her. Many possible designs were suggested and discussed. No decision had been made when once more Lila made her late and theatrical entrance. A tastefully simple camel-colored wool fedora matched the blazer that she wore with a straight black skirt. "This," Claire thought, "is how she should dress more often. She looks like the wife of a mayor instead of a call girl."

"Good, good morning, ladies. What a fine, fine day it is. Have you been discussing our wonderful fund raiser? Didn't the Brocks and I do a great job on it?"

Clara opened her mouth to say something but Meredith quickly placed her hand in front of the older lady's mouth. Lila didn't even notice since she was too busy demonstratively waving her arms as she described all of the work she imagined that she had done. Claire sat pretty much dumbfounded as she listened to her carry on. The rest of the group sat politely looking at Lila but with a glazed look in their eyes, since they really were not paying any attention to what she was saying.

Twelve

Claire was in the middle of baking cookies when the doorbell rang. She popped a glob of chocolate chip dough in her mouth and headed for the door. She was quite surprised to find Reverend Carlson flanked by six Cub Scouts, each dressed in his blue and gold uniform. She would have thought this was some sort of fund raiser for the scouts were it not for the minister standing in the middle.

"Good afternoon, Reverend Carlson, boys," she said.

"Good afternoon," Bill responded. He reached out and poked two of them in their backs.

"Good afternoon," the two added and the other four echoed the greeting.

"What are you men up to on this nice fall afternoon?"

"We would like to talk to you for a few minutes, if this is a convenient time," Bill said.

"I think you all should come in and sit down." The entourage had just entered the living room when Claire heard the buzzer in the kitchen. "I do have some cookies calling me. Please sit down and I'll be right with you." She hurried into the kitchen to save the cookies from getting too brown and retrieved them just in time. Taking them off the cookie sheet, her curiosity grew about what Bill and the scouts wanted to talk to her about. Since she had no idea how long they might stay, she decided that it would be a good idea to turn off the oven. She pulled a plate from the cabinet, grabbed a handful of napkins, and carefully transferred the warm cookies onto the plate. Armed with goodies, Claire headed back to the living room.

"I know that Reverend Carlson likes chocolate chip cookies but I don't think that you boys would," Claire said, handing a napkin to Bill and extending the plate to him.

"I like them," most of the boys chimed in, so she passed the cookies to five of the boys who were gingerly squeezed onto the couch. The sixth scout must have moved the fastest since he had one of the armchairs all to himself. As Claire passed him a napkin and the cookie plate she asked, "What was it that all of you wanted to talk to me about? I am quite intrigued." The boys looked at each other with puzzled looks on their faces.

"Mrs. Menefee means she is curious about why we all came. Would one of you like to explain?"

There were a few moments of silence while each boy tried to decide if he was brave enough to tell. Finally, Johnny Hornsby spoke up. "We want you to be our den mother."

Claire straightened up in her chair, bracing herself from what she had just heard. Of all the possibilities that had run through her mind while in the kitchen, this had not been one of them. "But I thought Jeff's mom was the den mother," Claire said with a tone of disbelief in her voice.

Bill turned to Jeff. "Do you want to explain to Mrs. Menefee?"

Jeff turned his little freckled face toward Claire. "My mom went to the doctor today and he said that she needs to stay in bed until the baby comes. So she can't be our den mother anymore."

Bill continued the story. "I was going to meet with the boys today anyway for one of their award requirements. Jane called me in tears when she got back from the doctor. I went over and talked to her for quite awhile. She came up with the idea that you might be able to take over for her until after the baby comes. It would just be for a few months. She said she would be willing to help you any way she could. She has lots of ideas. She just needs someone to follow through with them."

"Yeah," piped in Jeff, "She even said we still could meet at our house if we needed to."

"Oh I'm sure that is just what someone on bed rest would need – a den of scouts invading her home," Claire thought.

"When the boys showed up for their meeting, Jane explained the problem and they all thought that you would be a great replacement."

Joey Simpson added his opinion, "You know most of us anyway from working in the school and we figured that you must like kids and we all like you." And then, as if he didn't think that he had made a strong enough argument, he added, "And you are a pretty lady, too."

"You think that buttering me up will help?" she thought. "Now that is a problem for you boys. Let me think it over for awhile." Claire meant when she said "awhile" as a couple of days. The boys, however, took it to mean a couple of minutes. They all stared at her with pleading eyes. Even Bill gave her a beseeching look. All of those little faces, and the one big one, were harder to say no to than looking in the faces of cuddly, pudgy puppies anxious to be adopted and then walking away. Claire let out a big sigh, telling herself that she was an easy mark, and told the forlorn group that she would do it. The boys on the couch jumped up and cheered, almost knocking each other over.

"Boys, boys," said Bill. "You need to sit down. Remember, you are a guest in Mrs. Menefee's house. You need to use good manners." They immediately quieted down and sat like little angels on the couch. Claire wondered if she could arrange for Bill to attend every meeting. She liked his crowd control.

When the cookies were devoured and the boys and their partner in crime had all disappeared, Claire went back into the kitchen to sit down. The thoughts of what she had just committed herself to were sinking in. "Lesson plans again!" was what she first thought of and it was not a pleasant thought. She knew that Jane would be willing to help but Claire was the one who would plan the meeting agenda and purchase and organize the necessary supplies. For a brief moment she wished that the baby would come early but quickly pushed that unfair, selfish thought out of her head.

Claire thought she should call Jane but she really didn't want to. It was as if she was living in that mental state where the less you know the better off you are. Right now she would tend to her cookie project and eat lots of cookie dough. Maybe she could eat so much that it would make her sick like her mother always threatened that it would. Then the word would spread that she had been taken to the hospital and the town would feel bad and they would not make her be the den mother after all. Claire wondered how much dough that would actually take. She figured she probably didn't have that much anyway. Just then the phone rang.

Claire had barely gotten out a hello when a voice said, "You are a life saver and I owe you big time!"

Claire wanted to reply, "You are darn right and I will hold this against you for years," but instead she managed to smile into the phone and said, "I think it will be fun. It will be a challenge for me but it'll be fun." She wondered if she was trying to convince Jane or herself.

"Did Bill mention that you can still have your meetings here? That way I can still be of some help."

"I doubt that the doctor prescribed bed rest with six eight-year-olds running through your house once a week. No, we can meet here. It will be fine. This kitchen needs some young life in it, anyway. But I will need your advice on projects. The busier I can keep them, the better off we'll all be."

"You've got that right. You know what they say about idle hands. How is your schedule tomorrow? Maybe we could get together and make some plans then."

"I go to quilting group in the morning but the afternoon would work for me.

Now what can I do for you and your family? How about if I bring something for your dinner when I come tomorrow?"

"Oh that is a nice offer, but you certainly don't have to do that."

"I won't take no for an answer. It will have to be something simple since you know that cooking is not my forte. Oh, and by the way, am I correct in assuming that since this is Monday that all of the den meetings are on Mondays?"

"We've had some on Thursdays but the regular day is Monday. But that is your day at school isn't it?" Jane replied almost apologetically. "They wouldn't have to meet on Monday if there is a day that works better for you. The monthly pack meeting is the fourth Monday, so we don't have a den meeting that day."

"Mondays will be fine. My buzzer is going off. I need to go. I'll see you tomorrow. And Jane, remember doctor's orders. You take good care of yourself." Claire went to get the cookies out of the oven and unloaded them onto a cooling rack. "Well, I might as well make Mondays my little people days. That way I have the rest of the week and the weekend to recover," she said to the empty kitchen, which on the upcoming Monday afternoons would no longer be empty. Claire loaded one more cookie sheet, stuck it in the oven, finished off the remaining dough and wondered how easily six active little boys could make chocolate chip cookies.

Proving once again that word travels faster than a prairie fire on a windy autumn day, the news of Claire's agreeing to take over the Cub Scout den had reached many members of the quilting group. When Claire arrived she was greeted with a mixture of gratitude and pity.

"That was so nice of you to help Jane," said Grace. "Bill told me you didn't give it a second thought." Obviously Bill's idea of a second thought and Claire's were quite different but she felt this was not the time or place to argue the point.

"I would be more than happy to help with the refreshments at some of the meetings," offered Phoebe Peoples. Judging from her size Claire imagined that Phoebe did a lot of cooking and was tempted to take her up on the offer.

"That's very nice of you, Phoebe, but from what Jane tells me, the boys take turns bringing snacks. But if I get in a bind, I might ask you for some help."

Betty offered herself as a basic first aid instructor but after discussing it they decided that might be too much for active eight-year-old boys. Claire thought it might be more prudent to offer a first aid class to her and to the Cubs' parents.

"Farley could teach them how to tie knots. He did that for the Boy Scout troop a couple of times," Francine suggested.

"That old fool around those little boys? He'd probably bring his gun and end up shooting one of them," said Clara in her usual cynical tone.

"Mother, you know he wouldn't do that. I think Farley might enjoy teaching something he knows to the boys."

"That is a nice offer, Francine, but I don't think I am quite ready for them to be learning to tie knots. I can see them practicing them in all sorts of inappropriate ways. I know the Cub Scout leaders have a lot of resources available, and Jane has quite a few ideas that she was planning on using and she is more than willing to let me use those. Plus, I might be able to think of some myself. It might actually be lots of fun. And if I get in a real bind, I figured that we could just teach them all how to quilt." That comment was met with a resounding "NO!" followed by some laughter as the ladies talked among themselves about what an interesting experience that might be.

As they walked into Clarence's office, Mike said, "Clarence, as you may have guessed, I've made a decision. I have an idea that you, Chester and William might like. I've brought a few things to show you. Why don't we sit over here at your conference table so I can walk you through everything?"

Mike placed a worn but intricately tooled leather portfolio on the table. Noticing Clarence's raised eyebrows, Mike said, "Nice, isn't it? Or at least it was when it was new. That was a gift from my dad when I bought my seat on the Board of Trade. He said I should have something more impressive to go with my new position, instead of the old plastic thing I used to carry around. I thought this might be a good time to bring it out of retirement, too."

"I guess that means you've made a decision that we're all going to like – and profit from," said Clarence.

"After talking it over with Missy, and giving it a lot of thought…yes, I'm going to set up a private commodities fund with you three gentlemen."

"Great!" exclaimed Clarence. "Whom do we make the checks out to?"

"Whoa, whoa, let's not get ahead of ourselves. I promised to give you some background on myself, and show you what I've done for the last few years. First, let me give you a copy of my Registered Investment Adviser registration. If it looks like a government form, that's because it's a copy of what's on file with the SEC. They say I can put all the information from this Part Two into a brochure, but the people I've dealt with have never been very impressed with slick brochures. Anyway, all the information the SEC requires is in there."

Clarence glanced quickly through the pages, pausing only at the portion dealing with any prior criminal history or civil suits. Noticing that there were none, he scanned the remaining pages rapidly without really understanding what he was reading. "That looks good, Mike. I'll spend some more time later going over it in detail. What else do you have to show me?"

Mike pulled a thick stack of documents from his portfolio. "These are my personal investment statements for the last three years. I'll let you make your own judgment about what they mean, but let me point out what I said about this being risky. For two two-month periods last year, and one four-month period the year before, I lost money – big-time – but I've always been in this for the long haul, so I didn't let it worry me. I thought you should know, though. Why don't you start going through these and I'll get us another cup of coffee. I think I know where it is by now."

When Mike returned, Clarence had reviewed only the first year of statements. He looked up and said, "This is amazing. You started the year with a little over $300,000, and ended at over $700,000…and you had two months of losses! All I can say is, you must really know what you're doing." He returned to reviewing the statements.

Mike sat quietly and watched him, the excitement building inside but absolutely calm to all outward appearances. "I hope you don't mind if I catch up on my reading while you're looking through that information. I picked up your copy of the Wall Street Journal in the lobby."

A half hour later, Clarence looked up at Mike. "You really do have this commodities thing figured out. I see you're only working in agricultural commodities."

"I decided early in my career that it made sense to know everything about a relatively small field – pardon the pun – rather than try to know a little bit about everything. I can follow those markets pretty closely, especially here in the Midwest, and that strategy seems to have worked."

"I'll say it has," said Clarence. "Mike, I think you've been holding out on me."

"Wh-what do you mean," Mike stammered, starting to get a little uncomfortable.

"Well, according to this last statement, you have over 1.6 million in this trading account, and you only deposited $650,000 in my bank!"

"Oh," said Mike, trying not to show how relieved he was. "That's because I like to keep my money working for me. As you can see, most of that is tied up in commodities contracts."

"I understand. I was just pulling your leg. I knew it was possible to make a lot of money in commodities, but a 150% return every year is really incredible. I was hoping we could get 10% in a good year."

"As I said, there aren't any guarantees, but I'm confident we can average more than 10% every year."

"What's the next step?" asked Clarence.

Extracting a few more pages from his portfolio, Mike said, "Here's a fairly detailed outline of how this would work. In a nutshell, the investors give me the money to invest, I set up a special account to do the trading, and every month I'll provide statements and a check for any of the profits. Of course, if we lose money that month there won't be any checks. On the other hand, we could leave the money in the account and let it keep building each investor's value. Each investor can decide how he wants that part handled. All this will be part of the agreements we'll sign to make it legal."

"Who makes the investment decisions?" asked Clarence. "Do the investors have any say-so?"

"Let me be blunt," said Mike. "You guys – I mean gentlemen - are hiring me to make you money. This isn't something that can be done by committee – especially a committee that doesn't know anything about commodities trading. Part of the deal is that you let me make all the decisions. You can judge me on the results."

"I really like what I see here, Mike, and I trust you to do what's right to make this work. Frankly, I'm relieved we won't have to get into a lot of stuff we don't understand. Do you think you could spare some time the next couple of days to meet with Chester and William?"

"Sure, just name the time and place. Bud is pretty flexible with my schedule, so I'm pretty sure we can work around that. Oh, I almost forgot. I'll give you these extra copies of all the documents for our little partnership so everyone can look at them before we meet. I thought we could call our fund WC2 for William, Clarence and Chester. It can be sort of a code word when we're around other people."

Jane suggested that Claire use her plans to have the boys make totem poles out of toilet paper tubes. Jane had collected enough tubes for each boy and Claire had picked up the big sack full of them and decided to store them in the garage until Monday's meeting. As she set down the bag, she looked around the big double garage that had served as a carriage house and as a workshop for Edgar Blowers, the man who had built Claire's house as well as many of the others in the center of town. Edward and Shirley Hoffman, who had owned the property after the Blowers family, had wired electricity into the garage. Claire spotted the space heater she had deposited in the garage when she first moved in.

"I think this would work. Yes, I think this would work just fine," she said, turning and looking at all of the space. To make it even better, the Hoffmans had built a low workbench for their children when they were young. And they had been kind enough to leave Claire a very old, beat up table that they didn't want to bother to move. Claire had agreed that they could leave it there, thinking that extra surface area might come in handy some day. "Well, that day is here," she thought. She could envision the boys busily gathered around the work bench and the table totally engaged in their projects. Or at least she hoped that was what she would be seeing.

Claire moved the bag of tubes to the workbench and started collapsing the packing boxes she had tossed there when she was getting settled. She was embarrassed to think that she had not done anything with them since then. But now was not the time to wallow in guilt. It was time to get busy. When the boxes had all been flattened, Claire grabbed a broom and swept a few odds and ends off the floor. "Yes, this will work just fine." Feeling quite proud of herself, she shut the door and walked to the house.

The boys were excited when Claire explained the totem pole project to them. Their enthusiasm decreased considerably when she told them that they were going to have to do some research on the animals that would be depicted on the poles.

"Gee, that sounds way too much like school," complained Joey Simpson.

"Do we have to read and write both?" whined Johnny Hornsby.

"I don't think that is what my mother had in mind," added Jeff Dunn in a scolding tone.

"We will divide up the work. It will be fun. Things are always more fun when you work together." Claire didn't think her pep talk convinced them very much since the moans continued after her comment. The boys listed the animals they thought would be fun to put on a totem pole and they narrowed the list to six. Then each one picked an animal to study. Claire grabbed a notebook and stuffed some pencils in her purse and off they went to the Hayward library for their research adventure. She was pretty sure of the response they would get from Bertha Banter when they all walked through her front door. In fact, Claire was kind of looking forward to seeing the annoyed look on Bertha's face.

When they reached the front door, the boys were not overly enthused about entering. Claire really couldn't blame them. She felt it was a pity that the library held so many resources but the children never felt welcome to use them. She reminded the boys that they needed to use proper library behavior, including talking in very quiet voices. Since no one opened the door, she took advantage of the situation and they had a brief lesson on being polite and opening a door for a lady, for an older person or just for others. Jeff quickly volunteered. Claire thought he figured if he held the door for all of his friends as well as for her then he would be the last one in the library and could hide in the back of the group.

Miss Banter's head snapped to attention as the little group entered her sacred territory. She glared at them as Claire led the boys to the desk. "Good afternoon, Miss Banter," she said nodding to Bertha. Claire turned to the boys and quickly they got the hint. "Good afternoon, Miss Banter," they said in a group whisper.

"The boys are here to do a little research on some different animals. Could you please direct them to where they would find that information?" Claire was perfectly aware of where in the library they would need to go but she was determined that Bertha should be the one to guide them there. After all, it was her job to help the library customers, not Claire's.

Bertha raised her shoulders and gave a big huff. She pushed herself up out of her chair, straightened herself up and threw her shoulders back, trying to look as authoritative and intimidating as possible. She emerged from the sanctity of her desk and proceeded to march herself to the children's non-fiction section. Pointing at the shelves she said, "This is where you need to look. You need to stay in this area and not be roaming all over the library." She gave them all a scrutinizing stare. "Hands, let's see your hands. We can't have my books getting all smudged."

Trying to remain calm, Claire jumped in with, "I can vouch for the cleanliness of their hands. We all washed at my house before coming over here." At that moment she was thankful that the snacks that Bobby had brought that day had required thorough hand washing. "I can assure you that the city's books are in safe hands with these young men."

With another big huff Bertha turned and stomped off. Claire watched as she headed back toward the desk. She found it interesting that even though Bertha's body gave the impression of angry stomping, her feet hardly made a sound. Claire wondered if this was a technique she had developed over the years to keep her precious library quiet. The boys were actually quite self-sufficient in finding some books to use for their research. Each needed to find and write down five facts about his assigned animal. These would later be shared with the group. They actually seemed to be enjoying the project.

When each of the boys had made note of at least five facts, with most finding more than that, it was time to leave. The boys huddled together for a moment. Claire wondered what they were up to. Jeff Dunn picked up the book he had been using and approached the big checkout desk.

"Excuse me please, Miss Banter, but where would you like me to put the book I used?"

She looked up with her stern face and replied, "At the end of the shelf there is a cart for reshelving. Gently put it there."

Jeff politely thanked her and walked to the shelf as directed. Immediately Johnny headed for the desk and boldly stood in front of it. "Excuse me please, Miss Banter, but where would you like me to put the books I used?"

Bertha gave him her patented stare and replied, "At the end of the shelf there is a cart for reshelving. Gently put them there."

A few moments after Joey had placed his books, Jerry Smith headed to the desk, book in hand, and asked the same question. The rest of the boys were peeking through open spaces on the shelves, trying to keep from giggling, as once again, Miss Banter gave the same directions. This was followed by Joey Simpson and Bobby Secore with the same routine. Each time Miss Banter's patience decreased and her voice started to rise.

Gary Branford, the littlest of the group, went after Bobby. As he turned to the desk with the book in his hand, he never had the chance to ask his question. Instead Miss Banter rose from her chair, bent toward him over the desk and said in a voice quite close to a yell, "Put it in the cart and the end of that shelf. And tell all the rest of them the same thing!"

"Thank you, ma'am, but I won't have to. There aren't any more." As Gary walked back toward the rest of the group he had a huge grin on his face. After he had turned the corner and was behind the shelves, the boys all patted him on the back as they tried to stifle their giggling. Claire was glad that she hadn't known what they were up to sooner, or she might have told them not to go through with their plan. She got as much pleasure from it as they did, but she didn't want to let on to them how she felt.

"Now, boys, that wasn't necessary." Claire felt that had covered that topic sufficiently. "I will take your papers and save them for next week unless one of you would like to write more or practice what you want to say."

Bobby piped up with, "Let's do this in an orderly fashion. You first, Joey. Hand your paper to Mrs. Menefee." As he handed Claire his research, he dropped his pencil on the floor. Five of them scrambled to pick it up. She watched the pile of blue shirts on the floor thinking that this was much more how she expected these eight-year-olds to behave. Once the pencil was recovered, Bobby continued, "You next, Gary." As Gary started to hand it to Claire, Jeff blew as hard as he could and blew the paper under one of the tables. Four boys rushed to be the one to retrieve it.

Bobby, definitely taking over the leadership of the little band, called out the next name, "Jerry."

"Oh, I think I left it in my book. I'll look."

"I'll help!" piped up three of the boys.

It wasn't until Johnny handed her Jerry's paper that Claire realized that there were only three little blue men in front of her. She looked toward the desk and saw Jerry standing in front of Miss Banter, saluting her. "Good day, Miss Banter." Bertha looked at him in her harsh way and nodded with the least amount of movement that she could. Jerry turned around and marched to the front door where his little comrades stood waiting. Now Claire knew that the little darlings had plotted plan B and it was halfway carried out.

"Okay, boys. I'm on to you. Just hand me the papers, no more dramatics." They did as they were told but as Claire was organizing the papers and checking to make sure they were not forgetting anything, the other three marched themselves up to the desk. But before they could offer their snappy salutes, Bertha glared at them.

"Good bye. Go home," she said stretching out the "go home" part.

The last three went to the door as Claire went to talk to Bertha. "The boys did a very nice job today. I think I should plan some more projects where they can use the library. I think children should make more use of this fine facility, don't you, Miss Banter?" Claire gave her one of her nicest smiles.

"Oh, yes, that is just what I would like, more children in my library," she said with a disgusted look on her face."

"You have a nice evening now. We will see you another day." Claire smiled and turned to the waiting group. Then, in a very unlibrary-like voice, she said,

"Let's go home, guys." There was no hesitation about someone reaching for the door now. Jerry, who was the first to get there, actually did remember to hold it open for all of them. When they reached the first step, laughter broke out as they hit and punched each other. It was not an unexpected reaction of six young boys cooped up in a quiet, controlled setting for too long.

"Unless someone needs to come back to my house, you boys can just head home from here. I'll see you next week." They probably didn't even hear the last part as they ran down the steps and across the street to the park, where they continued to joke, push, and punch, and then broke off in the direction of their homes.

Mike breathed a sigh of relief as he left the bank building. He had thought about it all weekend but the meeting with the three would-be commodities tycoons had been easier and had not taken as long as he imagined it would. They didn't ask many questions, and seemed anxious to write their checks, sign the documents, and get their money working for them. The only uncomfortable moment had come when Mike said that they'd need a total of $50,000 to get started, and they balked at putting in any more than $10,000 apiece. He had let them stew over that a moment, then said he'd put up $20,000 himself. That seemed to bring everyone's confidence level up – just as he'd planned it. As he left the bank's board room, he told everyone that he and Missy would be going to Chicago for the week of Thanksgiving and he would get their new account set up. Once that was done he could start trading. He also explained to Clarence that the CW2 money would be kept in the brokerage account, not in the Hayward bank, and that checks for the trading account would be written on a Northern Bank and Trust account.

Claire was out in front raking leaves when Ben Miller moseyed down the street to visit. "I hear that you and your Scouts made a trip to the library."

"Yes, we did. How did you hear about it?"

"I got an emergency call from Bertha. She asked me to run to the drug store and get some aspirin for her headache, or as she described it, her 'horrible, sickening, throbbing headache.' She called right after all of you left and said she couldn't leave the library herself. She made it sound like she was going to die before closing time if she didn't have some relief right then."

"That was very valiant of you, Ben."

"I just couldn't tell her no. She sounded so desperate. I really did feel sorry for her. You all must have really been loud or unruly or something."

"We were not!" Claire kind of snapped at Ben. "I'm sorry. I didn't mean to sound like that but those little boys were the perfect gentlemen. They talked quietly, they did the research they were supposed to do and they replaced the materials exactly as Bertha asked them. They each even gave her their scout salute when they left. It was really quite cute. I was the only one who had anything close to a loud voice, anyone except Bertha."

"I suspected that she was probably exaggerating. She does tend to get overly dramatic."

"I don't mean to be snoopy, but do you see or talk to her often?"

"I wouldn't say often, but more like once in awhile. We have been to dinner a couple of times and, of course, we were at the fund raiser. Oh, and we did go to see a movie. It's just kind of nice to have company closer to my own age," Ben said, almost apologetically.

"I think it is good for both of you. But you're such a kindhearted, gentle man. You just seem like an odd couple. My hope would be that some of your easy-going personality would wear off on her."

Ben smiled. "Well, I'll see what I can do about that. Let me help you with that." Ben followed Claire around with the bushel basket and dumped leaves in the incinerator each time the basket got filled. As with most things, the job went much faster and was much more fun with two sets of hands.

Everything was already organized in the garage when the scouts started arriving Monday afternoon. They had their snack in the kitchen, and then the boys followed Claire out to the garage. They had no idea that this was going to be their meeting place.

"Wow!"

"Cool!"

"This is great!"

Claire thought it was a relief to them to think that they could be less formal in this atmosphere. After they looked around the inside of the old building, she told them what its original purpose was. She thought most of them already knew that these buildings along the alley had been built as carriage houses, but she didn't think any of them knew that the original owner of her house also had built many of the other Hayward houses, and that he did some of his carpentry work in this old structure.

After they had heard the history, Claire handed out the papers they had written about the animals. She gave them a few minutes to look them over and then each one gave his little report. The boys listened to each other politely. They even commented about some of the interesting information they had heard. Then they were ready to get on to the construction phase.

First they taped the tubes together. Then they covered the elongated tube with paper. So far, so good. Then came the part Claire was dreading, painting the individual sections with different colors. Thankfully, she had asked each boy to bring some type of covering since she didn't think their blue shirts would look too good if they ended up looking like a painter's palette. She stood back and just watched, waiting for trouble, but things went quite well. When most of them had finished their painting Claire realized that she had not brought out any rags and water for washing hands.

She made a fast dash inside, ran to the basement to grab rags and a bucket, made a short stop in the kitchen to get water, and headed back to the garage. Then she heard the raucous laughter and walked faster, apprehensive about what she would find when she walked through the door. The laughter stopped when her shadow hit the doorway. It appeared that her garage had been invaded by a bunch of Indians complete with war paint. The boys looked as if their hands had just been caught in their mothers' brand new box of chocolates. They knew it was wrong but the temptation had been too great.

"Okay, all you Indian braves." As Claire threw each one a towel, she said, "Time to go down to the creek and get washed. You need to be getting ready to go home to your teepees."

The boys laughed as they washed their own faces and hands and even helped each other remove all remnants of the war paint they had been wearing. As they headed home, each one thanked Claire for the fun afternoon.

The topic of the sermon was thankfulness and Bill touched on many areas on which he wanted the congregation to reflect. He specifically mentioned how thankful he was to live in Hayward. He cited many instances during the past year of the kindnesses shown to others within the community and in the surrounding areas. Claire imagined that many in the congregation had heard of some of these but to her most were news. With some of the examples Reverend Carlson attached names, while with others he let the people be anonymous. There were tears in many eyes as he related some of the stories.

The hymn Bill chose to follow his sermon was, he said, one of his favorites. It was also one of Claire's favorites and judging from the enthusiasm with which those sitting around her started singing, it was the favorite of many. Phoebe belted it out for all of her might on the organ. But over the organ came a very loud voice that was anything but pleasant to hear. The volume of the voice did not make up for the lack of quality and Claire saw the faces of others cringing as the cacophony continued. She finally determined that the disharmony was coming from Bill who was singing with much gusto the stanzas of *Come, Ye Thankful People, Come*. She momentarily thought about changing her mind about this hymn being a favorite. Then the "amen" was sung and relief reached everyone's ears. Bill delivered the closing prayer, wished everyone a wonderful Thanksgiving, and recessed down the aisle.

Betty, who was sitting next to Claire, turned and said in a quiet voice, "Bill forgot to turn his microphone off again. Grace will be scolding him about that this afternoon. He does love to sing but, unfortunately, few people like to listen to him."

Claire just smiled. She didn't know what to say so she thought that making no comment would be best. As they waited their turn to greet Bill, Claire scanned the crowd looking for Lila. Going to church was always enjoyable but checking out her headwear on Sundays added to Claire's enjoyment. When she thought she saw a pheasant floating above the crowd she was sure she had found her target. As she got closer Claire could see that it was not, of course, an entire pheasant. The crown of the hat was a dark grayish brown. At the front of the crown and extending to the sides was an arrangement of feathers that would have come from the breast and the wings of the pheasant. Along both sides and protruding out the back were the long brown and black striped tail feathers. It was quite a hat for this time of year, since Claire assumed it was probably hunting season. She guessed it was not a very good Thanksgiving for that pheasant.

The Cubs attached pieces of colored paper to their totem poles to make the features for their animals. While they worked, Claire read them a story about the Tlingit Indians of southeastern Alaska. The story, although fiction, told about some of the culture of the tribe. It also explained that the totems told silent stories. She really emphasized the silent part but it wasn't really necessary as the boys were very respectful as they finished their work and then explained about the animals on their poles.

Since they still had a little time Claire felt that she should fill it with what seemed to be the obligatory question this time of year. She asked each boy to tell what he was thankful for. She got the traditional responses – home, family, food, health, etc. – but she also got a few surprises. Gary said he was thankful that the paint he had managed to get on his pants last week had washed out okay. Joey said that he was thankful his family was not going to have to have duck for Thanksgiving again like they did last year.

"I'm thankful that my grandpa got his new false teeth because his old ones kept falling out," said Jerry. The boys all laughed at this and Claire had a feeling that was the reaction he wanted.

"I'm thankful that I didn't break any teeth when I hit my mouth on the handlebars when I crashed on Friday," said Bobby. The boys all commented with awe about what a great wipe-out that had been.

Jeff waited until everyone else was through. Looking bashfully at the ground he said, "I am thankful that you could take over for my mom so she could stay home and be safe and have a healthy baby." The boys nodded and mumbled in agreement.

"I am thankful that it worked out well," Claire paused, and then added, "for all of us. I hope you all have a wonderful Thanksgiving with your families."

The boys grabbed their totem poles and left, sprinting down the alley and giving the impression of a large blue six-headed creature on the run. Claire sighed and smiled. "And I am thankful that I have made it through three meetings."

Thanksgiving had been her favorite holiday since she left that egocentric childlike stage of listing all of the possible things she wanted for Christmas and reached a more adult outlook on the holiday. Thanksgiving also had a special meaning for Claire since some of her ancestors had come on the Mayflower and were mentioned in historical journals of life in Plymouth. And she was thankful that her great, great, great, however many greats grandfather had been one of the lucky children to have survived that first deadly year when half of the Plymouth colony died. Otherwise, she had often thought, "I would not be me today."

Claire had learned about two weeks before Thanksgiving that the culture of Hayward provides that no one should be alone on Thanksgiving, or Christmas or Easter either, unless she or he chose to do so. Betty Nutting was the first to extend Claire an invitation for Thanksgiving dinner and, or course, she was very happy to accept. But the invitations did not stop there. Jane Dunn's parents were coming for the long holiday weekend and Jane insisted that Claire join them. She thanked Jane, explaining that she had already accepted an offer. Bill and Grace Carlson also offered invitations but as it turned out they also were asked to the Nuttings and ended up there, too.

Susan Davis said that she was so thankful that Claire had come into her life and the life of the school library that she thought it only fitting that Claire spend the day with her husband's family on the farm. Claire had always had the secret desire to gather with a big family in an old farmhouse for a Thanksgiving celebration and was rather sad to have to say "no thank you" to this invitation. She hoped that there might be another chance in the future.

Elizabeth practically begged Claire to join Clarence and her at the Hayward family gathering to be held at brother Charles's house. Elizabeth knew that Lila was going to be her usual annoying self with her snide comments about Dorothy, whom she always looked down on. Elizabeth also was uneasy about what dishes Dorothy might be preparing. Elizabeth feared that while everyone else in town was having a nice traditional Thanksgiving dinner, her family might be eating some "gourmet" meal that Dorothy had concocted.

"One year when Dorothy was trying to prepare a more authentic meal, there actually was a turkey, but she had cooked the dressing and gravy with curry. In addition to that she had prepared clams and mussels, specially ordered for the occasion since she had read that these might have been at the 1621 feast. There was some rice dish with so many little extras thrown in that no one was sure what we were eating. The dessert was a sweet potato pie that neither Clarence nor I could eat. I made scrambled eggs and toast when we got home that evening because we were both so hungry. The next day we drove into Des Moines and found a restaurant that had some of their Thanksgiving dinners left."

This was an invitation Claire was glad she could not accept and wished instead that she could bring Elizabeth and Clarence with her to the Nuttings. She told Elizabeth that she was sorry that she couldn't come for moral support, and added that she would be anxious to hear all about it. Claire jokingly told Elizabeth that she would try to sneak some leftovers out for Clarence and her.

Even though she did not have to do the main part of the cooking, Claire had volunteered to bring whatever Betty wanted her to. She kept her fingers crossed when she asked, knowing that her cooking skills were still not, and probably never would be, comparable to those of these Iowa women. Betty made some suggestions and Claire quickly volunteered when she listed pumpkin pie. Pies were one thing Claire was comfortable making and pumpkin was a pretty easy one. She also said she would bring a gelatin salad. She knew she might be getting in over her head since she had the impression from what she had seen over the past few months that gelatin salads must have originated in Iowa. She had never seen such a variety. But she had one strawberry recipe that she had never seen turn up at any of the events she had attended. Claire was glad that she didn't have to deal with a turkey, and she wondered if Bryan Graves could stock enough turkeys for the entire town. But she had to make her own shopping list and not worry about anyone else's.

Since the Tuesday quilting group was canceled to allow the ladies time for their holiday cooking, Claire decided to go to school then instead of Monday. The day had a definite crisp feel to it and she enjoyed walking those few blocks whenever she could. Business in the library was light. Just a couple of classes came in so she spent time reshelving books. She was reaching to return a biography when out of the corner of her eye she saw something brown rush down the hall. She even thought for a moment that she heard a faint gobbling sound. Claire decided that her upcoming feast must have been on her subconscious. But then she saw Clifford Wilkens run past the door, followed closely by Theresa Stevens. Right behind them came Miss Hatcher who was yelling, "Catch it! Don't let it get away!" This time when Claire heard the gobbling sound she was pretty sure it was not her imagination. And when, a few moments later a turkey ran in through the open library doors, she knew it was not. In fact she was not sure who was more scared, the turkey or her.

Claire didn't know of any recorded incidents of turkey attacks, but having spent most of her life in cities or non-agricultural communities, she really didn't know what to expect from this frantic bird. It seemed like minutes but it was probably only seconds before the turkey posse swept into the library. A new member, a very small member, had been added to the group. The boy, whom she recognized as being in the kindergarten class, started to take charge of the situation. He shut the library doors so the feathered beast could not escape. Then he told the rest of them to stand still and be quiet. Slowly he approached the turkey, talking quietly and calling it by name.

"It's okay, Tallulah, no one is going to hurt you. You're safe now."

When he was close enough to Tallulah, he reached out his hand and touched her feathers. Then slowly he slid a lead over her head. By now Tallulah was calm enough that the boy could pet her and her gobbling was very different, more like a cooing, contented sound.

"It's okay now," he said. "I'll take her back to my room."

By now a few heads were peeking in through the doors that had been cracked open. Loretta Goering, the kindergarten teacher, entered the room. "Timmy, I think Tallulah has had enough school for one day. I think we should call your mother and have her take Tallulah home." Timmy looked disappointed but nodded his head in agreement.

Theresa took Timmy by the hand and they escorted Tallulah to the office.

"I am so sorry," said Mrs. Goering. "Since the children were to bring something for show and tell that had something to do with Thanksgiving, Timmy had brought his pet turkey. Everything was going well. Tallulah was behaving herself, not causing one bit of trouble. Then Wilma had one of her sneezing fits. The sound of those continuous sneezes echoing through the halls frightened poor Tallulah. She took off running and gobbling before Timmy could get a hold on her. I didn't know that turkeys could run that fast. I am so sorry."

"No harm done from my point of view," said Clifford. "I'll retrace her steps and do any necessary cleaning. That was the most excitement we've had around here since the ants." He turned and left with a happy step to his walk, whistling as he went.

As she walked home from school Claire tried to form a mental shopping list. When she was younger she could do that more easily. She had tried different techniques such as the one where she was supposed to envision the different items that she wanted in connection with different parts of her body starting with her head and going downward – loaf of bread on her head, sour cream on her nose, eggs in her ears, and so forth. But now she found it much more useful to write down what she needed. Otherwise, she would inevitably be making numerous trips across the square to the grocery store.

Claire had mentally run through the recipes in her mind as she walked and had a pretty good idea of what she needed. As soon as she got home, she sat at the kitchen table and wrote down what she could remember. Then she got out her recipes and compared them to her list. She really did quite well and was proud of her old memory. She did a quick inventory of the cupboards and added a few more things to the list. Then she grabbed some sandwich makings and had a quick lunch.

As Claire walked across the square she noticed that Farley was not sitting in his usual spot in front of Simpson's hardware store. Instead he was pacing back and forth, his rifle held across his arm. When she crossed the street in front of the store she yelled to him, "Hello, Farley, how are you doing today?"

He looked anxious and kept looking around while he answered, "Got to keep watch. Things might be happening."

Claire had no idea what he was talking about but she assumed that whatever might be happening was probably going to happen only in his mind. "Well, you just keep your eyes open." As she walked toward the grocery store she thought how hard it must be on the Simpson family to have Farley living so much of his life in this tenuous, fictitious existence. The whole family must have a great deal of patience.

"Good afternoon, Claire, how are you this fine fall day?" asked Bryan from behind the counter as she walked through the door. "I'll bet you're here to do some Thanksgiving shopping. Most people are doing that about now, don't you know. Is there anything special I can help you find?"

"No thanks, Bryan. My list is pretty ordinary. I just hope you have canned pumpkin. I'm not big on cooking and pureeing my own."

Bryan directed her to the pumpkin and then left her to continue finding the necessities on her list. She was almost finished when there was a terrible commotion outside with a lot of yelling. Bryan and Claire looked at each other, and without saying a word, both headed to the door to see what was happening. There on the sidewalk was an angry Clara, her arm held tightly in Meredith's grip. In front of the bakery was an enraged Farley who was being restrained by his son, Bob. There were many dark spots on the front of Farley's shirt and water was dripping from his face.

"Calm down, Mother," pleaded Meredith. "And give me that gun." Reluctantly Clara reached into her purse and handed over her squirt gun.

"That old fool. He deserved it. He had no right to point that old gun in my face. What did you do that for anyway, you old coot?"

"Just what did you say to him, Clara?" asked Bob, who was still struggling with Farley as he squirmed to get free.

"Oh I just asked him if he was figuring to shoot any turkeys as they flew down the street and the next thing I knew he pointed that gun in my face and told me to put up my hands. Nobody's going to get the drop on me so I reached in my purse and drilled him with my piece. The old fool!"

"Hold on a minute." Bob turned to his dad and Farley, after looking suspiciously over his shoulder at Clara, whispered something in Bob's ear. Bob listened and nodded. After about a minute he turned back to Clara and Meredith. "He said that lately he heard lots of people talking about turkeys. He looked up 'turkey' in his code book and found that it meant 'spy.' He said that the code book said anyone talking about flying turkeys was the head of the spy ring. I am so sorry, Clara. I hope he didn't scare you."

"He didn't scare me at all. I wanted to show him that he couldn't push me around."

"Well, I am very sorry, Clara. Dad, you need to apologize. She is no more a spy than Francine and I are."

Bob tried to shove his father toward the ladies without much luck. He did, however, manage to get his father to mumble a quiet and insincere, "Sorry."

Meredith, trying to soothe things over as best she could, looked sympatheti- cally to Bob and then turned to Farley. "Well I personally appreciate how you are always concerned about the safety of our town. I think that is very patriotic of you."

Clara rolled her eyes and muttered, "Hummph!"

"We should be getting on with our grocery shopping, Mother. We'll see you later, gentlemen." Meredith grabbed her mother's arm and headed her toward the door that Bryan was still holding open.

"Well that was sure something, don't you know," commented Bryan. Claire went back into the store and Bryan held the door for his two new customers. Claire finished getting the last things on her list, and a few chocolaty things that weren't on the list, and headed toward the checkout counter. On the way she passed Clara and Meredith and tried to act as if nothing out of the ordinary had happened.

"Hello, Clara, Meredith. Are you shopping for your Thanksgiving weekend?"

"We sure are," answered Meredith and before she could continue, Clara interrupted.

"If you are buying a turkey, don't tell that crazy old coot down the block. He's liable to blast you one."

"Luckily I don't have turkey anywhere on my list," Claire said, holding it up as if to prove to Clara that she was telling the truth.

"Does that mean that you are joining someone for dinner on Thursday? If not, you are more than welcome to come to our house. Our sons and their families are coming. It will be a full house but it will be fun."

"Thank you. I appreciate your offer but I am going to the Nuttings. I think they are going to have a houseful, too. I'm done with my shopping, so I'd better check out. I hope you and your family have a wonderful holiday together."

"Thanks, and you, too."

Claire went to the cash register and Bryan totaled her purchases. "Will you be with family for Thanksgiving, Bryan?"

"Oh, yes. Cooking for every relative she can round up for Thanksgiving is one of the highlights of the year for Vernina, don't you know. It is surpassed only by preparations for Christmas. I wasn't meaning to snoop but I heard you say that you are going to the Nuttings. That should be a lovely time. Betty and Vernina often share ideas and recipes for these holidays. So I imagine that Betty is well underway with her preparations, also. I think I might need to pull out the pants that I used to wear before I lost fifteen pounds. I figure I will eat at least that much on Thursday."

"And I'd better be lengthening my walks. I can feel my skirt getting tight just thinking about it."

Bryan handed Claire her two sacks of groceries. "Can you handle these all right?"

"I'll be just fine. I hope you all have a wonderful Thanksgiving. Maybe you will see me waddling home from the Nuttings."

Bryan laughed as he held the door for Claire and went back to wait on Meredith and Clara.

Claire woke up early Thursday morning in order to get in a long walk before going to the Nuttings. She knew her favorite walking partner would not be going with her this morning since she was quite busy getting ready for her numerous guests. Claire was hoping for a cool but clear morning. Instead there was a light snowfall. As long as the walks and streets were not icy, she would walk in any weather. She put on her coat and wrapped a scarf around her head and started out. There were not many people up and about but she did go by a few houses where families were loading children into cars, probably heading out to go "over the river and through the woods" to get to grandparents or other relatives or friends. Claire had always been envious of her friends who had gone to visit grandparents on holidays. For most of her childhood, her only living grandparent, her grandmother, had lived with Claire's family. It was truly wonderful to have her with them and there were many benefits to her being there. But Claire always wished that she could go to visit a grandmother's house. It was a romantic notion she always had and she was still somewhat envious as she saw these families packing up their cars for their visits.

After her walk, Claire took a shower and dressed for dinner. She was not sure how fancy she should get so she chose a fall skirt and sweater and wore flats instead of high heeled shoes. She figured that after she had gone through one year in Hayward she would know the appropriate dress for all these occasions. Claire really didn't want to wear a coat since the walk was so short, but with the snow still lightly falling, she didn't want to take a chance of having to walk home in what might be a heavier snow. So she put on a coat and precariously balanced the pie in one hand and the salad in the other and pushed the door open with one knee. Claire set the pie carefully on the swing, pulled the inside door shut and picked up the pie again. With both hands now full, she pushed the storm door tightly closed with her hip. "I knew those hips were good for something," she said as she carefully walked down the steps and onto the sidewalk. She was glad that there was no ice on the sidewalk yet since her balancing act was hard enough as it was.

Luckily Claire arrived at the Nuttings' walk at the same time that Ben Miller did. "Here, let me help you with that," said Ben as he took the salad from her cramped right hand.

"That certainly was good timing," she said shaking her hand to try to get her fingers to bend again. "Pretty day, isn't it. It kind of sets the mood for the holiday season."

"Yes, it is pretty but I would be just as happy if it didn't snow enough to make me have to shovel."

"Should you be doing the shoveling? Maybe you could get Steve Hornsby or one of his friends to shovel for you."

"Maybe, but he is so busy riding around in his car that he doesn't seem to be home much. He's probably out flirting with the girls. Believe it or not, I can remember being sixteen. I remember coming into town on Saturday and looking for girls at the soda fountain in the drug store. I would not have had much interest in shoveling anyone's walk either. Oh, to be young again."

"I don't know about that. I'm not sure I would want to go through those teen-age years again. They were not at all easy, as I recall. But our lives were certainly simpler than they are now – fewer choices and distractions. I think I'm glad that I grew up when I did."

A third voice interrupted their conversation. "Are you two coming in sometime or are you planning on spending the day out there?" Leonard held the door open for them. "We would like to have that pie and salad even if you decide not to come in for dinner."

"I don't know about Ben, but I'm ready to come in. It's cold out here and I'm getting hungry besides." Ben and Claire walked in and Betty met them to take the food, and then Leonard took their coats.

"Make yourselves at home. There are some appetizers to munch on. I heard someone say she was hungry," said Betty, directing them toward the dining room. The side board was filled with a wide variety of appetizers. Claire was very hungry, having not eaten breakfast before going for her walk, but she didn't want to spoil her appetite for the big meal. She did find a few things to snack on just to tide her over. Ben followed Claire to the food but he didn't use quite the restraint that she had. He filled his small plate and then headed for the rocking chair in the living room. Claire had chosen a wingback chair since she thought she would be better able to eat there.

They had just sat when the doorbell rang. It was Bill and Grace, armed with their contributions to the meal. They were just removing their coats when the bell rang again. This time it was Sally and Jen Jensen. Sally was the nurse in the clinic and her husband operated the service station at the edge of town.

After their coats had been removed, Sally handed Betty the bowl she had brought. "Is Tim here yet?" Sally asked. "I want to make sure to tell him that I put extra coconut into this ambrosia since I know how much he likes it." The way she said it made Claire think that he probably did not like coconut at all. Claire was the only one in her family that liked coconut so she always enjoyed dishes that included it. "Are the girls and their families coming, Betty?" Sally continued.

"No, they are all going to in-laws this year. But we get all of them for Christmas, and it will be quite a houseful."

The doorbell rang again and it was Tim Payne. "Happy Thanksgiving," he bellowed to those in the living room. Dr. Payne was a short man with a slight build, but his voice compensated for his size. Claire often wondered if he had developed the habit of talking loudly so his patients could hear him over the sound of his dental drills. She also wondered if he might be a bit hard of hearing. He handed over a box that Claire recognized as coming from the Taylors' bakery. "Homemade, of course, an old family recipe," Tim said with a big smile. "I was up late last night slaving over a hot oven. And I frosted it this morning. Sure hope that you all like it."

"I just hope it is as good as the ones that the Taylors bake," teased Sally. "And I hope it has coconut frosting because you know that is my favorite."

"Sorry, if you want coconut you'll just have to furnish it yourself."

"That's okay. I think I'll get my fill of coconut with what I put in the ambrosia."

"Oh, no! What a terrible thing to do to all of that good fruit! Knowing Betty, though, I imagine there will be plenty of other things so I won't go hungry."

Everyone went to get a plate of appetizers while Betty buzzed in and out of the kitchen. "Can I help you with anything?" Claire offered.

"Not right now, Claire. Things are under control at the moment, but I'll let you know."

The conversation in the living room was lively, covering a wide range of topics, including the need to repaint the clinic. Ben jumped in with, "If you need a good painter I can certainly recommend one or maybe even two." Ben looked directly at Claire. "This little lady can paint up a storm. You put her and Francine in charge and it would be done in no time."

"I might consider it, Ben, but I usually only take on painting jobs for handsome older gentlemen."

Tim put on a frown. "Do you mean that Leonard and I are not handsome?"

"Not at all. It's the 'older' part that eliminates you," Claire said, looking sympathetically at him.

"Heck, for once I wish I were older."

"Want to trade ages?" asked Ben.

Tim put his hand on his chin and stroked it for a moment as if in deep thought. "No, I guess I'll just stay the way I am."

The conversation continued at a lively pace. Then the doorbell rang again. Leonard opened the door and there was Bertha Banter. "Happy Thanksgiving, Miss Banter. We're glad you could join us. May I take your coat?"

Momentarily Bertha stood with her arms crossed over her chest as if bracing herself for the group watching her from the living room. Leonard stood patiently, appearing as if he was not sure whether or not she was going to relinquish her wrap. Finally she unbuttoned it very slowly with all eyes on her. Claire wasn't sure why they all looked at her the way they did, but it was somewhat of a feeling of disbelief that the town's social recluse, the person who could take the pleasure out of reading, the person who could put a gloomy cloud over any setting, was actually coming to this festive occasion.

They all rose as Miss Banter walked into the living room. Claire didn't think it was as much a polite gesture as it was fear that she was going to yell at one of them for not giving up a seat for her. Thankfully Betty emerged from the kitchen at that awkward moment. "Hello, Miss Banter. I am so glad that you came. There are appetizers in the dining room if you care for something. Dinner will be in about a half an hour."

"Never touch appetizers. What's the sense of having a big fancy meal if everyone snacks on something first. Appetizers are just silly, an unnecessary waste."

Claire was glad that she had finished snacking and Betty had taken her plate to the kitchen. She had a feeling that the rest of the guests wished that they were not sitting there with their snack plates. It was amazing how this ill-natured woman could make them feel like children who had just been reprimanded by their teacher. The conversation that had been energetic and often animated was suddenly nonexistent.

Grace broke the silence. "Isn't the snow pretty today?" While everyone else commented or nodded in agreement Miss Banter just sat and shook her head.

"I don't like it one bit. It is dangerous for walking and if it sticks around it only gets dirty and disgusting looking."

Claire was hesitant to say anything for fear of the retort she might get, but the silence was too uncomfortable. All that she could think of was, "Will the library be closed tomorrow for the holiday?"

She did not receive a verbal response right away. Instead she got a cold stare for a few moments before Bertha replied, "If you had read the note on the library door you would know the answer to that, now wouldn't you?"

Claire felt about two inches high and everyone's eyes avoided hers as they were embarrassed for her and the response she had received. But Ben was not about to let it rest.

"Well, I didn't make it to the library this week, Bertha, so I don't know. Will it be open or not?"

She looked at Ben with that same annoyed look. "No, it will not be open. It is hardly worth my time what with all the people out of town. And then there is all of that decorating going on around the square. People are too busy with trivial things to think about reading this time of year." She dramatically crossed her arms across her chest with this last statement.

Dead silence followed. After a few minutes Claire jumped up and said, "I think I'll see if Betty needs any help in the kitchen."

Leonard jumped up from his spot on the arm of the couch and said, "I was just headed there myself."

And almost in unison Sally and Tim also volunteered for kitchen duty. This left Bill, Grace, Ben and Jen, stuck with Bertha. For the first time since Claire had known Bill she saw an uncomfortable look on his face. But it was almost as if Betty had been listening, for she intercepted the deserters at the kitchen door. "Things are in good hands, folks. But I will let Claire give me some help since she asked first. The rest of you go back and visit for a few minutes. I will let you anxious helpers know when I need you."

Dejectedly the other three headed back for their seats in the living room, much to the relief of those who did not move fast enough to escape. Claire, on the other hand, breathed a sigh of relief and passed through the door to the refuge of the kitchen. "So what can I do to help?"

"How do you feel about mashing potatoes?" Betty asked.

"How do you feel about lumps?" she responded.

"I can take' em or leave 'em. It's either potatoes or gravy. Everything else is ready."

"That's a tough decision. I don't mind making gravy but I can never seem to make enough to fill all the gravy lovers and it looks to me as if you have a house full of them. So I guess I will stick to the potatoes." Betty tossed an apron in Claire's direction. She tied it on and went to work doing battle with the potatoes.

Betty bent over the stove thickening the gravy. "Was it really that bad with Bertha? I just didn't want her to be alone. From what I could tell from talking to others, she seemed to be the only one in town without a place to go for Thanksgiving. And since I knew that she had spent some time with Ben, I thought maybe she would enjoy coming."

"Right now things are not exactly chatty out there but I'm sure that it will get better. Maybe it just takes her a long time to warm up to a group," Claire said, trying to sound optimistic even thought she really wasn't.

"How long do you think it takes? She has been the librarian for over fifteen years and she still has not warmed up to the townspeople. I just don't understand why the Haywards haven't replaced her by now."

"Maybe she's blackmailing them," Claire said jokingly. But Betty looked pensive as if she were thinking over that possibility.

The potatoes and gravy were finished at the same time so Betty yelled for reinforcements to help put food on the table. Everyone, except one person, paraded through the kitchen picking up dishes to carry into the dining room. When they got there Bertha had already seated herself at the table. Claire didn't know if Bertha had asked Leonard where he wanted her to sit, or whether she just took it upon herself to pick a place. If Betty had to mentally juggle the seating arrangement it was not noticeable as, without skipping a beat, she told her guests where to sit. Claire knew everyone was secretly hoping that he or she would not get the short straw and end up next to Bertha. Claire was also hoping that she would not be seated across from her so she would not have to look at that grumpy face. She got lucky and was assigned a place a chair away from her with Ben in between them.

Bill gave a very meaningful blessing and then the food started around the table. And there was a lot of it. Luckily the Nuttings had lots of leaves for their table, which allowed not only for plenty of seating for the guests but also adequate space for the plentiful feast. Conversation continued at the friendly level that it had been before Bertha's arrival. In fact, had they not actually seen her there, the others hardly would know she was there at all. The only comments she made were when the food was originally passed and she passed judgment on the contents of the containers, stating not only what she definitely liked and didn't like but also how she thought the different foods looked. Although Claire really should not have cared at all, she was relieved when Bertha said that her strawberry salad looked "somewhat attractive." Claire would never know if she liked it, since she chose not to take any.

During the conversation Claire mentioned that she was very pleased to be invited, not only here but to so many other dinners, also. Grace said, "For years the community has tried to make sure that no one is alone for the holidays. It just seems like the friendly thing to do."

"The only ones I wasn't sure about were the Brocks," said Grace. "Do you know if they are going somewhere in town?"

"Francine said that they had invited them but Mike said that they were going to Chicago for the week. I think Francine was relieved about that."

"I like Mike. He's fitting in really well, but Missy still doesn't seem too comfortable here," said Betty.

"I think that Chester and Charles like him pretty well. I've seen them spending quite a bit of time together at Maude's," commented Tim. "Sometimes I run over there for coffee between patients and I often have seen them together."

"Now that is just what I want my dentist to do before he works on my mouth, rev up with a couple of cups of coffee," joked Leonard.

"It's probably better than having him fall asleep with his hands in your mouth," added Sally.

As usual, Claire ate much more than she intended. From all of the sighs as people leaned back in their chairs she thought almost everyone else did, too. Bertha sat as straight and stiffly as she had the entire time. She appeared to be the only one not feeling the effects of a tightened waistband. Compliments were exchanged about the delicious dishes. Betty said that they had gathered some of their family's favorite games that everyone could play while recovering from dinner and waiting for the desserts. Everyone moaned at the thought of more food but no one expressed a lack of interest in having dessert later.

All but one guest reversed the routine at the beginning of the meal and the table was cleared off very quickly. Board games were set up at both ends of the large dining room table and one more was put on the coffee table in the living room. Leonard offered to help Betty in the kitchen but Claire insisted that he let her help instead. He said he was going to go play Sorry and he probably was sorry when he realized that Bertha was also at that game.

After about an hour and a half of playing a great variety of games, Betty asked if everyone was ready for dessert. She got an energetic response so Sally and Betty started loading the sideboard with a variety of pies, cakes and ice cream. It was a delicious ending to a very enjoyable gathering. After a few cups of coffee, the guests gathered up the leftovers of what they had brought. Everyone thanked the Nuttings for their wonderful hospitality. Even Bertha, in her staid way, sounded sincere when she thanked them for "including her in the festivities." They donned their coats and headed out into a cold November afternoon.

Thirteen

The snow that had fallen on Thanksgiving morning had melted by late afternoon. Claire hated to see it disappear so quickly. However, it was probably a good thing that it did since Friday morning there was a flurry of activity around the square. She could see some of the activity from her windows but the courthouse blocked much of the view. She decided that it was time for a walk, both to see what was going on and to help work off some of the big Thanksgiving dinner.

As she turned the corner of Main and Oak Claire could see that the storekeepers were all decorating their windows in keeping with what were probably their own holiday traditions. Bryan Graves was straightening one of the two large wreaths in the windows of Hayward Foods. When he saw Claire he yelled, "How does it look?" She motioned to him that it needed to move a bit to the left and gave him a thumbs-up after he adjusted it.

Maude's had a curtain rod across the middle of the window which always held a pair of green and white checked café curtains. Now five stockings hung from that rod. A large red and white candy cane was in each of the holiday colored stockings.

Dale Taylor stood in front of the bakery store window giving directions to Irene, who was trying to paint the words "Seasons Greetings" across the top of the window.

"Good morning, Dale," Claire nodded.

"Good morning, Claire. How was your Thanksgiving? If you are still hungry, we have a few packages of rolls left that we'd like to have someone take off our hands."

"I think my stomach is going to need a few days to recover, but thanks for the offer. It looks as if Irene has quite a job going on there."

"Yeah. Every year she says I should do it but I just can't figure out how to paint those letters backwards. And despite how she fusses, she does enjoy it. She really is quite artistic. I could never do as good a job as she does. She insists that I do the bell that goes under the words, though. It's pretty hard to mess up a bell."

Claire turned toward the window, waved to Irene and mouthed the words, "It looks good."

"I'll come back later to check out that bell, Dale."

"When you do, stop in and I'll give you a cookie, maybe even one shaped like a bell."

The window of the hardware store was filled with a tree which Claire suspected was artificial. A young man was trying to untangle a mass of multi-colored lights. He was so busy fighting with the tangled wires that he did not even notice that she was watching him. She thought back to the many times Dennis had worked to straighten the strings of lights that always seemed to tangle themselves up after they had been put away after New Year's Day.

If the barbershop was getting any decorations, they were not yet in sight. It probably really did not need any more since the red and white barber pole looked quite festive by itself.

Bea Winters was arranging the reindeer that were pulling Santa in a sleigh in the window of the drug store. She looked up as Claire looked in the window. She picked up the hat that would go on Santa's head and, placing it on her own head, put her hands on her stomach, tilted her head back and mouthed, "Ho, ho, ho!" Claire smiled and waved.

Felton's Clothing Store was next on the block. Gladys was in the window removing a pair of dark pants from the male mannequin. The female form had already been dressed in a long red dress with fur trim. Claire suspected that the male would soon be Santa Claus but she assumed that padding would be added to the very slim and trim plastic fellow. She knocked on the window and waved at Gladys, who smiled in return. As Claire walked away from Felton's, she thought how different it was on this Main Street compared to the main streets in so many cities that were already crowded with shoppers out early trying to take advantage of the big day-after-Thanksgiving sales. That made her wonder how many people from Hayward and the surrounding areas did their Christmas shopping on this street. She had a feeling that many purchases were made through the Sears and Penney's catalogs.

The last business along the square was the bank. Its windows were hung with pairs of large gold bells tied together at the tops with big red bows bedecked with evergreen bows. The windows were very tastefully done. Claire had a feeling that Elizabeth Hayward had done the planning, since Elizabeth's own home was decorated so stylishly. In the window closest to the door was a red velvet bag with gold foil-covered candy coins spilling out of its opened top. Next to the coins was a sign that read, "Need ideas for stocking stuffers? We can help." Claire thought that this idea was Clarence's.

She continued away from the square and walked up and down the adjoining streets for about 30 minutes. Claire didn't mind walking in the cold weather, but she didn't like walking on snow or ice. She was dreading the Iowa ice storms that many people had told her definitely would be coming.

By the time Claire made it back to the square there was much more activity. Several groups of people were coming from the area around the court house. Each group had a bag or box. She could see a dark brown something in the area from where all the people had come. As she drew nearer Claire could see it was Lila, who was dressed from head to toe in brown fur—a full length coat, mink pillbox hat and tall fur boots which probably were fake. Lila waved as Claire approached. Claire could see that Lila carried a bull horn in one hand.

"Claire, oh Claire, did you come to help decorate the square? Isn't it wonderful that all of the people turned out to beautify our little ol' town? Even those cute Boy Scouts came to help. I'm sure you are just dying to do your share of the work but right now I think all of the tasks have been assigned. I will be walking around to make sure that everything is done correctly. You could walk with me, if you like. But please don't talk to the workers. You might distract them from their jobs."

"Thank you for the offer, but I was just heading home. I promise to go quietly and I'll try not to say a word to anyone."

"Good for you. Now I need to start supervising."

Claire waited until she was quite a few steps away before she said under her breath what she really wanted to say. She wondered what Lila was planning to do if she found too much unnecessary talking among the ranks of her volunteers. Claire knew she should have been happy that her neighborhood was being decorated for the holiday season, but for some silly reason she was irritated that Lila was the one in charge, or at least she seemed to think that she was in charge.

The big evergreen trees on both sides of the courthouse were being decorated with strings of multi-colored lights. Since Lila had headed in the other direction Claire ventured to say "Good morning" to the men working on the lights. It was easy to tell by their yellow vests that they wore over their coats that they were from the Lions Club. "That will look very nice. And I can enjoy the view from my house, too." The workers greeted her but said nothing more. Maybe they were worried about incurring the wrath of the officious fur lady.

Claire turned around the corner of the courthouse and could see that the bare trees around the square were being adorned with large plastic balls of many colors. The evergreen trees were having red bows tied onto the branches. The lampposts around the outside of the square and in back of the courthouse were festooned with large evergreen wreaths.

Remembering her specific directions from Lila, Claire walked quietly past a couple working on the other side of one of the large evergreen trees. They seemed to have missed the "no talking" part of their instructions and their conversation was privy to anyone in the close vicinity.

"I don't see why you dragged me out of my nice warm bed to stand here and tie these ridiculous bows on these stupid trees. It is colder than blue blazes out here."

"I told you. You need to look as if you are interested in these people and their frumpy traditions. We need to have them trust us. So you have to get involved and look happy even if I have to paint a smile on your face with one of your hundred tubes of lipstick."

Claire hurried by as quietly as she could and tried to give the appearance that she hadn't heard anything. However, she saw enough to know that it was Mike and Missy. Mike had always seemed like such a nice guy, although Claire didn't much care for his choice of words to describe her new hometown. Missy could turn the charm on and off like a faucet and this morning she was not being very charming.

When Claire got to her porch she decided to sit on the swing and watch the workers for awhile. She got tickled watching Lila scurrying around yelling at everyone with that bull horn. With the volume that she still had from her hog calling days they really could have heard her well enough without the horn but Claire was sure that it gave her even more of a feeling of authority. Though Claire had doubted that there could possibly be any harmony to this decorating scheme, things began to come together as the different parts were completed. Had she tried to write to her friends and describe what she was seeing, she would have given the impression of a hodgepodge of decorations. In actuality, however, the combination was really quite charming. She felt lucky that she would be able have the benefit of this colorful display.

The snow began to fall again. Claire rocked back and forth in the swing, mesmerized by the decorations and the workers hurrying to finish. As she sat, she debated whether or not to get a Christmas tree. She would be going to Michigan for Christmas to spend a couple of weeks with her children. "It's silly to go to all that work when you won't even be here," she told herself. But Claire was quire sure that in a couple of weeks she would be asking her neighbors where to buy a tree, and she would be in the middle of decorating her new home for the first time.

The Saturday evening before the first Sunday in Advent was the time when the Methodist church, and many others, were decorated for Christmas. When she saw the announcement in the bulletin inviting anyone who was interested to come and help, Claire decided that she would definitely like to participate. She had often wanted to do that in her Colorado church but the timing was never good. In fact last year she had been determined to go help, but a major snow storm kept everyone away and Advent was half over before the decorations ever made it up.

Snow was falling as she walked toward the church. It was a couple of inches deep by then but was not enough to keep away the hearty decorating regulars, many of whom were arriving as Claire got to the door. Everyone greeted each other as snow was shaken from coats and boots were removed. Claire had never thought of wearing socks to go running around in a church but that seemed to be the appropriate foot attire for this evening.

From somewhere, very large storage boxes had appeared in the sanctuary and the narthex. Many of the volunteers obviously had done this job before, since they looked at the label on each box and knew exactly where it was to go. Boxes were carried off in their respective directions and for a few minutes Claire watched like a lost soul. Then a familiar voice behind her said, "I'm so glad that you came, Claire. We can use all of the help we can get." It was Grace Carlson loaded with evergreen roping.

"What would you like me to do?" Claire asked.

"You just pick what looks like fun for you. Most of our helpers have done the same jobs for years and I am sure they would all welcome your assistance."

Claire was not so sure about that last statement since she had learned from years of trying to volunteer in various capacities that some old time volunteers are quite territorial about their jobs and are not always willing to have newcomers butt in. She was looking around when a hand landed on her shoulder. She turned to see Reverend Carlson smiling at her. But instead of his normal loud, clear voice he spoke in very hoarse tones. "Why don't you help with the sanctuary tree? Martha and Del Danielson usually help with that but won't be able to make it tonight." Claire walked with Bill toward the front of the sanctuary where a very large tree was being anchored into its stand. The smell of evergreen filled the air.

Bill hoarsely introduced Claire to the tree group, but she already knew Floyd and Lloyd Lavelle and Irma Fisher. She was rather surprised to see Irma in this group since she had the reputation of a Saturday night partier. Maybe the weather had prevented her from doing any more socializing than hanging around the church. Bill went on to explain to the others that the Danielsons were not going to be able to come. Claire felt that he was buffering her entrance into the group, as if to say that she was their substitute for the evening and therefore she could stay. A voice from the rear of the sanctuary yelled toward them, "You stop that talking, Bill, or you will have no voice by tomorrow morning." It was Grace. Claire had no idea that that petite little lady could holler that loudly. Bill nodded and wandered off to oversee another group of decorators.

Once the tree was secured, the little group began the decorating. Numerous boxes of ornaments lay on the floor in front of the first pew. Irma Fisher began opening the boxes and stated in a very matter of fact manner, "We'll use only the red ball ornaments and the white lights. And, of course, we need the white doves, too." Our group seemed to agree, so while the men in the group strung white lights around the tree, Irma and Claire carefully gleaned only the shiny red balls of all sizes from the boxes. The tree was so tall that three men worked together to decorate the parts the ladies could not reach standing on the ground. The Lavelle brothers steadied the ladder while the third man precariously leaned forward to reach the receding top sections. Claire was just waiting for the ladder to tip and send the top man careening into the tree, but luckily that never happened.

About half of the tree was decorated when three other people showed up. "We wondered where the ornaments went. We're working on the tree in the basement and need some."

Immediately Irma chimed in, "We are using the red ones."

"Well, we have chosen red, too," responded one of the basement workers.

Irma picked up a few of the boxes holding ornaments of many colors. "Here, why don't you take these? I am sure you can find some red ones in here." She shoved the boxes toward the workers and quickly returned to work.

As soon as they had left Irma turned to Claire and handed her a stack of boxes. "Look through these fast and see how many red ones you can find. Then hide them under the front row pew."

Claire admitted to herself that they needed to stick with the red and white color scheme they had begun. But when it came to hiding the ornaments, she couldn't agree. "Don't you think there are enough for both trees?" she asked Irma.

"Do you see the size of this tree? The other one is not so big. We still need as many as we can get." Irma was searching the boxes as quickly as she could, transferring ornaments to make up boxes filled with reds and then pushing them under the pew with her foot. "Find some more red ones and get them hung on the tree," she said demandingly and added a "Please" as an afterthought.

Claire was still uncomfortable with this plan but did some compromising by leaving some red ornaments in the boxes that were to be passed on to the basement crew. When all of the boxes had been searched and the treasured red ones stashed, they returned to the task of putting them on the tree. When two representatives arrived from below, Irma proudly handed over the boxes not realizing that Claire had undermined her plan and had actually shared the wealth of red.

"Why don't you take all of these? I think we will have enough here." She smirked as the two walked down the aisle loaded from waist to chin with the boxes.

Irma then changed her role from procurer of red ornaments to director of decorating. She walked around to various places in the sanctuary to see where more ornaments needed to be placed. Then she would yell at the decorators where to hang balls and birds. It was probably a good idea that someone did this but there was a bossy, know-it-all tone in Irma's voice that Claire found irritating.

At one point Lloyd Lavelle turned and glared at Irma. He looked as if he were going to say something when his brother Floyd put his hand on Lloyd's shoulder. "Just let her be. You know Irma. She's just trying to help. Besides, we're almost through."

When Irma gave her final nod of approval, they all stepped down into the pews and critiqued their work. "It is lovely," Irma said with a big sigh. They all agreed and stood in silence. When the moments for adoration were over they started to clean up the empty boxes and put them in their proper storage crate. While gathering up the boxes Claire discovered that they still had plenty of unused red ornaments. "Silly Irma," she said softly to herself. She gathered the remaining ornaments to take them to the basement.

Claire had just started down the aisle when a frantic Phoebe Peoples came hurrying toward her. "Have you seen the baby? The baby is missing!" Phoebe asked in a nearly hysterical tone.

"How terrible," Claire thought. "A baby lost in this kind of weather." Then she quickly got her wits about her. "What baby? Where did you see it last?" she asked.

"Last Christmas," she answered. "Baby Jesus is missing. You just cannot have a crèche scene without Baby Jesus."

"Here," said Lloyd, bending over one of the crates. "I think this is what you are looking for." He straightened up holding one rather bedraggled doll.

"Oh thank goodness," exclaimed Phoebe. "It must have been put in the wrong box last year." She lovingly held the doll to her ample chest and, after rocking it back and forth a few times, turned and headed toward the basement. Claire followed, red ornaments in her arms.

The basement was a hive of activity. The nativity scene had been set up at one end. Next to it was a very full fir tree adorned with only small white lights. At the other end of the room was another tree covered with red velvet bows and, of course, red balls.

"Do you need these? We had extras," Claire said, offering the boxes she held.

"Thank you. We can certainly use those. We were thinking that we might have to supplement with another color," said Edna Bemis.

"If you had to, silver would have been nice. It would complement the tree by the nativity scene."

"Silver! What a wonderful idea. We should have thought of that," exclaimed Edna. "And there are plenty of silver balls." The group decorating this tree looked at each other and smiled. Without saying one word they got busy and the red balls were quickly removed and replaced with the silver ones.

Irma entered the room as the silver balls were placed on the tree. She stood by Claire and looked in amazement. "What in the world?" she said.

But before she could continue Claire said, "Don't say a word. It was just a little last minute change of plans. It seems they did not have enough red ones to do an adequate job." Claire knew it was a little lie. And lying in church was certainly not a good thing. However, under the circumstances she thought it was the best thing to do.

Grace and Bill appeared from the kitchen and set out trays of cookies. Cups were already on the table and the coffee was ready. As the groups finished their areas, they joined around the table. "It looks wonderful," croaked Bill. "Thank you so much for your help. Stay as long as you want but when you leave drive carefully." Then he looked at Claire and added, "Or in some cases, walk carefully. And may God bless you all."

People stood and visited for a while. After a few minutes Claire chose to walk around and look at all the decorations in the room. She stopped in front of the crèche which looked very nice were it not for the fact that the blonde hair on Baby Jesus was sticking out in all directions and his face was rather smudged. She turned her head to different angles to see if different views improved the appearance.

"That is not quite how I envision Jesus to look, either," quietly said Grace who was now standing beside Claire. "The doll belonged to Phoebe's daughter, who died when she was eight. The Christmas after that Phoebe asked Bill if he would like to use it in the church's nativity scene. He really didn't want to but he said there was such pleading in Phoebe's eyes that he could not turn her down. So that doll has been with us ever since. Tonight, after everyone leaves, Bill and I will wrap it up so the hair does not show and just the sweet face does. Phoebe is happy to have the chance to see the doll for a little while each year and to know that her daughter still is contributing to the church at Christmas."

As she walked home Claire thought about what she had seen that night. A group of people, some of whom had driven miles from their farms, had braved the storm to ready a church for the Christmas season. With the exception of Irma, people had worked cooperatively, quickly and joyfully to do their assigned jobs, some of which they had done for years. Irma's fit of selfishness truly was the first behavior of this kind that Claire had seen in Hayward since she had arrived, and she was convinced that Irma was the exception to the generous spirit of the town. But what she would always remember most was the doll that gave a lonely woman a brief loving memory of someone she had lost, and how everyone understood why for a few hours Baby Jesus had straw-like blonde hair.

"I haven't made these for awhile," said Jane, "but I think I remembered the recipe correctly."

"I mixed it just like you told me so I guess there is only one way to find out," Claire said. "We might as well make some for practice. Do you use cookie cutters?"

"No, I just get some idea and go with it," Jane answered.

"You must be more creative than I am. I guess I'll try a teddy bear. That shouldn't be too hard." Claire took a glob of the doughy mixture and formed it into an oval. Then she attached a somewhat flattened circle for the head. Arms, legs, ears and a pointy little snout were attached.

"That looks good. How do you like my fish? I think I need to make some marks for the scales," said Jane.

Jane's fish looked really good. Next she made a clown that bore a strong resemblance to the elf Claire was crafting. They each made a few more pieces and laid them carefully on a cookie sheet, which Claire slid it into the oven to bake.

"These take a while," said Jane. "We have time for some tea and cookies."

"Don't you move! I'll get it. I am nervous enough about your getting out of bed to help me practice these ornaments." Claire heated the water for the tea and got the tea bags, cups and cookies.

They were on their second cup of tea when they were both startled by very loud popping sounds. They looked at each other with a bit of fear in their eyes.

Claire had never heard gunshots, that she knew of anyway, but she wondered if that was what they were hearing. She momentarily thought that maybe Farley had actually found bullets for his gun and was in pursuit of one of his imaginary enemies. There were more pops but this time they realized that the sounds were closer than they had first thought. In fact, they were much, much closer.

"The oven!" yelled Jane. "It's coming from the oven."

Claire jumped up and reached for the oven door, not really sure what she would find when she opened it. She was sure wishing that Jane could do it herself but Claire knew that she had to do this for Jane and the baby.

"Be careful. Please be careful," Jane said excitedly. Claire could have used some words of encouragement as much as words of warning at that point since she was already saying to herself, "Please be careful."

She cautiously and slowly started to lower the door when she heard another loud pop and pieces of dough shot out through the opening, hitting the apron that protected her midsection. She quickly shut the door again, not knowing the best approach to take to this explosion problem. She decided to turn off the oven, hoping that it would cool enough to stop the blasts. After one more bang Claire again slowly opened the door and this time was not hit by flying fish fins or teddy bear arms. Looking in the oven she surmised that all of the damage had probably already been done. She and Jane waited a few seconds for more popping noises, but heard none. As they gazed into the oven they saw nothing that resembled what they had put in there a short time before. Instead there were dried-up gobs of clay all over the oven.

Jane and Claire looked at each other and started to laugh. As Claire reached in and removed a couple of the little dried missiles they just laughed harder. Claire had to sit down as she continued to laugh. When Jane's laughter had subsided enough to catch her breath she said, "Well, I guess that wasn't quite the right recipe, was it?"

They finished their tea and cookies as they giggled about how they had initially reacted with fear when hearing those explosions. Jane promised to research the correct recipe for the dough so that they could use it at the next scout meeting. "I really think the boys would get a big kick out of it just the way it is," Claire said jokingly. "Little boys really like blowing up things." She promised to come back to clean out the oven later when it had cooled.

"Good morning, Clarence," came the voice over the phone. "This is Mike. How would you and the other CW2 partners like an extra $1500 to spend for Christmas? I figured right on some short-term cattle futures and we've made a little money already. I know we agreed to let everything ride, but I thought this time of year you might want a little extra spending money. What do you think?"

"Well, Mike, your call couldn't have come at a better time. I don't know about the other partners, but I'll sure take you up on that offer. I'm sure all of us can think of a way to use that kind of money. And if we can't, I am sure that our wives could."

"Great," said Mike. "As soon as the trades settle and the money is in the account I'll drop off a check. I assume you'll want me to bring it by the bank. I'll go ahead and call Chester and William and see what they want to do. I'll see you early next week."

Mike's call to Chester had the same result, with Chester sounding relieved that he'd have some extra money to cover Lila's ever-expanding Christmas party, not to mention her new holiday wardrobe. William, though, said everything was just fine as it was, so he'd rather keep his money invested.

From what Claire had gathered from her friends, this was the social event of the holiday season. She had always loved Christmas parties and this one was going to be special, for she was going to get to see the interior of the mayor and Lila's home. The current challenge was picking something to wear. She decided on a green silky polyester dress with a tie belt. It made her green eyes look even greener. Emerald earrings with a matching emerald on a thin gold chain, an anniversary gift from her husband, added a festive and dressy touch. Luckily the snow from the day before had been cleared from the sidewalks so it was safe to wear heels. Claire turned, examining her reflection in the mirror. "Not bad," she said aloud. "Not bad at all."

She went downstairs and put on her coat, tying the belt around her. "Whoever designed this coat without buttons should have to be here to wear it in this fifteen degree weather," she said in an irritated tone. Fortunately there was no wind. Claire could have driven, but it seemed silly when she had only one block to go. She turned on the porch light and the small light in the living room, braced for the cold, and headed outside. Up the block she could see others heading for the Haywards. She had seen the exterior of Haywards house decorated before but tonight it seemed even more festive than usual. Trees in the front yard were decorated with white lights. White lights were hung from the ceiling of the porch and followed the ceiling of the balcony as well as the railings on the balcony and along the porch. It was really lovely, but Claire had to laugh to herself about a story Betty had told her. It seems that the first year Lila decided to have this party she did all of the outside lighting in red, thinking that it would be a lovely contrast to the big white house. Someone said something to her at the party about the significance of red lights. The next morning she had poor Chester out in the bitter cold, removing all of them.

A huge evergreen wreath hung on the front door with a large red velvet bow at the bottom. In each of the large two front windows was a big tree decorated with multi-colored lights and shiny ornaments. A few people had arrived at the door just before Claire did so she did not have the pleasure of ringing the doorbell. She was curious about the bell and wondered if it just buzzed or if it played some elaborate chime.

Lila opened the door and ushered the small group in with a wide sweeping motion. She was decorated as lavishly as her house. Her off-the-shoulder floor length dress was of green velvet with a wide satin sash. Her head was encircled by a crown of pseudo holly leaves accented with small red berries. Baby's breath was intertwined with the holly setting off the dark leaves and berries. Lila greeted her guests, floating from one newcomer to another except for when she stepped on her dress and nearly tripped into the arms of her visitors. She never seemed to even notice her missteps but continued on warmly welcoming each and every one.

Steve Hornsby approached the new arrivals, offering to take their coats. Claire hardly recognized him since she seldom had seen him in anything other than jeans and sneakers. He looked quite serious dressed in his white shirt, black bow tie and black slacks. Even the sneakers had been replaced by a pair of black dress shoes that had been polished to a bright sheen.

"You look very handsome tonight, Steve," Claire said to him as he helped her remove her coat.

"Thank you, ma'am," he said politely in return, but then in almost a whisper added, "I feel like a fool but they pay really well. And the food's good, too." With coats over his arms he disappeared down the hall.

They followed Lila into the inner sanctum of this mayoral manor. Leaving the entryway they entered a large area that most would have called a living room, but Lila referred to it as the larger parlor. The main focal points were a huge tree by the window, decorated to the hilt, and a baby grand piano. Although Claire was certainly no expert, most of the furnishings appeared to her to be antiques or quality reproductions.

Since Claire was a newcomer to the house, Lila took a few moments to point out some of its features. The wallpaper was as close to the original as they could find. All of the pictures were hung on wires suspended from the ceiling railing. "That keeps us from having to put those nasty little holes in the walls," she explained. She pointed out the stained glass transom windows in the doorways between the living room and the dining room. The open doorways were finished with recessed oak woodwork. Lila made a point to draw Claire's attention to the inlaid oak floors in both the living room and dining room. "I usually have my authentic Persian rugs on the floors but they clash with my Christmas decorations so I like to have just the beautiful hardwood. Isn't it lovely?" Claire would have agreed with her but Lila was ushering her to the short lace curtains that adorned the top of each tall window. "They are handmade Irish lace. Aren't they just exquisite?" She turned Claire toward the fireplace and proudly pointed out the imported tile that rimmed the opening.

Again Lila was off, pulling Claire around the dining room to show off the two large built-in china cabinets. "And I really could use more to store all of our antique crystal and Haviland china." Then in a very quiet aside she said, "I would use it tonight but I doubt that everyone would be as careful as I know you would be, dear, if you know what I mean. So I'm just kind of slumming and using my Noritake." Claire was familiar with Noritake and was not too pleased to think that the set of china she and Dennis had saved for years to buy were just dishes to be used for slumming.

There was a small bay window in the dining room with oak window seats. Lila shooed Vernina and Bryan Graves off one of the seats. "And look here. These are actually storage areas. Isn't that the most clever idea ever?" Did this woman think Claire had just crawled out from underneath a turnip leaf? She certainly had seen window seat storage before, so she merely smiled and agreed that it was a great use of space. "Sit, sit, sit," Lila said to the Graves as she led Claire to the fully laden dining room table. "If you can't find anything you like here, there is much more food in the kitchen. And please do look in the kitchen. It's lovely and so efficient for all of my culinary projects. In fact please feel free to just look everywhere. I am sure you would like to see what a lovely home from the late eighteen hundreds looks like."

Claire thanked Lila but what she really had the urge to say, "And just where do you think I live?" Lila left Claire to visit with the other guests and hurried off to greet those who had recently arrived.

Claire knew most of the people. Everyone from Oak Street seemed to be there. Many of the teachers from the elementary school were in attendance as were the principal and football coach from the high school. All of the merchants from the Hayward businesses were present. The ministers from all of the churches had been invited but it was speculated that Reverend Stover from the Baptist church would not attend since he had never been to one of Lila's parties before. Sheriff Johnson stopped in for a short time but said he was on duty that night so he didn't stay long.

Ironically, Missy Brock, whom Lila had held in such contempt for so long, had been invited as had her husband. Claire also had heard, although she didn't know how true the rumor was, that the Brocks had quite a bit of money. That in itself would have made them popular with the Hayward family since much of that money was said to be in the town bank. Claire assumed that if Chester wanted them invited to this big Christmas gala Lila would have to agree, but she also imagined that there had been some rather interesting discussions about including them. Even though Mike seemed to fit in pretty well by now, Claire wondered if this town would ever get used to Missy and her fashion choices.

At that moment, the men in the room seemed to be enjoying Missy's presence. Although they might not have been engaging her in conversation, they were certainly engaging her with their eyes. The women were checking her out, too, but not with the same admiring looks as the men. Her attire included a very tight, very low cut off-the-shoulder fuzzy sparkly red sweater. Her skirt was equally tight and so short that Claire hoped Missy would not drop one of her large gaudy dangling diamond earrings. Trying to bend over in that get-up would not be a pretty picture, at least from Claire's point of view. Missy's legs were covered in black fishnet stockings and the heels on her pointed black shoes were so high and spiked that it was a wonder she could walk without losing her balance.

Suits and dressy dresses were in order for all of the other guests. Red was the predominant color in both dresses and men's ties. There were also some black dresses but color seemed to be preferred by most of these Midwestern women. Many of the dresses appeared to be homemade. Claire's green dress was also homemade but she hoped it didn't look like it. It was hard to see what Clara was wearing because she would not take off her coat. Aaron tried to convince his mother that she would be too warm, but she would have nothing to do with that idea. She just sat in the living room, her coat wrapped tightly around her and her purse clutched securely to her little body.

Betty spotted Claire from across the room and headed her way. "This is some shindig, huh? Have you had a chance to check out the house?"

"I was given a tour of this area. Lila told me to look around but I thought she was just kidding."

"I'm sure she meant it. Lila isn't happy until everyone in this town has seen her little palace from top to bottom. Let's go." Betty grabbed Claire's hand and off they went, wending their way through the crowd toward the front of the house. They stepped into the smaller parlor to the left of the front door. This was the location of the other huge decorated Christmas tree. "Lila calls this the smaller parlor or sitting room. I'd call it an office. I'm pretty sure that Chester spends a lot of time in here," said Betty. Looking around Claire could tell that this room was also richly decorated but a bit more masculine. Along the inside wall there were built-in book cases filled with an impressive assortment of books, including one of the biggest dictionaries she had ever seen outside of the library. There were also heavy oak doors that could be shut to close off this room from the entry way.

"If I lived with that woman I think I would spend a great deal of time in this room with those doors locked from the inside," Claire said to herself.

"Did you say something?" asked Betty

"I was just saying this is a comfortable-looking room where one could spend a great deal of time." As Claire looked admiringly at the loaded bookcases she thought of the town librarian. "Does Miss Banter ever come to these parties? I can't imagine that this would be her type of social activity but then I'm not sure just what kind of social activity would be her type. I get the feeling that if she can't be in control she doesn't want to participate. Besides, if she were here she probably would be going around telling everyone to keep their voices down."

Betty laughed. "She is something. I wonder how much more the library would be used if it were run by someone with a smile on her face." She nodded her head toward the stairs. "Do you want to go up?"

"Are you sure that we can?"

"Trust me, she would be insulted if you didn't look at the entire house. I say we go now before she finds some other newcomer to go with us. Then we might have to watch what we say."

Claire felt like a mischievous child as they started up the stairway. She really felt like the bad kid when they heard, "I caught you two!" They turned around and saw Lila grinning at them from the bottom of the stairs. "Betty, I am disappointed in you. I thought you first might ask if anyone else needed a tour."

Claire could feel the color rising on her face and was thankful that she was standing in a rather dim spot on the stairway. Betty, who was in full view, appeared completely composed. "Well I would have, Lila, but I truly didn't see anyone I felt was new and had not had the wonderful opportunity to tour your magnificent home." Betty had really turned on the charm.

"You two stay right there. I'll go check and see who might need to go with you."

Betty and Claire looked at each other like two kids who had just been caught with their hands in the cookie jars. Then Claire had a not too pleasant thought. "What if the Brocks want to come, too?"

"I wouldn't worry. I doubt that she could climb the stairs in that skirt and those shoes."

While waiting, Claire looked around. The wall was lined with raised oak paneling. The railing appeared to be hand carved but it was hard to see since it was wrapped in evergreen roping with red bows and baby's breath. The stairs were covered in deep wine carpeting. Claire was surprised that Lila had not ripped this up, too, since this color did not go well with her overabundance of red decorations.

The chandelier hanging above the entryway had a large glass globe in the center with eight arms extended, each holding a smaller glass globe with eight tear-drop glass pieces. It looked like a lighted octopus. About the only polite thing Claire could stay about it was that it did provide somewhat adequate light. It also was quite a dust collector. She was sure Lila would die from embarrassment if she realized that a large cobweb criss-crossed the chandelier. The rest of the house looked as if it had been spit-shined from ceiling to floor.

Momentarily, Lila returned empty handed. "I asked the Brocks but they said they would rather visit with the others. You two go ahead. Give Claire the full tour, Betty."

They continued up the stairs, stopping on the landing. "I can't imagine that Missy wanted to visit. I have yet to see that woman be civil to anyone," said Betty.

"I wonder if she is just quiet and doesn't like to spend time making chit chat."

"You are nicer than I am. I think she is just a big snob. I get the distinct feeling she thinks she is better than we are. She sure won't have many people at her funeral."

"At her funeral? Is she sick? I had not heard that."

"Not that I know of. I just said that to show that I am not sure how many people will care much about her when she treats everyone in this town like she does. Anyway, enough of her. Which way do you want to go first?"

Claire told Betty that she didn't care, that she wanted to see it all. They first went into the master bedroom with its white textured wallpaper, white floor length drapes, white cover on the large four poster bed and two over stuffed chairs both upholstered in a white fabric. Claire couldn't believe that anyone would feel comfortable sitting in them for fear of getting them soiled, and she wondered how comfortable Chester was in there.

They peeked in each of the other five bedrooms. Each one had a different style of bed and a different color scheme with floral arrangements to match. There was a variety of antiques in the rooms. Candles burned everywhere. Those made Claire wonder how many of these party goers were members of the make-shift volunteer fire department that would man the old fire truck that sat behind Hornsby Ford, or how fast the real fire truck from Livonia could get here. She hoped that she would never have to find out.

Betty pulled her into the last room. "Check this out," she said, opening the door to a very large walk-in closet. "Originally there was a secret closet inside this closet but Lila had the inside wall removed so she could use it for this." In front of them were shelves filled with hats and hat boxes that went from floor to ceiling. There were hats of every size and color, hats for every season and occasion. Claire knew Lila had lots of headwear but this display was greater than she had ever imagined.

All she could say was, "Wow!" After a few moments of staring she said, "Where do you suppose she gets all of these?"

"I don't know but I'm sure they don't come from Felton's."

"And Frank is probably not checking her source to add to his inventory, either."

Betty and Claire were headed toward the stairs when suddenly they heard a loud scream followed by yelling and barking. They looked at each other and said in unison, "Mellow!"

The two hurried downstairs so they wouldn't miss out on any of the excitement. When they got back to the dining room they saw Lila being helped up off the floor. A tray that had evidently held food lay on the floor beside her. Chester was on his knees, his arms wrapped tightly around the neck of the dog. Scoop Gibson was taking pictures as fast as he could. Betty asked Grace what happened.

"Evidently someone forgot that Mellow was in the backyard and opened the back door. He came running and went straight for the first food he could find. That happened to be on the tray Lila was carrying. He knocked her over and, with his feet on top of her, started gobbling whatever he could reach. Everyone stepped back because I think they're all scared of that dog. As soon as he could make his way through the crowd Chester pulled him off Lila."

Lila didn't appear to be physically hurt but her dignity definitely was. She pointed to Bruce, who was still taking pictures. "You will not publish any of those pictures! If you do I'll sue!" Lila brushed herself off and excused herself to go change. Chester, with some difficulty, dragged the panting dog back outside. Scoop Gibson just smiled.

Things were pretty much back to normal after Steve got the floor cleaned and Claire continued her tour. She wanted to see the kitchen and was not disappointed. Tonight it was a hub of activity with Maude Richards bustling around, refilling trays with hors d'oeuvres and finger foods. Irene Taylor was also a busy little bee although calling Irene little was not totally accurate. She and her husband both looked as if they did a lot of sampling of their delicious baked goods. Unlike many bakeries, they seldom sold day-old products. Claire suspected that any leftovers contributed to the Taylors' size. Irene seemed to be in charge of all of the baked goods. No one would go hungry at this party.

The kitchen was pretty much as she assumed it would be, very large and modernized. There was a lot of counter space in addition to an island work space in the center. A variety of pots and pans hung from a brass rack above the island. There were two ovens and all sorts of kitchen gadgets sitting on the counters. Next to the coffee pot was the largest mug tree Claire had ever seen. But this one had no mugs, only tea cups that she figured were probably antiques. She wondered if Chester had to have his morning coffee out of one of these dainty cups. One section of counter held cookbooks of every variety from *My Country Barbecue* to *The Art of French Cooking*. Somehow Claire didn't picture Lila as a dedicated cook, but perhaps she was wrong.

There was a fireplace on the outside wall of the kitchen. This one, like the one in the living room, was not lighted. The people in the kitchen who were constantly in motion were certainly creating their own heat and didn't need any more. This fireplace had a decorative mantel which was filled with a collection of Santa Clauses of all sizes. There were carved wood ones and ceramic ones. There were some that looked as if they were imported from Europe. The Santa display was the only decoration in the house that was light hearted. Everything else was elegant and much more formal.

Claire peeked out the window of the back door. Although she couldn't see much she could tell there was a large porch with what she assumed to be lawn furniture. It was hard to be sure since all she could see was a big pile of coats. "Well, won't those be comfortable to put on after being outside," Claire thought. Past the porch she saw movement. She saw it again and again. Then she heard sounds. It was Mellow who must have seen her looking out of the window and was jumping against the rope with which he was now tied. Claire decided that the neighbors, if there were any who were not at this gathering, did not need to hear that dog carrying on so she moved away.

When she turned around, she saw a small gathering of ladies in a corner. Claire decided they must be waiting to use the restroom. While upstairs Betty had mentioned there was a bathroom downstairs that she might want to see. Betty headed back to the dining room and Claire went to join the waiting line. They discussed the tasty food, talking loudly enough that their compliments could not be missed by Maude and Irene. They made idle chitchat as others came and went from the little group. The line seemed to move very quickly and soon it was Claire's turn. Was she glad that she had waited!

Upon entering, she was almost overwhelmed. She had to blink to believe what she was seeing. Red! Red everywhere! How could this have happened? For having every other room so tastefully decorated, what had Lila been thinking? Or maybe this was Chester's room to decorate. It made Claire wonder if some horrible murder had taken place sometime in this room and rather than trying to cover up all of the blood, red paint had been applied. The floors were oak but most of the floor space was covered with dark red throw rugs. The toilet itself was white but there was a red seat lid cover as well as a red tank cover. Upon closer inspection in the dark room Claire discovered that the walls were not painted but were covered with dark red wallpaper. She figured Lila must have gotten a good deal on that paper since she couldn't imagine that it was a popular seller. The sink itself was a traditional white, which stood out from the surrounding red counter top. In the corner of the counter were three fat red candles that had been fanned out as they burned. These reminded Claire of three very full pairs of lips protruding from three red mouths. The towels gave some relief. They were white fingertip with big embroidered red poinsettias. The white roll of toilet tissue was another welcome cool relief from the overwhelming hot feeling of all that red. The heat of the three candles in that small room added to the closeness. Claire could hardly wait to get out. She did what she needed to and hurried toward the door. Now she understood why the line waiting to use the restroom had moved so quickly.

She made her way through a group of people who had gathered in the kitchen. It made her wonder, as she often did, why so many people think the kitchen is the place to be. If she were Maude and Irene she would have asked everyone to leave but they did not seem to be the least bit bothered. Back in the dining room Claire got a plate. She realized that because of her extensive house tour she had not eaten anything. There was plenty to choose from. She figured she would be able to make more than one trip around the heavily laden table so she didn't put as much on her plate as she would have liked. "Better to look like a proper lady," Claire thought.

Vernina was making another trip to the table when she looked at Claire. "You looked flushed. Are you all right?"

"I'm fine. I just made a quick trip to the restroom. And…"

"Enough said," she interrupted. "Isn't that horrible? The first time I was in the house that was a nice powder room but then, for some reason, it got changed to that monstrosity. I don't know anyone who knows or has had the courage to ask why, don't you know."

The food had been abundant and the liquor had flowed freely. Everyone was in quite a relaxed mood, including Lila who had reappeared in a long gold skirt, long-sleeved white silk blouse and a large gold bow fastened across the back of her head. She was back to her usual gushing self as she directed her guests into the living room. She had already cornered Phoebe Peoples and had her seated at the baby grand piano. "We must try out my brand new piano. Isn't it beautiful?" Lila ran her hand lovingly across the shiny black surface. "Now all we need is someone to get us started."

Claire saw Grace Carlson trying to hide behind Jim Dunn, who looked even heavier than he was last time Claire had seen him. Maybe he thought he also was eating for two. The plan didn't work since Lila called, "Grace, where are you? We need you here, dear." Grace rolled her eyes and stepped out from behind Jim and slowly approached the piano. "We would love to have you lead us in some beautiful Christmas songs, wouldn't we, everyone?"

The response from the crowd was not exactly a rousing yes but more like a moan. But that didn't put a damper on Lila's plans. Besides, Claire thought Lila knew she had a captive audience. Once Grace got them started, the crowd seemed to catch the spirit. Lila worked her way in and out through the group as she sang. To Claire's misfortune Lila stopped right next to her. Lila could belt out a song. Unfortunately, just like Bill Carlson, who was standing on the other side of Claire, the quality of Lila's voice was not comparable to her volume. Like Lila, Bill had a passion for singing but everyone in his congregation was well aware of his tonal qualities. Bill and Lila were having a wonderful time, but standing between them was a less than pleasurable experience. Claire knew that sticking her fingers in her ears might look quite rude. If she had had a tissue in her pocket she would have gladly ripped off two wads and stuffed them in her ears.

She thought she could tough it out through this song, thinking that Lila would continue to rove during the next number. However, she seemed quite content to stay put so Claire had to come up with another plan. She could have feigned having to go to the restroom but she couldn't face that again. Instead, she pretended to get a tickle in her throat, gave a few fake coughs, smiled at Lila raising her hand to acknowledge that she was okay, and backed her way out of the singing throng. In the back of the room, still sitting in a chair, was Clara, clutching her purse, eyes closed, quietly singing the carols. Claire had the feeling that Clara was thinking of Christmases past, Christmases in a happier time in her life. It was one of the few times Claire had seen a contented look on Clara's face.

As Claire made her way to the kitchen to get a drink of water she heard various comments about the beautiful piano and what it must have cost Chester. Shortly the singing stopped and Steve appeared from the porch loaded with coats. Claire guessed that was a not-so-subtle way of telling everyone the party was over. She headed back to the living room and waited for the arrival of her coat. Betty and Leonard's coats were on the first load. They said they would wait for Claire, as did Vernina and Bryan, but she assured them that they could go on. As people exited, thanking Lila for the lovely evening, some commented on her new musical addition.

"Isn't it grand!" Lila gushed. "Not to brag but it was a bit pricey. We used the money that Chester just earned from his new investments. It was quite a windfall. That's where Clarence got the money for Elizabeth's new diamond ring."

Elizabeth was busy visiting with some of the other departing guests and did not hear that last statement. However, Clarence, who was in earshot of Lila, stared at her. He shook his head putting his finger to his lips. "Shhhh! Don't blow my Christmas surprise," he exclaimed, loudly enough for people close to him to be aware of Elizabeth's upcoming gift.

It took awhile for Claire to get her coat, which arrived at the same time as Clarence and Elizabeth's. Elizabeth hugged her brother and sister-in-law. Clarence and Claire managed to get away with just a handshake. Claire thanked the Haywards for a lovely night and the three headed out into the cold night. As they descended the stairs, Elizabeth held onto Clarence's arm not to aid her but to steady Clarence who had done a lot of socializing around the bar. He was in a jolly mood and thought the three of them should continue to sing all the way home. Elizabeth and Claire passed on that idea but Clarence was not to be deterred as he belted out a solo version of *Deck the Halls*. Claire noticed that the Nuttings and the Graves, who were almost to their own houses, turned around to see who was bellowing.

Clarence offered Claire his arm so they headed home three abreast. He had toned it down to a loud hum but was still having quite the good time. "Doesn't Lila have a lovely home?" Elizabeth said, trying to draw Claire's attention from her staggering husband.

Clarence turned his head to Claire, "And did you get to that hideous red bathroom? Isn't that the most revolting thing you've ever seen?"

"That's not very nice," Elizabeth said embarrassed by her husband's candor.

Laughing he continued, "Now, you know it's true. That room is a nightmare. Lila spent a lot of money on the other rooms. When she wanted to redo that bathroom Chester told her that they couldn't afford the cost of another professional decorator. So Lila promised that she could do it by herself. He told her she didn't have an artistic bone in her body and she insisted she could. So he told her to go ahead." He rolled his head back, laughing heartily, almost causing him to lose his balance. Elizabeth and Claire tightened their grip on him.

"Once it was done Chester hated it but he didn't tell her because she would insist that they should have it professionally redone. I think she made it that way just for that reason. Now neither one of them will give in, so they live with that mess. Chester will not even use that bathroom. He says he'd rather climb the stairs than go into that red devil room."

Now they were in front of Claire's house. She looked at Elizabeth and mouthed, "Do you need help?" Elizabeth mouthed back, "No thank you."

As she stepped onto the porch, Claire heard Elizabeth reprimanding Clarence. "That story was supposed to stay in the family. Now I suppose everyone will know." Considering the state he was in, Claire doubted that Clarence cared. He might feel differently in the morning but now he was feeling no pain. The next time that Claire saw Elizabeth she would have to assure her that their story would be safe with her.

With Christmas less than a week away, the quilting group held a Christmas tea at Claire's house instead of having its regular meeting. She had not done any entertaining since moving to Hayward and was a little nervous. Even though she knew these ladies quite well by now, and they were all very positive and friendly, she still was concerned about having everything perfect. Since Claire was leaving for Michigan on Thursday, she had baked the same things she had made for her family for years. There was a variety of holiday cookies as well as three different kinds of breads – pineapple, cranberry and apricot. And, of course, she made her favorite, fudge. She liked to eat the cooled fudge but what she really liked was eating the warm gooey fudge that was left in the pot after most of it had been poured into a pan to cool. And, of course, she always purposely left more in the cooking pot than she should have. Dennis never had caught on to why she always made the fudge after he went to bed until the year their son took a picture of Claire with her new daughter-in-law participating in the late night fudge eating splurge. Claire figured that doing this just once a year wasn't going to kill her.

The foods were on trays on the dining room table, the good china and silver were out and the coffee and tea were ready when the first guests arrived. In fact, they all came at the same time. It was almost as if they had met down the street before coming to the door. The ladies piled their coats in Claire's arms after they came through the door and with a nod of her head she directed them toward the food. Everyone chose a variety of treats and then found a seat in the living room. It always amazed her how people would eat so much more during the Christmas season than they would ever choose to eat at other times of the year.

"Your house looks so festive," said Betty. "And your tree is perfect in front of the window."

"I thought you said that you weren't going to decorate a tree this year," commented Grace.

"I didn't think I would but the more I thought about I decided that it just wouldn't seem right without one. I have had one in my house every year that I remember, so I decided that this would not be the year to break with tradition."

The ladies talked about their Christmas plans and about interesting gifts they had purchased. Some of them even shared what they were hoping to get. For the most part, their requests were quite simple – a slow cooker, a set of knives with a wooden block holder, the new edition of the *Iowa Delicious and Simple* cookbook. About the most personal gift that was mentioned was a new set of bathroom rugs complete with a toilet seat cover.

Then someone brought it up – the diamond ring. Claire knew these ladies never would have let the surprise slip if Elizabeth had been there. But several of them had been at the Hayward gala on Saturday and had heard Lila comment about the ring and then had heard Clarence's shushing right after that.

"I wonder if Elizabeth suspects that she is getting that ring?" asked Meredith. "I can't image that she would have asked for one. That just doesn't sound like something she would put on her list."

"I really don't know him well, but I never saw Clarence as a big spender. I always got the impression that he was pretty thrifty," said Vernina. "I don't mean that he is a miser but he and Elizabeth just don't spend money the way I think a banker and his wife would, don't you know."

"And if we're talking about spending money, how about that piano of Lila's?" asked Phoebe. "I know pianos and that one is a dandy. It was an absolute delight to play. I couldn't give you an exact figure but I can tell you that it was very expensive."

"I think I heard Lila say something about some new investments that Chester and Clarence had. Oh, that I should invest and do that well," said Ellen.

"Investments can be pretty risky," added Betty. "I feel more secure with government bonds."

There were some more comments about the pros and cons of investing, which then lead to talk about budgets and then to secret stashes of cash that most of these housewives had. Claire was a little surprised until most of them said that was the source of money they used to buy gifts for their husbands at Christmas and birthdays. Since she had worked most of her adult life she had never had to stash money for occasions like these. Claire momentarily thought this interesting. And then she remembered that she, too, had saved change from the grocery store in a sock. She had forgotten all about it and had the urge to run upstairs and rummage through her sock drawer to see if it was still there.

As the party broke up the ladies thanked Claire for hosting the get-together and holiday wishes were passed around. After the last guest had left, Claire closed the door and turned to look at the plates and cups that needed to be washed and the remainder of the food to put away. But she knew she had to get her priorities in order so she rushed up the stairs and into her bedroom. She pulled open the bottom drawer of the dresser and rummaged through the pairs of socks. And then she found them, the red argyles. Claire gently unfolded the socks and there in the middle, carefully folded, was a group of bills. She unfolded them and counted out a total of one hundred and twenty dollars. She sat on the floor holding that money that had been tucked away for years and started to laugh.

"I guess I fit in with these women more than I thought I did."

The women of Hayward were not the only ones whose interest had been aroused. Across the square, some of the gentlemen of the town were asking questions, too. At Maude's, the Lavelle brothers were taking their morning coffee break from the furniture store when Bud Hornsby walked in and joined them.

"Howdy, Bud, how are you doing? It was good to visit with you the other night," said Floyd.

"Lila and Chester sure know how to throw a party, don't they?" commented Bud. "They always have such good food. I don't know about you two, but I sure ate too much."

"Yeah, the food was something and so was that piano. Whew! That must have set Chester back a little. What do you think that cost him?" asked Lloyd.

"I have no idea but I'd sure like to know just what Lila was talking about when she mentioned Chester's investments," said Bud.

Lloyd and Floyd looked at each other with a puzzled look on their faces.

Bud continued, "You must not have heard her comment as people were leaving. She said something about this investment, whatever it was, being a windfall. Then she made some comment about Clarence being involved, too, and using his money to buy a diamond ring for Elizabeth. But that part is supposed to be a secret so don't mention that to anyone."

Floyd thought for a moment. "I wonder how willing one of them might be to share their secret."

"I would sure be willing to listen if they are willing to talk," said Lloyd.

The three sat quietly sipping their coffee. Finally the silence was broken when Bud said, "So which one of us is going to talk to them?" Again there was silence. They all wanted to know but not one of them had the nerve to ask.

"We could draw straws, if we had any," Floyd said smiling.

Maude came over to their table and topped off their cups, "Can I get you gents anything else?"

"That should do it, Maude. Thanks," said Bud. As she walked away he suggested, "In lieu of straws, how about this? Whoever Maude sets the check closest to will be the one to ask either Chester or Clarence. What do you think?"

The Lavelle brothers nodded in agreement. Then all three sat waiting nervously for Maude's return. When she did, she diplomatically placed the check in the middle of the table. The three sat and looked at it. "Well," said Lloyd, "I guess that didn't help a lot, did it?"

"Oh, I'll ask," said Bud and pointing to the bill added, "but one of you gets to take care of the check. I'll let you know if I learn anything. I've got to get back to the store. Talk to you later."

Bud left the restaurant while Lloyd and Floyd resolved the current problem by doing what they had done for years to make decisions. They played a round of rock, paper, scissors. Floyd won with his rock breaking Lloyd's scissors. He laughed and handed the bill to his brother. "Here you go. If we get in on Chester's big investment, I'll get the next one."

Frank Felton sat nervously in the chair while Tim Payne looked in his open mouth. "How did you say you broke your tooth?" Tim asked.

"I bit into something the wrong way at the Hayward's the other night."

"It doesn't look too bad. I think we can take care of that pretty easily. Just relax, Frank."

It might have been easy for Tim to relax but Frank's anxiety only increased as Tim raised a large needle and readied it in front of Frank's face. "Open up," said Tim with a smile. "I'll let that work for awhile." Tim left the room for a few minutes then returned and sat on the stool next to the reclined Frank. Tim started the repair work and the talking at the same time. "That was a very nice party the other night. Lots of good food. Or maybe you don't feel quite that way about it. Anyway, I enjoyed it. And what about that new big piano? That was something, wasn't it?"

With the dentist's hands in his mouth it was impossible for Frank to respond to any of these questions. All he mustered was a very small nod of his head. "I know I wouldn't have room for it in my house. How about you, Frank, would you have room for that?" Another nod from Frank. "I would like to know what a piano like that costs. What do you think Chester had to pay for that?" This time Frank just shrugged. "We're surely not paying him that kind of money to be our mayor, are we?" Tim said laughing. "I guess the Hayward-owned businesses in town must be doing really well." At this point, Frank held up his hand. "Did you need to spit?"

"No, I need to talk. Didn't you hear about Lila's comment at the end of the party? She said something about Chester's new investments paying off really well. And then there was some comment about a diamond ring, too. Whatever that investment was, I sure wish I had a piece of it." Frank opened his mouth again and Tim returned to his repair job.

"Did she say anything about what kind of an investment it was? Did she give any clues?" Frank, of course, said nothing. "I wonder if we could find out. Maybe your wife could ask Lila. I'd ask my wife to ask her, if I had a wife." He stopped work long enough for an answer.

"I don't think that would work," said Frank. "Gladys has never been too fond of Lila, if you know what I mean. I can't imagine her cozying up to Lila to ask her about anything like that." Tim knew exactly what Frank meant about Lila but he didn't want to say so since he figured it might be good not to reveal how he felt about the honorable, and apparently prosperous, mayor's wife. "I think you know Chester better than I do. And I think it might sound more respectable if a professional like a doctor or dentist asked instead of a clothier."

"Lean back and open up. Let me think about that. It might just be about time for Chester's annual checkup. Maybe I could see if he would want to come in for a cleaning. Okay, I'll see what I can do."

"Hello."

"Hello, Mom."

"Rita, Rita, is that really you, baby?"

"It's really me, Mom. Mom, please don't cry. Please."

"Oh Rita, are you all right? I've been so worried about you. Why did you leave in such a hurry without even telling me goodbye? Where are you?"

"I've missed you, Mom. I'm sorry that I couldn't tell you we were leaving but I just couldn't."

"Lots of people asked about you right after you left."

"What'd you tell them?"

"I didn't tell them anything? How could I? I don't know anything, Rita."

"Are you doing okay? Is your back feeling better?"

"I'm doing okay. My back is about the same, but I would be better if I was sure that you were okay. Where are you, anyway?"

"I can't tell you, Mom. I wish I could. I will tell you that it sure gets cold and icy here."

"I suppose Tony is there, too. I never did like him or trust him, either. When are you coming home, baby? Give me your number so I can call you, please."

"I don't know when I'll be home, Mom. And don't call me. I'll try to call you again. Bye, Mom. I love you. Oh, and Mom, Merry Christmas."

"Did you get that?"

"Yeah, I got it. But it's not worth nothin'. About all I know now is that it ain't Florida, Arizona or Hawaii."

Fourteen

Claire's Christmas trip to Michigan, where all of the children and grandchildren had been together, had been wonderful, and it was hard to leave growing grandchildren. But it was also good to get home. She had thought about Jane quite often, so after depositing Christmas gifts and suitcases, calling her was the number one priority.

The phone was picked up after the first ring. "Hello."

"Hi, Jane, it's Claire. How are you doing?"

"I am so glad that you're back. I'm going stir crazy," Jane answered in a mournful tone.

"I thought your parents were there to keep you company?"

"Oh, they were here all right. I love my parents dearly but a week at Thanksgiving and two and a half weeks at Christmas was almost more that I could take. My mom would let me do nothing,"

"I kind of thought that was the idea when you are supposed to be on bed rest."

"Yeah, but she didn't let me have a say in anything, either. She picked the menu for Christmas Eve and Christmas without even asking what I wanted."

In somewhat of a surprised tone Claire said, "I guess I figured that what you chose to prepare for your family would have been somewhat similar to the traditions you had while growing up. I know we always had the same menu that my mother had fixed for both Thanksgiving and Christmas."

"You obviously did not grow up with my family. They had very consistent ideas about Christmas Eve dinners. We always had twelve courses, allegedly one course for each of the disciples."

"I think that sounds like a very nice idea. What was wrong with that?"

"Probably nothing if you liked fish. The house smelled of fish for days because almost all twelve courses contained some kind of fish. There was herring prepared in more ways than you ever dreamed that it could be fixed. There was perch and sole and oysters. Yuck! I could hardly wait to get married so I could get away from all of that fish."

"Oh poor little Jane," Claire said, feigning sympathy. "After I get acclimated and organized I'll come over and we'll do something fun. Did I miss anything interesting?"

"Let me think." After a pause Jane said, "Nothing really much. Old Zeke Myers did too much celebrating on New Years Eve and started playing his trombone in the square. From what Betty said they would have let it go if he had just played for a minute or two at midnight but when it went on and on, Leonard went out and asked him to stop. I guess Zeke yelled at Leonard that he was a terrible doctor and an interfering old busybody and told him that he was not going to stop. So Leonard called Butch Johnson. When the sheriff arrived Zeke didn't want to cooperate with him, either. Betty said that Butch ended up chasing Zeke around the square and was surprised that Zeke could run that fast, especially since he was so drunk."

"I'm glad I missed that," Claire commented. "Have you talked to Elizabeth since Christmas? Did she say anything about the diamond ring?"

"She came to visit a couple of days before Christmas but didn't have it on then. When I talked to Betty yesterday I didn't think to ask. But Jim said that the neighborhood scuttlebutt has been about the piano and the investments that I guess Lila said something about. He did the mail deliveries the week before Christmas. He does that every year because everyone is happy to get Christmas cards and they are happy to see him coming. He says they are not so happy to get mail in January when the bills come. Anyway, he said lots of people wanted to talk about those mysterious investments, but he didn't get any real information. He said lots of people have ideas about how they got that money. But as far as Jim can figure, no one except Clarence and Chester know for sure."

"I guess it is really none of our business, is it?" Claire commented.

"No, not really, but it would sure be nice to have some extra money, especially with another little person on the way."

"It was good to talk to you and I'm glad that you are doing okay – bored maybe, but okay. You be good and I'll talk to you later."

"I didn't realize it was time for my checkup already," said Chester as he climbed into the chair.

"You had been coming once a year but I think that at your age it's important to start coming every six months or so," answered Dr. Payne.

"Then I guess I should get Lila to come in, too, shouldn't I?"

"Oh, yeah, well... I'll give her a call to set up an appointment."

Tim took more time than usual with this cleaning process. He was trying to find the right way to bring up the subject that was really on his mind. In the meantime he verbally danced around the topic, chatting about almost everything else he could think of. And since Chester couldn't talk much with the cleaning apparatus in his mouth, the conversation was pretty much one-sided.

As he finished and removed the paper bib from around Chester's neck, he could put it off no longer. "That was a great party you and Lila had before Christmas. As usual, you outdid yourself with the food. And that piano is beautiful! Was that Lila's Christmas present?"

"She had wanted a grand piano for a long time, and things just worked out that this was the year."

"When I was leaving I heard her say something about some investments you had made. They must have been good ones if that is what let you get the piano."

"Yeah, I guess they did pretty well."

"Boy, I sure wish I could find some good investments. I would like to do some updating of this office but I can't see that happening very soon without some extra cash."

Trying to act indifferent, Chester looked around. "Yup, you could stand to make some changes around here."

"I know some people don't like to talk about their finances but I would sure appreciate it if you could give me some advice on how I could make a little extra. Frank Felton and I were talking and he's really interested, too."

Chester's eyes continued to wander around the room as if he was not one bit interested in Tim's request. After a few moments he said, "I'll have to think about it, Tim. I'll have to talk it over with my financial advisor. I'll get back to you." Chester ran his tongue over his teeth. "They feel great, Tim. Thanks for getting me in." As he grabbed his coat and opened the door he looked back and added, "Just send me the bill."

As the door closed, Tim quietly said, "Oh, don't worry. I certainly will."

The call from his secretary had told him who was coming through his office door. "Come on in, Bud. How are you doing?"

"Great, just great," answered Bud.

"What can I do for you? You have that look in your eye."

"Well, Clarence, I just thought I'd let you be the first to know that I am supposed to get three new cars in toward the end of the week, a Mustang convertible, a Thunderbird and a Torino. That Mustang would be a nice little gift for Elizabeth."

"I'm sure she would love it but I did splurge on her at Christmas." Clarence, thinking that everyone in town had probably heard about the ring, paused and waited for Bud to comment. Instead Bud played unaware and just looked at Clarence, waiting for him to continue.

Clarence obliged. "I surprised her with a diamond ring."

"Oh yeah, I think I did hear Ellen say something about that." Bud paused. "Now that makes a little sense."

"What makes sense?"

"I had heard rumors about your making some good investments. I didn't think much about it but I guess there must be some truth to those rumors. I sure wish I could find a way to make some solid investments. With a family it would be good to be able to build up some money for college and some extras, too." He stopped there, trying to read Clarence to know how hard to push. "Would you be willing to share your secrets? I'd really like to check into it if you would."

"I don't know. Some investments can be pretty risky, especially for a family man. If I were to let you in on what I know, you would really need to think it over. I'm not promising anything, but I'll think about it. And there is someone else I need to check with. I'll get back to you."

"I appreciate that, Clarence, I really do. And by the way, pass the word about those new cars coming in, will you? They're real beauts."

There were a few things that Claire needed at the drugstore. The bell over the door jingled when she entered. "Good morning, aaah… Claire?"

"Good morning, Ron. I'm surprised to see you. I thought you were back in school."

"I'm here to intern with Uncle Rudy. What can I do for you today?"

"I just came in for some odds and ends, but I know where they are."

"Just holler if you need me," he said as he walked to the back of the store.

She was getting the last thing on her list when she heard the bell jingle again. She looked up to see Meredith and Clara coming in. Clara headed to the soda fountain while Meredith headed toward the makeup. Claire walked over to Meredith. "I see you survived the holidays."

"Oh, hi, Claire. Yes, we had a very nice time. How about you?"

"I had a wonderful time. It was fantastic to have that time with the grandchildren, but they sure wore me out. I feel as if I'll need a week or two to recover." She looked over at the counter where Clara was shaking her finger in Ron's face. "I guess Clara must be setting Ron straight on how to make her fountain order."

"It looks like it. And I'll bet he'll never forget whatever it is she is telling him."

"Maybe I'll go over and say hello."

Meredith laughed. "Good idea. I think Ron would be thankful for that."

Claire walked over and sat on the seat next to Clara, who jumped when she saw Claire out of the corner of her eye. "Geez, don't scare an old lady like that. You need to wear a bell or something."

"I'm sorry, Clara, I didn't mean to startle you. I just came over to say hello. How was your Christmas? Did you get everything you wanted?"

"You must be kidding. I think I got every old lady gift they could find – an apron, house slippers that look like they came from some nursing home, a housedress that looks like something my mother would have worn, and a box of hankies. Have they never heard of Kleenexes? And then there were the soft center candies. Not even a caramel in the whole box. I still have darn good teeth and they're all mine, too. See." Clara turned, opened her mouth and gnashed her teeth a couple of times. "And there wasn't even any chocolate, either!"

As if on cue, Ron showed up with the chocolate shake she had ordered. "Extra thick with double chocolate and no straw?" Claire asked.

"Yeah. I hope he'll be able to remember that like Rudy does," Clara said, nodding toward Ron.

"Oh, I'm sure he will," Claire said smiling at Ron who winked at her in return and then walked away. "What were you hoping to get for Christmas?"

"A piece."

"A piece? A piece of what?" she innocently asked.

"Don't you know anything? A gun, I wanted my own gun, a real gun."

The thought of that made Claire shudder. Two senior citizens running around with real weapons did not seem like the best thing for Hayward or its residents. By now Meredith had walked up to the counter.

"Mother, you do not need a gun."

"Well, if that old coot down the street can have one I don't see why I can't. This town is scary. That old coot and those two crooks down the street and that killer dog at the corner. We all should be packing heat to protect ourselves."

"You've been watching too much television. The Brocks are not crooks and Mellow isn't dangerous. He's just loud. Besides, you know that Davy gave you that new squirt gun. And it looks very real. Show it to Claire."

Clara gave Meredith a disgusted look and then reached in her purse, pulled out and held it up in Claire's face. "Wow! That looks pretty real to me. I think that would fool a lot of people."

At that moment, Ron walked by, looked at Clara and her gun and threw up his hands. "I give up!" he said. "Take all of the chocolate you want."

Clara just glared at him. "See what I mean. I couldn't fool even the kid."

Ron put down his hands and glared back at her, not appreciative of her reference to his being young. He got over his irritation quickly and said, "No, Clara, I think that looks pretty real. I think you could hold off someone with that."

Claire got up from her stool as Clara shoved the squirt gun back in her purse. She took her few purchases to the cash register where Ron totaled them. "I'll bet it's always interesting in here, isn't it?"

"You're right," Ron said smiling. "Never a dull moment."

William sat fidgeting with his cup of coffee, waiting for Clarence to return to his office. When he got the call from Chester, he didn't know exactly why Chester and Clarence wanted to meet with him. He was worried that it might be bad news about their investment group although there had been nothing in the tone of Chester's voice to indicate any trouble. One of the bank employees had shown him to the office while telling him that Mr. Lambert had not yet arrived for the day. Now the longer he had to wait, the more concerned he became. After what seemed like hours, when actually it was only minutes, Clarence came into the office followed by Chester.

William rose as they entered and there were handshakes all around. "Glad you could come, William. We have some things to talk about." William's knees were shaking as he returned to his seat. "Mike is coming, too. I guess we could talk a few things over before he comes." William was feeling a bit better noticing that Clarence and Chester seemed calm and unconcerned. Chester continued, "Has anyone asked you about our investments?"

"Well, no. But then no one knows but you two, and of course, Mike, do they?"

Chester answered, "As far as I know, nobody but the four of us knows anything about it except that Clarence and I came into some money. The thing is, William, both Clarence and I have had inquiries about how we got that money."

The phone on Clarence's desk rang. "Yes? Have him come in."

A couple of seconds later the door opened and in walked Mike. The smile that he entered with disappeared when he saw the three serious faces looking at him. Momentarily he worried that maybe they had put their dull money-hungry brains together and figured out the truth. Trying to quickly compose himself, he made the rounds, shaking hands and greeting all three. "This looks pretty serious. Did someone die?"

Chester broke a faint smile, "Oh no, nothing like that. We just had a couple of questions to ask you."

Mike was still uneasy. He pulled up a chair, tried to act nonchalant and asked, "What did you want to know?"

"First we need to explain. Thanks to a comment that my wife made a few weeks ago, both Clarence and I have had, shall I say, 'inquiries' about how we made the money to purchase the grand piano and Elizabeth's ring. Some others in town are wondering if they could get in on the information about our investments."

"And what did you gentlemen tell them?" questioned Mike.

Chester and Clarence looked at each other. Clarence answered, "We both said the same thing. We told them that we would get back to them. We knew that we would need to talk it over with William and you first. In fact, this is the first he has heard about it."

Mike turned to William. "So now that all three of you know, what do you think?"

A variety of questions were posed. "Will more people cut into our profits?" "Would more investors make more money?" "How many more people would it be wise to include?" "Do we want to alienate some of our friends by turning them down?"

After the last question, Mike jumped in. "Or do you want to alienate those friends if the investments don't pay off and they blame you. You have to admit that you were very lucky to turn that big profit as fast as you did. You, and they, have to realize that investments like this can go south just as easily. If we did take in more investors I would manage all of the investments just as I did for you. I think it is basically up to the three of you whether you want to increase the size of your group. If you decide to, we would need to get together with the others and bluntly explain to them that investments like this can be risky. Money can be lost just as easily as it can be made. You know who these people are. You know better than I do about their financial situations and how any losses might hurt them. I'll leave the final decision up to you. What I think I'll do is just head back over to Bud's so you can talk it over. You can let me know what you decide. If it's yes, we can go from there." Mike stood up. "I will talk to you gentlemen later. Have a good day."

Mike walked out, closing the door behind him. "Well, what do you think?" asked Chester.

"Tell me who wants in," said William.

"Doc Payne talked to me," said Chester, "and said something about Frank Felton being interested. Also, my brother Charles has been fishing for information."

"Bud talked to me. It was really hard to keep from telling him that the information was right under his nose."

William thought for a minute. "Tim's dental practice seems to be doing okay but I don't know much about Frank. And I'm sure that there is a lot of income from the grain elevator that your family owns." When he said this he looked at Chester who averted his glance. "Bud's dealership only seems to be growing so he could probably handle some loss, if necessary. But I'll bet there is someone in this room who would know better than I who has the financial backing to get involved. But I know there are confidentiality factors so I won't ask."

"Thanks," said Clarence.

"I guess it wouldn't hurt to meet with the others but I think we need to stress that we don't want them talking about it to anyone else. I think we need to keep this as hush-hush as possible."

"I agree. How about you, William?"

"Sounds okay to me."

"Okay, I'll call Bud and we can set up a meeting with the others."

William stood up. "Just let me know when and I'll see you then." He breathed a sigh of relief as he walked toward the front door of the bank, feeling much more secure and relaxed than he had when he entered.

Claire had never been overly fond of cold, icy weather but the spell of extremely frigid temperatures with highs in the single digits seemed to have broken and the temperatures in the twenties were very welcome. Her agreeing with the boys to get together for an ice skating party had meant that she had one less meeting activity to organize. The Cubs had decided to meet at the small lake just off of the creek by the city park. On this rare occasion she had driven and not walked to the park. She knew it would be impossible to carry the large thermos she had borrowed from the church. Just before leaving home, Claire had filled it with hot chocolate and had packed cups, chocolate bars, graham crackers, and marshmallows into a bag.

Shortly after parking as close as she could get to the little lake, the boys started arriving. They came in threes. Claire wasn't sure if that was because of location of their houses or their preferences as friends. It had never appeared to her that some boys got along better with certain others. They all seemed to be one happy, jovial little bunch. Jeff, Johnny and Joey arrived a couple of minutes before Jerry, Bobby and Gary.

"Hi, Mrs. Menefee," the first three boys said almost in unison.

"Hello, boys, it's good to see you again. Did you have a nice Christmas?"

As the boys related what they had received, the other three joined them and added to the conversation. While they talked they pulled off boots and put on skates. Luckily others had used the lake for skating before they arrived and had shoveled the snow that had fallen during the holiday storms. Claire had no doubt, however, that there would have been six volunteers to do that job since two large shovels lay by the discarded piles of snow.

"When are you going to put on your skates?" asked Joey.

"I don't have skates anymore," she answered.

"What'd you do with them?" questioned Gary.

"I'll run home and get my mom's," said Joey and then as he looked at the size of Claire's feet added, "or my dad's. They wouldn't mind."

"That is a very nice offer, but I don't skate anymore."

Six little faces looked up at her in disbelief. She had heard that skating was a big wintertime activity here since the lake and usually the creek were frozen for weeks at a time. The looks on those faces affirmed that.

"Well, the last time I went skating I fell and got hurt."

Now she really had their interest. Boys always seemed to be interested in injuries and Claire thought they were hoping for something pretty major and bloody. She could have dramatized the event to make it more to their liking but instead kept the story simple and to the point. "I broke my wrist, had a severe concussion and a slight skull fracture."

"Cool!" said Bobby.

"Did your head bleed a lot when it cracked?" asked Jerry.

"Did your bones poke through your arm?" asked Gary.

"Wow! I bet that hurt!" said Joey, shaking his head as if to shake off the thought of the pain.

Claire answered all of the questions and added, "Since then I have had no desire to skate. But I'll bet you are all ready to go." She didn't have to say anything else as they were off their bottoms and onto their skates in a flash of silvery blades. She was impressed with the skating ability of these young boys and wondered at what age most children learned to skate around here. She figured that skates were probably passed around from family to family as they were outgrown. Claire had not had skates until she was in high school, when she convinced her parents that she would use them whenever the lake a few blocks from their house was frozen. She got the skates and did use them with her friends when the ice was solid, but unfortunately that was not all that frequently. So her skating abilities were not very good. And even as an adult she could never have matched what these boys were doing.

Since she had started working with the boys Claire had witnessed many moments of male horse play – pushing, shoving, punching, and tickling – but on skates they managed to keep their hands and feet off each other, with the exception of an occasional game of tag, played with a surprising sense of restraint so the tagging was done gently and caused no one to fall. Oh, there were some falls but they were all part of skating and of six boys experimenting with new moves and trying to impress. It was very pleasant just to sit and watch for awhile.

Claire could have watched longer but then she remembered that she needed to get a fire going. She had set everything down by one of the cooking pits so she didn't have to go very far away to start one. She didn't need a large fire, just one big enough to get some good coals for toasting marshmallows. As the fire got going Claire realized that she was cold. She had not even thought of it as she watched the boys skate. Sitting by this new warmth added to the ambiance of the afternoon.

The fire was starting to turn to coals at just about the right time and Claire gave the boys a five minute warning. When the five minutes was up she told them it was time to stop skating. There were some complaints until Claire said, "Oh, that's fine with me. That means I get more hot chocolate and will get to have all these smores myself." She didn't have to ask again as it became a race to see who could get skates off and boots on the fastest. The boys needed no directions on how to make smores. Claire figured that was something that every Boy Scout, Girl Scout and Camp Fire Girl must know. Claire passed on the smores, choosing to eat her marshmallows and chocolate squares in their original forms.

When everyone was finished, they all helped clean up and made sure that the fire was safely out. As they were almost finished loading things back into the bag, Bobby looked up at Claire very seriously, his arms held innocently behind his back. "Mrs. Menefee, I know you don't do ice skating anymore, but I'll bet you still do snowballs." The angelic look instantly disappeared from his face as his hands came out from behind his back and unleashed two snowballs at the same time. One hit her in the shoulder.

"You bet I do!" Claire said as she picked up some snow and formed it into a ball as quickly possible. The group spread out in different directions as snowballs flew hither and yon. Claire seemed to be the major target but luckily the throwing skills of these boys did not equal their skating abilities. The majority of missiles aimed in her direction missed. She, on the other hand, managed to land some good hits. After a few minutes she called a truce and decreed that it was time for a brush off. They all stood in a circle and brushed the snow from each other's backs. Then they all walked back to her car while some of the boys helped carry the supplies. She offered to give them a ride home, predicting that no one would accept the offer. She was right; no one did. After saying goodbye the little groups of threes headed off for home. Claire sat watching from her car for a few minutes. And for a moment, a fleeting moment, she hoped that Jane was not in a hurry to return as den mother after the baby came. Then she saw the pushing and shoving and punching return as the threesomes walked away and decided that maybe she would just volunteer to babysit instead.

The three partners were curious to see who the other interested men would be. They knew about Charles, of course, who was sitting in the Haywards' living room waiting for the others to arrive. "Thanks for setting this up, Chester," William Swan said. "Your coffee is even good. Did you do this all yourself or did Lila have to show you how to work the coffee pot?"

"I sent Lila on a shopping trip to get her out of the way. I knew that if she overheard any of this that it would not be long before everyone in town knew."

"Good plan, but I'm sorry that Elizabeth went with her. Sometimes Lila's enthusiasm for shopping is contagious and Elizabeth comes home with stuff that she really doesn't need," said Clarence.

"But haven't you learned after being married all of these years that what may seem unimportant to you might be important to your wife?" replied Chester.

William laughed. "I wasn't married for many years before Elaine died, but I learned that lesson fast. She wasn't a big shopper but she did buy some quirky things. I often didn't like the things she bought to set around the house as decorations but I figured that she spent lots more time in the house than I did so she should decorate the way she wanted. Had she tried to decorate my office, however, I would have had a few things to say about that."

They sat making small talk while they waited for the others to arrive. When the doorbell rang, the other three looked at each other momentarily while Chester went to open the door. They listened to the voices at the door and recognized one as that of Tim Payne. His was easy since they heard it a lot on their visits to his office. The other turned out to be Frank Felton. The men greeted each other with handshakes all around. The two newcomers barely had been seated when the doorbell rang again. Now the five looked at each other, listening. This time it was the Lavelle brothers, Floyd and Lloyd.

They came in, shook hands and sat down with the others. Except for brief conversations about the weather and the upcoming Super Bowl game, there was uncomfortable silence. Chester didn't sit but paced back and forth in front of the door. The bell rang for the third time. The newcomers were very curious about who would be coming in next but the originals knew who was still to show. This time it was Bud Hornsby. He entered the room and greeted those already seated. "Were you all waiting for me? Was I holding up the meeting? I was closing a deal on that new Torino. I didn't want to leave until I got the signature on that lovely sales agreement. I left Mike to turn over the keys."

The big three all nodded their heads. Chester passed out coffee to the six newcomers and placed a plate of cookies on the table in front of the couch. When Chester sat down he cleared his throat and said, "We could start now but we are waiting for one more person. I would prefer to have that person explain everything to all of you." The would-be investors looked around the room sizing up who was there and wondering who was still to come. They were all thinking the same thing – who else in this town would have information on investments or projects big enough to make serious money? They were all nervous but tried not to let it show. Finally the bell rang again and Chester rose to open the door.

"Hello, come on in," said Chester motioning for the mystery person to go in to the living room.

Most of the group looked up in surprise when Mike Brock entered the room, everyone but Bud. "Mike, did I forget something in the Torino deal? I thought I had given you both sets of keys and a copy of all of the paper work."

Smiling Mike answered. "You did, boss. But that's not why I'm here." Bud now understood and was just as surprised as were the other five. Chester motioned to an empty seat and offered Mike coffee and cookies. He declined both as he confidently sat down, leaned back in his chair and crossed his legs. He sized up the group as they silently stared at him, still in a state of shock. He waited to speak, not knowing if Chester was going to make one of his long-winded speeches or if he was just supposed to start. Chester must have had similar thoughts, for they both began talking at the same time. "After you, Mr. Mayor," Mike courteously said, tipping his head toward Chester with deference.

"Here is our financial genius," Chester said, tilting his head toward Mike. "Clarence, Will and I appreciate what he has done for us so far. You were curious and wanted to know about it, so Mike is here to explain."

Mike stood up and gave pretty much the same explanation that he had given to the big three about two months before. He told them of his background and offered to show them his licenses and registration forms as well as some the statements from his investments.

"I saw them and checked them over. They were all in order," interjected Clarence with a voice of authority and expertise.

Mike went on to explain how their investment group had been set up, pointing out that he himself was one of the investors. Then he emphasized the risk just as he had to the original three. "You need to be fully aware that there are no guarantees. You could lose your investment just as easily as you could make money, maybe even easier. I am sure you must have questions."

The six would-be investors sat for a few moments as if formulating their questions. There were not many and Mike was able to readily provide answers. Then came the big question from Tim, "Just how much money are we talking about here?"

"I think it only fair that any additional investors come in with at least the same amount that the founding three did, "Ten thousand each. And I put in twenty thousand myself."

"Whew, that's a lot of dough," said Frank.

"I know, and that is something you really need to think about. If you can't afford to lose it, then don't risk it," said Mike with a sympathetic tone. "You don't have to decide right now. Go home and think it over."

"When do you need to know?" asked Floyd.

"Let's see. This is Saturday. How about letting Chester know by Tuesday? If you're in, can everyone come up with the money by Thursday?" asked Mike.

Clarence nodded, but Mike couldn't tell if he was agreeing with the suggestion or verifying that he knew they could come up with that amount by then.

"Does anyone else have any questions?" There was dead silence. Mike didn't know if that was because the men truly had no questions or if they were still in shock about the ten thousand. "Since you all seem to understand and have nothing to ask, I think I'll head home. I haven't eaten lunch yet. My boss is quite the slave driver, you know." He smiled at Bud as he spoke. Then he shook hands with each of the prospective partners and left.

"Who would have ever guessed!" commented Bud.

"Yeah, I figured the mastermind must have been you, Clarence," said Lloyd.

The men sat and talked for a few more minutes, now feeling more comfortable to ask questions of their old friends and acquaintances than of someone they had known for just a few months. William told them that the three had made a fast profit of $1,500 after just a few weeks. That was indeed a solid selling point for the newcomers. Chester reminded them to let him know by Tuesday whether or not they were in. "And one more thing, I think we should keep all of this just between those of us in this room. And I think that should include wives. I know my wife has a habit of blabbing when she should just keep her mouth shut."

"And we are sure glad that she does," said Tim, "or we wouldn't be here right now. But I guess Lloyd, Floyd and I won't have to worry about that. I knew there had to be some advantage to being single."

The group broke up and the men walked together until they broke off to go to their businesses. Visions of dollar signs danced in their heads as they thought much more about the gains they might have rather than the losses they could face. But then that was the positive, optimistic attitude of the people of Hayward. They expected good things to happen and when the bad things on occasion did occur, they were used to having friends and neighbors offering support to pull them through those tough times.

Mike whistled cheerily as he walked home with his arms swinging briskly. "There's a sucker born every minute, or in this case, nine suckers," he said as he strode toward his house. He was feeling so proud of himself that he waved to his next door neighbor who was sitting on his porch, keeping vigil over the comings and goings on the block. "Howdy, Farley. Nice day for January, isn't it?" Farley looked momentarily at Mike and then started thumbing through this code book that lay in his lap. "What a nut case!" Mike said, but of course not loud enough for Farley to overhear.

He was just about to open the door when a voice called to him from behind. "Hello there, Mike. I've got some mail for you." He turned to find Jim Dunn walking towards him. "Hard to believe this is January, isn't it? Usually we have cold weather this time of year. I am darn thankful that the weather is like this and that we aren't having one of those killer ice storms like we had a year ago today. Man, you couldn't get anywhere unless you had ice skates." Jim continued to talk but Mike tuned him out and instead just focused on his face with its continuously moving mouth. "Don't you think?" Mike did catch that phrase and nodded even though he had no idea what he was agreeing with.

"Did you say you had some mail for me?" Mike asked in hopes of getting the mail carrier moving on with his route.

"I sure did. Here you go. Now you have a nice afternoon, you hear?" said Jim with his familiar smile.

"You betcha I will," answered Mike taking the letters from the outstretched hand and then without another word reached for the doorknob and entered the privacy of his home. "What a square. What's with these hicks? They are all so happy. It's just not natural. Hey, Rita, where are you?"

"No Rita here, fella. You must be in the wrong house," Missy said sarcastically poking her head around the kitchen door. "Where have you been? You're late for lunch."

"Yeah, and I'll bet I've been missing a real feast, too."

"You don't like what I fix, fix it yourself." Missy plopped a grilled ham and cheese sandwich onto a plate. "You want chips?"

"Yeah, fine. Now sit down and listen to this. I met with six more suckers at the mayor's place. They all sat staring at me while I dangled the hope of making big money in their naïve faces."

"Did they all go along?"

"I don't know yet, but I think so. They're supposed to let our illustrious mayor know by Tuesday. Here, the dufus mailman handed me the mail." While Mike ate, Missy started shuffling through the mail.

"Anything interesting?"

"No, looks like just bills."

Mike started opening the envelopes as Missy got up and started looking through the cabinets for the package of chocolate snaps that she had bought last week.

"What is this? What have you done?" Mike yelled. Missy turned around to see Mike clutching a paper in his fist. His face showed rage that Missy had seldom seen. She didn't know what he was holding or what had caused that reaction.

"What are you talking about?"

He was not yelling anymore but there was still seething in his voice. "This is the phone bill. It lists our long distance calls." Now she knew what he had seen.

"I just had to call her. I just couldn't let Christmas go by without talking to her." Missy's voice trembled. "We just talked for a minute."

"What did you tell her?"

"I didn't tell her anything, I promise. She asked me where we were and all I said was that we were okay and that it was cold here and then I said Merry Christmas. That's all. I promise." She was whimpering by now.

"Oh, don't cry. Just don't do it again. Do you understand? You can't call her again!"

"I know, Mike, I'm sorry. I won't do it again."

Mike had barely simmered down when the doorbell rang. The two stared at each other for a moment, the phone call fresh in their minds. "Do you want I should get that?" asked Missy, trying to get back on Mike's good side.

"No, I will. Try to look relaxed." Mike went to the door, wishing it had a small window so he could prepare himself for whom or what was on the other side. He quickly slid opened the drawer in the end table beside the door and then cautiously opened the door a crack. On the other side was a familiar face and Mike discretely shut the drawer. "Come on in," he said with a sigh of relief.

The visit complete, he got into his car and made a u-turn, heading back to the center of town. Rather than parking on the main street he decided to park in the small lot behind the Methodist Church. Out of habit he locked his car and then wondered if that was really necessary. He headed south on Oak, again admiring the architectural beauty of these well-maintained old residences. At Elm he intended to cross the square on his way to Maude's but changed his mind when a woman carrying grocery bags in both arms tripped as she started up the steps of the corner house. He hurried across the grass toward her. "Are you all right?" he yelled.

She looked around to see who was talking and saw a stranger almost even with her. "I'm okay, although I am a bit embarrassed."

He bent over and helped her up. "I hope you didn't have eggs in here," he said as he helped her put the groceries back into the two bags. Luckily they hadn't torn in the fall. "I'll carry this one to the door for you." When they reached the door, Claire opened it and set one of the bags on a table right inside.

"Thanks for your help. I don't believe we've met. Are you from around here?"

"No, I'm more or less passing through. An old friend of my brother lives here and I stop by just to say hi when I'm in the area."

"Well, whatever the reason, I'm glad that you came along when you did. By the way, my name is Claire."

"Nice to meet you, Claire. I'm Daniel. I'm glad I could help." He turned and headed back toward the street. "Maybe I'll see you next time through." Daniel continued on through the square toward Maude's. "This place is even more attractive than I thought it was," he said, smiling.

At Maude's the lunch rush appeared to be over. Daniel didn't head for a back table this time but instead picked a table right in front of the window, one that gave him a good view of the house on the corner. Maude presently brought him a menu and lingered for a moment. "I'm pretty good with faces," she said, hands on her hips and tilting her head from one side to another. "Weren't you in here sometime last fall?"

"Good memory, you're right." Then in hopes of not needing to offer any further explanation, he quickly asked, "What do you recommend for lunch?"

"To be honest, everything on that menu is good. But today I'd say that the pork sandwiches with the potato salad are exceptionally good."

"That sounds great. And add a cup of coffee to that, please." He handed the menu to her and she was off to place the order. It was just a minute or two before Maude was back and was artistically pouring coffee into Daniel's mug. "I have a question for you. Last time I was here, you mentioned that the town was planning a fund raiser for something, the school, I think. How did that turn out?"

"It was great! They made a lot of money, can't remember the exact amount. It just shows what can happen when the people around here work together. And that Mike Brock did a great job of being in charge of the whole thing."

"Mike Brock?"

"Yes, do you know him?"

"He's a friend of my brother. I stop and see him when I'm in the area. I just can't quite see him as being in charge of a big community project like that, but good for him."

"Yeah, his wife was supposed to be his co-chairman but I don't think she did too much to help. Not to bad mouth your friend's wife, but she just never seemed too happy about the whole thing. I think he dragged her into it."

Mike smiled slightly and nodded in response. "That must have been a big job keeping all those people working together, keeping track of expenses, counting up all the money."

"It was a big job, but he did have lots of help. And he certainly could not have kept track of all of that money by himself." Daniel nodded, making no comment but taking mental notes.

Maude went off to take care of other customers. When she returned with his lunch and he declined the addition of a dessert, Maude left his ticket and encouraged him to come back again. "And next time maybe it will be sooner than three months."

Rather than heading directly back to his car, Daniel decided to stroll the main street. He didn't get far because he had just passed the barbershop next to Maude's when the smells from the bakery were too much to resist. He was barely inside the door when he was greeted by a smiling Irene. "Good afternoon. What can I get for you?"

Daniel took his time looking at the display cases and found that there were too many delicious temptations to make a quick decision. Finally he said, "I think I'll have a brownie. No, make that two." His mouth watered as he spoke. Irene started to put them in a bag when Daniel told her to bag just one and he would eat the other one right away. He put the money on the counter and in one hand carefully took one fudgey-looking rectangle, surrounded by crisp white tissue, and in the other the white bag. Upon leaving, he struggled slightly trying to open the door without squashing his purchases.

He continued on his tour as he devoured his brownie, next passing a store with "Hayward Hardware" painted on the window. Daniel looked in the window and decided that a more appropriate name might be Hayward Hodge Podge. He saw a lot of items that were not what he would classify as hardware. "This might be a fun place to visit sometime. Maybe next trip," he thought.

A few people passed him on the sidewalk as he strolled. Everyone spoke or at least gave him a friendly smile. Even the children gave him a quick, "Hi!" Hayward Drugs was next. Daniel decided it would be good to make a quick stop and pick up some more aspirin. He quickly ran his hand across his lips to brush away any tell-tale crumbs and pushed against the door. His entry was announced by the bell and a "Howdy, how are you doing this fine day?" A smiling face was looking at him from beside the old cash register.

"I'm doing just fine. I just stopped in to pick up some aspirin."

"Oh, I hope you don't have a headache. Those can really get you down. I'll show you where they are." Daniel figured that in a store this small, finding aspirin really couldn't be that hard but he willingly followed the clerk down an aisle. "There you go. You have some different brands to choose from. I'll meet you up in front unless there is something else I can do for you."

Daniel assured him that was his only need at the time and the man disappeared around the end of the shelf. Daniel found the brand he needed, but rather than heading right back to the front, he meandered through the small, welcoming store. It reminded him of the old drug store in the town where he had been raised. As he passed the soda fountain, he paused and his eyes slowly moved from one end of the counter to the other. A slight smile appeared on his face as if seeing that counter and the accompanying red padded stools had brought back some pleasant memories.

"Can I get you a soda, a sundae, a malt, a shake? Folks around here say I make the best shakes. I also make a wicked limeade but those don't sell too well in January."

"If I had not just devoured a brownie from the bakery up the street I might take you up on that."

"I'll tell you, those Taylors and their baked goods do cut down on my fountain business in the winter. But I get even in the summer. Folks would rather have cold things for their summer treats rather than going into a hot bakery. So are you all set there with your aspirin?" Daniel paid for the small tin and, as Rudy was about to drop it into a bag, said he would just put it right in his pocket.

As he handed Daniel his change, Rudy said, "I'm sorry, I didn't introduce myself. I'm Rudy. It was nice to have you visit this afternoon. Hope you come back again soon. And I hope you don't need that aspirin for a really long time."

As Daniel left the store the bell jingled once more. "Man, these people are friendly. It must be something in the water. Or something that Rudy is slipping into the limeades." The next store was the clothing store. He looked in the window as he passed but felt no need to visit there. On the corner was a dominant feature of the street, the large white stones on the ends of the building that were in distinct contrast to the red brick. "I wonder how well Mike knows the banker. Or maybe I should wonder how well the banker knows Mike," he thought.

Daniel crossed Main Street to the end of the square. He paused for a moment, staring at the large pillared building across the street. "Now that's one heck of a library! That must have cost something to build." Rather than continuing straight across to the sidewalk on Oak, he decided to walk through the square so he could get a better view of the houses. "I can see why people would want to live here. It seems so quiet and peaceful. This part of town looks as if it was preserved in some kind of time capsule." He quickly glanced around to make sure that no one was there to hear him talking to himself.

When he was almost to the end of the square, he crossed over Oak and headed up the walk at 101. He rang the old fashioned bell and waited somewhat nervously. When the door was opened, he was greeted by a surprised look. "Hi, Claire, I brought you a little something from the bakery."

Claire opened the bag and looked in. "A brownie! How did you know that I'm crazy about chocolate?"

"You just looked like the chocolate type. I just had one and it was so good that I thought you deserved one, too. I thought it might help ease your pain or your embarrassment from your fall."

"Thank you very much. That was very thoughtful."

"I hope your husband won't mind that I brought that to you."

"My husband died a few years ago, and he was well aware that I loved chocolate."

"Well, I'd better be going." Daniel turned and headed down the steps.

"Maybe I'll see you if you come through town again."

Daniel wanted to say, "You can count on that," but all he did was wave.

Claire knew that Monday was going to be a busy day at the library. The new books that had been purchased with the fund raiser money were ready to be catalogued and shelved, and their cards needed to be added to the card catalogue. She still had classes coming in and had to prioritize her duties. She decided that it would make more sense to shelve the books in order to alleviate some of the clutter that was taking up space in the library.

She was making good progress when Mrs. Fossel's second grade class came into the library. They followed the routine of coming to the open space in the room and waiting for Claire to join them. She would have been with them sooner had not Mrs. Fossel wanted to talk.

"It certainly took a long time to get all of these books here," she said in a disgruntled tone, a tone Claire had come to know accompanied her wherever she went.

"I know that Susan did the best that she could. And believe me, there is no one who is more anxious to get these into the children's hands than she is."

Mrs. Fossel turned with a "humph" and wandered over to the stacks of books. Claire hurried over to where the girls were talking and giggling and the boys were talking and wiggling. She sat down and apologized for being late and thanked them for waiting so patiently. She hoped that by continually using the term "waiting patiently" the children some day would actually do so. She had picked a picture book about winter to read to them. Mrs. Fossel had not been pleased when in the fall Claire had started reading her students these books that she felt were too easy for them. Claire had explained that many different literary skills could be demonstrated with books like these. Mrs. Fossel didn't agree, but she was so relieved to not have to deal with her class for that brief period of time that Claire probably could have read anything to them. When she had finished reading the story, Claire took her station at the checkout desk and supervised the children as they dutifully signed their names to the cards from the book pockets and handed them to her. They then found chairs and read quietly while waiting for the entire class to finish.

"It's time to go, class," bellowed Mrs. Fossel and the children rose, pushed in their chairs and lined up in an orderly manner. Claire had the feeling that they did this as much out of fear of verbal retribution as they did because they knew it was the proper thing to do. "You may pass." The children were almost out of the library door when Claire noticed that Mrs. Fossel's arms were loaded with books. Claire hurried around the desk and caught up with her just as she reached the door.

"Excuse me, Mrs. Fossel. We would prefer that you not check those out until we have finished with them all."

"Well, excuse me, but I need these. I need to use them now, today."

Claire looked at the stack she had cradled in her arms. "But these are not ready for circulation yet. They may not leave the library."

"This is how it is. I work here and you don't. You certainly have no right to tell me what to do."

Claire forced her body, inches taller and but certainly not wider than Mrs. Fossel's, in front of her. Claire braced her feet in the doorway. Although she could not see the children since she had focused her eyes as sternly as she could on Mrs. Fossel, Claire could hear the shuffling of feet behind her. Claire straightened her shoulders, trying to add even a few more inches of height and tried to keep her voice low and calm. "No, this is how it is. At this moment I am in charge of this library and these books are part of this library and they will stay in here. If you wish, I can write down the names of these books and save them for you. Then you can have them when they are ready. But you may not take them now."

From behind her a voice whispered, "You tell her, Mrs. Menefee." She had not intended that this be a battle in front of the children. There is nothing worse than a teacher losing face in front of her class but there was a principle here and Claire was not giving in, unless she was bulldozed out of the way by Mrs. Fossel whose weight was definitely greater than hers.

"Oh here," she said, thrusting the books into Claire's midsection. "I've changed my mind. I don't want them anyway."

Claire stepped aside and Mrs. Fossel marched with her nose in the air through the crowd of small bodies that had gathered around the door. There were many wide-eyed looks from the children as they fell into line behind her as she stomped down the hall. "Way to go, Mrs. Menefee," said one boy as he walked by. Claire had a feeling that the atmosphere in that classroom would not be very pleasant for the rest of the day. But then she remembered something she had found out about Mrs. Fossel. "Maybe she'll feel better after she takes her lunchtime nap," Claire said and headed back to return this load to the other new books.

The quilting group was well underway with a totally new pattern that had been started in November right after the fund raiser. For this quilt every lady was to make a square that depicted some building or something special about Hayward. Claire had asked if this was selected for a special occasion such as a centennial. Evidently it was an idea that someone had suggested for Founders' Day and the rest of the group jumped on the proverbial bandwagon.

Claire had learned that Founders' Day was held to recognize the date that Hayward was officially recognized as a town in 1854, eight years after Iowa had become a state. The day had been celebrated in a variety of ways over the years but there were always fireworks over the town. Many years there had been contests such as those to select the town bird, the American goldfinch, and the town tree, the white oak. The folks in Hayward did not stray too far in their selections from the state bird, the eastern goldfinch, and the state tree, the oak. The contest for their own flower was more interesting with it having been, Claire was told, a close race between the early sunflower that bloomed along the area roadways, and the winner, the great blue lobelia that could be seen in late summer adding color around the area creeks. She had also heard that there had been strong support for Joe Pye weed but the mayor, whichever Hayward it was at the time, had refused to have the town flower be a weed. Contests to select the town rock, soil, and insect were also proposed but had not been held.

Since all of the houses in the main block of Oak were considered historic buildings, those who lived in those houses had the opportunity to portray their own residence for the quilt, or they could pick something else. Claire had thought about all of her roof lines and decided she didn't have the sense of perspective to depict that. Instead she picked the bank. She figured that she could handle a big red rectangle with white edges and tall rectangular windows. Claire knew the stone arches over the windows would be a little harder but felt they were well within her appliqué skills. Fittingly, Grace was given the Methodist church. The other well known buildings were easily divided as were the very old houses. For this meeting all were working on their individual pieces, most of which were nearly finished. It was interesting to see the various ways that the different structures were being recreated.

Claire happened to be sitting close to Ellen Hornsby, Gladys Felton, and Elizabeth. Ellen and Gladys were sharing their curiosity about the meeting their husbands had at the mayor's house on Saturday. They questioned Elizabeth since Bud had let it slip who was there but that was all that he would share. Elizabeth, who always tried hard to have no knowledge of her husband's business dealings, truthfully pled ignorance about the matter. "In fact, Lila can testify that I was in Des Moines that day shopping with her."

"Oh, I'm so sorry," said Gladys. They all laughed. Claire thought that Gladys had made that comment for two reasons. First, Lila had quite a reputation for her shopping trips. And second, she and Frank would probably have loved to have Lila shop in their store and leave her money in their pockets.

Vernina was sitting across the circle from Claire when she asked her, "How did you like your brownie the other day?" She had to think for a moment and then she knew what Vernina was talking about. "I hear that he was quite handsome, don't you know." Little did Vernina know just how handsome. He was so good looking that if he had had any brownie crumbs left on his fingers Claire would have begged to wipe them off.

"How did you know about that?"

"Let's see. Oh, yeah, Irene told Maude that some cute stranger had bought two brownies and had taken one of them in a bag. Maude knew who she was talking about since we don't get strangers around here very much, let alone really handsome strangers, don't you know. Well, Maude had to go to the store to buy some stuff for the restaurant and she told Bryan about it. He also knew who she was talking about. Bryan had been loading groceries into a car when he saw someone he didn't know walk to your door carrying a small white bag. He said he was a little concerned for a minute since he didn't know what the guy was up to. But when he handed you the bag and then left right away he figured everything was all right.

"You bet it was all right, it was great!" Claire wanted to yell. "Oh the good old Hayward grapevine," she laughed, "Always faster than Western Union."

"Who was it?" asked Vernina.

"I really don't know. He said something about knowing someone in the area but I don't remember if he said who." Little did Vernina know, or need to know, that Claire had been too busy looking into his green eyes to listen to everything he was saying. "Earlier I had fallen and he happened to be walking by and helped pick me up. He said he brought the brownie to make me feel better."

"Oh, how romantic!" said Elizabeth.

Never liking to be the center of attention Claire wanted to change the subject. "Okay, everyone back to your quilt blocks."

"Ladies, may I have your attention please." They all stopped talking and working and turned their attention toward Reverend Carlson. "I just want to remind all of you about our annual Valentines Day red rose dessert sponsored by our youth group here at the church. Put in a good word with your sweeties and after they take all of you out to dinner..."

This was met with a lot of "Oh, sure" and "Who are you kidding" kind of comments.

"Well, bring them over here that evening. It's two dollars a couple for coffee and either pie or cake with ice cream and a red rose for the ladies. Or you can give the rose to your gentleman if you want. Please spread the word. Thanks for your time. Now I'll let you get back to your work."

Claire wondered what the chances were that Daniel Dreamboat would be back in town on Valentines Day. She figured the odds were slim and tried to put the idea out of her head, but it was still fun to dream.

"Good afternoon, Hornsby Ford and Tractor," Bud said when he answered the phone. "Oh, hello Chester. He's right here. It's for you, Mike."

"Hello, Chester. How you doing? Okay. Okay. Right. Okay. Sounds good. I'll see you then."

Bud had busied himself and tried to look as if he was not eavesdropping but he had a definite interest in the call. After Mike hung up, Bud turned to him with a questioning look.

"They're all in. Or I guess I should say we're all in. This will be good. It will make it a good sized investment, better for us all." He reached across and shook Bud's hand. "Congratulations, partner."

On Thursday afternoon Mike picked up six checks each made out to the WC2 Fund for ten thousand dollars. He assured Chester that he would deposit them right away in the Chicago bank account that had been set up in November. He and Chester shook hands and Mike left his office and then walked out of the door of the bank. His whistling started as he headed for home. He was thinking about the paperwork he would need to get Missy started on, paperwork to show the group the account and how it was doing. They were getting pretty good at coming up with these official looking documents. But then as he walked by the Mayor's house he said, "There's no fool like and old fool. And I have nine old fools." The whistling continued.

Claire was engrossed with the murder mystery she was reading. She was at a very suspenseful place where the electricity had just mysteriously gone out and the main character was groping through the dark when Claire's phone rang. It startled her so much that she almost dropped the book. "Hello," she tentatively answered, almost expecting the murderer to be on the other end.

"Oh, Claire. It's Jane. My water just broke and my contractions are just minutes apart. I called the office but Dr. Nutting is out. I called Jim but he's making a special delivery run to the Johnson's farm. I called Betty and there was no answer. I need you to come." There was a long painful moan followed by, "You need to come, Claire. I need you now!" Jane yelled.

Claire had the almost uncontrollable urge to yell, "I don't know nothing 'bout birthin' no babies," and hang up. Instead she told Jane that she would be right over. After hanging up the phone, she ran into the kitchen and stood for a moment wondering what she needed to take with her. Rubber gloves? A kettle to boil water? Dish towels? A tranquilizer? She opened a drawer and pulled out clean white tea towels and then headed on a run out the back door. As she passed through her yard and crossed the alley she tried to remember all that she could about the delivery of her own children. About all she could think of was the pain and then the relief when she heard their shrill cries. But she really had no good idea what had been going on beyond her bent knees and draped abdomen. For a short time in her youth Claire had thought she wanted to be a nurse, but a few months volunteering in a hospital had rid her of that notion. She was known to faint at the sight of blood, hers or anyone else's. She had even lost consciousness the one and only time she tried to donate blood. She tried to put these images out of her head as she approached the Dunns' back door, telling herself over and over that she could do this, that she had to do this. Boy, did she hope she could do this! "Jane, I'm here. I'm here. Are you upstairs or down?"

"Up!"

Claire rushed up the stairs and found Jane on the bed, knees pulled up toward her chest, in the middle of a contraction. Claire dropped the tea towels on the foot of the bed and went into the bathroom and put cold water on a washcloth. She went back to the bed and put it on Jane's sweaty forehead. The contraction having passed, Jane could talk again. "Downstairs, on the washing machine, Jim did laundry last night. Bring up the some clean sheets and some towels." Then as an afterthought she added, "Please."

Claire had not even left the room before another contraction hit. Instead of making a laundry run she went back and held Jane's hand. Letting a woman in the advanced stages of labor squeeze her arthritic hand had about the same effect as putting it in a vice, but she tried not to show the intense discomfort. Jane would not have noticed anyway since her eyes were scrunched shut. When Jane's pain eased, so did Claire's and she pried open her fingers as she continued on her hunt for linens.

Under Jane's direction, Claire managed to wedge some of the towels under her. Noticing the tea towels, Jane thanked her for thinking of those – like Claire had any idea what she was doing – and had her tear off a narrow strip. "Oh, I think I have to push!" she said, again grimacing in pain. Claire was about to ask her if she could please reconsider when she heard a voice downstairs.

"We're up here," Claire yelled. She heard footsteps and at that point didn't really care who it was. All she knew was that some kind of help had arrived. But she was extremely thankful when Betty came through the door. Betty took one look at what was happening on the bed and said, "Are you two doing okay here or would you like some help?"

There was not even time for Claire to think of some sarcastic comeback before Betty jumped into action and before Claire knew it a tiny wet head had made its appearance. Then in a couple of seconds out slipped the rest of the tiny little body. The loud wail brought a smile to three of the four faces in the room. "It's a girl!" announced Betty as she placed the wriggling little body in the sheet that Claire held in her arms. She held the precious bundle gingerly as Betty used the strip of towel to tie the cord.

The next thing Claire knew Betty was on the floor beside her, shoving a pillow under her head. "She's coming to," Betty assured Jane.

Claire didn't even remember handing the baby safely to Jane. All she felt now was embarrassment. "Just lie here for a few minutes, Claire. I'll finish cleaning up here."

Claire didn't argue but stayed quietly on the floor until Betty was through bustling around. "It's safe now," she said and helped her to a standing position. Claire's timing was perfect, since the moment she was upright they heard more footsteps as well as a thumping sound on the stairs. Through the door burst a worried looking Jim followed by Dr. Nutting. Leonard stopped in the doorway but Jim rushed over and sat on the bed beside his wife and new daughter.

Feeling that she did not want to intrude any further into this special family moment, Claire whispered in Betty's ear, "My work here is done. I'll see you later." She quietly descended the stairs on somewhat shaky legs and headed home.

Rita dropped the coins into the pay phone and told the operator the number that she wanted. Then she deposited some more. "Hello," came from through the ear piece.

"Hi, Mom, how are you?"

"Rita, baby, is that really you?"

"Yea, it's me Mom. I just wanted to call and wish you happy birthday. I hope you are going to do something fun to celebrate."

"You just gave me the best birthday present. How are you, darlin'? Are you doing okay? I worry about you and miss you so much."

"I'm just fine, Mom. Really I am. And I miss you, too."

"Just tell me where you are and I'll come see you."

"Oh, Mom. You know I can't do that. But I will tell you that you'd laugh if you could see this place – the middle of Iowa with a bunch of small town hicks.

There are so many people and places around here with the same name it's not hard to figure out how this dippy little town got its name."

"Please deposit fifty cents," the operator interrupted.

"I've got to go, Mom. I love you." Rita quickly hung up the phone. She leaned against the phone booth and cried a few silent tears. Then in an instant change of emotion she left the booth, slamming the door hard behind her. "Dumb jerk! Mom warned me about him!"

"Did you get that?"

"Yea, but it doesn't tell us much."

"What do you mean? She said Iowa."

"Right, but do you have any idea how many small towns there must be in Iowa."

"No I don't, but you'd better find out and start checking every blessed one until you find them!"

Fifteen

"Is Mr. Lambert in this morning?" Mike asked the woman sitting at the big desk closest to the door with the big brass nameplate.

"Just a moment, Mike, I'll see if he's available." She made a quick phone call and then told him he could go on in.

Clarence stood as Mike walked in and studied the solemn look on Mike's face. "What is it, Mike? Is it bad news?"

Mike just stood and hung his head. He shook it a little as he reached in his pocket and then handed Clarence an envelope. Clarence took the envelope with some trepidation. "I warned you gentlemen that you cannot always expect profits like we were lucky enough to get in December." He tried to avoid looking Clarence in the eyes.

Clarence felt his knees get weak and decided that sitting down would be an appropriate thing to do. He reached back with his hand, assuring himself that his chair was there before actually sitting. He stared at the envelope for a few moments and then carefully lifted the flap that had not been sealed. He peeked in and saw multiple thickness of paper. "This looks bad," he thought to himself. He reached in cautiously, almost as if he were expecting some unknown thing in the envelope to snap at his fingers. He pulled out the entire stack of papers and looked at the words on the top sheet. He first saw his name and then he saw a number, $856.43. He looked up at Mike with an open mouth.

"Surprise!" said Mike.

"You had me scared. I was expecting the worst."

"Well, I was afraid you might be disappointed with a much smaller profit this time so I thought I would just let you think you'd probably lost some. So now that gain looks pretty good, doesn't it?"

"You bet it does," Clarence grinned thumbing through the rest of the checks.

"They're all there, all nine. I decided to just let my money ride. But I thought the timing was pretty darn good. Maybe you married guys will want to buy some special little trinket for your wives for Valentines Day. I figured you could pass out the checks since most of them probably come in here to do bank business and it would look more natural for them to come here than for all of them to come traipsing over to Bud's."

Clarence stood up and extended his hand across his deck. "Thanks, Mike. Thanks a lot."

Jane was feeling well after the birth of little Jessica and was actually anxious to get back to the Cub Scout den. Claire told her that she would have the first meeting in February and Jane could take it from there. The project for the week was making placemats and little paper baskets that would be taken to the nursing home for Valentines Day. Claire was in charge of this, the easy part. Jane would take over next week when the boys were actually going to make some kind of cookies or candies - she had not yet decided which - to put in the baskets.

The boys were finishing their snacks out in the garage when Claire remembered that she had not carried out all of the necessary craft supplies. She went back in the house and had not been gone but a few minutes when Jeff came running up to the back door, yelling hysterically. "Mrs. Menefee, Mrs. Menefee, Bobby fainted!"

Never being good in an emergency and especially in one where there might be blood, she yelled back, "Run down the alley and get Mrs. Nutting. Hurry!" By the time Claire made it to the garage the rest of the boys were circled around Bobby who was by now sitting up and looking quite proud. "Bobby, are you all right? What in the world happened?"

"Nothing much, except I won."

"Won? What did you win?"

"We had a contest to see who could hold his breath the longest and I won."

By this time Betty appeared in the doorway, quite out of breath. "Is Bobby all right? Jeff said he fainted?" She studied the proud, smiling face framed by his yellow neckerchief. "He looks pretty good to me."

"I'm sorry, Betty. But I guess Bobby was just practicing the breath holding requirement for his Wolf badge."

The boys all laughed at this but Betty turned to Claire, put her arm sympathetically around her shoulder and whispered, "How many more weeks do you have?"

"This is the last one."

"We'll celebrate tomorrow," she said and headed back down the alley to her house.

The placemats and baskets turned out very cute and the boys even seemed to enjoy making them. As they worked, Claire told them some funny stories about her grandmother and said that she missed being around her. Without being prompted the boys joined in with stories about grandparents and even great grandparents. She thought that helped them take their project more personally.

Before they left Claire told them there was something she wanted to try and bet them that they couldn't do it. She knew that would be the best way to get them to try their hardest. She pulled an old Cub Scout neckerchief out of her pocket and laid it on the floor. "I'll bet all of you can't stand on it at the same time." There was a mad dash with resulted in bodies bouncing off each other. Then Gary took control and had each one stand with only one foot on the cloth. The boys cheered. "Now you get on, too," they yelled. Claire looked at the neckerchief, their feet and then the size of her foot. There was no way. But when they said they would help her she couldn't turn them down. She put the tip of her foot on the small patch of yellow that remained, raised up on tiptoe and leaned into the group to maintain her balance. For a brief moment they were all on it and then the weight of Claire's body forced the rest of the group to lose stability and they all tumbled on top of each other. They lay on the floor and laughed for a moment, and then it was time for the meeting to end. Claire told the boys she had enjoyed getting to know them and they each in turn hugged her and said thanks. Then they hurried off into the cold late afternoon, not lingering this time for the usual post-meeting jostling.

Ever since Dennis died, Valentine's Day had not seemed very important to Claire. She didn't begrudge others for celebrating it but was just content to try to let it pass by without much thought. But in an elementary school that is not always easy. Even though Monday was not the fourteenth, many children had planned ahead and throughout the morning many little people made extra trips to the library to drop off their cards for Claire. By the time her stint was over, she had such a pile that she needed to track down Cliff Wilkens to see if he had any extra bags she could use to take them all home.

This Valentine's Day promised to be different, since she had volunteered to baby-sit for the Dunns so that Jim and Jane could get out for an evening alone. Claire was a little nervous about it. She had taken care of baby Jessica during the Monday scout meeting but that was only for an hour. This was going to be different – they were aiming for an early dinner at Maude's, the first seating at the church youth fund raiser and still wanted to catch the eight o'clock Valentine special at the movie theater. The theater normally only operated Fridays and weekends but this was something that was done every year. That gave some of the teenagers, as well as older couples, a close, fun place to go with their special someone.

Claire was just about ready to head out the back to the Dunn's when the doorbell rang. She opened it to find Steve Hornsby standing there with a dozen yellow roses. Claire had the urge to say, "Oh, Steve, I didn't know you cared," but was afraid he might take her seriously and it would embarrass him, so all she said was, "Oh, they're lovely."

"There's a card inside. And you are the only one getting yellow roses today. Anyone else getting flowers is getting red ones."

"I didn't know that you worked at the flower shop."

"Oh, I just help out on different holidays if it doesn't conflict with baseball or basketball or football practice. Well, I've got to go. I have a couple more deliveries."

Claire barely managed to remember to say thanks in her haste to open the card. She read it out loud since she always felt that cards were best when read that way. "These roses aren't red, these roses aren't blue, but for being our den mother we want to thank you." Added below the poem in parenthesis were the words "They are a Cub Scout color. That is why they are yellow." Following that were six names written in very nice second grade penmanship and in obvious alphabetical order – Bobby, Gary, Jeff, Jerry, Joey, Johnny. Mrs. Fossel would be proud.

She rummaged through the cabinets to find an appropriate vase and arranged her new treasure. "These are coming with me. If I am to have Valentine flowers then they should be with me on Valentines Day." Carefully carrying them, Claire went through the back door on her way to the Dunns.

Claire had just returned from a brisk walk, the best kind of walk for February in Iowa, when Jane called and invited her over for coffee. She quickly showered, dressed and paused for a few minutes in the kitchen to admire and add water to the beautiful roses. Then she was out the door to hear all the Valentines Day news. Claire hated to call it gossip. News sounded much more refined.

Jane had seen her coming through the back gate and already had the coffee poured by the time Claire got to the kitchen. She had put out some freshly baked coffee cake. Claire had told herself to not have anything except coffee but as she smelled the still-warm cake she thought it would be rude to turn it down. That was the kind of rationale that allowed her indulgences such as these.

Jane sat down and started nursing Jessica. "Well," Claire said and then paused.

Claire pulled her chair closer to the table. "First, thanks for watching the children. It was so nice to get out with Jim and not have to worry."

Claire wanted to say, "Fine, now get on with the news," but politely nodded and told Jane that she too had enjoyed the evening, which she had.

"There were lots of people at church. Ben was there with Bertha. I'll tell you, that man has the patience of a saint. Bertha looked so bored and ungrateful and he simply smiled and tried to get her involved in conversation the entire time they were there. Dr. Payne was there with the tall, good looking redhead that I've seen him with quite often over the past couple of years. She showed off a ruby heart pendant she said he had just given her. It was a nice piece of jewelry."

"Wow, I wonder just how well he knows her."

"But wait. That was just the beginning. The Feltons were there and Gladys was wearing a new string of pearls. She had on a black sweater that made those pearls really show up. And she kept fingering them and looking at them. I didn't hear it from her but someone told me that Frank had given them to her as a Valentine gift. And then there was Ellen Hornsby who was flashing the new emerald and diamond bracelet. She was so proud of it. She sat with her hand in the air with her elbow resting on the table and kept flipping her hand back and forth. It sparkled like crazy in the light."

"Then there was Dorothy Hayward. She is usually so down to earth and doesn't go out for a lot of flashy stuff. Well, she was wearing a big pair of diamond earrings. She was even wearing her hair pulled in a twist. In all of the years that I have lived around here, I have never seen her wear her hair any way other than down and curled gently around her face."

"And there were the Lamberts. You know that Elizabeth isn't a showoff, and I didn't think that Clarence was either. But they were wearing matching watches, of course hers was smaller than his. But they both had little diamonds around the crystal. They were definitely not Timexes."

"You are making it sound as if their husbands pulled off a jewelry store robbery or something."

"Oh, it wasn't just jewelry. The room was pretty much full when who do you think made a grand entrance in a new mink coat?"

"Lila."

"You guessed it. She came in whirling and twirling as she went from table to table visiting with everyone she could reach. And Chester followed behind her, shaking hands and wishing all of his voting public a happy Valentines Day. It was quite an ostentatious display."

"Do you think that it was just a coincidence that all of these pricey things showed up at the same time or was love truly in the air this year? And if it's not a jewelry store heist and if Lila hasn't been raising minks in the basement, then where did all of the money to buy these things come from? Oil hasn't been discovered around here lately, has it?"

"Not that I know of. It is just the strangest thing, all of this jewelry on these ladies that have never seemed like the expensive jewelry type. But I guess I could be wrong. Anyway, I thought you would find it interesting."

Jane was right. Claire had hung on every word and was now as curious as Jane. Jessica, on the other hand, did not seem one bit interested. She had finished eating and was sleeping peacefully in her mother's arms, perfectly content not to be nosey about other people's lives.

Claire was at the bank and visiting with Meredith when all of a sudden there was a lot of yelling. Claire could tell by the look on Meredith's face that she recognized one of the voices before she even turned around.

"What did you do that for?" yelled a man dressed in overalls and a winter coat.

Claire noticed that the front of his jacket was covered with numerous dark spots. She then looked at Clara who stood with her water pistol still pointed at him. Meredith rushed over to Clara. "Mother, what are you doing?"

"He was robbing the place!" Clara stated emphatically.

"I was not, you crazy woman!" the man yelled back.

Clara raised the gun toward him but before she could fire another drop Meredith grabbed it out of her hand. Clara defended her actions. "Yeah, he was. I looked over here and he's holding a gun in his pocket. And Ruby is standing there with her hands up. Now you tell me that is not robbing a bank."

By now Clarence had come running from his office and every employee and customer had gathered around. The angry customer, still wiping his face, replied, "That wasn't what happened at all. Just ask Ruby."

Ruby looked a bit shaken as she stood behind her cashier's counter. "Sam's right, Clara. He had just asked me how I was recovering from my shoulder surgery. I was showing how much movement I had regained. I lifted my left arm, my good arm, and then I put up the right one to show that I could lift it just as high. That must have been what you saw."

"Yeah and then the next thing I know she's yelling 'Put up your hands. I got you covered.' I didn't even have a chance to do anything before she starts squirting me."

"You were getting ready to bring your gun out of your pocket."

"I was not. Look, all I had was my checkbook." Sam reached in his pocket and lifted out a gray checkbook. "See!"

Clara still was not satisfied. "So why did you have your hand in your pocket."

Sam got an annoyed look on his face. "Let's see. It's winter. It's eighteen degrees. I forgot my gloves. I had just come in and was warming my hands. Any other questions?"

Claire was pretty sure that he really did not want her to ask any more questions. Knowing Clara she would be sure to think of some if given the time. Clarence stepped up, deciding it was time for him to take over the situation. "I am terribly sorry, Sam. It sounds as if it was an unfortunate misunderstanding."

"I am so sorry, Sam, Clarence. You know she was only trying to help," said Meredith once more apologizing for the less-than-conventional behavior of her mother-in-law.

"And, Clara, it is good to know that you are watching out for the bank's welfare but in future robbery attempts it is probably best not to interfere." Claire wondered how well Clarence knew Clara if he felt that was a real possibility. "Okay, folks, I think we can all get back to our normal business now. Sam, let me get you a cup of coffee, a new check book cover, a pen, a towel."

"Nah, I'm fine. But I will take that coffee." He and Clarence walked back toward Clarence's office and disappeared behind the heavy wooden door.

"Come on, Clara. It's time to go home."

"Did you get done what you came for?" Claire asked sympathetically.

"No," Meredith answered, "but right now I can't even remember what it was. See you later, Claire." Meredith grabbed hold of Clara's arm and steered her through the door. The remaining people all just stood and watched, some just shaking their heads in sympathy.

Two of the members of the quilt group had sewn all the squares together and the stitching was ready to begin. The design of the quilting stitches in each square was up to the person who had made that square. Claire's was one of the next squares to be worked on. There were several conversations going on as they sat around the large quilting frame. But among those that Claire could overhear, the jewelry that had made its debut at the Valentines dessert was a popular topic. Those who had merely seen it complimented those who wore it. Those who wore it compared notes on their gifts.

"It was just so out of character for Frank to splurge on something that he didn't view as an essential. Ever since we got married, he seems to hold on to every penny that he has ever made. I was just flabbergasted when I opened that box." Gladys seemed as if she still couldn't believe that she was the owner of that lovely string of pearls.

"My birthstone is the emerald," said Ellen, "but I was really surprised that Bud remembered that. He told me years ago that when the business got going he would get me something with my birthstone but I figured that he had forgotten that he had ever said that."

"Clarence told me that his watch wasn't working and when he went to replace it he found a very good two-for-one sale. It sounded too good to be true but now we both have very nice watches and mine doesn't gain five minutes every week like my old one did. Every Sunday before I went to church I would turn it back." Then Elizabeth switched to her sister-in-law. "I loved Dorothy's earrings. They looked so nice on her. In fact, she looked so pretty with her hair all done up like that. She should wear it like that more often."

Just then there was a flash of something large and brown coming through the door at the bottom of the stairs. In her typical Johnny-come-lately style, Lila swooped in, holding the sides of her new coat out, giving her the appearance of a large furry kite. "Good morning, ladies. It certainly is a cold morning, isn't it? Thank goodness I have this to keep me toasty warm." She swirled in the middle of an open space and then proceeded to pass by every lady very slowly. "I was just too surprised when Chester gave it to me. I had hinted for years that I wanted a new mink but he always said I didn't need another one and it was just too, too expensive. I don't know what made the dear man change his mind but I'm sure glad that he did."

Lila sat down with the coat still wrapped around her. She had not done the square for the quilt that represented her house, although Claire thought the Hayward's house would have been rather easy to do – just sew on a big white rectangle and slap on some tall skinny rectangles for the pillars. Instead Lila said that she had come to give moral support. Claire already had thought the room was warmer than usual and figured that Bill Carlson had boosted the thermostat to try to stay ahead of the frigid outside temperatures. As she sat there chatting Lila's face was getting somewhat red.

"Aren't you a bit warm with that coat on?" someone asked.

"Oh, not at all," she answered as beads of perspiration were popping out on her forehead. "I am quite comfortable. I do think I will go get a drink of water though." She stood up and hurried through the kitchen door.

"I think I could use a drink, too," Claire said and quietly headed for the kitchen. Elizabeth followed and nudged Claire's arm as they got to the doorway, holding her finger to her mouth to tell Claire not to make any noise. They quietly pushed open the door a crack and silently watched Lila as she stood in front of the large upright freezer that, ironically, had been a gift to the church from her family. She held the coat open with one hand while frantically fanning the door to the freezer. Claire looked at Elizabeth and nodded back to the rest of the group. They let the door close without a sound and went back to their quilting.

"We thought you were going to get a drink," one of the ladies said to Claire.

"Oh, I changed my mind. After two cups of coffee I decided that a glass of water would just send me to the little girls room too many times this afternoon." Claire really didn't think that she wanted an answer, since she was probably well aware that they had been peeking to see what Lila was up to, but she gave a semi-plausible answer anyway.

After a few minutes Lila exited the kitchen. "I think I'll head home now, ladies," she yelled in their direction. "I need to fix lunch for the mayor. Taa taa."

The group sat in silence for a few moments. It was if everyone was thinking something similar and had to wait for more polite thoughts to come to mind before saying anything. Luckily Claire soon thought of a legitimate question. "This is to be finished by Founder's Day but what happens to it then?"

One busy quilter looked up, her needle still for just a moment, and said,

"I assume that we present it to the mayor." Many of the ladies nodded in agreement.

"That sounds good," Claire continued, "but what does he do with it?"

There was silence while everyone pondered that question. Someone spoke up and suggested that it could be hung in the courthouse but that idea was discarded since not everyone who did business in the courthouse was from Hayward. Someone else suggested that it be placed in the town hall. That sounded good until Claire mentioned that she had never even been in the town hall and a few others admitted that they had not either.

"What about putting it on display in the library?" recommended Vernina. "Lots of us go in there from time to time, don't you know."

There was unanimous agreement that the library would be the logical home for the Hayward quilt. "There is only one problem I see with that," said Grace, "and that is Bertha. How will she feel about that?"

"There is only one way to find out," Claire said.

"Yeah, let's ask Ben to ask her," laughed Ellen.

"That sweet man probably would, too. But I think the request should come from us," Elizabeth said.

"Maybe Lila could threaten that the librarian's position would not be funded if she didn't agree," suggested Gladys.

"We could keep that as a backup plan, I guess," said Grace, "but I think a group of us could approach her and ask." Everyone agreed that was what should be done. Then Grace added, "And I will pray about it."

Since they all had dealt with Bertha, Claire had the feeling that they were all thinking the same thought. "That will take prayers from all of us."

Word about the jewelry acquisitions was noticed not only by the ladies in the town but also by many of the men. Questions were asked and guesses were made about why this group of husbands had gotten so generous so suddenly. By a week after Valentines Day all of the husbands and Tim Payne had been asked by at least one person about the source of wealth. And when news got around that both of the Lavelle brothers had purchased new color television sets the curiosity was greater than ever. Some inquiries were made half jokingly while others were serious about how they could get in on whatever was adding so quickly to the wealth of these select few.

William Swan, who had decided to reinvest his profits, smiled to himself as townsfolk gossiped to him about the purchases of the others. He just acted ignorant of everything and pretended that he was not even aware of what the others had done. He liked being the truly silent and parsimonious partner.

Throughout the week the investors drifted into Clarence's office, sharing with him the inquiries they had received. Clarence listened and nodded to each, not really knowing how to respond. Finally he called Mike. "I'm just curious. We've had lots of people asking. Would it be a good thing or not to increase the number of investors in our group?"

This was just what Mike had been waiting for. He paused for a moment, trying not to show his excitement. He also had to think of exactly what to tell Clarence. Rather than giving him an immediate answer he said he would think about it and weigh the pros and cons. Clarence really would have liked an immediate answer but told Mike that he would be anxiously waiting to hear Mike's decision.

When Mike got home that afternoon, he could hardly contain his excitement. "This is turning out much better than I ever thought," he explained to Missy whose legs were draped over the arm of the couch letting the newly applied fire engine red polish dry unobstructed on her toes.

"So how much longer are you going to keep up this little scheme? Does that mean that we can blow this dump pretty soon?" she asked with enthusiasm that Mike seldom saw in her.

"I'll need to think this through really well. I can't make any mistakes. The timing will have to be just right."

Betty and Claire were bundled up and were walking very briskly, not only because the faster pace was better exercise but also because the temperature was in the twenties. "Tell me what happens on Founders' Day."

"It kind of varies from year to year depending on what the planning committee decides. Sometimes there is a big community sing in the theater with patriotic songs as well as folk songs. Sometimes different community awards are presented. One year they were all funny awards. A couple of times the theater showed a movie about pioneers or the western expansion. The best was when they got *The*

Music Man and at the end the high school band marched across the stage playing *Seventy-six Trombones*. There have been plays put on by the school or by different community members. It's always fun to see what the committee comes up with. But no matter what happens at the theater during the first part of the evening, there are always fireworks. They are shot off from the park but people gather in the square to watch them."

"But isn't it too cold to be outside in early March watching fireworks?"

"Sometimes, but some years it has been mild. But there is not much we can do about the date."

"No, I guess you can't go back over a hundred years and hold off the paper work until summer. Do you have any idea what is being planned this year?"

"No, but I'll give you three guesses who is chairing the committee."

Claire didn't have to think very hard before saying, "Lila."

"However did you guess?" laughed Betty.

"Then my guess for this year would be a drama, and I do mean a drama. She is about the most theatrical person I have ever known. Maybe each member of her cast could wear one of her hats."

"Just the members of the cast? I think she could probably provide headwear for everyone in the theater." They both laughed at Betty's comment.

"I am going to completely change the subject and ask what you think is going on with all of the jewelry that showed up on Valentines Day? For some reason it just didn't seem like what I think of as typically Hayward behavior. I know this was my first Valentines Day here but those seemed like pretty extravagant gifts."

Betty nodded. "I agree. That certainly was quite a display of jewels. I know it sounds as if I'm jealous, but really, I'm not. It just all seemed out of place to have so many expensive things show up at the same time. But it's none of my business. However, if Leonard gave me that bracelet or those earrings, I would think he was up to something. In case you hadn't noticed, there aren't a lot of black tie events that go on in this town."

"Hey, maybe that is what Lila is planning for Founders' Day and she and her committee are just getting a head start on their outfits."

Mike sat comfortably in Bud's office, leaning back with his feet up on the desk and exuding complete confidence. "I've thought it over, Clarence, and I think the decision needs to be up to the nine of you. It is your, our, investment group. It should be agreed on by the group. And one more thing. I think that the select few, and it should be just a few, that want in now should be putting in fifteen thousand instead of the ten that you all did. I'm going to just let you talk to the other gentlemen and see what they think. Then you give me a call and we'll go from there. I look forward to hearing from you, Clarence. Bye."

Mike hung up the phone. "This is easier than shooting fish in a barrel. And the more fish that jump into the barrel the better the shooting."

Claire was not quite sure why she was lucky enough to have been one of those selected to talk to Bertha about having the Founder's Day quilt displayed somewhere in the library. The group had talked about ways to approach her that might get the most positive results. But the one thing they all felt about Bertha was that no one knew of any sure way to get on her good side. Claire even had asked Ben if he had any suggestion of things they might say. He didn't. All he could say was, "Good luck."

The little group - Grace, Elizabeth, Vernina, and Claire – assembled in front of the library and after a brief huddle, and a short prayer offered by Grace, headed up the stairs. Claire didn't know if Bertha was curious about why four adults were entering her realm all together or if she didn't think much about it. One could never tell from the ever-present irritable look on her face just what might be going through her head.

Grace had been selected as the spokesman of the group. She was always so tactful and was least likely to make some sarcastic comment. "Good morning, Miss Banter, how are you this morning?"

"Fine," was one of her typical, inhospitably brief responses.

Undaunted, Grace continued. "We represent the interdenominational quilting group that has met and produced many quilts that have been made with care and donated to different individuals and causes for many, many years. It's the group that made the quilt you won at last fall's school raffle." Grace waited momentarily. Getting absolutely no response, she continued. "We are just finishing up a very special project, a quilt that shows some of the wonderful and historic buildings in Hayward. It will be presented to the town at the Founder's Day celebration. But after the presentation, there needs to be a place for the quilt to be displayed. Our group unanimously agreed that here in the library would be the most appropriate spot. So we are here to talk to you about that possibility." Grace finished her little speech with a sweet smile.

There was no immediate response from Bertha and again there was no indication from the look on her face of what thoughts she might have. Her facial expression had not changed one bit, except for her brief utterance of "fine," since they had come through the door. The four stood patiently, not knowing whether it was time to bring up some of the other points they had considered.

Just as Claire was about to say something, Bertha shook her head and said, "This is a library, an institution where a collection of books and other reading and or research materials can be safely kept. This is not a museum, a place to house a variety of objects that are put on display." They really did not need to hear her definitions of a library and a museum. They wanted a yes or a no that they could start arguing against.

Elizabeth, however, was quick to pick up on the museum comment. "You are right. This isn't a museum but you know full well that Hayward doesn't have one, not even an historical museum. The closest thing we do have is the local history in the reference section. Putting the quilt somewhere in that section, if possible, would be very appropriate since many of those buildings are referenced in some of your resources."

Vernina dovetailed on Elizabeth's comments. "I think having the quilt on display would be especially appropriate for the children in town."

"Oops," Claire thought. She didn't think Bertha wanted anything that might appeal to the town's younger generations.

"They study about local history in second grade. And when the children come into the library they could see the quilt and be able to understand what they were seeing. It would make their trips to the library more interesting for them, don't you know."

Claire's turn was next. "Many libraries in larger communities are becoming more multi-dimensional. Some display artwork on a rotating basis. Some even check out pieces of art like they do their printed materials. Displaying local crafts has also become quite common in many libraries. By doing this the community becomes more aware of different types of artistic activities that they might not see in their normal day-to-day routines. This also tends to create more interest for the library patrons in researching these activities or learning how to do them themselves. This increases the circulation of books that deal with these topics."

Grace spoke up next. "Just hanging the quilt somewhere in here would increase the aesthetic appearance and give it a warmer, more inviting look." Grace and Claire had stated some good reasons from the committee's point of view, but again Claire didn't think Bertha wanted to make the library more inviting. That would only bring in more people to interrupt her peaceful solitude and handle her precious books.

Again they paused and waited for a response. Still seated, Bertha cleared her throat and said, "Well, that is all well and good, but I repeat that this is a place for books and it is not an art gallery. So that means that there will be no quilt hanging in here." She finished her proclamation and demonstratively folded her arms one over the other across her chest as if to put a final exclamation point on her decision.

The group was ready to play their final card, one that they didn't want to have to use unless it was absolutely necessary. Elizabeth took one step closer to Bertha and leaned slightly over the desk. "Did you remember that the library funding committee is having its annual meeting next month? Did you know that five of the six members have already told me that they will be out of town that day and have appointed proxy voters for them at that meeting? I believe that committee has the ability to fund and staff this library. Is that not correct?" With a slightly concerned look on her face, Bertha nodded.

"Well, let me introduce to you three of those five proxy voters." Elizabeth acknowledged her cohorts with a sweep of her arm, "I am number four. Lila Hayward is the fifth. And her house is shown in the center of the quilt." Elizabeth smiled confidently as she finished, looking like an attorney who had just presented damaging evidence for the prosecution.

Bertha silently stared at Elizabeth for a few moments. Then she quietly rose from her chair, turned around and faced the research section at the rear of the library. Her head turned slowly as she appeared to scan the area. Pointing to an empty section of one wall she said, "I believe it would fit nicely into that spot."

That was all she said, but the ladies knew that they now had a home for their heritage quilt. Before leaving they all thanked Bertha and assured her that she was providing a service to the community. As they started to descend the stairs, Claire thought they all had mixed feelings about what had transpired. They were glad they had accomplished their mission but they had hoped that it would not have taken such heavy-handed tactics.

"I feel like we just committed blackmail," said Grace.

"Let's just look at it as tough persuasion," said Elizabeth.

"Just how much power will proxies have at that next library committee meeting?" Claire asked. "Can we institute an attitude change?"

"Never underestimate the power of a group of women, don't you know," said Vernina.

"And I do believe in miracles," said Grace. They laughed as they continued down the steps.

The days had passed too slowly for Mike since his last conversation with Clarence. He was anxious to hear how many new suckers would be contributing to his bank account. He had worked extra hard for Bud to help keep his mind off the WC2 partnership. His days had been productive, however, since he had taken orders for a new tractor and a reaper. These only had confirmed his belief that there were some very wealthy farmers in the area.

Finally he got the call he was awaiting. Clarence had told him that they had lined up eight new interested investors, none of them from Hayward but from the surrounding areas. Mike didn't care at all who they were. If they had the money to throw his way they could have been anyone from anywhere. It was decided that their checks for the fifteen thousand needed to be to Clarence by four-thirty on Wednesday, March 7th so Mike could get them into the mail the same day. Mike told Clarence that way he could get them before the bank closed and still make it to the post office in time to get them mailed off to be deposited into the account. Clarence thought that was a good day since that was Founder's Day and many of the new members would be coming to town that afternoon anyway for the evening events. Mike knew that would give him enough time to get everything organized.

Sixteen

Most winter days were too cold for Farley to sit outside guarding the hardware store and the town. So he either stayed home or was relegated to a chair out of the way in the store. That is where he was on March 6th when Mike and Missy came in to shop.

"Good afternoon, folks. What can I do for you?" asked Bob Simpson.

"We need some jumper cables," answered Mike. Farley's ears perked up.

"Having some battery trouble? I'd be glad to give you a jump," offered Bob, tying to be helpful.

"It's not that bad yet but when the little Mrs. said that the car was acting funny I gave it a spin and I think it is just getting close to needing to be replaced. These are just precautionary."

"Good idea. They're over there on the end of the third aisle. Yell if you need help."

When they reached the end of the aisle and Mike started looking at the cables, Missy hit Mike as hard as she could in his arm.

"Ouch, what did you do that for?"

"Don't you ever, ever, ever call me 'the little Mrs.' again as long as you live. Do you understand?"

"Yeah, I understand. But don't you understand that it just helps us fit in with these country bumpkins?"

"Okay, but never again."

Mike took the cables to the cash register and after he gave Bob a twenty dollar bill, he got more than change in return.

"Tomorrow is the big day. Everyone is getting pretty excited," Bob said.

Mike knew why he was excited about tomorrow but he wasn't sure what Mr. Simpson was talking about. Mike thought that maybe he was one of the new investors.

"I guess I don't what you're talking about," replied Mike.

"Oh, that's right. You two have never been here for Founders' Day before. There are sales in all of the stores tomorrow. Maude serves her traditional Founders' Day stew all day. You should make sure you go over and try some. At 7:30 there is a presentation of some kind in the theater to honor the founding fathers, mainly the original Haywards. Then following the program there are fireworks at 8:30."

"Fireworks?" asked Mike.

"Yeah, they fire them off from the city park and people gather in the square to watch them. Bring some blankets and join your new neighbors. The Lions Club sells hot chocolate. It's a great family event."

"How long do they last?" Mike asked.

"Usually about fifteen minutes. It's not the greatest display you'll probably ever see but it is still pretty and really noisy." Then Bob added, "If you decide not to come, don't plan on going to sleep early. Can I put those in a bag for you?"

"Oh, no thanks. They're fine this way."

"You better get that battery replaced before you get into trouble when there is no other car around."

"Right," said Mike. "I've ordered one at Bud's. It should be here by Friday." Mike picked up the cables and then went to get Missy who had wandered over to look at a display of dishes. He grabbed her by the elbow and led her toward the door. "Did you hear that?" Missy shook her head. "There's some big celebration tomorrow night and there are going to be fireworks."

"Fireworks?" questioned Missy.

"Fireworks, at 8:30. This could work out just right." He pushed the door open and walked through leaving Missy to catch the door as it started to close behind him. She pushed through it, an irritated look on her face, and followed him down the street.

Farley pulled his well worn notebook from his pocket. "Jumper cables," he said quietly flipping through the pages. Then he mumbled, "Fireworks, twenty thirty hours," and began another search through the book.

When Mike and Missy got home Mike immediately deposited the cables in the trunk of their car that was parked in the alley in the back of their house. When he returned to the house he made Missy sit down on the couch and look at him so he knew that he had her full attention.

"Okay, let's go through this once more. You start getting everything packed tomorrow while I'm getting the checks and mailing that phony letter I addressed yesterday. Make sure you close all of the drapes. And don't forget to get the gun out of the drawer by the door. Then I'll stop in at Maude's and get a couple of orders of that whatever-you-call-it stew to go. I'll say that you are not feeling well and I am bringing dinner home to you. Then we put everything that is coming with us just inside the back door. At exactly 8:30 we take everything out the back, put it in the car. We need to get it all packed in ten minutes before the fireworks end. Then we drive down the alley."

"What if that stupid mutt next door starts barking?" asked Missy.

"That's why we go the minute the fireworks start. If it barks either people won't hear it because of the noise or they will think he is barking because of the fireworks."

"Won't the people in the square notice us coming up the alley?" asked Missy again.

Mike with an exasperated look on his face said, "We're not going to drive toward the square. We're going to drive away from it. And we won't use the head-lights. Then at the end of the block we head west and not even the people setting off the fireworks from the park will be able to see us. It should all go like clock-work. This stupid celebration is just what we needed to help us get out of here unnoticed."

"Hey, boss. I think I've found it."

"Have you found them?"

"No, but I'm sure this is the place. The name of the town is Hayward, a real small dump and everywhere you look you see that name. Hayward Drugs, Hay-ward Hardware, Hayward Library, Hayward Market. Even the name of the mayor is Hayward. In a place this small I should be able to spot him just by walking around the town or asking a few questions."

"Good. And Marco, let me know when it's done."

"Yes, sir. You're lucky. We have one room left. You must be here for the Founder's Day Celebration. That brings in people from around the area. In fact I just rented a room to another gentleman I didn't know. When I asked him if that was why he was here, he said he wouldn't miss it for the world. Here's your key. I hope you enjoy your visit."

Daniel took the key and walked to room four, the one next to the end on the front side. Before entering, he walked around the end of the building to see what the back of the Snooze Inn looked like. The back was nothing more than that, the back of the building. There were no more rooms. "Good thing I came when I did since tourist season seems to be in full swing around here," he said as he walked back to room number four. He unlocked the door, deposited on the bed the few things he had with him, locked the door and walked the few blocks to Oak Street.

Daniel turned south on Oak and again about jumped off the sidewalk when the barking and growling of what sounded like a very large, very angry dog startled him. "I would hate to tangle with that guy," mumbled Daniel under his breath. He walked up to the door of the next house and rang the old door bell. Missy cracked the door and then opened it so Daniel could enter. Mike was seated at the kitchen table with some papers in disarray. When he saw Daniel he shuffled them back into a more orderly pile.

Without being invited, Daniel sat down on the couch. "Hi, Missy, Mike. I need you to tell me just what is going on."

Missy and Mike looked at each other. Missy's back was to Daniel so he couldn't see the frightened look on her face. Mike tried not to show how worried he was and instead feigned a look of confusion. "I really have no idea what you're talking about," he said with a slight tone of defensiveness.

Daniel looked at Mike, then at Missy and then back at Mike. Mike's eyes drifted toward the end table by the door. Then Daniel continued, "I mean this Founders' Day thing. What's it all about?"

Relief rushed through both Missy and Mike. Missy answered quickly, "I guess it's a big thing with sales and fireworks and stew." Daniel looked puzzled so Mike jumped in to explain it as thoroughly as he understood it himself.

"I heard it mentioned when I checked into the motel."

"You checked into the motel?" asked Mike.

"I've been on the road for awhile and I thought I might hang around this place for a bit." Daniel didn't think they needed to know anything about his hoping that he might run into Claire again. "I think I might take in the program if it sounds interesting, hang around for the fireworks, and then hit the sack early and leave town tomorrow morning. Are you planning on going?" There was no immediate response so Daniel just stood up and walked to the door. "I assume that everything else is going okay. No problems of any kind?"

Mike smiled as Daniel reached for the doorknob. "Everything is great. In fact it's really much better than we ever thought it could be. Thanks for stopping by."

"Glad to hear it. Well, maybe I'll see you later." Daniel walked out the door and immediately crossed the street. That didn't stop the dog from barking but at least his growling and scratching on the fence were not as intimidating from across the street.

Daniel had barely left when the phone rang. Mike answered as he always did. "Oh, yes sir, Mr. Mayor. Yes, I had heard that. Well that is quite a surprise. All right. All right. Fine. Thank you, sir. I'll see you then." Mike turned to Missy. "Well, isn't that one fine kettle of fish."

"What was that all about?" asked Missy.

"It seems that we are to be honored tonight at the Founders' Day program. They want us there at 7:25. Let me think about this." Mike paced around the living room. After a moment he said, "I think this will still work. I will keep with the story about you not feeling well. I'll go to the program and get honored. Then I'll say that I need to be home with you, so I leave early. And then things go just as planned. Yeah, that will still work okay. No one will have a clue."

"I don't care how you work it out," said Missy, throwing her arms around his neck, "just as long as we get out of here tonight, Tony."

"We will, Rita, we will."

Daniel walked around the square twice, both times letting his glance wander over to 101 Oak. Nothing special caught his eye so he continued on to Maude's. Maude saw him come in and led him to a table by the window. "I thought this would give you a good view of our…ah….lovely town square. What can I get for you?"

"I hear you have a special stew for today. That sounds good to me."

Maude hustled away and was back in no time with a large bowl of steaming beef stew, two large biscuits, a small bowl of warm cinnamon applesauce and a mug of hot coffee. It was delicious and was the closest thing to home cooking that he had had in a long time. He told her that when she came back to refill his coffee mug.

"Are you planning on attending the program tonight?"

"I'm thinking about it."

"I don't think that Claire is going with anyone else."

Daniel tried to act nonchalant. "Who?"

"That nice looking woman who dropped her groceries when you were here a few weeks ago? I've heard that she really appreciated your help that day."

"Oh, I remember now. I was just glad that I could be there to help. I might keep an eye open for her."

Daniel was finishing the chocolate layer cake he had ordered when he saw Mike come in. He just stood by the front door and waited until Maude came back with a brown paper bag and handed it to him. Then he left and walked up the street.

When Daniel was finished he asked Maude for directions to the program. "And if you want a good seat you should go early." Daniel thanked her and headed out into the cool March evening. He checked his watch. He still had almost two hours before the program was due to start. He decided to walk back to the motel, rest, and freshen up a bit. He figured that would give him time to get back, linger around the theater and keep an eye open for Claire.

Claire was just coming out of the drug store when she ran into Mike, almost causing him to drop the package he was carrying. "I am so sorry. Are you all right? I hope I didn't damage your package."

"Oh, I'm fine. I was just taking home some of Maude's Founders' Day stew for Missy. She is coming down with a cold and is not feeling very well."

"I'm sorry to hear that. I have a cold, too, and I know how crummy that can make you feel."

Mike didn't want to stand there chatting, but he forced himself to be somewhat congenial. "I guess it is that time of the year. Hope you feel better soon. I'd better go before this cools off too much."

"I imagine I'll see you later at the program."

"Yeah, I guess you probably will." Mike turned and hurried down the street.

As Claire headed across the square she decided to take Missy some of the leftover chicken noodle soup she had made for herself two days ago. She had used a recipe from her grandmother's little hand written notebook with her favorite recipes. Claire had never understood what the magic was in that soup but it had been the preferred cold treatment for her family for as long as she could remember. She had made a batch for herself and figured that the neighborly thing to do would be to take some to Missy. Claire figured that she could just drop it off on her way to the theater.

When Claire rang the doorbell, Missy barely cracked the door in response. "Hi, Missy. I ran into Mike and he said that you were getting a cold. I brought you some of my grandmother's famous chicken noodle soup, guaranteed to make you feel better." Missy reached through the small opening in the doorway to take the container from her. "Oh, it's too hot. That's why I have this towel wrapped around it. Let me take it to the kitchen for you." While it was true that it was hot, Claire was really quite curious about the Brocks' house. As far as she knew, no one else had been inside since they had moved in.

Claire pushed her way past Missy and charged inside. She headed straight toward where she thought the kitchen would be and was surprised to see suitcases and boxes piled by the back door. Claire was about to make some comment about the luggage when an angry voice behind her said, "What is she doing here?"

"I was just bringing some soup for Missy's cold," Claire explained. Then sensing that she had seen something that maybe she should not have, she felt it best to get out—fast. "I'll just be going now," she added heading quickly toward the front door.

"I don't think so," Mike said glaring at her. He grabbed her arm as she tried to reach the door. He twisted it behind her and gave her a shove. "Get into the bedroom. Missy, tear up one of those sheets and help me tie her to the chair."

"I don't think that is necessary. I could just sit here and read a magazine or something."

Mike didn't appreciate her comment and, despite Claire's fighting as hard as she could to loosen his grip on her arms, pushed her into an old, very uncomfortable straight back chair. Missy handed him the fabric and he methodically tied Claire's struggling hands behind the chair and her thrashing legs to the splintery legs of the chair. Claire had the feeling that Mike had probably done this before. He grabbed Claire's head, stuck a strip of sheet in her mouth and tied it tightly behind her head. He then turned off the light and closed the door, leaving her to sit terrified in the dark. The gag in her mouth was doing its job and was making her gag. So Claire took a couple of deep breaths to try to calm herself and evaluate her situation. At that point two thoughts immediately came into her head. First was that she wished she had taken up the suggestion to have Farley teach a knot tying class to the scouts. Then she might have been able to figure out a way to release the knots that bound her. The second thought was that she would have to apologize to Clara about not believing her warnings about the Brocks. She vowed that she would do that for sure—if she ever had the chance to see Clara again. For the present, however, she sat wondering what in the world she had stumbled into, what was going on in the other room and what was to become of her.

The crowd started gathering outside of the theater about twenty minutes before the program was to start. Even though the doors were open, most chose to stand and visit with neighbors and friends. The night was chilly but not a bad temperature for enjoying a fireworks display later in the evening. Betty was lingering, wondering where Claire was and hoping that Leonard would soon return from a visit he had made to a farmer who had an unfortunate run-in with a very mad rooster. Even though the wife had come to the rescue and kicked the bird over the henhouse, it had inflicted many beak and claw wounds on the farmer and the wounds had subsequently become infected.

Betty was not the only one looking for Claire. Daniel milled around the outside of the crowd, wondering if maybe she had come earlier and he had missed her. As the performance time got closer, people headed inside. Leonard arrived at 7:25 and he followed Betty through the door. At 7:30, Daniel figured that Claire must already be inside and went in to find a seat. He sat on the aisle, something that he did whenever possible. In his line of work he never knew when he might have to make a quick exit.

The program started soon after he was seated. It began with the sixth graders singing the state song of Iowa. Then Lila took command. In normal conversation Lila could be dramatic and loud, but with a microphone in her hand her voice took on a brassy quality that mimicked her garish clothing styles. In her bright turquoise suit she was quite the standout on the stage. The beads on her suit sparkled in the spotlight and could be seen well even by those in the back rows. Sitting low on her forehead was a matching pillbox that had a large tall bow pressed flat against the hat. From out of the center of bow came another triangular piece of cloth. It looked like a bird sitting on a nest with only the wing visible above the nesting materials.

She invited all of the members of the quilting group to join her on stage. No one took her up on her invitation so she was the only one on stage when the curtains behind her parted and the quilt hung charmingly from some of the stage rigging. She then explained the project. After she had droned on for much longer than necessary, a group of children came up on the stage. Each child gave a brief history of one of the buildings portrayed on the quilt. This was followed by a long round of applause.

Then Lila invited Miss Banter up on the stage. Ben Miller stood up and helped pull a reluctant Bertha to an upright position. She then walked on down to the stage with an obvious lack of enthusiasm. When she was in place, Lila put her arm around her. It was easy to sense Bertha's discomfort with this action. "Miss Banter has agreed to house our beautiful quilt in the research area of the library. This will allow everyone to enjoy its beauty. For the entire town, we thank you, Miss Banter." There was more applause and after another embarrassing hug from Lila, Bertha returned to her seat in less than half the time it had taken her to go the other direction.

Next Lila introduced the mayor and stood proudly beside him. Chester made a speech about what a good year Hayward had since the last Founders' Day. "Also, we gained some new productive citizens during the year. I would like to have one of those citizens join me on stage." Mike Brock stood up from his seat in the front row and walked up the steps.

"We were hoping that Mrs. Brock could join us, but unfortunately she is not feeling well tonight. Nevertheless we are so glad that Mike could be with us. Thanks to the efforts of this fine couple…"

Daniel had heard from Maude about the success of the fund raiser but he still could not believe that these two were capable of doing anything to deserve these accolades. Chester continued, "…we had an incredible community effort to raise funds for our school's library. To thank you for all that you did for us, especially since you were newcomers, I want to present you with a key to the city." There was applause as Chester handed Mike a large brass key. Mike mumbled a quick thank you to Chester and then headed back to his seat.

Lila then invited Phoebe Peoples to come on the stage. She plopped herself down at the piano that had been pushed out from behind the hanging quilt. While she wiggled around to get comfortable students went to the ends of the aisles passing out song sheets. Then Lila announced that there was going to be a good old fashioned community sing. She had barely gotten out her last word when Phoebe started belting out the beginning notes of God Bless America. Everyone, or at least almost everyone, started singing along. The crowd had barely made it to "From the mountains to the prairies" when Mike stood and walked up the aisle. With "God bless America my home sweet home" he was beneath one of the rear lighted exit signs. Daniel watched with curiosity as he saw Mike make his exit and decided to follow him.

Daniel was not the only one who saw Mike walk out of the theater. "That's him," said the newest arrival in Hayward under his breath and he, too, headed for the door.

There were a few people already staking out spots to spread their blankets for the fireworks as Mike hurried down Maple Street across the end of the square. But instead of turning on Oak as if heading for his house, Mike kept going on Maple past the Hayward mansion. Then he turned and headed down the alley. Daniel followed, but at enough distance that Mike would not notice. And behind Daniel came another man, lurking close to the fence.

Mike was amazed that Mellow didn't raise a fuss. He figured that he must be asleep or inside. "You can bark all you want to later, you stupid animal. Raise a ruckus. I won't care at all," Mike thought as he rushed down the alley. When he reached his car he quietly opened the doors on the driver's side and hurried to the back door. He almost tripped over the suitcases that Missy had placed in front of the door but he caught himself as he stumbled forward by grabbing the doorframe.

"Missy, where are you?"

Missy came out of one of the bedrooms. "I was just checking to make sure she was still tied up and to make sure I didn't forget anything. Everything is by the door just like we planned." Mike looked at his watch. It was eight-twenty, ten minutes until getaway time. He started pacing nervously. "What's the matter?" Missy asked.

"Nothing. I just want to get out of here."

"We could start now, couldn't we?" she asked looking at him as he paced by her.

"We stick with the plan. The fireworks will cover up any noise. They're the perfect distraction." Mike left to make another check of the rest of the house, not so much out of distrust of Missy's packing ability but as a way to pass the time until the first loud explosion. He cracked the bedroom door and saw Claire still tied to the chair. Though she was unable to speak, the look in her eyes conveyed her contempt for him.

At 205 Oak, the house next to the Brock's, a figure rose from the chair on the front porch. He came down the porch steps and then cut across the grass. As he got closer to 203, he dropped to his stomach and did a low crawl across the grass, cradling a rifle against his chest. When he got to the front door, he came to a crouching position and checked his watch.

At 207 Oak, another figure came slowly into the silent darkness and walked quietly up the sidewalk on thick, rubber-soled shoes. It lingered behind a tree at the corner of the lot at 203.

In the alley behind the Brock's house, Daniel crouched behind the car wondering how Mike had opened the two doors without the overhead light coming on. He could see the outline of what looked like boxes gathered around the opened back door. Missy and Mike were moving around in the living room.

Pushed up against the fence, the stranger stood silently observing one of the men he had followed move around the car in the next back yard. As he stood in the silence he could hear strange muffled noises coming from the other side of the fence, kind of a snoring sound, but still a noise he could not identify.

The first round of fireworks went off at exactly eight-thirty. "Let's get moving," said Mike as he turned toward the back door. But at that moment the front door burst open and a figure rushed through and leveled a rifle at the pair. "Get your hands up!" yelled Farley. "I don't know what you two are up to but it can't be good. I'm pretty sure you're spies. Now move over here and sit down," he ordered, pointing toward the couch."

At first Missy was so startled and scared that she couldn't think straight. Then she remembered that she had not done a thorough job gathering all of their belongings and realized the gun that was still in the table by the couch. When Farley took his eyes off her and glared at Mike instead, she made a split second move and pulled the gun from the drawer.

"Now you drop it!" she screamed. Farley, taken by surprise, and knowing that he really had no ammunition in his rifle, did as he was told. "Now it's your turn to sit on the couch, you stupid old man." She and Mike stood up and moved to face the couch.

Daniel, who had crept up close to the back door, could not believe what he saw happening in the house. He didn't know who the older man was but Daniel figured that it was time for him to take over this bizarre situation. Drawing his pistol from his shoulder holster as he rushed through the back door, he yelled, "I've got you covered. Drop it, Missy." Mike and Missy turned in surprise but Missy did what she was told.

The third man who had been in the alley had moved up closer to the house as soon as Daniel had made his way toward the back door. As he stood where he could see the Canellas standing with their hands up, his heart raced and his anticipation built. He had no idea who it was holding a gun on his prey or who the old guy on the couch was. But this hit had been assigned to him so he was ready to get in on the action. "This will be about the easiest job I've ever done," he thought with a sly smile on his face.

All of the loud voices had drifted over the neighboring fence and now he knew what the noise next door had been. A dog, apparently a large dog that had been sleeping heavily, had been awakened and was barking and throwing itself against the fence. Between the sound of the fireworks and the barking and all of the confusion in the living room, the stranger came through the back door without being noticed. He rushed through the door of the kitchen right behind Daniel and yelled, "And I've got you covered. So everybody make sure you drop everything and put your hands up."

His attention was then immediately drawn toward the door where an elderly lady was standing with a purse draped over her arm. "And that means you, too, lady." At these words, the other four turned toward the front door in surprise. They were all so busy looking at her that no one noticed the growling and barking getting louder. And until it was too late, no one saw a snarling Mellow until he was in the air headed right for the head of the stranger holding the gun on the other five.

When Mellow made contact with the man, the gun flew out of his hand.

Daniel was the first to pick it up and immediately retrieved his own gun as well. In the same movement he kicked Missy's revolver out of reach. Farley was next to retrieve his weapon. "Help! Help! Get him off of me!" the man screamed. "Shoot him! Shoot him!"

"I'll get him," yelled Clara as she pulled her revolver out of her purse. She held it out in front of her and approached the struggling man and dog. She took aim right at Mellow's eyes and fired repeatedly. The dog instantly stopped his attack and ran out of the kitchen door, yelping as he went. The rest of the group stood watching in amazement. "Lemon juice works wonders," she said nonchalantly.

Farley kept his rifle aimed at the Brocks while Daniel produced a set of hand-cuffs from under his coat and put them on the wrists of the man on the floor. He helped him struggle into a chair and looked at him for a minute. "Well, I'll be. If it isn't Marco Malone. I have a feeling that you've met this charming couple before," he said, nodding toward a dejected looking Mike and Missy. "I'm not sure just what you two were up to but I will find out. Ma'am, will you please call the sheriff for me while this gentleman and I keep an eye on these three."

"Gentleman?" asked Clara. "You mean that old coot?" she said looking at Farley with scorn in her eyes. The timing was perfect for just as Clara picked up the phone the fireworks stopped.

Since the house had become quieter with no more yelling, Claire decided that whatever was going on must be over. She figured that if she could make it to the door maybe she could somehow knock on it to draw someone's attention. As she wiggled against the chair the rough wood was embedding slivers in her legs. But the sound that rickety piece of furniture made was even more unnerving. It made a creaking sound that warned her of what was about to happen. With one more wiggle she heard the crack and one of the legs broke from the seat. Both the chair and Claire tumbled toward to door. It was probably a good thing there was a gag on her mouth or she might have yelled something very unladylike.

Slowly the bedroom door opened and she looked up to see Daniel staring at her in wide-eyed amazement. "Claire, what are you doing here? Are you all right?" He quickly removed the gag from her mouth.

"I think I'm fine—now," she said, trying not to cry.

He bent over her, gently but quickly untying the bonds. Smiling he said, "I thought you were coming to the Founders' Day program."

"I was planning to but I got a little tied up at the last minute," she answered smiling up at him.

"You missed an interesting show," he said finishing the last knot.

"It sounds as if I missed an interesting show here, too," Claire added as he helped her up.

"Yup, it was quite something. Come on out here and I'll tell you all about the fun you missed."

Little did those sitting in the park know just what fireworks were going on a few blocks away from the town's pyrotechnic display. Word had traveled fast, which was not surprising since Sheriff Butch Johnson had come roaring south on Oak with siren blaring and lights flashing in a display just as bright as the fireworks. His patrol car had come to a screeching halt in front of the second house from the corner. Those getting ready to leave the south end of the square had a good view when he exited his car with such speed that one would have thought his car was about to explode.

Deputy Burton Taylor, who was off-duty and was also watching the fireworks, decided that he should probably be in on whatever was happening and ran south, pushing his way through the crowd. Doc Nutting, feeling that his help might be needed, took off in the same direction.

Many in the crowd headed down the street to see what the excitement was but were held back by Burton who was able to find a volume and authority to his voice that he probably never knew he had. Even the mayor, who had been sitting on the corner of his own lot, was not allowed any closer. Instead he acted very official as he tried to assist Burton, who really did not need any help, in keeping back the curious.

Everyone was sure that whatever was happening was more than another arrest of the town's perpetual drunk, Zeke Myers. Some, judging from the location next to the Simpson house, suspected that Farley had finally gone off the deep end and actually shot someone. Others speculated that Mellow had jumped the fence and mauled someone. In only a few minutes, the news started to spread back through the anxiously waiting crowd. The stories became a variation of the game most children played in school where one person would whisper a sentence to someone and they in turn would repeat it to the next person. By the time the sentence reached the last person it seldom resembled what had originally been said.

"Farley shot a robber going into Clara's house."

"Clara was caught sneaking into the Brock's house."

"Some stranger shot and killed Mellow. Poor old dog."

"Some stranger tried to set the Brock's house on fire."

"Clara and Farley had a shouting match outside the Brock's and they called the sheriff."

Meredith and Aaron were quite concerned since they had left Clara home alone after she absolutely insisted that she was not going to the program at the theater, a program that, according to Meredith, had always been one of her favorite events. Aaron forced his way through the crowd and hurried down the street afraid of what he might find. Burton allowed him through and when he reached the scene he found Clara and Farley sitting on Farley's porch looking proud as peacocks about something. Once he realized that she was all right he returned to report to Meredith what he had learned. "She told me to just go on about my business. Said she would tell me about it later, if she felt like it. The sheriff is still in the Brocks' house, but things seem to be under control."

Within seconds of Aaron's return, the crowd was bombarded by the booming voice of Lila who had appeared on her front lawn with her bull horn. "Everything is fine, folks. No one is hurt. I hope you enjoyed the Founder's Day evening and you should all go on home now. My husband, the mayor, has everything under control."

Claire had trouble sleeping because of the excitement and because of the ache in the hip that had hit the floor when the chair broke, so she got up earlier than she had planned. She figured that was just fine because she had baking to do for the get-together that had been planned for weeks. Claire thought it best that she get dressed, complete with makeup, since she always seemed to run out of time when she tried to do more than one thing at a time in the kitchen.

She made it downstairs with some discomfort and tried to prioritize what needed to be done. She decided that instead of baking one coffee cake as planned she would do two. "People will undoubtedly be hungry after being up so late last night." She really didn't find much logic in that statement but it still seemed like an acceptable reason. After the dishes were in the oven, Claire got two pots of coffee started and began mixing a fruit compote, a favorite recipe from a well-known Colorado cookbook.

Next she got out the cups, saucers and plates of the good china from the utch. One would have thought that she was entertaining a Presidential entourage rather than just having over some friends and neighbors. She was disappointed that she couldn't find the small monogrammed dessert napkins. "Rats! I don't even remember unpacking those." Luckily she did find some cute paper ones that were decorated with small bouquets of shamrocks, not too bad considering that St. Patrick's Day was just around the corner.

Claire had just finished arranging things on the table when the timer went off. "Perfect timing," she said, feeling pretty proud of herself for actually getting everything done before the guests arrived. She checked that clock – nine-twenty. Ten minutes to spare. Or at least she thought she had ten minutes to spare when the doorbell rang. "I hate it when people come early," she grumbled, stomping begrudgingly to the door. She forced a smile as she opened it to the early arrival.

"Good morning, Claire." Daniel must have noticed the flabbergasted look, because then he added, "I hope I'm I not disturbing you. I came by to make sure you are all right."

Claire felt an awkward pause and then came to her senses. "No, you're not disturbing me at all. Please, do come in."

It didn't take Daniel any time at all to notice the dishes on the table. "I'm sorry. You must be expecting company. I just wanted to…."

She cut him off before he could tell her what he just wanted to do. She immediately realized that was kind of silly. She wished she had let him finish. Instead, she jumped in with. "I'm having some friends over for coffee and I would love to have you stay. I'm sure you would enjoy meeting some more people from Hayward." She added a, "Please," with as much of a coquettish manner as she could muster. Being a coquette had never been her modus operandum but thought it might come in handy on this occasion.

Daniel looked at his watch. "Well, I might have a few minutes. It would be fun to meet some of your friends. Is there anything I can do to help?"

"Follow me," she said leading the way into the kitchen. "Do you think you can handle cutting this coffee cake into sections?" Daniel looked a little worried as Claire took a knife out of the drawer. "Now, you're not afraid of a little knife, are you?" She handed him the knife and told him how to divide it. The doorbell rang and as Claire left the kitchen yelled over her shoulder, "Could you please do the other one the same way?"

When she opened the door it looked as if all of her guests had agreed to meet on the porch before ringing the bell. Claire wondered if this was another Hayward custom. At least that saved a lot of getting up and down. She took their coats and ushered them toward the living room. She offered, in an encouraging way, to take Lila's hat, too, thinking that the hat with an extremely wide brim of hunter green felt would take up extra space in what was going to be a very full room. But not surprisingly, Lila declined and with a typically dramatic motion swept into the room. People were not even seated before they started talking about last night's excitement. But the conversation came to a dead halt and all heads turned as Daniel emerged from the kitchen, followed by Jane and little Jessica who had entered through the back. "Good morning, folks," Daniel calmly said as all eyes scrutinized him.

"That's him. That's the one!" stated Clara emphatically. "He and I took care of those crooks last night."

Now everyone was staring at Clara. They were all used to her accusatory comments about all strangers being crooks. But now she was claiming that this stranger and she had dealt with genuine crooks. Heads turned back and forth between the two unlikely heroes, wondering if Clara really knew what she was talking about. Claire smiled as she stared at Daniel, too. Prior to last night she really didn't know anything about him other than that he appeared to be quite the gentleman and he was as handsome as handsome could be.

Claire finally managed to come up with some words, which wasn't easy since her brain was in somewhat of a fog. "Let's get something to eat and then we can hear all about what happened last night."

Daniel stood at the end of the table in a rather uncomfortable manner. Had a newcomer not known better she might have thought that he was the butler, standing attentively ready to provide help as needed. Claire volunteered to hold Jessica as her mother filled a plate and continued to snuggle with her so that Jane could eat. It also gave Claire an excuse to stand somewhat away from the others so they might not notice her frequent long glances in Daniel's direction.

After the ladies were seated, Daniel put a piece of each kind of coffee cake on his plate, filled a cup with black coffee and stood at the end of the table until Clara made Meredith move over on the couch. "Sit here," she ordered. "That way we can tell them what happened." Daniel looked at Claire as if to say, "Can't I just stand here?" but all she did was shrug. "Don't be shy, I don't bite. There's plenty of room. Sit down!" said Clara in her characteristic, demanding way. Daniel was learning what the rest knew, you don't argue with Clara. She patted the spot Meredith had vacated and reluctantly Daniel maneuvered his way to the center of the couch.

Claire was amazed how quiet everyone had remained. It was like there was a big secret that they were about to be let in on. As soon as Daniel was seated, Vernina blurted, "Tell us, for heaven's sake. We can't stand the suspense, don't you know."

"Well, this I what I know about last night," offered Lila.

"Butt out, you weren't there!" snapped Clara, which brought a look of discomfort to Meredith's face.

Daniel looked at Clara, "Go ahead. You can tell them."

That was all that Clara needed. "It all started when I decided not to go to the program because of that old fool, Farley."

"Mother, that is not a nice thing to say." They all knew that it was not a nice way to refer to anyone but in all honesty, the description did seem to fit the poor fellow.

Clara glared at her daughter-in-law. "I call 'em as I see 'em. As I was saying, the kindly delightful gentleman was acting even stranger than usual," she continued in a sarcastic tone. "He had been walking in a circle around his house all afternoon. I wanted to see what the old goat... oh, I mean what the marvelously enchanting fellow was up to. I was watching him through the window when I saw him sneak off his porch so I decided to follow him. It was a good thing that I did, too, since the fool got himself into trouble in the Brocks' house. He tried to arrest the Brocks, seemed to think they were enemy agents or spies or something. But the broad got the drop on him. Then this here man comes roaring through the back door guns a blazing."

"Now, that isn't exactly what happened, Clara," Daniel interrupted.

"Okay, so his guns weren't blazing but he did get the drop on the Brocks. Well, no sooner had he come in than some other guy comes crashing through the back door with his gun out," Clara stated, pointing to Daniel. "Then things got really interesting."

"That obnoxious dog of the mayor's jumped the fence and attacked that new guy. Mellow had him in a good grip when I plugged that flea bitten mutt with my rod." Had not everyone known just what Clara's rod really was, they would have all been quite appalled the think that she might have shot the dog. "Then I called the sheriff and that was that."

Everyone sat in stunned silence, surprised at what they had heard but feeling that there were a few facts missing in Clara's abbreviated version. So all eyes shifted to Daniel who calmly said, "That's pretty much what happened."

"There is a bit more to it than that," Claire said. "Like who was the other man?"

Daniel paused and then said, "Okay, this is what I can tell you. Evidently Farley thought something was up."

Francine jumped into the conversation. "He said that he heard the Brocks talking about jumper cables and fireworks at 8:30. So he looked in that old code book that he always carries and seemed to think that meant that there was going to be a rendezvous of some kind with spies and terrorists at 8:30. He felt it his duty to prevent this from happening." This part of the story made perfect sense to anyone who knew of Farley's inability to leave World War II behind him.

Daniel continued. "So he walked in the Brocks front door at exactly 8:30 to arrest them. But it seems that the Brocks had a gun stashed in a table in their living room, and Missy got to it and got the drop on Farley. I had been watching this from the back yard, and when Farley got into trouble I came in. I thought I had everything under control until this other man, Marco Malone, sneaked up behind me and forced me to drop my gun. That's when the dog came bounding through the door and jumped on Marco. He was screaming, not as much from pain, I think, as from fear. Clara was standing in the doorway by then and drilled the dog square in the eyes with the lemon juice that she had in her squirt gun. It was a perfect shot."

Daniel had barely finished when Jane asked, "Who is this Marco person?'

"That is kind of an interesting story. Marco works for a mob boss in New York City. He had been searching for the Brocks."

"Why the Brocks?" Jane asked the question that everyone else was probably thinking.

"From what Marco begrudgingly told me, the Brocks, who by the way, are not really Missy and Mike at all but are Rita and Tony Canella, had stolen a great deal of money from the mob before Tony agreed to testify against them in a federal case. The Canellas were put in the federal witness protection program and that is what brought them to Hayward."

More questions for Daniel were coming from almost everyone.

"How do you know the Brocks or who ever they were?"

"How do you know this Marco person?"

"Why were you hiding in the back yard?"

"Why do you have a gun?"

"I heard that there are three people in the jail. Does that mean that that Marco person brought some of his mob thugs with him?"

And then came Claire's favorite question, from Lila, no less. "Oh my goodness, are you one of those mobsters, too?"

"Whoa, ladies. Let me take one question at a time." Little by little Daniel started to untangle the mystery. "I know the Canellas because I am a US Marshall and I was assigned to help them in their relocation as protected witnesses, and to check up on them periodically. As a US Marshall, I always carry a gun." Clara's eyes were getting wider and wider as Daniel continued, but when he came to the part about always carrying a gun, it was obvious that Clara had a new hero in her life.

"I had been here a couple of times, as some of you know," he said, looking in Claire's direction. She felt her cheeks begin to flush. "I recognized Malone from my assignment to this case and the information provided to me about the hit men from the New York mob. I had noticed that Tony left during in the middle of the program last night. I thought I would just catch up with him and see why Rita had not come with him. But when he headed down the alley instead of just going down the walk, I decided that looked a little suspicious and it might be a good idea to follow him. Unfortunately, I had no idea that someone else was following him, too."

Clara's rating of Daniel as a hero dropped a bit with those words. "That was not very alert of you was it, flatfoot?"

"No, Clara, it wasn't. I should have been more careful."

"So are there three people in jail like I heard?" asked Grace.

"Yes, Malone as well as Rita and Tony."

"But why those two? I thought they were under protection by the government," said Elizabeth.

"They were but we had not planned on their running a scam here in Hayward."

That comment brought looks of total astonishment. "Well, first of all, one of the terms of their protection is that they can't possess a gun. And now it seems that Tony talked some of your leading citizens into investing a good deal of money in some ponzi commodities scheme. But instead of investing it for them, he cashed the checks and deposited them into his own private account."

Those words had barely left Daniel's lips when there was a loud sigh from Lila who proceeded to collapse onto Jane who was sitting next to her. After a lot of fanning and shaking, Jane and Betty brought her back to consciousness. Claire provided a cold rag that Lila pressed tightly to her forehead under the wide though somewhat askew green brim. Elizabeth and Ellen Hornsby didn't look too well either since they had learned only recently about the investments that their husbands had made.

Daniel, who had stopped his explanation, continued. "Oh, we didn't mention Claire's exciting evening, either."

Puzzled faces turned toward her. She tried to shrug off the attention but with prodding told as quickly and briefly as she could about what had happened to her in this scenario. Then she turned it over to Daniel to continue with his explanation.

"When all of the confusion ended and the sheriff had the three in handcuffs, we looked around the house and it was obvious that Tony and Rita were packed and ready to run. Had they made a successful getaway we might never have been able to track the money, but Tony was really good with figures and about keeping records. That was what got him in trouble with the mob, too. So it might take a little time but all of the money they haven't already spent should be recovered." A collective sigh of relief was heard from Elizabeth, Ellen and, of course, Lila who by now was almost fully revived.

Daniel stood up. "Well, I've enjoyed our visit, ladies, but I really need to go. I have some prisoners to transport to Des Moines. It has been a pleasure meeting all of you." The group nodded and replied with the standard polite comments. Daniel made his way to the door. In her attempt to make it to the doorway before he left, Claire practically threw a sleeping Jessica into her mother's lap and somehow avoided tripping over the many pairs of feet filling up the room. She managed to get to the doorknob before he did. She opened the door and followed Daniel out onto the porch, closing it behind her.

As he descended the steps and headed down the walk she decided to follow him. "You have a lovely little community. I can certainly see why people like living here."

"You certainly did add some excitement to our routine lives. I have a feeling people will be talking about this for years, especially Clara and Farley."

"It's always good to see things like this have a happy ending. Everyone's money is safe and the only ones who got hurt are those three waiting for me over there," he said tilting his head toward the courthouse.

Daniel was about to cross the street and head for the jail when he turned, reached out and took Claire's shaking, cold hand in his. He didn't seem to notice the cold as he smiled and looked into her eyes. "It's been a pleasure seeing you again, Claire."

"It has been nice seeing you, too, Daniel. You really ought to come back and visit sometime when you're not tracking down or babysitting some bad guys. You should come back in the spring. It is really lovely here in the springtime."

He squeezed her hand and smiled. "I might just do that." He lingered for a brief moment, released her hand and walked across the street. Claire watched for what seemed like a long time but it was probably only a matter of seconds before she started walking backwards toward the house, watching him as he walked away. When he was almost to the corner of the building he turned and waved. She had a feeling he knew she would be watching.

As she turned to go up the steps and get back to her guests, Claire thought about the last words she had said to him. "That was a pretty stupid thing to say," she reprimanded herself. "You have never even been here in the springtime yourself. Oh, well, I imagine that it is lovely." She smiled and sighed, thinking about just what spring might be like here and what possibilities and surprises it might hold.

About the Author

Mary Ann Seymour received a bachelor's degree in psychology from Colorado State University and teaching certification from the University of Colorado. She has taught elementary school for 30 years and is currently teaching kindergarten in Fort Collins, Colorado, where she lives with her husband, Bob, and a hyperactive Bichon Frisé. She has two sons and one granddaughter. In her spare time she enjoys walking, counted cross-stitch and kids' sporting events.

Those who have enjoyed Jan Karon's *At Home in Mitford* and *A New Song*, and Dorothy Cannell's *Bridesmaids Revisited* and *The Spring Cleaning Murders* will undoubtedly enjoy *Around the Square*.

TATE PUBLISHING *& Enterprises*

Tate Publishing is committed to excellence in the publishing industry. Our staff of highly trained professionals, including editors, graphic designers, and marketing personnel, work together to produce the very finest books available. The company reflects the philosophy established by the founders, based on Psalms 68:11,

"THE LORD GAVE THE WORD AND GREAT WAS THE COMPANY OF THOSE WHO PUBLISHED IT."

If you would like further information, please call
1.888.361.9473
or visit our website
www.tatepublishing.com

TATE PUBLISHING *& Enterprises*, LLC
127 E. Trade Center Terrace
Mustang, Oklahoma 73064 USA